Begin Again

Also by Emma Lord

Tweet Cute
You Have a Match
When You Get the Chance

Begin Again

Emma Lord

WEDNESDAY BOOKS
NEW YORK

First published in the United States by Wednesday Books, an imprint of St. Martin's Publishing Group

Designed by Jen Edwards

www.wednesdaybooks.com

The Library of Congress Cataloging-in-Publication Data is available upon request.

ISBN 978-1-250-78336-3 (hardcover)
ISBN 978-1-250-78337-0 (ebook)
ISBN 978-1-250-89776-3 (international, sold outside the U.S., subject to rights availability)

Our books may be purchased in bulk for promotional, educational, or business use. Please contact your local bookseller or the Macmillan Corporate and Premium Sales Department at 1-800-221-7945, extension 5442, or by email at MacmillanSpecialMarkets@macmillan.com.

First Edition: 2023

10 9 8 7 6 5 4 3 2 1

To my best friends (it's a tier!!) — I love you and also I'm sorry that I'm probably late to all the group chats right now, on my way

Begin Again

Chapter One

To be clear, I don't believe in fairy tales. After the past eighteen years of existing, I'd have to be pretty silly to put any stock in those. But I do believe in destiny. Specifically, in our power over it.

Which is why, against all odds, I'm here—standing just outside my dream school as one of the record few mid-freshman-year transfers that Blue Ridge State has ever had. I kept it under wraps over winter break since I was scrambling to figure out the financials of it, but as of today, everything's official. For once, everything is falling into place.

I squeeze the "A" charm on my mom's old necklace, slide it back under my coat, and knock three times on the door of the off-campus apartment in front of me.

"Who's there?" someone calls from inside.

"Um." I've mentally rehearsed this moment so many times this morning that my brain can't shake the expectation of Connor swinging the door open, his amber eyes wide and so happy to see me he sweeps me off my Keds. Instead I lean in and say to the stranger, "It's Andie? I'm Connor's . . ."

Girlfriend, I'm going to say. Which I am, even if we've barely seen each other since August, when he moved two hours from home to study here, and I stuck around at the local community college.

A boy opens the door a crack, squinting at me. "Uh, I only just moved in. But I don't know any Connors."

"I mean Whit," I correct myself. Connor's teammates have always called him by his last name, to the point where I'm pretty sure they don't remember he has a first one to begin with. Even his Instagram bio just says "Whit" now.

"No Whits, either."

"Oh." I step back to check the address. It looks like the same one I've been sending care packages to every month, but maybe in all the pandemonium of shoving my life into two suitcases and a backpack, I got the numbers jumbled.

I pull my phone out of my pocket to call Connor. "Sorry to bother—" The door shuts in my face. "You," I mumble, taking a step back.

I press the phone to my ear, but it just rings until it hits Connor's voicemail. "Snickerdoodle," I cuss, an admittedly weird habit I've picked up from Gammy Nell, who refuses to use actual swear words and makes a big show of flinching when anyone does within ten feet of her.

I was hoping to catch Connor before the kickoff event for the school's annual ribbon hunt, a tradition for freshmen I've only been dreaming about for—well, pretty much my entire human existence. According to the livestream I caught of the school's underground radio show *The Knights' Watch*, it'll start on the quad at ten o'clock. But today's already going to be stacked with a quick move-in and new classes and trying to find a decent work-study job as it is, so maybe catching up with Connor later is for the best. It's not like we're short on time, now that we're going to the same school again.

I walk back to the car where my grandmas are waiting for me, flashing what I used to call my syndicated-talk-show smile, the one so practiced and reflexive that it's almost stopped feeling fake.

"I forgot," I say as I open the car door. "He's at an early soccer practice."

One of Grandma Maeve's perfectly penciled eyebrows pokes out from behind her hot pink sunglasses. "Is he now?" she asks, turning her key in the ignition.

We both know I'm lying for Gammy Nell's sake, so I press my lips back at her in the rearview mirror in acknowledgment that I've been busted. Better that than letting Gammy Nell go on another one of her doomsday spirals—she can take "Connor's not picking up his phone" to "Connor's been kidnapped by a cult that's going to harvest his organs" in two seconds flat.

"Off to Cardinal, then?" Grandma Maeve asks, referring to the dorm I've been assigned.

Gammy Nell pouts, turning back to look at me with the same big blue puppy dog eyes she gave my dad, and my dad gave me. "I wish you'd let us come up."

I lean forward from the back seat. "I don't mind if you want to—"

Grandma Maeve waves me off. "And ruin your street cred with two bickering old ladies before you can so much as bat your eye at one co-ed?"

"I have a boyfriend," I say patiently.

This earns me a scoff. Grandma Maeve isn't Connor's biggest fan at the moment, since he talked about taking a break last semester when the distance got to be too rough. But in his defense, Blue Ridge State is known for putting students through the wringer. I'm sure it's why I didn't get in when I applied out of high school— none of my otherwise shiny academic and community feats could make up for the string of Cs I got sophomore year, which was more than enough of a reason to put me in the "reject" pile at the most competitive school in the state.

"And *I* don't bicker," says Gammy Nell primly.

Grandma Maeve pats her on the shoulder with the hand that isn't trained on the wheel. "Sure you don't, Nellie."

The thing about Grandma Maeve and Gammy Nell is that they have precisely two interests in common: a years-long, borderline-concerning obsession with Ryan Reynolds, and me. Other than that they might as well be night and day. Grandma Maeve is all sass and flashy accessories and telling you how it is; Gammy Nell is all sweetness and cotton cardigans and not telling you how it is, but passive-aggressively letting you know she doesn't like it. The only reason they haven't blown our house in Little Fells sky-high is that seven years ago, when my mom died, they both decided to move in with my dad to help raise me.

Well, "help" might be a generous word for it. With Gammy Nell long since widowed and Grandma Maeve divorced multiple times over, they did their fair share of it, then pretty much took over after my dad landed a job two hours away and I stayed put to finish high school. It wasn't long before the two of them were so well-known in our neighborhood that the neighbors practically camped out on our porch, hoping to hear about another misadventure behind one of Grandma Maeve's tattoos or score some of Gammy Nell's famous chocolate cherry jam.

There's this pang then that I've been doing a pretty decent job of ignoring for the past few weeks, ever since I got my transfer acceptance letter. It's been a weird childhood, but a mostly good one. They'll only be a two-hour drive away, but it still feels like a whole lot more.

We roll up to the entrance of Cardinal and my heart skips a beat. I'm trying to think of something to say as we all get out of the car, something to reassure both them and myself, but then Gammy Nell nudges Grandma Maeve and says, "You forgot."

Grandma Maeve scowls. "Forgot what?"

"I knew you would. The rib—"

"Oh, you're right. Shit."

Cue the trademark Gammy Nell flinch.

"Hold up, chicken," says Grandma Maeve, pulling something out from the glove compartment.

She presses a stack of three ribbons into my hand, one red, one yellow, and one blue, all of them stamped with a faded version of the Blue Ridge State logo of a knight. She waits to give me the fourth ribbon last—a white one marked with my mom's signature "A" in permanent ink.

My throat goes tight. I haven't seen these since my dad put them in storage; I wasn't even sure we still had them.

"I dug them out of your mom's old things," she says. "She'd have wanted you to have them."

Neither of us likes to talk about my mom in front of other people. After our tiny town of Little Fells watched her grow her local radio show into a statewide syndicated one, she was so universally loved as the "hometown spitfire" that everyone jumps at the chance to share memories of her. But there's always been this private, almost sacred grief between me and Grandma Maeve and my dad, in the rare moments he acknowledges it with us.

So I'm not surprised when Grandma Maeve immediately changes gears by pressing a bag full of quarters into my hand for the laundromat. A beat later Gammy Nell yanks out an entire grocery store aisle's worth of snack cakes and candy she's stuffed into a tote bag and hands them to me, nearly spilling out individually wrapped Ring Dings and Tastykakes onto the sidewalk.

"For all your new friends," she says excitedly.

I grin back, the seams of my coat itching at the anticipation. The minute I had that acceptance letter in hand I promised myself that this wouldn't just be an academic fresh start, but a fresh start for making new friends, too—something I don't have a lot of experience with, growing up in a small town full of people I've known my whole life. Lightly bribing the dorm with snack cakes seems like a good place to start.

They hug me in turn, Grandma Maeve with that deep, sharp squeeze like she's jolting my bones with love, then Gammy Nell all soft and full and smelling like the apples she put in the air fryer this morning. I swallow back the extremely unhelpful balloon of fear in my stomach.

"Call us when you're settled," says Grandma Maeve as they get back into the car.

"And every day!" Gammy Nell demands.

Then Grandma Maeve blows me a kiss and steps on the gas as Gammy Nell squawks in protest, trying to take my picture through the open window in vain. I wave as they turn the corner, smile still fully intact, then open my suitcase to its hidden pocket and press the ribbons inside, safe and out of sight.

Chapter Two

Cardinal dorm is on the fringes of campus, nestled between a row of other dorms and the woods behind the school. The campus is every bit as stunning as all the brochures I've collected over the years promised, and the ache in my chest feels deep enough to bruise. It's not just the faded red brick of the buildings and the idyllic tree-lined paths and the sweeping mountain views from the campus's highest hill. It's that I've seen them all before, in the background of pictures of my parents I found in a box under my dad's bed. Blue Ridge State is where they met.

I square my shoulders. This is my story, not theirs. And seeing as I have an entire floor's worth of new friends to make, an entire schedule of classes to wrangle, and eventually a dimpled soccer star to surprise, my work here is cut out for me.

An elevator takes me up to the fourth floor, where I've been assigned. I pass a group of students in the hallway, all of them carting sleek laptops and textbooks and laughing about something that happened at a finals party last semester. A few of them cast me a curious glance, but they all seem so at ease with one another that I clam up before I can remember which hand I've got the snack cakes in.

I take a deep breath, promising myself to give it another go later, and knock on the RA's door.

"Nobody's home."

I laugh nervously. "It's Andie Rose? The transfer student."

There's rustling on the other side of the door, which then opens to the more modern Blue Ridge State logo. I blink, then look up from the T-shirt into the eyes of an overly tall boy who must be the Milo Flynn I've been emailing with, blinking right back at me with the bewilderment of someone who clearly hasn't slept in a week. He hovers in the doorframe, his shoulders slumped but his eyes considering mine so intently that my face burns from the unexpectedness of it. He clears his throat and we both glance away.

"Transfer student. Yes," he mutters, more to himself than to me. He runs a hand through his dark curls. "Shit. Is it Monday?"

His voice sounds familiar to me, enough that I'm about to ask if he went to a school near Little Fells. But I'm immediately distracted by his room, which is littered with coffee mugs, the majority centered around a tiny, single-serve Keurig placed dead center in the room like a shrine.

"Yup," I inform him. "You okay there, Milo?"

"Peachy," he mutters, moving his hand to rub his thumb and pointer finger over his eyes like he's trying to rub his face back to life. "Cool, okay. I got this. You're with Shay."

Now this is the one part of the whole Blue Ridge State experience I've actually been looking forward to—having a roommate. Especially considering my only past roommates, bless their hearts, both qualify for social security and spend most of their nights arguing over the division between the tomatoes and strawberries in the backyard garden. I squashed the hope my kid self had for siblings a long time ago, but I can feel the glimmer of it now—someone my age. Someone who doesn't think that watching *The Proposal* eighteen times a month is a personality trait. An actual, legitimate *peer*.

Milo leads me down the hall on legs so long that I half jog to keep up, then knocks on 4A. There's no answer.

"Shay's probably in the shower," he says, pointing vaguely down the hall. "So, uh—bathrooms are down there on the left. Just past them is a study room. End of the hall is the rec room."

"Got it."

"Rules. Uh . . . quiet hours start at nine. If you're going to drink, please don't do it in front of me, I don't have the time or the will to write you up. This is your key," he says, pulling it out of the back pocket of his jeans and pressing it into my hand. His own is warm in that way of someone who's recently been asleep. "Don't lose it, they're expensive to replace."

I close my fist around the key like a talisman. "Anything else?"

He takes an exaggeratedly long breath. "Probably. Sorry. Long night. Do you have any questions?"

"No, thanks." I read through the student handbook so thoroughly that I probably know more about the rules than he does. I don't do anything halfway.

"Good, because I'm not alive enough for them yet." He gestures at the closed door. "You lucked out. Shay is my favorite person on this floor."

"Why's that?" I ask, eager to hear more about her. The only information I've been able to glean about Shay Gibbins is from the Bookstagram she runs, where you can scroll into an endless abyss of beautifully pastel-filtered books on bedspreads and shelves paired with coffee and knickknacks and cozy socks. I only know what she looks like because I managed to find pictures her sister and friends tagged of her—she has this close-lipped, conspiratorial kind of smile and full cheeks and a seemingly endless collection of knit sweaters that would make Gammy Nell proud.

Milo leans down to meet me at my level. He's just awake enough now that I can see the celery green of his eyes, and the absolute resolution in them. "She respects quiet hours. Quiet hours are very, very sacred to me. Understood?"

I laugh. Milo does not.

"Understood," I say, saluting him.

He straightens himself back up to his overly tall self, so I have to crane my neck to look at him. "Good," he says. "And, uh . . . godspeed with the whole midyear transfer thing."

"Thanks?"

"Anytime," he says, and then stops himself. "Except during quiet hours."

There's a pink-robed, flip-flop-clad Black girl walking down the hallway that I instantly recognize as Shay. She and Milo high-five each other without breaking their strides, then Milo disappears back into his room, and Shay pulls her key out of her robe pocket.

"You must be Andie," she says, her smile just as warm as it is in pictures.

I hold myself up straight, trying to project the same warmth even as my stomach does a quick backflip. "And you're Shay."

"For better or worse," she says, twisting the key in the lock and opening the door. "Sorry in advance—my side of the room is kind of, uh . . ."

"Whoa."

I have no idea how she meant to end that sentence, but I'm so swept up by the aesthetic that I probably wouldn't have heard it anyway. Her half of the room is littered from wall to floor with candles and books and pillows, with glossy Blue Ridge State stickers from the school's literary club and Campus Pride, with framed and hanging pictures of herself with friends and her parents and sister. Everything is so personal and cozy that I don't even want to cast my eyes at my bare side of the room and wreck it. I make a mental note to head to the craft store down the road and see if I can curate anything half as cute as her setup.

That is, if I have any money left over after the school's work-study program comes to collect. Tuition does *not* come cheap.

"Yeah. Well. You're welcome to the bookshelf anytime," says Shay.

"Holy guacamole," I say, peering closer to look at the titles. It's a mix of everything—romance, young adult, historical accounts, sci-fi, fantasy, horror. I only look away because there's a zombie skull on the binding of one of them that rattles me. "You must read like, an entire book a day."

"Sometimes two," she confesses.

"In *this* place?" I ask, setting my bags down on the bare mattress of my bed.

She shrugs. "I don't have a major yet, so. Things aren't super intense for me." She pulls off her shower cap, revealing her intricate pattern of zigzagged cornrows cinched in a ponytail, and plucks a book with a very steamy cover from her bedside table. "How about you? Picked your poison?"

"Psychology," I say, hoping she doesn't take one look at me and know that the only two books I own are celebrity-authored hybrid cook- and lifestyle books.

Shay looks up at me from the pages of her novel, wincing. "Well—good, I guess. Makes sense for you to be here, since the psychology program is so intense. Nearly knocked my older sister off her ass, but she's in grad school now and glad for it."

I try not to wince back, focusing on unpacking the backpack I put all of my essentials in.

"Yeah. Not looking forward to that."

Shay shrugs. "If you managed to elbow your way in as a mid-freshman-year transfer, I'm guessing you'll be fine. That's basically unheard of."

And this time I do wince, pivoting on my heel before she can see it and turning my attention to the overflowing snack-cake bag. It's not basically unheard of. It technically *is* unheard of. According to the registrar, not only am I the only freshman transfer they took, but the first one in years.

It's not that I didn't get good grades. I worked my tail off in my first semester, wrote fifteen drafts of my application essay, and got glowing recommendations from my two most favorite teachers.

But I can't help suspecting that a huge part of why I got in is because—well. For lack of a better phrase, the "dead mom" card.

See, when you have the "dead mom" card in your playing deck, everything in your world is just a little bit tilted sideways. The kids you were close to growing up suddenly hesitate to talk about their own moms in front of you, or even the rest of their problems, like they're worried to bother you with them when they think it doesn't compare to yours. The adults in your small town are extra nice to you, sneaking you gumballs at the grocery store checkout line, showing up in full force whenever you host a car wash fundraiser. And eventually you get a little older and look around and realize that there's a mark on you that's followed you around, some shadow that's colored everything that's happened to you since. Marked you as an "other" with your friends, so you can never quite relate to them the same way you did. Given you little boosts with everyone else, like they could ever make up for the worst thing that ever happened to you.

It's why I loved writing the anonymous advice column for our high school paper so much, and why I've kept doing it long after graduation. Nobody has ever known who I am. It was a way to help friends with their problems, once half of them felt too uncomfortable about my situation to keep coming to me with them. And I know the reputation I've built with it is all my own, and not because I'm Amy Rose's daughter.

Blue Ridge State, on the other hand, I'm not so sure about. My mom was just as well-loved here as she was back at Little Fells. As happy as I am that it all worked out, there's some part of me that's wondered exactly whose merit I got in on—mine or hers.

"Got any friends here?" Shay asks.

I clear my throat, securing the smile back on my face. "Yeah. My boyfriend, Connor," I say, a little more brightly than I meant to.

"Your boyfriend?" says Shay.

"Yeah. Of three years. But we've been friends for like, ever." I put down the shirts I was pulling out of my suitcase and take a step closer to the edge of her bed. "Actually, my being here is kind of a surprise. I haven't been able to tell him yet. Still brainstorming the most romantic place to go about it."

Somewhat unhelpfully, my thoughts keep straying to the arboretum, a huge chunk of woods on the edge of campus full of trails to explore and hidden spots with bridges and gazebos and a whole tree grove full of birdhouses. There's a lake smack-dab in the middle of it with a trail that goes all the way around, one just as picturesque as the big lake my parents used to take me on nature strolls to as a kid. On a whim I even unearthed my old hiking boots, only to abruptly realize upon seeing the Hello Kitty pattern on them that I no longer had ten-year-old feet and they wouldn't do me any good here.

But Connor's always been too restless for that kind of thing. If he's outdoors, he wants to be competing in soccer matches or training, doing something "productive." Considering all the times he dodged my attempts to take him hiking back in high school, I doubt he'd appreciate getting dragged all the way out there when I could have just as easily met up with him somewhere less muddy.

Shay watches me curiously. "Huh," she says. "Well—as long as you don't ditch me to join the cast of a reality show like the last roommate did."

I flip my ponytail over my shoulder. "I'll try to keep MTV's casting directors at bay."

Shay lets out a small snort and we share a cautious smile. We've messaged back and forth the past few weeks, but it was mostly about moving arrangements. But as nervous as I've been to make friends here, I can already tell that Shay and I are going to get along just fine.

"Zebra Cake?" I ask, pulling one out of Gammy Nell's bag.

Shay's eyes widen. "Um, yeah, always."

I toss one over to her and she catches it with ease, tearing open the wrapper. I grab one of my own, then walk over to cheers it with her.

"To new roomies."

My phone buzzes on top of my mattress. I apologize quickly before turning around to answer it.

"Hey, Andie. Sorry I missed your call."

Just hearing Connor's voice makes the world feel a little smaller again, a little easier to manage. We've known each other since kindergarten. Sometimes his voice sounds just as familiar to me as my own.

"No problem. Um, are you at your apartment? Or on your way to class?"

Connor lets out that easy laugh of his, the one I can feel in his whole body when my hand is pressed against his chest. "Funny you should ask . . ."

"Tell me where you are," I say, grabbing my key off the mattress. "And stay put."

"I'm outside your psych building."

I stop at the door. I can feel Shay's eyes on me. "Like, the psych building at Blue Ridge State?"

"No, Andie, *your* psych building."

The key suddenly feels so heavy and bulky in my hand that I nearly drop it on the dorm room's linoleum floor. "Why would you be . . ."

"I transferred to Little Fells Community College. To be with you."

My eyes sweep up to Shay's, knowing she just heard every word through my old tinny phone. My jaw drops, and so does hers, just before she lets out a low, sympathetic "Holy guacamole."

Chapter Three

When you're a teenager and you tell people one day in the nearish future you're going to write a book that's part self-help, part memoir, you're bound to get more than a few laughs. But that's never made my vision of the book any less clear: *Through Rose-Colored Glasses*, it'll be called. A little on the nose, given my last name and my reading glasses, but relentless optimism is kind of my brand, and I've never been one to apologize for it.

The thing is, though, if you're going to sell a book on how to find happiness, you need to be an authority in it. You can't just sell people on a happy ending based on your advice; you need to *be* the happy ending. You have to earn it.

And I intend to. I'm nowhere near the brightest person I know, but I am one of the hardest-working. I'll get my bachelor's and do whatever it takes to earn my way into a program for my master's. I'll find mentors in the field, and then strike out on my own, and become a mentor myself. And I'll tie up all that success with the sweetest, most beautiful bow: the proof that love really can conquer all.

"Connor . . ."

"Yeah?"

I purse my lips, pressing the phone closer to my cheek. "I transferred to Blue Ridge."

Shay's wincing again, and I don't blame her. I know what this sounds like: some lovesick girl who upended her whole life, Elle Woods-style, for the sake of some boy. But it isn't like that. This school has been my plan since I was basically in utero. My mom always talked about this campus like there was magic in it. Other kids dreamed about Narnia or Middle Earth or mythical worlds, but I was staring at maps of Blue Ridge's campus on my dad's mug and curled up on the couch in my mom's Blue Ridge scarf.

And even if it *were* like that—Connor isn't just some boy. He's the thread that has run through every part of my life. The kid who took me to the school nurse when I skinned my knee playing lava on the playground. The boy I swapped ghost stories with at the town's annual s'mores cookout in Little Fells Park. The crush so in sync with mine that when we were fifteen, we both asked each other to Homecoming at the exact same time, in equally cheesy, public ways. The boyfriend who's invited me and my grandmas to all of his family's events, from birthdays to Thanksgivings to Christmases. After my mom died it felt like there was a strange distance separating me from a lot of our old friends, but Connor always made sure I was part of his world.

Even now, all these miles from him, I can see Connor closing his eyes and breathing the impossibility of this out like he's two feet in front of me.

"You did?" Connor asks, his voice low.

I turn my back on Shay, just in case my eyes prick with tears. Usually I've got myself on lock, but this situation is a decidedly unprecedented one.

"Yeah," I say miserably. "Are you . . ."

"There's no way for you to transfer back?" he asks.

Something seizes in my stomach. "I . . ."

"No. Sorry. Of course not," he says quickly, apologetically. "Plus—you probably just used all your savings, didn't you?" He may not be paying his own tuition, but he knows from all the part-time jobs I saved money from that I am. "I don't deserve you."

I shake my head, the pit in my stomach still clenched. *It wasn't just for you,* I want to say, but I'm too busy trying to blink myself out of this absurd dream to really latch on to the thought.

"I can't believe—if I'd known you were . . ."

"*Shh,* Andie, don't. If anything, it just shows how much we love each other."

Love. That's a word I haven't heard from him in the past few months. I'm not proud of myself for knowing that, because I don't believe that love is about keeping score. But there's such an immediate relief at hearing him say it again that I can't pretend it hasn't worried me.

"Let me see what I can do on my end," I say, holding on to the idea that we can fix this like it's a lifeline.

"Yeah. Me too. It's—it'll be fine, okay?" he says. "We've both got classes starting today, so—let's take it one step at a time. Go to class. Then figure it out."

Like I can go to class now without acting like the guilt is eating me alive. If I'd just told him. If I hadn't been so stubborn about wanting this to be a surprise. It's the Homecoming mix-up all over again, except I sincerely doubt either of us will be laughing about this anytime soon.

"Worse comes to worst, we're apart for one more semester," says Connor. "We'll figure this out. We always do."

"We always do," I echo.

After we hang up I take a beat. When I was in middle school I read an article on how to stop tears from coming out of your eyes. The first step was to breathe in four seconds, then breathe out two. I stare at the wall and take that breath.

"Shit," says Shay. "Are you gonna cry?"

There's something in her very frank but empathetic delivery that makes me laugh, and snaps me right out of it. I shove my phone into the pocket of my dress and turn back to her. I can tell from the steady way she's looking at me that the laugh is exactly what she'd intended.

"No," I say thickly. "At least, not if we take these Zebra Cakes to the face right now."

Shay nods, holding hers up as she shifts off her bed. "Good. Because I've got to get to my ten-thirty shift."

"Cheddar cheese and Ritz *crackers*."

She takes this oddity in stride a lot faster than others have. "I appreciate the specificity." She reaches for a plush gray beanie. "Do you have class?"

"Not until stats at eleven. But I need to get to the quad," I say, helping myself to the mirror she propped up by the bookshelf. Somehow, impossibly, I look every bit as intact as I did five minutes ago—blond ponytail still immaculately styled and curled, eyeliner unsmudged, berry-pink lip stain still smiling tentatively back at me. Given the number of legacy Blue Ridge kids with trust funds and immaculate test scores, I wasn't sure what to expect when I got here, but I made sure to try to look the part.

"I have to cut through it to get to work." Shay hauls a tote bag full of books approximately half her own size. It is safe to assume, based on the titles on the bindings poking out of it, that 90 percent of them are not part of Blue Ridge's core course curriculum. "I can take you there."

"Thanks," I say, tightening my ponytail and grabbing my Zebra Cake for the road.

When we emerge into the January chill the campus is teeming with students, the sidewalks and little winding paths so full of them that it feels like they've shoved the entire population of Little Fells into a few square blocks. At first I'm so dumbstruck by the sheer number of *kids*. It feels like someone raptured all the authority figures. I can't stop staring at everyone, accidentally making direct and aggressive eye contact enough times that people start to give us a wide berth.

"You look like you just got dropped into another country," says

Shay, who has been lightly steering me by tapping my arm every time we're going to pivot in another direction.

I shake my head. "Little Fells is kind of tiny. I'm just not used to so many . . ."

"Hungover co-eds in pajamas?" Shay supplies.

So much for me looking the part. I look more like someone about to teach a class than take one. But before I can answer, class lets out from a nearby building and a group of students nearly flattens us. Shay yanks me into the grass before we get caught in the maelstrom of elbows and bright blue coffee cups, and we watch them go by like Simba on the edge of a wildebeest herd.

"My life may have just flashed before my eyes," I say after we're in the clear.

"Was it pretty?" asks Shay.

"Honestly, there was a lot of scrolling through Instagram."

Shay squints at the crowd we just dodged as they sharply pivot to the quad just ahead. "Oh, right. The Knights' Tour. Is that what you're headed to the quad for? You're trying to get into one of the secret societies?"

I pick up the pace to keep up with the crowd in front of us, but slow when I notice Shay doesn't change her stride. "Yeah. You aren't?"

"Eh, probably not," says Shay. "I'm busy enough as it is. And besides, whatever's at the end of this ribbon hunt might just be a waste of time."

I think of my mom's ribbons, still tucked away safely with my things, and am suddenly glad I didn't pull them out in front of her. "But you don't know that."

"And you do?" Shay asks, raising an amused eyebrow.

I open my mouth to defend it—the ribbon hunt, the secret societies, my compulsion to be a part of it all—but the truth is, I don't know much at all. Only that it's so much a part of my mom's legacy that it all feels inextricably tied to me, too.

Off my look, Shay pivots and says, "Well, if you know about the kickoff event, I take it you've been listening to *The Knights' Watch*."

I nod, grateful for the change in subject. "Yeah."

But "listening" is an understatement. "Living and breathing" might be a better one. I've been keeping up with *The Knights' Watch* since I was a little girl, either on the livestream or the downloadable version that always pops up as a podcast after it plays.

"So what do you think?" Shay asks.

We've reached the edge of the quad now, and I'm half distracted by the small crowd of students gathering on the grass near the open concrete stage. "Of the show?"

When I look back over, Shay's wearing a smirk I can't read for the life of me. "Yeah. And of this year's Knight," she says.

I flush and hope against hope that she won't notice. By "this year's Knight" she means the anonymous student hosting *The Knights' Watch*, who gets rotated out every time their predecessor graduates. They all usually have some kind of schtick, but their role is mostly to give updates on whatever is happening on campus, including every spring semester when they're tasked with releasing the locations and times for the scavenger-hunt tasks—freshmen show up, complete some kind of task, and are given either a yellow, red, or blue ribbon. Each of the ribbons represents a different secret society, and if you have enough of one of the colors at the end of the semester, you have the option of joining the society of that color.

Trouble is, nobody's sure just how many is enough to qualify. Hence the scramble to get as many ribbons as you can, and why anyone participating hangs on the Knight's every word.

"I think he's phenomenal," I say quickly, willing my face to un-heat itself. "The one before him was great too, but the new guy is just hilarious. I can't listen in public anymore because I keep laughing out loud."

Shay tilts her head at me. "Wait, you were listening even when you didn't go here?"

I let out a nervous laugh. "You might have caught on to the fact that I'm a *little* bit of an over-preparer."

"Well, at least you'll fit right in here," says Shay, eyes sweeping over the campus. "Can't take a step without running into a fellow nerd."

I cling to the words like a lifeline. In that case, maybe connecting with people here will be easier than I think. Maybe I'll even feel comfortable enough to launch some kind of advice column here without hiding behind a fake name to do it.

But while it's true that I am an over-preparer in every sense of the word, that has nothing to do with my *Knights' Watch* obsession. Or the fact that I not only know about the last Knight, but the one before that and the one before *that*, all the way back to the very first broadcast of the show, some thirty years ago.

See, my mom's the one who started it all. The original Knight.

Chapter Four

You know how when you hear the premise of *Footloose* for the first time and you're like, "Wow, a bunch of adults seriously banned kids from dancing? That's ridiculous." But that's also kind of like Blue Ridge State in the nineties, because apparently they flat-out banned new student organizations from forming. They said there simply weren't enough professors to act as supervisors, but according to my mom, a loudmouth journalism major with an uncanny knack for uncovering secrets, it was because the current school president was misusing alumni funds that were meant to go toward student-driven programming. And apparently she said so—right on the air of the school's radio show that she was hosting at the time.

Somewhat unsurprisingly, she was fired from her role ten minutes later. But instead of backing down, she banded together with some friends, figured out how to get back on the air using an underground channel, and started *The Knights' Watch*—a radio show reporting on what students needed to know, but the school didn't necessarily *want* them to know.

Over the years it's evolved into what it is today—less of a rebellion and more of an alternative news source on campus. It's not part of our broadcast major, so it's not necessarily school-sanctioned, but school-tolerated. Each of the Knights is known for being outspoken and often critical of goings-on on campus. The current Knight goes on rants about the cost of tuition and the lack of decent work-study opportunities so often that I can't say I'm not nervous about trying to find one. But different Knights have all had their own things—one was a budding comedian, another was super into discovering local bands.

My mom's "thing" as the Knight was the first-ever Knights' Tour. The school had banned new organizations, but not events. So when a group of students came up with the idea to go behind the school's back and start new organizations on campus, and wanted to throw the administration off with scavenger hunts to access information about them, my mom gave them a platform. She would announce the day of where people were supposed to meet off campus. Then she'd go and participate in the ribbon hunts herself.

That's why the ribbons always had a certain lore. My mom laid hers out on her dresser right alongside all the family photos. She had enough to qualify for any of the societies, but every time I asked her which society she ended up in, she'd tap me on the nose and say it was a secret. That I'd find out when I was older.

Turns out, as a nod to the secrecy of the organizations when they first started up, it's tradition for members not to reveal themselves unless you qualify first. It's part of the reason why I was so determined to get in right now instead of waiting the year out—second semester freshman year is the only chance to participate. After all these years, I might finally get to know which society she was in, and what it meant to her. What it could mean to me.

That is, only if I collect enough ribbons for all three.

Shay and I are interrupted by the pinging of my phone. It's Connor, responding to a text saying I'd be at the kickoff event and then class, but would call him later.

Shit, his text reads. I'm gonna miss the whole ribbon hunt, huh?

My stomach drops.

"Yikes," says Shay. "What's that face about?"

Oh, nothing. Just the pit of my guilt opening up into an endless

abyss. "My boyfriend—he wanted to collect rib**b**
plain.

"Ah," says Shay. She knows as well as I do that y**o**
ticipate in the spring of your first year here. "That

I perk up so fast that Shay looks around us i**n**
spotted a predator. "I could collect ribbons for bo**t**
ize. "Right?"

Shay scrunches her nose. "I guess. I don't think
you got them."

I nod more to myself than to her, saying it ou**t**
speak it into existence: "I'll just go to as many eve**r**
enough ribbons for me *and* for him. Then he'll co**r**
mester and everything will be back on track, just li

We reach the fringes of the crowd in the mi**d**
and Shay veers slightly to the left, in the directi
street in town. I clutch my bag harder to myself, u
ing it this way. As far as first impressions go, this
exactly painting me in the most flattering light.

But Shay just sighs. "Look, I'd warn you not
plans on someone you're dating, but maybe that's
have to learn for yourself." Shay shudders. "Like m
AP Gov for my ex-girlfriend senior year. God, I h**o**
is burning in hell."

"I'm not pinning my plans on him," I say qui
a chance to clarify. I stand up a little taller, whic
as a five-foot-one person can. "I already have a**r**
mapped out. I also just know that he's part of it."

Shay looks amused. "Okay, I'll bite. What's y**o**

I suck in a perilously deep breath, and com**r**
tor pitch for the next two decades of my life. "I
therapist. I'll get my degree in psychology, my m
psych, then for the first seven to ten years it'll b
and me building up a presence as my advice-gi

social media through my syndicated advice column, and then I'll evolve to writing my memoir from there."

I actually have a lot of air left over, but I breathe it out. There used to be more to that dream. I was going to be like my mom—have a whole public persona, one I could use for good. It was maybe precocious for an eleven-year-old, but I had a mom in the business, so back then my plan was set: I'd book some podcasts and local spots, get an agent, and work on my brand as a relatable expert in the field until I could be a personality. I'd leverage it into getting interviews on morning talk shows, posting on social media under my own name, becoming a full-known force of nature. Maybe even start a talk show of my own.

But I moved on from those parts of the dream a long, long time ago.

"Wow," says Shay when I'm done. "Imagine having even half that much figured out. Couldn't be me."

I only gave her the SparkNotes version, but there's a line between mildly alarming and fully alarming someone, and Shay and I don't know each other well enough yet to risk crossing it.

Her face settles into an uneasy expression as she looks out at the quad. "I mean, I can't even decide on a major."

"Well, we've got time, right?"

Shay gives a quick shake of her head. "We have to apply for one by the end of the semester if we want to keep our work-study benefits."

Right. I forgot about that. I was so stressed out trying to secure myself a spot in the work-study program before the semester started that I skimmed the rule about deciding on a major—I've never had to wonder what mine would be.

I square my shoulders and beam at her like I can use it to will the crease between her brows away. "In that case, we'll just have to start workshopping ideas for your major tonight."

Shay cracks a smile. "Oh, will we?"

"Yes," I say chipperly. If there's one thing I'm good at, it's problem-solving. And Shay can be my first crack at doing it with an actual person here. "After dinner. I'll have an idea board ready."

"An idea board, huh?" says Shay in amusement, like she's trying to decide if I'm exaggerating. We're interrupted by the bells starting to ring in the tiny little church on campus, warning us that ten o'clock is fast approaching. "Gotta jet. Good luck with Hutchison."

The fact that she knows my stats professor by name despite never taking one of her courses does not exactly bode well for my academic future. I feel a flutter of fear in my rib cage and bleat out a "Thanks."

Chapter Five

I'm so amped from the aftermath of the kickoff ceremony that the walk to class feels almost dreamlike. It's finally hitting me that I'm *here*. That I'm not just at my dream school, but for the first time, I'm on my own. I can go off to any of the upcoming ribbon-hunt events without checking with my grandmas. I can pick which dining hall I want to grab lunch in without factoring in anyone else's schedules. And if I want to wander to the arboretum after class this afternoon, I can just pick up my bag and *go*.

All this time I've been so eager to get here that I didn't think much past beyond doing it. Now it feels like there's an entire new world to consider. I'm so giddy from the potential of it that I want to break into a run, swallow this entire place whole.

For now I take a steadying breath, pressing my grin into a close-lipped smile as I tuck my white ribbon into my bag. It's the qualifying ribbon—the one you can only get at the kickoff event and sign with your name, the same way my mom did all those years ago. All the other events will take place on weekends, giving people multiple opportunities to get each color—January for the blue ribbon, February for the red, and March for the yellow—but you only get one shot at the qualifying ribbon, and you can't play without it.

Which is to say, I'm ready to guard it with my life.

The only trouble is that given the nature of it, I could only get one. I doubt there will be a way to get a second one for Connor, but I owe it to him to try. I square my shoulders with resolve and reach for the door to the lecture hall.

The extremely locked door to the lecture hall.

I take a step back. Open up the class schedule I have saved to my phone, to my computer, even printed out somewhere in my bag. I'm definitely in the right place.

I try the door again, just to see if it's jammed, and when it doesn't open I tentatively knock. I hear some murmuring on the other end and step back, certain it's a student in one of the back rows getting up to let me in, but instead I find myself face-to-face with an older woman in a floral button-down tucked into no-nonsense slacks who can only be Professor Hutchison.

"You're late."

The words echo through the lecture hall. One quick glance behind her is all the confirmation I need that a hundred pairs of eyes have turned around to stare at me.

Just like that, I'm only half here. The other half of me is twelve years old again, my face an inch from a microphone at a school assembly with just as many eyes on me, my chest suddenly so tight I don't know how to breathe. I blink the memory away, forcing myself to look Professor Hutchison in her very impatient eyes.

"Um—sorry, I was—"

"With that noisy group on the quad?" she says disdainfully.

I follow her gaze to the incriminating white ribbon poking out of my bag.

"Yes," I say.

My phone lights up and informs me that it is, in fact, several minutes past eleven. I was so swept up in the excitement of my newfound freedom that for the first time in possibly my entire memory, I lost track of time.

"On the first day of class, which you well know from my copious emails is the day of your placement exam?"

"I—I didn't." My brain sidesteps the words "placement exam" only so I don't end up choking on my own spit. "I'm a transfer. My email didn't get set up until yesterday."

My heart is racing fast enough in my chest that it feels like there are two of them. I can't fail this class. Not if I want to graduate in this major. Not if I want to keep my entire life plan from crashing into the ground.

She narrows her eyes at me, but steps aside, holding the door open. "You get one pass. But first, hand that over." She's staring at the ribbon.

"But I—"

"Now, young lady."

My hand grazes the ribbon, but stops there. I keep waiting for some kind of punch line, but as I feel the weight of several dozen eyes and the sound of muffled laughter, it's clear the joke is me.

I hand over the ribbon. "I'm, uh—really sorry," I say, and now it's *my* voice echoing into eternity, like I've thrown a boomerang and had it come back and knock me on my butt.

She doesn't acknowledge the apology, just takes the ribbon from me and puts it in her pocket. My soul separates from my body just enough that I'm able to find a seat in the back row and plant myself in it. Professor Hutchison sets a fresh exam down in front of me. I take a breath. Four seconds in, two seconds out. I'll reason with her later. I'll get the ribbon back. I've got this.

Then I look down at the page and realize it might as well be gibberish. Our high school didn't offer statistics, only algebra and pre-calc, and I didn't take either first semester at the community college because I knew the credit wouldn't transfer here.

I glance up to see if anyone else is having a silent near-breakdown at their desk, and see every single person with a calculator propped next to their exam. I close my eyes and can see mine very clearly, stashed deep in my duffel bag back at the dorms, which is precisely the least helpful place it could be.

Ten minutes pass. Ten minutes of me staring down at the exam and wondering whether I should try to fake it or ask for a calculator or just write "SORRY" in all caps over the front page and run for my life.

Okay. Deep breath. I square my shoulders, preparing myself for whatever embarrassment is on the other end of me fessing up that I need to borrow a calculator, but then my eyes catch a scrawled letter on the desk—a neat little "A" with a distinctive swirl at the end of it.

Before the thought even connects, I'm touching the charm on my necklace. It has that exact swirl. I'm certain if I unclasped it right now and set the charm down on the scrawl, the "A" would fit into its exact dimensions—it was my mom's way of signing everything. Checks to pay the power bill. Autographs to fans of her show. Her white ribbon. My dad got the necklace specially made for her sometime before I was born, and she's wearing it in just about every picture I have of her.

There's no way it's her scrawled letter on this desk, but there's also no way it isn't. My throat tightens so fast I have to clear it before I choke. I've been mad at my dad for hiding all the pieces of her for so long, but now that I'm closer to her than I've been in years, all I can think is that I'm already letting her down.

I stand up.

"This exam is worth a significant portion of your grade," Professor Hutchison snaps from the front of the lecture hall. "If you leave this classroom, you're not coming back."

I open my mouth, but this time words don't come out. I feel all the eyes on me and I'm twelve and eighteen at the same time, so self-conscious that all I can do is nod vigorously like a bobblehead doll and back away toward the door. She looks away first, with a sharp shake of her head and a *tsk* that I can't hear, but can still see.

Then I'm out of the door, out of the building, beelining back to the quad so fast I'm on autopilot. But the upperclassmen and all the white ribbons are gone, and my chance to do the ribbon hunt right along with them.

I don't cry on my way back to the dorm. The whole thing is too absurd, too bone-deep. The Connor thing was a setback, sure. But now the ribbon is gone. Now I understand just how in over my head I am academically. I spent eighteen years trying to get here, and it only took an hour for it to fall apart.

Thanks to the wonky way my schedule was made to accommodate getting a work-study, I don't have any other classes today. I was going to use that time to start knocking down doors to actually *find* a position for work-study—it's not built in for transfers, and the current Knight hasn't been exaggerating in his rants about how hard the school makes it to find decent ones—but that can wait. I need to go home. I need to see my grandmas, to regroup with Connor. I need to Google the bus schedule that goes between here and Little Fells and—

"Don't tell me you're already sick of this place, new kid."

I stop short in the middle of the dorm hallway, my hastily repacked backpack slung over my shoulder. In front of me is a slightly more awake version of Milo the RA, his curls freshly showered with this faint citrus smell wafting off him that tricks me into a momentary calm.

I adjust the backpack, trying to look less ridiculous than I objectively do in the midst of running away from campus after approximately one hour of living in it. "I'm—I'll be back tomorrow. I'm just going home for the night."

Milo considers me for a moment that same way he did when we first met this morning, except this time his eyes linger. I try not to look away, frozen in place even as a loose hair falls into my face. The ponytail is coming undone, then. God only knows what the rest of me looks like.

After a few moments he shakes his head. "Nah, you're not."

He reaches a hand out for my backpack as if the matter is settled.

I cling to it stubbornly. When he moves his hand again I'm expecting him to drop it, but instead he presses it on my shoulder, the weight of it firm but bizarrely comforting coming from someone who looks like they haven't slept since the 1800s.

The gesture may be soothing, but his words are blunt. "Look—I know that face," he says. "That's the 'I'm in over my head' face. And I'm telling you, the last thing you want to do when you have that face is go home, because then it's only going to get worse."

I nod numbly, wondering how he knows about that face. Then I remember he probably had an hour's worth of RA training specifically devoted to that face.

But then my nod turns into a head shake, and I cling harder to my backpack strap. The last time he dealt with terrified freshmen, they were in this together. I'm out here by myself. That fresh slate I thought I'd be able to get here—the one where nobody knew about my mom, where there wasn't some invisible buffer between me and fitting in with everyone else—it never existed. They've already made themselves fit, and now I've made a new kind of buffer all on my own.

"I've already screwed everything up," I blurt. "Connor's not even here, I'm going to get a zero on an exam in my hardest class, I don't even know where to start on getting a work-study position, Professor Hutchison took my white ribbon—"

"Professor Hutchison?" he asks in mild surprise.

"You know her, too?" I ask, wondering just how terrifying this woman is if the only two people I've formally met on campus recognize her name.

"Of her. But listen." Milo squeezes the hand still on my shoulder, looking me directly in the eyes. Now that he's mostly conscious I can see the full array of green shades in his, striking against his dark hair. I'm just thrown off enough that this time, when he reaches for the strap of my backpack, I ease it off my shoulders and let him take it. "The work-study bit? That can wait. Use today to clear your head or something. Give yourself some time to adjust."

"But . . ."

I almost feel unsteady without the weight of the backpack on me, but watching Milo's resolute steps toward my room evens me out again.

"And hey, if you've still got that look on your face in a few weeks, you can always just ditch this place like I'm gonna at the end of the year," he says, moving out of the way so I can unlock the door.

"Wait. *You're* trying to leave?" I ask, all at once so indignant that I consider snatching my backpack right out of his hands.

"Tried, past tense." Once I let us in the room he pauses at the door, taking in Shay's intricate array of books and kitschy things. "Damn. This is a nice setup. Hope we don't have any earthquakes."

"Why are you trying to leave? You're an RA, won't you be a senior next year?" I ask, following him so close I nearly bump my nose right into his shoulder as he sets my backpack on my bed.

He seems unfazed to see me an inch away from him when he turns back around. "I'm a sophomore. And unlike you I didn't get accepted by any midyear transfers last semester, so I probably have a better shot this time around."

If there's any more of my stomach left to sink, it just hit the metaphorical floor. "Is this place really so bad?"

Only then does Milo pause. "Nah. School's fine. You'll be alright." His gaze falls back on me. "Besides. You don't seem much like a quitter. That is, if the three-page introductory email you sent me and the dorm supervisors is any indication."

He's right. I'm not a quitter. I've watched every season of *Grey's Anatomy*. I led a school-fundraiser car wash during a hurricane. I once ran an entire 5K matching pace with Connor despite never having run a full mile in my entire life.

And then I find it: some shred of what I was looking for. The stubborn part of me that doesn't know how to hear the word "no." The Amy Rose in me. It's a little thing, maybe, but it's enough. The world slows down for a moment. I take a breath and look back at Milo.

"You read it?" I ask.

"Your proposed matching T-shirt designs for the dorm weren't bad. Financially unfeasible, but not bad." He takes his hand off my shoulder so unceremoniously that I might have imagined it, then heads back toward my door. "I'm going to class. Tell Shay to hide those candles if there's a fire drill."

"Okay."

Except the word doesn't come out all steady like I'd planned. I'm hoping he'll ignore it, but then Milo turns back to look at me, leaning against the doorframe and taking me in. I take him in right back, and wonder why he seemed familiar to me earlier. Those sleepy eyes and dark curls are pretty distinctive, but he doesn't look like anyone I've ever met.

"And just . . . take a breather. Unpack your stuff. Go walk around campus." He makes a vague gesture at our window. "I feel like you won't have any trouble making friends."

I smile then. Not the syndicated-talk-show smile or even a power-past-the-tears kind of smile. An actual one, so surprising that for a moment I'm not sure of my own face.

"Thanks," I say.

One of the corners of Milo's lip tugs up, like a smile snuck up on him. By the time he waves me off, all traces of it are gone. "You know where to find me."

The door closes, and the brief reassurance goes with him. For the first time in a long time, I don't know what to do. That's the thing about having your goals set in stone—you always have a road map. The path might not be easy, but at least it's clear.

Now it's hazier than ever. I have all this energy, but I don't know which way to direct it. I step toward the window, staring at the campus at my feet, and try to imagine myself here in a real way, instead of the daydream way that I have since I was a kid. But even then, I see the faint shadow of someone else—a girl who was already making her mark. A girl who didn't just make plans, but brought them all to life. A girl who left a distinctive swirl at the end of her "A," and didn't follow any road maps, but made her own.

I can't help looking out at these winding paths without seeing her footsteps in every one of them and wondering if I'll ever be able to fill her shoes.

Chapter Six

Grandma Maeve doesn't laugh. She cackles. And this particular cackle goes on for so long that I almost have to hold the phone away from my ear.

"I had a feeling something would go topsy-turvy with your whole plan to surprise him."

"We both did," Gammy Nell chimes in.

I'm on speaker, which has informed me that despite threats from both grandmas to "find a place of their own" the second I was gone, they're still very much living together in our house. I don't even realize how worried I was about that until the relief of it is washing over me.

"Then why didn't you *say* something?" I demand, crossing my arms over my chest to try to stave off the cold. It's plenty freezing in Little Fells in the winter, but Blue Ridge State is just elevated enough to somehow make the bite even sharper.

I sit down on a bench on the borders of the lake in the arboretum, breathing in the freshness of the air. The lake is all frozen over right now, gleaming in the sunlight, looking prettier than it has any right to on this day when I may have unconditionally messed up my entire future.

Despite it all, there's something grounding in being here, something calming. I'm glad Milo convinced me not to go home. Glad that I can feel the unfamiliar relief that comes with being alone and wandering at my own pace. It feels like there's infinite space out here, enough that for once I don't need to worry about making myself fit.

"Because, chicken. You were supposed to go there either way," says Grandma Maeve.

"And I love that bagel place off campus," says Gammy Nell. "Good for lunch visits."

"You let me fly solo on the most monumental decision of my life for *bagels*?"

For once, Gammy Nell takes the reins on the conversation. "No, dearie. We did it because you're a grown woman now, and you have to forge your own path."

My chin feels uncharacteristically wobbly. I press the phone closer to my cheek, like I can use it to make them both closer to me. "It's weird that you guys are so far away."

Neither of them says the thing we're all thinking, which is that I was going to have to move out sooner or later. But we sidestep it, and they tell me what I need to hear most instead.

"Andie Rose. You know we will zip up there any day to see you," says Grandma Maeve. "Even days *Deadpool* is on cable."

Gammy Nell hums in agreement. "And you can come home anytime you want. We'll pick you up whenever you say the word."

My eyes are stinging, but I don't bother with my four seconds in and two seconds out. My grandmas are the only two people I've never had trouble crying in front of. They know me inside out and backward.

"Okay." I'm too overwhelmed to say anything else.

There's a pause then. The kind of pause so telling that I know exactly what Gammy Nell is going to ask before she asks it.

"Did you call your dad back yet?"

I fix my eyeline on a group of ducks waddling around the ice. "Oh," I say, the sincerity so false that it hurts even my own ears. "I meant to. I just—forgot. In all of the pandemonium."

There's silence from all three of us then, but their silence is different from mine. Their silence is strategic, the two of them doing that grandma thing they do when they're both trying to convince me of the same thing, but can't agree on how to approach it. My silence, on the other hand, is strictly out of hurt.

See, my dad asked me a few months ago to send him clippings from my advice column, "Bed of Roses." The one I'd spent most of high school hesitant to tell him about in the first place. And after I did—after I sent him the back catalogue of all the people whose questions I'd answered, each of the clippings painstakingly collected, printed, and put into an envelope—he never said a word about it. Not a single one.

"He's so excited you're at Blue Ridge State," says Grandma Maeve, which is how I know for a fact he's been calling the house about it. She isn't the conductor of the Make Amends With Your Dad train, the way Gammy Nell justifiably is, being his mom and all. "It might make you feel better to talk it out with him."

"You're right," I say automatically, even though I'd sooner try to figure skate on this half-frozen lake. And then, mostly just to move the conversation along, I ask, "How are your sourdough starters doing?"

Just as predicted, this launches them into a ten-minute back and forth defending the sanctity of their respective starters and which one they're going to use for that week's loaf ("Hers is *too sour*," Gammy Nell complains, to which Grandma Maeve responds, "What, did you want dull dough?"), so the focus is squarely off the dad talk. By the time we hang up the whole thing's all but forgotten.

I spend the rest of the day unpacking my stuff and staring at my phone, trying to decide whether to call Connor or wait for him to call. Eventually the question just chases itself in circles enough times that Milo's advice to "take a breather" falls on the back burner. Desperate for something else to focus on, I start emailing potential leads for work-studies—I know full well there are no open positions on campus right now, but I figure emailing the heads of a few different departments won't hurt. Once I've exhausted my options, I whip out the very large sketchpad I had tucked into the rolling suitcase, stare at Shay's half of the room, and write down all the words I can think of. It starts with "books, candles, cozy sweaters, Instagram, pastels, coffee." Then I do some light stalking of her Instagram and add "sister, bubble tea, sunflowers, hiking, rom-coms, horror movies, woozy face emoji, true-crime podcasts, Instagram-famous dogs, Janelle Monáe, photography." By the time Shay comes back with a massive to-go box full of food, I'm so far into my idea boarding I realize I didn't even notice the sun going down.

"Uh-oh. Did I miss dining hall hours?"

"If you love yourself, you'll never step foot in our dining halls. Here. I grabbed this for you," says Shay, opening the to-go box and handing me a bagel stuffed to the brim with cream cheese.

The smell of it alone is beautiful enough to make me swoon like one of the characters on the covers of her romance novels. I take a bite and the bagel is so perfectly pillowy on the inside and toasted on the outside, with this sweet, tangy cream cheese unlike anything I've tasted in my entire human life.

"This is . . . otherworldly." If this came from the same place Grandma Maeve was talking about, it's no wonder she was so willing to sell out my future for carbs. "How much do I owe you?"

"I do my work-study at Bagelopolis, so I get them for free," says Shay, unwrapping her own bagel. "They have like, twenty cream cheese flavors, but I guessed at cookie dough for you. Seems like you have a sweet tooth."

"My blood is ninety-eight percent sugar," I confirm. "Also, you can do work-study off campus?"

Shay jerks a thumb toward the hallway. "Talk to Milo. He has a zillion brothers and sisters, and they have all the best work-study connects."

I'd thank her, but I take a bite so large I might need a backup mouth to accommodate it. Shay pauses on her way over to her bed, justifiably concerned.

"Sorry," I say, wiping my face with the back of my wrist. It's the kind of thing I try not to do often, especially considering how tidy Connor and his family are, but every now and then I get excited and manners go out the window. I get a few more vigorous chews in before I swallow. "We just have a *lot* to get through before tonight's dorm catchup."

"Catchup?"

"The one I saw the flier for in the hall."

"Oh. People don't actually go to dorm-sponsored events here," says Shay. "Milo just puts up the fliers out of like, legal obligation. Sort of like that RA comment box outside of his room nobody actually uses."

I furrow my brow. "Well—maybe I can fix that." Shay opens her mouth, presumably to ask me how, but I interrupt her by putting my sketchpad of words in her lap. "May I present the idea board for your major."

"Wow." Her eyes comb over all the words I've piled on, taking a bite of cheddar bagel and letting it soak in. "This looks like you took a screenshot of the inside of my brain."

"That's the plan. Map out your brain." I point at the blank area I left for her. "You can fill in whatever I missed, and then we can take a good long look at it, figure out what you're meant to do with your life, and backtrack to find you a major from there."

Shay sighs in that exasperated but affectionate way I know all too well from a lifetime of inserting myself into friends' problems. When they would hesitate to come to me with them after my mom died, I'd usually have to take matters into my own hands when I wanted to help. I'd be discouraged if my track record for solving them weren't near spotless.

"Listen, I appreciate this," says Shay, trying to hand me back the sketchpad. "But the problem is, all I really want to do is read."

"Oh." I settle down on my bed, bagel still in hand. It almost seems anticlimactic for everything to get resolved so easily. "So English, then."

"I only read books I *want* to read," says Shay. "And Blue Ridge State's English department is run by some geezer who only pushes books from dead white men anyway."

I wince. As progressive as Blue Ridge State's student body is, I suppose the same can't always be said for the curriculum—even if it's making progress with each year of students and new professors coming in, it's nowhere near where it needs to be. Nothing like Shay's Bookstagram, which she uses to post weekly roundups of new releases from queer, BIPOC, and marginalized authors on her stories while highlighting her favorites on main. She may review books across all genres, but she's vocal in her captions about how important it is as a reader to see herself in the characters, for everyone to be able to see themselves in stories. People would get a much better education in literature from her grid than most college programs.

"Good point." I mull it over, going back to those captions of hers in my mind. "Maybe you're a writer," I say, the thrill of a challenge reignited.

She shakes her head. "The only writing I do is book reviews."

It's unfortunate that I choose that precise moment to take another massive bite of bagel, because I nearly choke on it in my enthusiasm. "Oh! Journalism."

Shay, to her credit, seems entirely undaunted by my theatrics. I'm glad that she's acclimating to me quickly. People usually do in the end, but it takes a little longer for some than others.

"You could be a book critic!"

"In this economy?" she asks, wrinkling her nose.

Fair point. "Chunky Monkey," I mutter in frustration. "Okay. I'll keep thinking."

"It's nice of you to get this invested in my collegiate future and all," says Shay, "but please, save your energy for literally anything else. I'm a lost cause. A cute one. But lost nonetheless."

If anything that just makes the fix-it urge even more powerful. "I've got this *thing* about solving problems," I tell her.

Shay lowers her chin. "You don't say?"

"I'll totally stop if you want me to, though," I say, lifting up the small fraction of my remaining bagel like a white flag. "I know I'm a lot."

My mom's general rule was that you can't help someone who doesn't want to be helped. So even though I am aggressive about offering it, I try to make sure it's actually wanted before I take off with it. Otherwise trying to help is like yelling at a boulder to move, or trying to convince my grandmas to watch movies without Ryan Reynolds in them—a fruitless effort in the end.

But every now and then I'm so full of ideas I get ahead of myself, and I have to double back.

Shay considers me for a moment. "I mean . . . I do have to figure this out before the end of the semester. So. Definitely let me know if you have thoughts. But don't like, waste too much time on it," she says with a shrug.

Before the end of her sentence I've already started mapping out a four-month plan to get her in the right major by the end of the semester, complete with a vision board, several personality quizzes I've vetted online, and internship options in the larger Blue Ridge State area.

"Sweet."

Just then an alarm goes off on my phone.

"Do you have somewhere to be?" Shay asks, frowning curiously at it.

"Yup." I adjust the headband Connor's mom got me to wear for my graduation photos, shaking my hair back so I can get just the right amount of volume on top, the way she taught me, then reach

for the absurdly large bag of snack cakes Gammy Nell dropped off
with me this morning. "The dorm catchup."

Shay follows me to the door as I'm yanking it open. "Look," she
says. "I don't want you to get your hopes up. Cardinal dorm's not
exactly known for its fraternizing."

I digest this, but also commence my two-point plan by steadily
knocking on all the doors I pass. Step one: Get everyone's attention. Step two: Lure them into the rec room with an abundance of
snack cakes. If I still have a shot at a fresh start here, I'm going to
have to rip off the Band-Aid now, before anything else can happen
to psych me out.

"Everyone just . . . studies, mostly," says Shay, at a light jog to
keep up with me. "And Milo's not kidding about quiet hours."

"We've got one more hour," I say, making a point of knocking
loudly on Milo's door, too.

I can hear his muffled response as I make my way up the floor.
"Has anyone lost a limb?"

"No," Shay calls back.

I continue zigzagging back and forth between the doors on either side of the hall, knocking just firmly enough that people start
poking their heads out.

A boy with a textbook the size of a toddler opens his door first.
"Hello?"

"Did you leave your key in the door again?" another girl asks
her roommate.

"I have cake!" I say, thrusting the grocery bag over my head.

They look justifiably startled, but within a minute I have a
small trail of undergraduates following me to the end of the hall
like a sleep-deprived parade. Shay wasn't kidding about the fraternizing thing—the lights aren't even on in the rec room. I find a
table and dump the contents of Gammy Nell's bag, pleased to see
the whole gang is here: we've got Ring Dings, Hostess CupCakes,

Kandy Kakes, Twinkies, Donut Sticks, Yodels, Moon Pies, Zingers, Cosmic Brownies. It's enough sugar to make a dentist feel faint.

I stick my hands into the pockets of my dress, a thrill running up my spine. As unfamiliar as I am with it, I really do love meeting new people. I'm pretty sure I was a labradoodle in a past life. "Do you mind introducing me to the people you know?" I ask Shay.

Shay edges closer to me, talking out of the side of her mouth. "Uh. I don't really know anyone."

"Huh," I say, waving at the confused faces on the other side of the glass door approaching. "I didn't peg you for an introvert."

"I'm not," says Shay, eyeing the cluster of people who followed us here. "All my friends are from book clubs and the school literary magazine."

By the looks of things, I've lured just enough people in here to know that by the end of the night, we're going to change that. I grab a chair to prop the door and drag it over, yanking the door open with a merry "Hello!"

"Hi?" says one of the boys, adjusting a Blue Ridge State baseball cap and blinking at us in confusion.

"Help yourself," I say, gesturing at the very unstable mountain of cake I've created. "I'm Andie, by the way. If you want to head back to study, that's fine, but if you want to stick around I have a fun game we can all play."

"Are you our new RA?" a girl in a Spider-Man onesie asks.

"No, no, our RA is Miley," her friend, carting around a half-finished embroidered shirt of a dumpster on fire, corrects her.

Shay sighs deeply enough to power a windmill, but sticks close by me and grabs a peanut butter Kandy Kake, so I know I have at least one taker.

"It's called Werewolf," I say. "Everyone gets randomly assigned to be a werewolf, an angel, or a villager. After everyone closes their eyes, the werewolf chooses a victim and—"

"Oh, sick," says the boy in the baseball cap. "I played a version where vampires could randomly attack and kill werewolves, if there was more than one."

"Love that," I say, handing him a Ring Ding. "Let's do it."

The girl in the Spider-Man onesie immediately snaps to attention, clearly besotted with baseball-cap boy. "I'm in."

The girl with the dumpster-fire embroidery smirks at me, her lip ring glinting. "We called it Mafia, where I'm from. And there was booze."

"Well—I have cake?" I have a feeling Milo would not take too kindly to me helping intoxicate half the freshmen on his floor the first day of the semester.

"Fair enough. I'm Tyler, by the way," says baseball-cap boy. "Hold up. I'm gonna grab the guys." He pauses. "They're in Bluebird dorm, is that okay?"

"The more the merrier!"

Tyler ducks out, leaving a dazed Spider-Man-onesie girl in his wake. Dumpster-fire embroidery nudges her to snap her out of it.

"I'm Harriet. The pajama-clad arachnid here is Ellie. And we need more players," she says, glancing back at the three other people who are starting to wander in. "I'll round up more of the floor. But only because I'm a Cosmic Brownies bitch."

Harriet uses some fear-based tactics to round up a few more people hesitating in the hallway and Tyler brings half a floor's worth of Bluebird, along with several half-eaten party-size bags of tortilla chips and a massive tub of salsa someone clearly snagged from the dining hall. We sit in a big circle on the floor, quickly learning one another's names to avoid any confusion and launching right into the game, adding mismatched, ridiculous rules from everyone's childhood version of it as we go.

The longer the night goes on, the more I start to get the lay of the land in Cardinal. There's Harriet with her cuttingly hilarious commentary on the status of everyone's mortality throughout the course of the game. There's Tyler with his booming laugh and his army of friends who keep the energy mounting all through the night. There's Ellie with her shy smiles and her little squeals every time Shay and I declare that yet another villager has "died," and the way she scoots over to Tyler when they're both eliminated from a round. There's Shay, who gets caught up in it so fast that she takes over narrating duties, stringing elaborate, ridiculously creative stories behind the deaths of every villager at the hands of the werewolves and vampires. For a little while, it's like we've all entered some separate realm—some place where all our worries are so far gone that we can just forget them.

And for a little while, I forget, too. I forget I was apprehensive about making new friends here. I forget I messed things up with Connor. I forget about my ribbon burning a hole somewhere in Professor Hutchison's desk. I forget that I'm in over my head here at this school full of overachievers who were probably all in the top 10 percent of their graduating class. I forget that I'm away from home for the first time in a real, semipermanent, non-summer-camp way.

I don't forget the bone-deep things—the things so far buried in me that they're just there on a dull, constant hum—but I forget the scary ones. The immediate ones. For an hour or so, they aren't pulling at the edges of me, and I'm laughing and yelling and swapping embarrassing stories with everyone else.

That is, until the door to the rec room opens, and one very tall, very sleep-deprived RA says groggily, "What on earth is going on in here?"

The recently murdered villagers are closest to the door, so Ellie lets out a "Ruh-roh" and Tyler jokingly tries to hide behind the hood of her onesie. Shay, whose arms were fully extended in a theatrical depiction of Harriet's death at the hands of a vampire who lured her backstage at the school's production of *Mamma Mia!* and used a pair of prop overalls to tie her limbs together before suffocating her with glitter and draining her of all her blood, clears her throat and leans back against a chair. The kids from Bluebird look at Milo with total apathy, but the kids from Cardinal all clear their throats and glance around the room like they've been busted mid–bank robbery.

Milo takes all of this in while blinking like he thinks he might have sleepwalked into it and is waiting to wake up from an odd dream.

"It's past quiet hours," he says lowly.

I offer a half wince, half smile. "Were we being too loud?"

Milo zeroes in on me so fast that there's no doubt he knows I'm the responsible party. "I heard someone yell 'Avenge me!' from eight rooms away."

"And yet not one of you has," Tyler mutters pointedly.

Milo's nostrils flare, but he doesn't break eye contact with me. I gesture back at the mountain of cake, which is more like a small hill now that we've collectively dug into it. "Snoball?" I ask.

Milo narrows his eyes, but does take a few deliberate steps toward the table. The room is still utterly silent, all parties transfixed as he scrutinizes the table, picks up a package of Tastykakes, and opens it while looking at all of us in turn.

"If this is going to continue, I need it to be at least eighty decibels quieter. Am I clear?"

"Crystal," says Shay, before I can answer.

Milo nods at her solemnly, and it's clear he'll trust her word over mine, so I keep my mouth shut. Then he takes a very large bite of Tastykake and points himself toward the door, leaving the room as ominously as he came.

There are a few beats of silence and then some muffled laughter.

When Shay speaks again, her voice is only slightly above a whisper. "We'll just . . . be super quiet, okay?"

Harriet sighs. "You're literally killing me softly, huh?"

I muffle my own laugh, giving Shay the "one sec" gesture before ducking out of the rec room and following Milo down the hall—no easy feat, considering every one of his steps makes up about two of mine.

"Hey."

Milo doesn't stop walking, but does significantly decrease the length of his tall-person steps so I can keep up. "You again," he says, without turning to look at me.

"Me again," I confirm. "So—first of all—sorry about the noise."

He takes another large bite of Tastykake. "Apology mostly accepted."

"Good. Um. But the thing is, Shay mentioned you might be a good person to talk to about work-study?"

Milo stops walking, but sure does take his time chewing. For a few moments it's just the two of us standing in the hallway, me craning my neck to watch him, Milo considering me like we've both walked into a high-stakes business negotiation.

"How about this," he says. "I help you get a good work-study, and you agree to stop causing ruckus in my dorm."

I bite my lip. "I can agree to try?"

Judging by what little I know about Milo I'm not expecting this response to work, but he's evidently too tired to push back. He looks into my eyes, then at the half-eaten pack of Tastykakes in his hands, and then back at me.

"Are you a morning person?" he asks.

I perk up so fast that he raises a hand to interrupt me. "Why did I ask," he says, more to himself than to me. He extends his arm out, only hesitating for a moment before he pats me on the shoulder again. "Be at Bagelopolis at nine A.M. tomorrow."

"Really?" I ask, two times louder than I meant to. "You're sure?"

"Sure I'm sure."

I want to take him up on it, I do—it's just that it feels like a pretty big favor, and aside from snack cakes and keeping the dorm quiet, there's nothing I can offer him in return.

Milo must see some of it playing out on my face, because he

pauses at his door, running a hand through his curls. "Look, new kid. This place is overwhelming enough, and the work-study program is a mess. Might as well get through it all as easily as we can."

I wonder if the next moment catches him by surprise, too. The moment when our eyes connect, and something else does, too. A sadness. An uncertainty. The kind that I only see for a flash, but recognize too fast for it to be anything else—it looks just like mine.

Whatever his hurt is, it's none of my business. But if he stands here with me for another three seconds, the fix-it urge is going to be too much for me to resist.

"Well, thanks," I say, squashing it down. "See you tomorrow, then."

Milo cuts a glance down the hall, his face so neutral I might have imagined what I saw, if I still didn't feel the shadow of it. "Only if you promise me I won't wake up to any more werewolf howls tonight."

"I will." I salute him. "Swear-wolf."

Milo groans in response, then eats the last bite of Tastykake before disappearing behind his door.

I head back down the hallway to rejoin the group when my phone buzzes in my back pocket. It's not a text, but a voicemail from Connor. The kind you leave when you bypass calling so you can go straight to the voicemail box. I know because my dad used to do it when he first moved away, and when he did call there wasn't much I wanted to say.

I hold the phone to my ear, listening to Connor's voice on the other end. He's calm. Composed. Like he practiced it in his head before calling.

"Hey. So I've been thinking. Let's just—do the best we can this semester. Maybe I can transfer back. We'll see how we feel at the end of the semester and figure it out."

We'll see how we feel. Meaning it's not just school that's up in the air. We're still up in it, too.

The message doesn't say anything else, and I don't call him back. I take a breath, doing the only thing I can to soothe myself, and start mentally sorting through everything I'm going to have to do in the next few months to make this right.

Whatever goes down between then and now, I know the next chapter of my future memoir just got a *whole* lot more complicated.

Chapter Seven

I never set an alarm because my entire life I've been wired to wake up at 7 A.M. on the dot, like a human sundial. I laid out all my shower stuff and an outfit the night before so I wouldn't wake up Shay, but when I look over at her side of the room, it is distinctly Shay-less; the bed is already made with its mountain of fluffy pillows, and her coat isn't hanging by the door.

In the quiet of the early morning there's this new kind of potential, like maybe the sun just needed to come up and reset yesterday. I breathe a little easier in the steam of the shower, walk a little bit lighter when Ellie plugs in her hair dryer next to me at the mirrors and asks if we can make Werewolf a weekly thing.

The sting of yesterday is still raw enough that as I'm packing my bag, I scrap my usual routine for the second day in a row and don't listen to the episode of *The Knights' Watch* recorded earlier this morning. It's only going to stress me out if they reference any ribbon clues, knowing I've already blown my chance at playing. I allow myself one indulgent moment of self-pity, thumbing through my mom's old ribbons where I splayed them out last night on my desk, then square my shoulders and tighten the scarf around my neck to leave.

Bagelopolis is only about a mile from Cardinal, just off the main road that divides campus from town and nestled within a bunch of other small shops—a bakery, a toy store, a local artisan's shop, a mini grocery. The sidewalk is wide with cobbled brick, with lots of space for outdoor tables and chairs, even if nobody's sitting in them in the January chill. It looks like a quaint little painting, and for a moment I feel like part of the scene. Like someone would paint me in here on purpose. Like I'm exactly where I'm supposed to be.

"Andie!"

I turn my head and see Shay poking out of Bagelopolis, gesturing for me to come in. "We need reinforcements."

I hustle into Bagelopolis, which feels like getting hugged by a very large, warm loaf of bread. The smell of fresh oven-baked bagels hits my nostrils and the warmth of it goes straight to my chest and all the way down to my fingers and toes. The space is small and cozy, with just a few cushioned chairs and tables scattered throughout, but the bright, rainbow-color-coded menu is large enough to take up most of one of the walls. The display case at the register has at least two dozen cream cheeses and infinite bagels in all different colors and cheeses and salts. I skim some of their names, my mouth watering: Everything Pretzel, Chocolate Chip Sourdough, Peanut Toffee Crunch, Strawberry-Streaked Rainbow Pride, Cheese-Crusted Salt.

Before I can fully get my bagel bearings, Shay tosses me a powder-blue apron with a bagel and the name of the shop embroidered on it. "I assume you can work a register."

"Oh. Wow. I thought I was just interviewing—"

"So did we, but Milo's brother Sean's car won't start, so . . . congratulations," says Shay, pinning a white card on a lanyard to my apron pocket. "You're hired."

I finish tying the strings around my back and roll up my sleeves. "These aprons are so cute."

Shay types something into the register, then pulls the white card up to a scanner and grants me guest access. "That's half the reason I took this job, but trust me, everything's going to look a lot less cute in a few minutes."

"What's happening in a few minutes?"

The phone rings and Shay holds up a quick finger to answer it. I go back to staring at the menu, which is so prolific it deserves to be adapted into a novel and a Netflix original movie. Then the bell to the store jingles, and in comes a group of freshmen loudly speculating about whether the first event for the ribbon hunt will drop this weekend or next.

"Wow. I turned my back for like, a second. What's the look of abject despair for?" asks Shay.

I swallow down the bitter taste in my mouth. "I can't collect any ribbons. My professor took my starter one."

Just then a hand interrupts my line of vision. A hand holding a white ribbon with my name inked on it.

"What the . . ."

I look up to find Milo looking somehow even more sleep-deprived than yesterday morning, but nonetheless conscious and holding what might as well be a winning lottery ticket.

When I'm too stunned to move, he puts it in my apron pocket and says, "Hutchison and I go back."

"Milo, I . . ." Absurd as it is, I have to blink back tears. "Thanks."

I want to ask him how he managed this feat, but he's already waving me off, attending to a coffee machine behind us that's large enough to have its own zip code. I assume it must have something to do with one of his "zillion" siblings Shay mentioned.

"Well, problem solved," says Shay. "Except don't you have to get one for Connor, too?"

"Who's Connor?" asks Milo.

"Her boyfriend. She transferred to surprise him, but then he'd already transferred out to surprise *her*. It's all very rom-com of them."

"I didn't transfer for him." I'd press that point, but I'm too over-whelmed by the miraculous return of my white ribbon to care. I put my hand back in my apron pocket, skimming the silky surface of it with my thumb. "And . . . I'll figure it out."

"Eh, why bother. Love's dead anyway," chimes in Milo, feeding a massive bag of beans into a coffee grinder. Before I can ask where that grim pronouncement has come from, he shakes the dregs of the bag and says, "Hold on. Need more beans."

"Don't mind him," says Shay as Milo ducks into the back, re-vealing a massive setup of ovens and a boiler and a seemingly in-finite mound of bagels in every flavor imaginable. "His brother Harley stole his girlfriend, and he now refuses to speak to or ac-knowledge either of them, resulting in a Flynn family schism of epic proportions. Hence, why he's trying to flee the state like some kind of CW teen-drama antihero."

Milo swings the door back open with a fresh bag of coffee beans slung over his shoulder. For a moment I see it flash again— whatever it was I saw in his face last night, before we both pushed past it as fast as it came. But his voice is steady and flat when he says, "You're making me sound very dramatic."

"You're brewing a special blend of coffee you call 'Eternal Dark-ness,'" says Shay, lifting the cap on the grinder for him. "I think you've got your own drama covered."

"Eternal Darkness?" I ask.

Milo nods as he pours another batch of beans in, squinting at them as he measures. "It's about as caffeinated as you can legally make coffee. But the special ingredient is having no regard for your mortality."

Shay nimbly moves from the coffee grinder over to the front counter, where there are several cups full of coffee perched in wait. "Here," says Shay, handing me a cup. "This morning's test batch."

I hold it up to my nose and try not to gag. There's no way I could allow it near my human form, let alone my mouth. "It smells like death."

"It smells like resurrection," Milo corrects me.

"Is this why your sleep schedule is so wonky?" I ask, handing it back to Shay. To my concern, she shrugs and tips it back herself, in the manner of someone taking a shot. "Because you're chugging five cups of this a day?"

"Three cups," says Milo, affronted.

"Plus ten more out of the Keurig in his room," says Shay out of the side of her mouth. She turns back to me. "You might have noticed there's an entire HomeGoods worth of mugs in there."

"Look who's talking, Barnes and Noble," Milo shoots back.

"Books don't destroy my sleep schedule, though." Milo opens his mouth to protest this, but Shay amends, "Usually."

"Eh," says Milo dismissively. "I was gonna try and cut back over winter break, but then I thought to myself, I'm not dead yet, so."

"Have you tried switching to tea?" I suggest.

Milo's eyebrows rise up into his unruly curls. He turns to Shay. "You heard that too, right? You heard the new kid try to murder me."

We're interrupted by the sound of the coffee grinder and the sudden nearness of the group of freshmen at the register, their eyes alight with the promise of carbs.

"Hi, what can we get for you?" asks Shay, who moves aside to let me work the register but thankfully stays close in case I muck the whole thing up.

Even as I'm inputting all their orders in the system for the line cooks in the back, I'm acutely aware of just how many co-eds are lining up behind them. I ring up their order without a hitch, then quickly ask Shay, "What is going on?"

"The first-period rush hour," she explains. The next kid must be a regular, because she taps in the order before he even opens his mouth. "Half the campus is hooked on Eternal Darkness."

Shay is not exaggerating. A good hour later I feel like I've rung up enough orders for Eternal Darkness to make Satan himself mad for stepping on his toes. Shay and I make an excellent team swapping between the register and the coffee orders as Milo relays bagel orders to the back kitchen, only pausing to chug another cup of coffee so fast it looks like he's competing in a sleep-deprivation Olympics.

"That *can't* be good for him," I say as he heads to the kitchen to collect another round of orders.

"I think he's been like this awhile," says Shay. "He'll be fine."

"Really?" I ask doubtfully. "A few minutes ago I watched him walk into a trash can and apologize to it."

Shay's face registers mild concern, but not necessarily surprise. "He's a little overscheduled," she says, just in time for us to watch Milo return from the kitchen while popping a coffee bean into his mouth and eating it raw. "Okay. Maybe a lot."

I examine him as he hands a group of students their bagel orders, taking in his mildly bloodshot eyes and unkempt curls and overly tall but nonetheless slouched posture. "Hmmm."

"Oh, no. I already know that look," says Shay.

"What look?" I ask innocently, smiling at the next wave of students coming up to the register.

"The little miss 'I'm gonna fix this' look," says Shay. "And trust me, when it comes to Milo and his common-law marriage with caffeine, you're setting yourself up to fail."

She's probably right. But the thing is, Milo has helped me, and now I feel compelled to help him, too. I know that whatever is going on with his brother and his ex is none of my business, but coffee isn't personal.

"We'll see about that," I say through my smile, which I then aim at a group of fellow students clutching their laptops like lifelines. "What can I get you?"

We get through the morning rush without a hitch. I take about a bajillion orders as fast as I can, and even then manage to make enough meaningful conversations to get invited to two parties, a neighborhood knitting club, and a rock-climbing gym.

I'm trying to decide whether or not my sneakers would survive such a feat when Milo appears, seemingly from out of nowhere. He hands me an ID badge that says "Andie" on it, spelled in the precise right way. "In case it wasn't clear that you were hired," he says.

I secure it to my apron, beaming. "We're officially coworkers now."

"Despite your aversion to my masterpiece," he says, turning toward the coffee grinder. The gesture is short, but still long enough for me to see the slight way he almost seems to tremble at the movement, like there's too much energy to contain.

This time I'm the one who reaches out and touches his shoulder. He's done the same for me twice now, and both times I found such an immediate calm in it that it feels almost instinctive to do the same for him. But the moment I place my hand down—the moment my palm connects with the warmth of his skin, with the unexpected taut muscle of his upper arm—I feel a beat of hesitation so unlike me that I almost forget to speak.

I clear my throat. "Feel free to tell me to buzz off. But what if I had an idea to help with this coffee situation of yours?"

Milo's lip quirks. "I'd say you're fighting a losing battle."

"You're sure?"

Milo's shoulder shifts slightly under my hand, the movement of it so subtle that it's almost like he's leaning into my touch. "You know what? If you've got any ideas, hit me with them. But know if they have anything to do with those wet leaves you call 'tea,' you're fired."

I beam at his back as he walks off. Eventually the rush passes. Midmorning classes start, and it's evident that none of us has one on Tuesdays, because we're all still here cleaning up in the aftermath.

Only once the dust settles does an unwelcome thought start to settle along with it. I try to busy myself with restocking the napkins and plastic cutlery, but all the while I'm replaying all the conversations I'd overhead in my head—other freshmen excited about the ribbon-hunt events, coordinating plans to meet up with one another. They were all so stressed about getting enough of each color. I wanted to join in their excitement, but all I could think about was the impossible task of trying to get ribbons for Connor *and* for myself.

I pull the white ribbon out of my apron pocket for what must be at least the tenth time today. Once I've felt the edges of it and tucked it back in, I find myself face-to-face with Shay.

"I saw the ribbons on your desk. The super old ones," she says quietly, so Milo and the line cooks wandering out for their breaks can't hear. "Your whole thing with *The Knights' Watch*. There's more to it, isn't there?"

"Yeah," I say carefully.

The strange thing is, I want to tell Shay about my mom. I do. I'm familiar enough with her blunt warmth that I know she's not going to get uncomfortable and shy away from the grief of it, the way so many of my friends back home did growing up. That telling her isn't going to open that same kind of gap it felt like it did back then.

But I've spent so many years avoiding the topic that it feels like too much of a risk to take—not when Shay and I are just starting to get to know each other. Not when this was supposed to be my fresh start as just Andie, and not Andie with a loaded past.

But Shay just nods solemnly, her eyes as steady as before when she offers a resolute "Okay."

"Okay?"

"Okay, I'll help you," says Shay, heading over to the coffee machine counter. "Get ribbons, I mean."

I shake my head, catching the washcloth she tosses me so we

can start wiping down the coffee and tea area in the back. "Oh, you don't have to—"

"I mean, I can't collect any myself. But if you need to switch a shift to get to one of the events or something, I'm in," says Shay, moving the coffee syrups out of the way.

It's difficult to put up too much of a fight when you're trying to uncrust toffee syrup from a counter, but I sure do try. "Shay, seriously. I appreciate it, but there's no reason for you to."

Shay stops scrubbing for a moment to look back at me. "You're gonna help me figure out my major, right?"

I unconsciously clench my fists at my side, my energy renewed. "Absolutely."

"So let me help you, too. I have zero desire to join some secret society, but I don't mind lending a hand. Lord knows I read enough rom-coms that I'm game to see this ridiculous one through." She puts down her rag, holding her other hand out for me to shake. "We got a deal?"

I bypass the handshake and go straight in for a hug. Shay lets out an *oof* of surprise before hugging me back.

"Should've seen that coming," she mutters, patting me on the back.

We're interrupted by the sound of a *ping* from her pocket. Shay winces. "We get notifications whenever our test scores come in," she says, pulling her phone out.

I was supposed to have that set up too, but my phone is too old to sync with the app's notifications. I follow Shay's lead and open the student app, and immediately regret it with every bone in my body.

"Strawberry Eggo waffles," I mutter.

"Slept-on flavor," says Shay approvingly, looking over my shoulder. "What happened?"

I show her the big, red, resounding zero I got on my stats test.

The one that's worth an alarming portion of my grade. I'd figure out how much, but ironically, I can't do the math.

"Yikes. Here," says Shay, taking my phone and tapping a few buttons on the app. "What are you doing at three P.M. tomorrow?"

"Staring into a metaphorical pit and questioning every math-related life choice I've ever made?"

"Well, reschedule, because I just booked you a stats tutor in the campus library." Shay pulls the phone away from her face to show me the screen. "Also, your dad's calling."

"Oh. I'll talk to him later," I say, taking the phone back from her and putting it in my apron pocket.

"You can take your break now if you want," says Shay, tilting her head toward the back. There's a little break room decorated with watercolor prints of bagels and about a dozen coffee-stained mugs that no doubt belong to Milo.

"Yeah. Okay," I say, heading toward it.

Only once I've settled into one of the cozy chairs, I don't bother calling my dad back. I stare at the phone until enough time passes that I know I better get back to work. I tap on my voicemails, pressing my dad's to my ear as I walk back out before the next rush between classes begins.

"Hey, A-Plus. Hope the first day went well. I'm going on a quick trip for a few days and won't have a lot of service, but I'm passing you on the way up today—let me know if you want to grab lunch."

The shame is quick and sharp, and the anger that follows it more muddled and harder to define. It's not that I don't want to see him. It's that he had all the opportunities in the world to see me over the past few years, and he still chose to move away. And only recently did he decide to do anything about it. He's been in touch more, and we did spend Thanksgiving and Christmas together. It was fine. Sometimes more than fine. Sometimes good enough to trick me into thinking it had always been like that, and always will.

But it wasn't, and it might not be. So I do things like this even though I know I shouldn't—ignoring calls, letting plans fall to the wayside, taking forever to text back. Keeping him at arm's length so he can't get close enough. Never fully letting him in so he never gets another chance to leave.

I tap out a quick text—Sorry I missed you! Maybe next time. Enjoy your trip!—and shove the phone back into my coat pocket. I breathe out long and hard, watching it fog up the afternoon air, and wish the guilt could evaporate with it, too.

Chapter Eight

In my defense, I don't wake up on Wednesday morning with the intention of unearthing Milo's deepest secret and upending the sanctity of one of Blue Ridge State's most prolific traditions. And also in my defense, I was just trying to be a good roommate when it happened.

It's still pitch-black when I wake up to the sound of the door clicking shut. I flick on the light by my bed just to confirm Shay is gone and check the time. Two things register: one is that it's six in the morning, and the other is that I still haven't written a worthy response to the "Bed of Roses" column I took on this week. Everything's been such a whirlwind I haven't even been able to put myself in the headspace for it.

I let out the kind of sigh I know means I'm not going back to sleep anytime soon, stretching just enough that something glints from Shay's side of the room—her room key, sitting on top of her fully made bed.

"Brown Sugar Cinnamon Pop-Tarts," I mutter, grabbing the keys and shimmying into a pair of sweatpants and the slippers by my bed.

I see Shay and Milo both getting into the elevator at the end of the hall as I poke my head out, but the doors shut before I can holler.

I take the steps as fast as I can and bolt out braless and coatless, so cold that the air feels like the inside of a sno-cone, but when I call out Shay's name she doesn't so much as flinch.

Shay and Milo abruptly pivot to the psychology building near our dorm and walk inside, so I follow with the half walk, half jog of someone who is both freezing and attempting to use their own forearms as a makeshift bra. It's not just that I'm going to be busy with class and a tutoring session all day, so I won't be able to let Shay in—it's also that my brain can't reconcile these two non-psychology majors wandering in there before most psych majors have cracked an eye open. I'm too curious not to follow.

By the time I get inside I see Milo unlocking a door and Shay following him in, but they still don't hear me—they've both got headphones on—so I have to drag my slipper-clad self to the un-marked door and catch it with my hand just before it closes.

Shay spots me first, and greets me with an "Oh, shit."

"Your key," I blurt, holding it out to her, my hand shaking from the cold.

Only then, when Shay and Milo both freeze in place, do I take in our surroundings. The soundproofing foam on the walls, the soundboard propped on a table, the comically small booth behind clear plastic with chairs and mics dangling in front of them. A weathered-looking sign reads BLUE RIDGE UNDERGROUND.

"Oh, yikes. Thanks for that," says Shay, taking the key from me. She glances at Milo with a sheepishness I can't decipher. "Uh . . . my bad."

But Milo's already shucking off his jacket and tossing it to me.

I catch it, but just barely, because my eyes have already snagged on another sign. One on the wall to the left that reads THE KNIGHTS' WATCH has a bunch of pictures of students framed under it. The one closest to the top is a picture of Milo, looking slightly less sleep-deprived and smiling this wry, genuine smile that I saw just a hint of on my first day here. One that snaps the situation into place so fast that I can't help it when my mouth falls open, and I blurt out the one thing they're probably hoping I won't say.

"You're the Knight," I say, gaping at Milo. "*The Knights' Watch*—you're the one recording it."

It's why I thought I recognized him when we first met. It had nothing to do with his face, and everything to do with his voice. I've spent the last six months with Milo in my ears—early mornings sitting in my grandmas' garden, walking around the community college campus, lying in bed and watching the sun come up early enough to listen to it live.

The heat that floods into my cheeks is so searing that I don't need Milo's coat or maybe any kind of coat ever again. Shay winces, but Milo just lets out a loose shrug.

"Sorry," Shay tells him. She turns back to me. "It's supposed to be a secret."

"Oh, I know," I say, my eyes trailing all over the tiny room—everywhere other than the pictures on the wall, or Milo's sleepy face.

"No, not just the Knight. Like, this whole setup." Shay pulls down a rickety mic stand to settle it in front of a stool. "The broadcast and journalism programs don't exactly love that the show is more popular than all of theirs after all these years, so we've been relegated to this, uh." Shay looks around. "Is 'closet' too generous of a word?"

"But why the psych building?" I ask.

Milo shrugs. "It's always been this way, is what I was told."

My mom always told me they'd done the broadcast somewhere secret, but I was a kid back then. I'd imagined some edgy bunker or off-campus facility, somewhere hidden that would involve a fingerprint scan or password to get in. But I suppose in their case it might have made more sense to hide in plain sight. I've passed this same door plenty of times now and never even noticed it.

"Were you also told what to do about not one, but now *two* of your dorm residents finding out your big secret?" says Shay.

"Eh," says Milo. "We'll just make her sign an NDA and threaten to kidnap her firstborn if she rats on us. It's fine."

"I won't tell anyone," I say quickly.

"I know," says Milo, his eyes momentarily so intent on mine that my cheeks somehow burn even hotter. I chalk it up to embarrassment. I can't believe I had no idea it was him. "It's fine. Besides, even if you did tattle, nobody on campus outside our dorm's floor knows my name."

I back up toward the door. "Okay. I'll just, uh . . . head back and never speak of this again?"

Milo taps the mic, one ear pressed to a headphone, the other still bare and listening to us. "You can stick around if you want."

"Oh, I wouldn't . . ."

But I would. Now that I'm here in this room that's clearly older than all three of us combined, it's like I can feel some echo of the energy in it. In the musty smell of the carpets, in the dim, moody lighting from the overhead lamps, in the way everything in here feels muffled and contained and . . . safe.

Shay nudges the chair next to her with her foot. I almost don't take it. This all has a kind of surreal quality to it, like I stumbled into a dream, or maybe one of my mom's. I sit down, acutely aware that somewhere on that wall of photos her eyes are watching me.

"You work on the show, too?" I ask Shay as she fires up a laptop and Milo busies himself with the mic.

"A few times a week, for extra work-study hours. I help consolidate the stuff the school sends so Milo can write it up. Mostly I just look at listener emails and questions."

I end up sliding Milo's jacket on anyway, only because it will become abundantly clear just how braless I am if I don't. It's soft and flannel and has that distinctive woodsy citrus smell that makes me want to pull my knees up to my chest and burrow into it.

Shay pulls up the account and I let out a low whistle at the 173 unanswered emails.

"Oh, that's just left over from New Year's. We had listeners email about their resolutions." I almost blurt out the words "I remember that" before Shay adds, "I keep meaning to go through and delete them, I just . . . I don't know. Felt weird."

"Weird how?" I ask.

"Like, some of them are kind of . . . personal? I don't know. I should probably just clear them out."

We're interrupted by Milo tapping the bottom of a travel mug, sucking down the last dregs of his coffee. He blinks a few times, still trying to wake himself up. "I should have brought a second," he groans.

Shay rolls her eyes. "You're on in two," she reminds him, tapping the print button on her screen, where there's a bare-bones outline that says things like "weather 27 high 19 low clear skies" and "parent banquet date switch feb 22" and "trivia ribbons-tbd." Before I can zero in on that last bit, a dusty old printer in the corner whirs to life, and Milo plucks the sheet from it.

"What would I do without you?" he asks.

"Deeply alarm our peers. Are you ready?"

Milo slides the panel to the recording booth shut, gazing mournfully into his empty coffee mug. "As I'll ever be."

He turns a dial and I hear the notes of a Bruno Mars song coming to a close—in between the radio show and the other occasional student programs on the station, the station just plays Top 40 hits from the past few years—and the telltale *ding ding ding!* that always chimes in to introduce the show. Milo sits up straight on his stool, and the transformation is so immediate that it almost seems like a trick of the light. His eyes brighten, his back straightens, and the wryness in his voice has an electric kind of energy to it that makes him impossible not to watch.

"Well, I'd say good morning, but we're kicking off today's broadcast with news that yet again a bunch of you opted to bring back 'Hot Dog Breakfast Wednesday' in the latest student dining hall poll," says Milo, easing into the top of the show like he's sliding on an old favorite sweater. "Your efforts succeeded, you monsters. So, very bad, possibly cursed morning to you all. And with that, the weather . . ."

For the first few minutes we both watch him in hushed silence. The way he takes the bare bones and riffs off them ("The parent banquet has been rescheduled to February twenty-second, which will henceforth be known as our one and only Student Sobriety Day"), making jokes about campus goings-on ("I have been told to remind you all that the arboretum is a place of learning, not a place of cavorting; but whoever is cavorting there, for the love of god, I hope you brought a decent coat"), talking into the mic with the warmth of a close friend.

But the moment he really comes alive is when he's discussing ongoing efforts for the school to reform its work-study program, a common thread he follows up on every week. He leans into the mic with his full body, muscles tense and eyes alight with a new energy.

"If anyone else is keeping score out there, we're on day five million and fifty-two of the administration ignoring that its overblown tuition hikes have caused the work-study applicants to outnumber the available positions for the program," he says, his voice just as engaging as before, but with an edge. "To everyone who signed the online petition for the school to freeze tuition hikes and expand the work-study options to more local businesses, thanks. To everyone who didn't, you're dead to me. And probably also too rich to know this is even a problem, so I will accept an apology by way of a free sandwich or car."

It's not the first time this morning I've had to muffle a laugh. It's like watching Gammy Nell tend to the themed crusts on her pies or Connor scanning the soccer field to figure out which team-mates are open—someone clearly in their element, and enjoying every moment of it.

But watching him also makes me ache in a way I'm not used to anymore, at least not with such a full and immediate force. There was a time this made me happy, too. Using a platform and connecting with people in real time, whether it was talking at school assemblies or helping host the town's annual talent show for kids or even the few times my mom let me "guest spot" on her radio show growing up. There was a time when I assumed I'd be doing that kind of thing my whole life.

"The brave one of us," my mom used to brag to her coworkers, which seemed silly to me at the time. With her unapologetically blunt humor, willingness to navigate hot topics with guests, and relentless commitment to local causes, she was the bravest person I knew. She was a breath of fresh air on the radio, the host people tuned into every morning to wake them up and make them laugh, to set a tone for the morning that would follow them through their whole day. She was far from conventional, and she was beloved for it.

But she had stage fright of her own. She never wanted to make any appearances outside of radio, preferring the focus and quiet of being behind the mic. I was the one who dreamed even bigger; I was the one who dreamed so big that as a kid I felt limitless, like there was so much potential in the future that I could run in any direction and never meet the edge of it.

Now I can't even bring myself to use my real name on a column for a high school I don't go to anymore.

I wait for the ache to fade the way it normally does. These past few years it's been more of a phantom feeling than a real one. But if anything it seems to spread deeper, claiming back old territory, making me unsettled in my skin.

"Wow," I whisper to Shay, trying to pull myself out of it. "He's so good at this."

An understatement if there ever were one, but Shay just nods. "He only just pulled out of the biology major last semester." She turns back to the laptop monitor. "I'm guessing he'll apply to the broadcast program here."

I nod back carefully. Milo's identity as the Knight isn't just a secret for school tradition, then. If the broadcast and journalism heads don't love the idea of this radio show, being publicly known as the host of it probably won't put any points in his favor.

"Makes sense," I say. "Why would he major in bio when he can do *this*?"

Shay clicks back into the overflowing inbox, but I don't miss the way her smile falters in the light of the laptop screen. "Biology was Harley's major, too. I think he was gonna follow him to med school or something. They were super close."

Don't overstep, says that part of my brain that knows all too well what will happen if I do. *Don't get involved.* So even though I am itching to ask Shay for more details about this Harley-Milo-Girlfriend situation, I lean over her shoulder and decide to make strangers' business my business instead.

"Let's knock out some of the resolution emails while he's at it."

Shay blows out a breath. "I would," she says, her eyes skimming the inbox. "I just don't know what to say to people."

I scan the subject lines like I'm running diagnostics on strangers' brains. "I can answer some of them."

"You really want to?"

I flex my fingers over her keyboard. "Let me at 'em."

Since the emails are anonymous, I fall into a familiar rhythm, answering them with the same ease I answer my "Bed of Roses" column. Except the more I read, the more it feels like I'm finally part of something bigger here—like getting this glimpse into the day-to-day issues of other students makes the barrier I keep feeling between me and them fall away. Like I know this student trying to make a savings goal, or the one in a petty argument with a friend, or the other with chronic first-date jitters. People with problems so personal but so universal that it reminds me, the way running an advice column often does, that at our cores we're all more alike than we think. Hung up on the same worries, wishing on the same stars.

It doesn't quite make the ache from before go away, but it makes it quieter. Easier to ignore.

"Wow. Down to one sixty-seven," says Shay, closing out of the browser at the end of the broadcast.

"Barely a dent," I say. "I can do more."

"We only have access to the server from this building. I assume you don't want to get up at six in the morning to follow us here." Before I can even fully hit her with the gleam in my eye, Shay smirks. "Never mind. Forgot who I was talking to. I'm just going to poke my head down the hall to make sure the kid who's supposed to edit and upload the podcast version is fully functional."

Shay heads out and Milo is busying himself with the soundboard, setting everything back the way he found it. I glance and he doesn't glance back, so I figure he's absorbed enough in what he's doing that I can steal a glimpse at the wall.

All I have to do is take a few steps, and there she is—instead of chronologically, which would put her picture first, my mom's frame is smack-dab in the middle of all the others. She's beaming in it so widely that it makes my own cheeks hurt, her blond hair parted down the middle and draped over her shoulders, a version of her I don't think I've ever seen. A version of her so close to my age that the resemblance isn't just startling, but unsettling.

I look away, zeroing instead on an engraved piece of metal that says AMY JANSON, FOUNDER OF THE KNIGHTS' WATCH, along with the years she went to the school.

"You ready to go?"

I take a sharp step back from the wall. "Yeah." Milo doesn't miss it, looking at me quizzically. I clear my throat. "Great show, by the way."

He shrugs the praise off, grabbing a set of keys out of his pocket. "I try my best for our seven listeners."

I lightly swat at his arm as he locks up. "It's gotta be at least a few thousand. You really have a knack for this."

Milo makes a face like he's about to brush the compliment off, but we round the corner to the window and see a flurry of snow starting to fall so fast it looks like someone shook the campus up in a snow globe. Shay catches up to us in the hallway and joins us in our staring, her eyes going wide.

"It's so beautiful," I say quietly, already wondering how it will look in the arboretum if I manage to break away long enough to catch a glimpse.

"It'll be even *more* beautiful if they cancel classes," says Shay.

Milo nods. "Your mouth to the weather gods' ears."

I shrug off Milo's coat. "Thanks for—"

He's already walking toward the door, waving me off. "You can give it back at the dorms."

"But it's your coat, and it's snowing, and—"

"I'll be fine. Besides, if you freeze to death, it's a hell of a lot of paperwork I'd rather avoid."

He's smiling, but something in his tone tells me it would be a waste of breath to argue. I'm starting to recognize it—the stubbornness of the way he cares. The way he really only pretended to strike a deal with me before helping me get a work-study position. The way he acts like he dreads his RA duties and yet seems to accidentally-on-purpose leave his door open for people to wander in and out during the day.

I shrug the coat back on, at ease in its warmth, but uneasy with something else—at the feeling of being taken care of, when so often I'm determined to be the one who takes care. At the surge of gratitude, but also something else that follows it, too warm and indistinct to name.

I wrap the coat around myself as tightly as I can, letting the fresh sting of the cold chase it away.

Chapter Nine

I'm back in my own coat a few hours later when I'm trudging through the snow to the library to meet the tutor Shay scheduled for me. I scan the tables near the coffee stand at the front for her, and only one of them is occupied—or at least, I think it's occupied. There are so many books piled on it that I have to circle all the way around before spotting a girl with thick, glossy brown hair and high cheekbones frowning into a paperback, her hand poised over a notebook.

"Valeria?" I ask.

Her head snaps up so fast I almost apologize for startling her. "Oh. You must be Andie," she says, blinking hard like she's trying to bring herself back to the library from somewhere far away. She pushes the notebook aside as she stands up and hovers over the two piles of books, trying to figure out which of them to move first to make space for me. "I'm Val. Sorry. I just completely lost track of time."

"Here. I'll take the romance pile, you can take the . . ." I squint at the spines of the books, which all seem to feature daggers, skulls, and thorny roses. "Murder pile?"

"Fantasy pile," says Valeria. "And thanks."

I heave a portion of them and set them on the floor, but even then barely make a dent. "So did you accidentally join fifteen book clubs?"

Val lets out a laugh, her voice low and warm. "I wish. I was trying to cure my writer's block. Thought reading anything I could get my hands on might help."

I maneuver the other empty chair out of the way of the precarious piles we're making and plop my bag in it, rooting around for my textbook. "Huh. I figured you'd be a math major."

"Oh, I am," says Val. She pats the last pile of the books on the floor with the energy of a parent tucking a kid into bed. "Writing is just something I do to pass the time."

This, I've been learning, is a typical Blue Ridge State response. Everyone here is so ridiculously talented that it's not a matter of whether they can succeed in anything, but a matter of choosing which things they feel like succeeding in.

I glance down at the stats book in my hands. All Val will have to do is glance at my attempt at this week's practice problems to know that I'm an exception to that rule.

"What's blocking you, then?" I ask, moving my bag and settling into the seat.

"Oh." Val sweeps her curtain of bangs behind her ear, pursing her full lips. With her striking dark eyes, thick lashes, and gentle smile, she fits right in with all the beautiful heroines on the books at our feet. "It's a long story."

Ordinarily I might pry, see if it's a story she wants to tell. But now that I'm here, about to reveal to another student just how in over my head I am with this class, I can't help the unwelcome nerves that seem to have an agenda all their own.

"But I did manage to change a character's name three times." Valeria picks up the notebook full of her scribbled notes and squints at it. "So, baby steps."

"Well. You've made more progress than I have with my stats homework," I confess.

Val's lip curves. "Well, *that* I can do something about." My expression must relay my unease, because she adds, "Trust me, I've been with the tutoring program for almost a year now. Wherever you're starting from, we can turn it around."

As it turns out, the nerves were for nothing. I'm usually self-conscious about how long it takes for me to pick up concepts and how much *longer* it takes for me to actually apply them to problems, but Valeria just patiently guides me though all of it, occasionally falling quiet when she knows I can work something out on my own. I don't get in my head about it, the way I sometimes used to back in high school when I got put on the spot.

Halfway through our tutoring session Val gets up to grab another coffee, and I'm relieved to see several texts from Connor pop up on my phone: one with a meme of our old high school mascot, another with a selfie of him in front of my old psych building at the community college. His sandy hair is perfectly tousled under the beanie I got him for his birthday. Call tonight? he asks. I press the phone to my chest in relief.

"What's that smile about?"

"Oh, just a text from my boyfriend." It feels like a relief to say it out loud, like affirming it with the universe. Everything's normal. Everything's fine.

That is, until something in Val's expression flickers. "Oh," she says brightly, to make up for it.

"Oh?" I prompt her, half teasing.

She twists her lip to the side. "Ugh, it's silly. I've already talked my roommate's ear off about it today. But my ex broke up with me over winter break and I'm really trying to get over it, but he's still texting me every now and then in this way that's like—not clear exactly what he wants?"

I nod understandingly. "Like he's just trying to make sure he's still got you on the hook or something?"

"Yeah. Like that. Because the minute I respond, he basically just ghosts again. It's driving me nuts."

But it's not her phone she glances at when she says this. It's the notebook, so well-used that it's tattering at the edges.

"Hence the writer's block?" I ask.

Val puts her face in her hands, groaning. "It makes no sense. I mean, I started this story before we even met. But every time I actually sit down to write my brain just fixates on whatever his deal is instead."

"Aren't there literary clubs on campus?" I ask, looking around for a flyer I'm almost certain I saw on the way in. "Maybe if you talked to other writers or shared some of your work, they'd be able to help."

Valeria shudders. "Oh, no, no, no," she says, the words coming out so fast they almost tumble over one another. "If anyone actually read it I'd be like, mortified."

"Why?"

"Because it's . . . mine." Her cheeks tinge a deep and adorable red. "And if anyone read a book about a bisexual, half-Spanish, half-Italian heroine who uses math in a magical realm to save the day, there isn't a single person in their right mind who wouldn't be like, 'Oh, this is a self-insert fanfiction.'"

I lean into the table. "Yeah, but aren't *all* books kind of self-insert fanfiction?"

Valeria taps the stats textbook, drawing our attention back to the task at hand. "This one sure isn't."

I let out a laugh, resigning myself to the math ahead. "Touché."

Chapter Ten

"If he dies, I had nothing to do with this," says Shay.

"It's for his own good," I say decisively, opening the door to our room and heading into the hall. In my hands is several days' worth of trial and error: a bag full of a ground half-caf blend that tastes so close to Eternal Darkness that maybe even Milo, despite confusing coffee for oxygen, won't notice the difference.

Naturally, I needed Shay's taste buds to help perfect the batch, because I'm pretty sure if I had more than a sip of it myself I'd go supernova. And while Milo did say he was fine with me helping get ahold of his coffee consumption, he did not consent to peeling me off the ceiling.

Milo's door is open when we reach his room. Shay walks in the way she normally does and I follow, but the room is decidedly Milo-less.

Shay cranes her neck down the hall. This isn't an uncommon occurrence—sometimes he'll do a quick round of the dorm just to make sure nobody's crying to the lo-fi focus beats playlist on Spotify, which has happened enough times in the study room that I'm more than a bit apprehensive about my GPA. But Shay and I don't have time to wait around tonight.

"We can just find him later," she says.

I sigh. "He'll be on his ninth cup by then."

I consider just leaving the bag in his room, but am unwilling to risk it being buried under the pile of mugs that say things like POSSIBLY TODAY, SATAN and SCIENCE: IT'S LIKE MAGIC, BUT REAL!, and another that is an inexplicable collage of pictures of chickens.

Shay calls Milo's name down the hall to see if he'll appear, and I take a step back to take in the rest of his room. It's all done up in cool navies and deep reds, with the kind of cozy look of things that were well-used and well-loved before they got to him. Things with a history to them, like a little hand-me-down home. I accidentally brush the down comforter with my knee as we make our way out, and the soft wear of it makes me wistful—a part of me has always wanted siblings, wanted to pass stories and advice back and forth with people who knew me inside and out.

I'm snapped out of it when Shay walks back into the room and jerks her thumb toward the door. "Leave it in the comment box."

I follow her out, plopping the coffee grounds in the box, and use the notebook in my bag to fashion a note, propping it on the top of the box so he won't miss it: "Semi-Eternal Darkness—try switching to this after 2pm!"

"I maintain that the word 'semi-eternal' makes no logical sense," says Shay.

I pat her pale pink coat sleeve. "Save that big brain of yours for trivia tonight."

It's a high-stakes situation for us both—yesterday before the broadcast, Milo got word from the Knights' Tour organizers that the blue ribbon hunt events were starting this weekend, and would run on random Friday and Saturday nights for the rest of January. You could either participate on campus in the dining halls or opt to go off campus to a few participating restaurants that had their own incentives. I was resigned to eating what Milo affectionately called "an insult to food" alone on campus each weekend to collect enough ribbons, but it turns out Shay's book club already has a trivia team that meets at a restaurant near Bagelopolis, and was more than happy to absorb me into it—particularly because the prize for trivia night is always a fifty-dollar gift card to the bookshop in the historic part of town.

Shay heads out to meet up with them beforehand, which gives me enough time to go on a long walk and center myself. I head toward the arboretum, which I've wandered along the edges of enough times to have a few favorite spots. One of them is a bench half buried in an overgrown bush—I can see out to the lake and the edges of campus, but unless they're really looking, nobody can see me.

Once I'm there I take a breath and pull out my white ribbon, skimming my fingers along the edges of it. It's strange to feel it so light in my hand when it has such a significant weight in my heart. A weight I've been carrying so long that it feels strange to be here now, about to do something with it for the first time.

It sounds ridiculous, but I'm almost scared. Like I've spent my whole life anticipating this ribbon hunt, but it never once occurred to me that I might fail at it. That it might be as hard of an adjustment as so many other things here have been—the struggle with keeping up academically, the strangeness of trying to fit into this new world, the tension of not quite knowing where Connor and I stand. The ache of sitting in the studio and answering listener emails, trying to avoid my mom's static gaze from the picture on the wall.

Most of the time I can bury it. The faster I move, the more I keep busy, the easier it is to ignore. Because it's not just the thought that I might fail at the ribbon hunt—it's the understanding of how fragile everything really is, when I try to account for it. How easily plans can come undone. I spent my entire childhood with dreams that got smaller as I got older, but I've held fast to them. Now with every little setback I can't help wondering if they'll get smaller still.

I press the ribbon back into my bag and pull my coat tighter around myself. I'm not sure why I keep coming out here. Maybe I thought if I let myself feel it, the fear would go away. Or at the very least, become something I could better understand. But sometimes the longer I sit the more I feel like I'm in a tug-of-war with two versions of myself—the one who wants to face my fear head-on, and the one who doesn't want to admit to having any fear in the first place.

Connor calls. For the first time I can remember, I consider not picking up.

"I am so sorry I missed our FaceTime date last night," he says by way of hello. "I was totally slammed. My dad's making me take on extra hours at his office."

I wince, because I know how much Connor hates working part-time at his dad's real estate company. Mr. Whit runs a tight ship, and when Connor's on the clock, he's no exception.

"Don't worry about it," I say, genuinely meaning it. I don't bother telling him I was slammed, too. It feels almost rude to tell him too much about what I'm up to here, like I'd be rubbing it in his face—*I'm here and you're not.* "How was it?"

"About as fun as a root canal. What are you up to tonight?"

For a moment I feel this stupid little thrill, certain he's asking because he's considering coming down here or asking me if I want to come up. But the last buses between Little Fells and Blue Ridge State leave midafternoon, so he can't mean that.

"Actually," I say, pressing the phone closer to my face, "the first blue-ribbon event is tonight."

"Oh, shit. You're still grabbing them for me too, right?"

"Right," I say, a fresh panic hot in my throat.

I've planned for that since I got here, but only now am I starting to understand how much of a wrench it's going to throw into my life. We won't know where or when on the weekends the ribbon-hunt events are until the Friday before. So if I'm really dead set on getting to as many as I can for both of us to have enough, I'll never be able to make solid plans ahead of time.

"Just—you know it's not going to work without a white ribbon, though?" I remind him.

I'm expecting him to blow out a breath, but instead I can practically feel the charm of his smile in the words: "I'm not worried. I'm sure it'll work itself out."

I stiffen a bit. For the most part, it's unspoken, but there's always been a bit of a divide between Connor's situation and mine. His family is better off than most in our small town, and between that and his boyish good looks, he's not someone used to hearing the word "no." I don't think he realizes just how hard the rest of us are paddling under the surface to stay afloat with him.

Or how hard other people work to keep *him* afloat. Because if he's not worried, that probably means he'll let the worrying fall to me.

"I wish I could be there," says Connor, his voice so earnest that I feel myself softening. "I really miss you."

I get up from the bench, heading in the direction of the restaurant, an idea forming in my head. "You only have one class on Fridays, right? We could do something for Valentine's Day. Shay is already going to spend the night at her sister's, so we'd have the whole dorm room to ourselves."

"Ah, I wish I could, but . . . I'm doing this big open house with my dad. You know how it is."

"Of course." I clear my throat. "Well, I'll be back in the next few weeks."

I'm not sure which week, though, and Connor doesn't ask. Instead we talk about what our old high school friends are up to, and some spoiler that dropped for a show we used to watch together. The conversation falls into such a familiar, simple rhythm that if it weren't for the bustle of Main Street jolting me back to campus, I might have thought I never left Little Fells at all.

By the time I reach Barb's, a tiny restaurant not too far from

Bagelopolis, Shay is there and waving me over to a table she secured in the back. It's already overflowing with a mountain of cheesy nachos, a plate of mozzarella sticks, and a pile of wings with enough dipping sauce options to drown in. Connor happens to get an incoming call from one of our friends just then, so we say our goodbyes just before I get close enough to the table for my jaw to hit the floor.

"Is this all for us?"

"Barb likes me. And my good-for-nothing book club friends who just ditched for yet another Jane Austen movie marathon," Shay grumbles, plucking a nacho off the mountain and sinking her teeth into it. "They think trivia's going to be too loud with all the extra teams competing for the ribbon hunt, but we can't compete unless we have four players."

I glance around. "Maybe another team will absorb us?"

Shay narrows her eyes at the other clumps of students, and only then am I aware of the heightened tension of pre-competition in the room. It's like the beginning of one of Connor's soccer games, except with a lot less Gatorade and a lot more underage kids trying to pull out fake IDs for cheap beer.

"Team Bad & Bookish merges with no one."

"Well . . ." I do another glance and spot a curtain of thick, shiny dark hair catching the light near the exit. "Val!"

She stops at the door, turning around with one of those beaming, close-lipped smiles of hers. "Andie," she says warmly. "Good to see you outside of a library for once."

"Are you here for trivia?"

"Oh, no, I was just finishing a tutoring session," she says, gesturing to the back.

"Do you *want* to be here for trivia?"

"Oh," says Val. "Um . . ."

"You can split the gift card to End of Story if we win," Shay calls from the table.

Val raises her eyebrows by just small enough of a fraction that I know we've got her. "You have my attention," she says, shifting her purse off her shoulder and heading over.

One down, one to go. I whip out my phone for an SOS text to the Cardinal dorm group chat I made earlier in the week. Ellie answers with no less than ten emojis that she's visiting relatives, Harriet's at a movie, and Tyler is finishing an out-of-class assignment in the astronomy tower.

Just when I'm about to pivot to plan C and accost strangers, my phone buzzes.

Remove me from your godforsaken group chat, Milo writes.

I roll my eyes. Only if you come to trivia.

He starts to type an answer back, then stops and starts again. Tell Shay she owes me.

I swing by the registration table to put Milo's and Val's names next to ours. By the time I return, Val and Shay are in such a heated conversation about the protagonist of a recent romance novel that neither of them notice me approaching.

"That's just the *thing*, though, it's the 1867 version of a Hallmark Christmas movie," says Shay. "If she didn't have to go back to her small town—"

"But in this case, New York really *was* all wrong for her," says Val, the two of them leaning in so close that they might literally butt heads if they're not careful.

"It's a reverse *Little Women*, is what it is," Shay insists. "Jo March is rolling in her grave."

Val gasps. "Jo March is immortal. How dare you."

Shay laughs so loudly she has to abandon the nacho she was aiming at her mouth. "I'll give you that. But not much else, since it looks like we're disqualified."

"I texted Milo," I say, planting myself in the seat across from them.

Shay laughs again, this time hard enough to shake the table. "Oh. Andie."

I tilt my head at her. "What?"

"You could threaten Milo with his mortal life, and I'm pretty sure you couldn't get him into Barb's on a Friday n—" Shay's jaw drops. I follow her gaze, whipping around to see Milo walking gingerly into the establishment, dodging a drunk co-ed with a pint of beer sloshing in his hand. I yank up my arm to wave him over just as Shay mutters, "Well I'll be damned."

I turn back to her, smug. "See? He's got your back."

Shay raises her eyebrows. "I sincerely doubt he is doing this for me."

Before I can protest, the mic at the front lets out a sharp whine and the trivia host steps up to get us all started. Milo sits down so gracelessly that half his limbs brush mine, unwrapping his scarf and yanking off his hat to reveal red, wind-whipped cheeks.

"Did you teleport?" I ask.

"I was with my brothers in the Bagelopolis lot."

I suspect by the way he says this more to his coat than any of us that there's more to the story, but just then trivia night kicks off in earnest. I'm about to confess that I'm borderline useless at trivia when the host announces, of all things, that the first category is vampires in pop culture.

"Shit," says Shay, burying her head in her hands. "I haven't read *Twilight* in at least five years."

"I . . . have a box of Count Chocula left over from Halloween," Val offers.

I pull up my sleeves. Connor and I marathoned our way through *True Blood*, *The Vampire Diaries*, and *Buffy the Vampire Slayer*, not to mention watched every film adaptation of vampire novels from *Dracula* to *Interview with a Vampire*.

"You better hold on tight, spider monkeys," I say under my breath.

Thanks to my alarming vampiric knowledge we dominate the first round, which then leads into another round, this one on geography. Milo runs a resigned hand through his curls before telling us that his sister Jeanie started her career as a high school geography teacher, then casually crushing everyone in the bar around us down to the capital city of Cyprus.

"Cheers," says Milo, holding up his Coke to my hot chocolate, "to the *masterminds* of team Bad & Bookish."

I knock my glass with his, returning his satisfied half smile with a grin of my own. Luckily the two of us peak right then and there, before our smugness can become our downfall. We are utterly useless for the rounds on obscure dog breeds (Shay's wheelhouse), celebrities' real names (Val's specialty), and Broadway musicals (both Val and Shay nearly knock their own arms out of their sockets raising our whiteboard up with their answers).

In the end we win by a landslide. We're such a force to be reckoned with that we decide to reconvene next week and let Shay's book club friends off the hook, calling ourselves the "All-Knighters" (inspired in part by Milo's utter disregard for sleep). I'm so relieved to have a built-in team for the month of this ribbon hunt that I'm almost dizzy, and Shay and Val are so overjoyed by the gift card that they entirely forget about the food at our table. Someone hands us two to-go boxes, which Milo starts shoving leftovers into for breakfast tomorrow morning.

In the meantime I go up to the host's makeshift podium and show her my white ribbon and collect a blue one, along with the participating players in the teams that came in second and third. I wander back to the table in a daze with it pinched between my fingers, waiting to feel something other than relief, or the thought that immediately chases it—*one down, so many more to go.*

"Hey," says Val, grabbing my arm. "You guys wanna go to karaoke?"

"A bunch of other teams are going to the place down the street," says Shay, her eyes shining from the high of the bookstore gift card.

I shake my head apologetically. "If I try to sing I will put every dog in a mile radius in pain."

Milo is already halfway to the door. "I don't acknowledge the word 'karaoke' as a noun or a verb. But godspeed."

It takes me a minute to put my coat back on and secure our portion of the leftovers in my bag, so I'm not expecting to see Milo waiting outside the restaurant, leaning against the exterior of the building with his hands shoved in his jacket pockets. I catch sight of him before he sees me, seeing a rare moment of his face at rest—the thoughtful set of his brow, the keenness of his eyes, the slight weariness underneath them. It makes my chest warm in this familiar way, like when you spot a face you don't just recognize, but have started to know well.

"Are you meeting your brothers?" I ask him.

Milo shifts himself off and falls into step with me, and I realize he was waiting so we could walk back together. I press down a smile, knowing he'll say something to rebuff it if he sees.

"Eh, I think they've seen enough of me this evening," says Milo.

I notice his eyes flit over to the Bagelopolis sign, unlit for the night now that it's closed. We both hear a clang from the back that can only be someone taking out the garbage, and Milo picks up his pace enough that I have to go into overdrive on my short-person legs to keep up.

"What are they up to?" I ask.

"Oh, nothing new. Just another bimonthly attempt to get me and Harley to bury the hatchet."

It's as close as I've gotten to an invitation to butt into this situation, but I'm not sure whether I should take it. It's not just me worrying about overstepping. Milo actually seems willing to talk about it. But judging from the look on his face, I'm not sure if he should.

"Are you alright?" I ask instead, giving him the option to dig into it or deflect in that Milo way of his.

He goes for option B. "As alright as a person whose blood is surging at half its usual caffeinated rate can be," he says wryly.

The immediate skip in my step makes it easier to keep up with his absurd pace. "You tried my blend!"

"I tried your . . . concoction," Milo concedes. "And it's not bad for only being *semi*-eternal."

I shrug. "I considered 'Light in the Dark,' but that seemed too off-brand for you."

"Well, so is being this tired at ten o'clock at night."

"I think that's called a circadian rhythm," I say, with just enough slight sarcasm that I can tell Shay and Milo are rubbing off on me. "Anyway, if you like it, I've got the rest of the test batch in the kitchen at Bagelopolis. Also, I did some quick research, and apparently there's a roasted tea that has the same consistency of coffee you could try."

I wait for Milo to take a cheap shot at tea drinkers like he usually does, but he's gone quiet, his pace slowing. Just as we're about to hit the part of campus where the tree line hides the main road from sight, Milo casts another glance toward Bagelopolis, then back down to the ground.

"Do you want to talk about it?" I ask.

We stop at the crosswalk, and instead of answering, he looks me directly in the eye. "Shay said you have a fix-it thing."

"Oh," I say, my cheeks burning. She's not wrong. It's been so ingrained in me that I can't remember a time I *wasn't* like that. One of my earliest memories was petitioning the teachers to lower the tire swing in the recess yard so the pre-K kids could play on it, too. "I mean, yeah. That's fair."

"So I'm warning you right now, this is the kind of thing that can't be fixed."

I nod carefully. "That doesn't mean it isn't worth talking about, if you want to."

The walk signal comes on, but it takes a moment for either of us to move. Milo slouches against the cold, but his eyes are still on me as we trudge onward.

"Why do you care so much?"

He doesn't ask it out of annoyance, but genuine curiosity.

"You're my . . ." "RA" seems too clinical, but "friend" seems too presumptuous. At least when it comes to Milo, who seems to put a lot more stock in action than words. "I care about you."

This time Milo's the one to look away. "I meant the rest of it," he says, pulling one of his hands out to gesture vaguely at the air in front of us. "The whole fix-it thing."

I clear my throat.

"Oh—I don't know." I flash him a smile, giving an answer that feels safely general, pulling myself out of it as far as I can. "We've all got stuff we're going through. Seems like we could all use an extra friend now and then."

Milo tilts his head at me, his curls picking up with the slight breeze. "Huh."

I tilt my head back. "Huh?"

He shifts his gaze back to the sidewalk. "That . . . smile you did just there," he says, gesturing at it without looking at me. "It didn't look like your usual one."

It was, in fact, my syndicated-talk-show smile. I suppose I haven't had a reason to pull it out in front of Milo before—I'm happier squeezed into that recording closet with him and Shay than I am anywhere else.

I rub my chin with my wrist, scratching some invisible itch as the smile slides off my face. "Well. Offer still stands, if you ever want to talk brother stuff."

Milo reaches up and rubs the back of his neck. "I appreciate it. But this thing with Harley—our dad died a few years back. Car accident. So. That's kind of tangled in this whole mess, too."

My heart reacts before I do, pinching in my chest and stopping my breath. "Oh." I look up at him, and when our eyes connect, I am taken back to how familiar he seemed when we first met. Maybe it wasn't just that I knew his voice. There's a specific kind of grief that comes with losing someone you love, the kind that is always skimming just under the surface; the kind so universal that you can't help recognizing it in someone else, even if you don't know what you're seeing yet. "I'm sorry. I didn't know."

His tone is cautious. "But you get it."

I suck in a breath to deflect or change the subject, the way I've done whenever parents come up since I got to campus. But this isn't like that. For the first time, I don't worry about the distance it might put between us, telling him about my past. I worry about the distance it will put between us if I hold it back. If I swallow down the words that I want to tell him, knowing he's one of the few people here who can understand.

I let the breath go. He's trusting me with his own hurt. I can trust him with mine.

"Yeah. My mom died when I was eleven. Cancer." I almost shrug, trying to ease some of the bluntness of it, but there's something about this walk—the quiet in the chill, the way we seem so separate from everything else—that takes all of the tension out of me. "And my dad . . . just never really dealt with it. Put away all her stuff. Got a job two hours away, so he didn't really have to deal with me. My grandmas raised me, mostly."

My jaw tenses, waiting for some shift between us. For something to change in the dynamic, now that we've both laid out the worst things that ever happened to us.

But Milo just knocks his arm into my shoulder, so gently that I feel a faint smile trying to curl on my lips. "I'm sorry, too," he says.

I don't say "thanks," because we both know by now it's a word that never quite makes sense. I just knock my shoulder back into him. A quiet give-and-take.

He's quiet for a few moments, but there's nothing uncomfortable about it. Just thoughtful, his eyes still on me, like he's waiting for me to go on. When I don't, he says, "And that segued into solving everyone else's shit because . . . ?"

"Because . . ."

The ache is back, but it isn't just an ache anymore. It's sharp and demanding. It knows I'm changing shape here, and it's changing, too. And what it wants is for me to meet Milo's watchful gaze and tell him the truth—a truth I didn't know existed until he just made so much space for it. A truth I don't understand well enough to explain.

Because there is a part of me that genuinely enjoys giving advice and helping where I can. Not just because it feels like a natural progression of what my mom did with her own career, but because it's something I feel good doing. Something that most of the time, I excel at.

But in the past few years, it's become more than that. Not just a passion, but a crutch. And if I think too long about exactly what it is I'm using it for, I might look all the way down to the bottom of something I don't want to see.

I settle for part of the truth, if not the whole of it. "It just makes me happy, knowing there are things that can be fixed. That I might be able to help take a problem off someone's plate."

"Oh. So my messy love triangle is just a serotonin hit for you, huh?" Milo teases.

I let out a breathy laugh, relieved to pivot. "You caught me."

Milo's quiet for a few more strides. "That's rough about your dad, though," he says. "I feel like my mom did the total opposite. She's like, aggressively involved now. Which you'd think would be harder with seven kids."

"Seven kids," I marvel.

Milo kicks a stray twig off the sidewalk with his boot. "Honestly, it's a miracle I even remember my own name."

"It must be nice, though. I always wanted siblings."

Milo lets out a derisive snort. "Yeah, well."

I stop in my tracks. Milo stops a beat later, his expression quizzical.

"I'm gonna level with you, Milo."

He sizes up all five foot one of me. "Uh, good luck with that."

I square my feet on the pavement and look up at him. "I probably do have a fix-it thing. And I am trying *very* hard not to inflict it on you and your brother. So hard that I have at least eight abandoned coffee cups of failed 'Semi-Eternal Darkness' blends in the trash can behind Bagelopolis that should never see the light of day."

Milo's lip quirks. I gravitate a little closer to him, lowering my voice.

"And maybe I can't fix anything. But maybe it would help just to talk about it."

Milo leans back on his heels, staring out at the quad behind me. "I mean, you already know the details."

"Kind of."

I know that Milo had a girlfriend, and their relationship also had a strong Andie and Connor vibe to it—they'd been next-door neighbors and grew up together, so the whole thing was just kind of fated. I also know that in October of last semester Milo caught her and his brother Harley making out in the back row of a showing of *The Nightmare Before Christmas* a few towns away from campus, which is why he now hates both that movie and the idea of true love.

I also know he hasn't talked to either of them since.

"Look, new kid. The long and short of it is the same anyway. Family's complicated." Before I can say anything, he adds, "Like, this thing with your dad. You know the score, right? And it doesn't change anything. It doesn't undo what happened."

I'm not used to being caught off guard, especially this many times in a row.

"I guess . . ." I can't lie. Not to Milo, or anybody, really. "I mean, he's been trying to fix things, I think. In his defense."

Milo shrugs. "So has Harley. Doesn't mean things are fixable."

That's not true, I want to say, but I don't want to get into the pots and kettles of it all. I can't argue that Milo should try to fix things with Harley without digging myself into a hole where I'd have to be open to fixing things with my dad, too.

"Maybe . . ." I find myself saying, just to fill up the silence before my conscience can. "Maybe it's just a matter of being ready."

"Well, let me know if you ever are, because I'm sure not."

I have to bite the inside of my cheek to keep back the tidal wave of guilt, and the irritation that follows it. I don't want Milo to be right. But I also don't want to feel obligated to fix things with my dad, either. I wasn't the one who left.

"Hey." Milo settles a hand on my shoulder. Only when I glance over at him do I realize my entire face has twisted into this not-quite scowl, something so far from the syndicated-talk-show smile that I don't know how to categorize it. "Doesn't mean either of you are the bad guy or anything. There are just some things beyond help."

We've reached the dorm. Milo uses his ID card to let us in, and we make small talk in the elevator that I know we're both only half paying attention to. Underneath the banter about the cafeteria menu we're both raw and uncertain, like coming in from the cold slammed us back into reality—the mom-less, dad-less, uncertain reality that we just shared with each other, for better or worse.

We reach my room first and come to an abrupt stop.

"Well—g'night," I say, my throat tight.

"Semi-night," Milo corrects me.

I let out a laugh that borders on a wheeze, leaning closer to him. Or maybe he leans closer to me. All I know is that one moment we're both hovering uncertainly in my doorway, and the next his arms are wrapped around me, and mine around him. The hug is quiet and firm, and as I lean into the warmth of it, into the familiar citrusy, clean smell of him, I realize it's been a long time since I've really hugged anybody. An even longer time since I hugged anybody and felt this kind of mutual understanding in it—that sometimes words might not fix things, but this can make them hurt less.

We're just starting to pull apart when we're interrupted by an ear-piercing wolf whistle from down the hall. The noise is so loud that I stumble backward, and Milo steps back and lowers his arms so quickly that it almost seems impossible that they were the same ones that wrapped around me a split second ago. I follow his eyes down the hall to the student who catcalled us, ready to glare, but they've already ducked into the bathroom.

"Well," I say, putting my hands on my hips, "that was rude."

But when I glance up at Milo, his head is bowed so I can't see his face. He just mumbles a "good night" at me as he turns and lets himself into his room without looking back.

Chapter Eleven

"Uh, I think it's safe to say we've been banned from the food science department until further notice," says Shay, muffling a laugh in her scarf as we hightail it away from the science building.

I glance back as if afraid we'll be followed, trying to wring out my very wet ponytail. "Well, on the upside, at least we know how to set off a LaCroix bomb now?"

"Ah, yes. Can't wait to get into that specific vein of supervillainy with you." She stops me, raising a thumb to wipe off the mascara under my eye. "Hold up, you look like you just got broken up with at prom."

I sigh and let her fix my face, grateful that when we did, in fact, set off a small geyser, most of it spilled on me and not Shay or the other unsuspecting people around us.

Our shenanigans in the science building aside, two weeks into the semester, things are considerably looking up. Thanks to Valeria, I'm no longer failing statistics—once we showed Professor Hutchison my emails weren't set up, she let me retake the exam. Thanks to Shay and the trivia team, I have accumulated enough blue ribbons to match pace with the other students, both for me and for Connor. And thanks to me . . . well. Shay isn't necessarily any closer to finding her major, but she is certainly closer to finding out what it *isn't*.

I pull up the list-making app on my phone and cross "Food Science" off the list. This recent disaster is one of three "let's find Shay's major"–related adventures we've taken already, which included an invitation from the premed students to watch a pig dissection (we made it about five minutes before peacing out and watching several episodes of *The Great British Bake Off* to bleach our brains), a workshop on connecting with your inner child from the drama department (they had us crawling on the floor and making animal noises; I've never had a full-grown woman *moo* at me with as much resentment as Shay did that afternoon), and an interactive experiment with the food science department that, well. Didn't *not* end with us ricocheting a drink cap into a light fixture and onto a professor's head.

While the progress on finding Shay's major is approximately zero percent, the two of us, at least, are forever bonded by the mutual horror of Blue Ridge State's curricula.

It's helped that we've gotten into a familiar groove—Shay's alarm goes off in the morning and I head right out to the recording studio with her and Milo, mostly to answer the emails (we've cleared out half of them now, I can't help myself) but also because it's an easy way to find out firsthand when ribbon events are happening for my sake, and when other departments are doing open classes for Shay's. That, and I do feel just a *little* responsible for Milo's well-being, considering I am weaning him off a legal drug one version of Semi-Eternal Darkness at a time.

But as it turns out, I am justified in my meddling. A few mornings after we started half-caffing him, Milo showed up to the studio looking slightly more alive than dead. And now, as Shay and I make our way to the studio for the prep meeting they always have on Sunday afternoons, he looks downright human. The skin under his eyes is considerably less dark, and for once he doesn't look like he's on the perpetual verge of a yawn.

"You know we're not paying you, right?" Milo asks when we

walk in, his customary greeting for me most times I've followed Shay here.

"Our company is priceless," says Shay.

Milo looks up with a smirk, then zeroes in on me fast. "What happened?" he asks, with undisguised concern.

It's more eye contact than I've gotten from him in the last week, ever since that awkward moment when we hugged in the dorm hallway. I haven't worried about it *so* much—I knew it would resolve itself on its own if we just let it. It's not like either of us is actually interested in the other, especially given that I am in a committed relationship and Milo has declared on multiple occasions that love is a scam.

Even so, I'm surprised by the heat in my face when I touch it. "Oh—uh, we had a small calamity."

"You still look like a cautionary teen tale." Shay groans. "Here, I've got a mirror somewhere in my bag."

I wave her off, thumbing my eyelids to scrape at the last of the mascara. "It's fine. Only the computer screen can judge me."

"Plus that wall of former Knights, ever watching," says Shay wryly.

My eyes flit over to it, immediately locking on the picture of my mom. I could give a hundred reasons why I keep following Shay here. I enjoy their company. Answering these emails makes me feel a bit more like I have a role in this big campus where I haven't found my place. It's nice to have some kind of routine.

But those are just the little things that add to the big one: it's the closest I've felt to my mom in a long, long time.

I still feel Milo's eyes on me when I look away.

"Looks like a pretty slow week on campus, so we'll mostly be on the lookout for local news," says Shay, handing over the emails we printed earlier from the student board, campus organizations, and academic office.

"Thanks," says Milo. He barely glances the pages over before he shifts in his stool, looking at each of us in turn. "But, uh, are we going to address your whole 'Dear Abby' situation ending up on the air, or . . ."

My ears burn. Shay and I both had early shifts at Bagelopolis on Friday, so we weren't here for the broadcast. But of course I heard the full thing afterward, including a listener using "Call-in Friday" to thank the Knight for the advice he gave on time-management strategies for double majors. Milo was fast on his feet—"I'm only the Knight, not the cavalry answering the emails, but I'm glad it helped"—but it was definitely an unprecedented moment in the history of *The Knights' Watch*.

I clear my throat. "So, I might have gotten carried away answering those New Year's resolution emails."

"Shock me," says Milo, with a hint of amusement.

"But I can totally stop," I add quickly, even though the idea of it makes my stomach turn.

The emails have become more than just practice for giving advice. They're a reason for me to be here, close to my mom, when I don't have any real business being here. And they're also a way to distract myself from the ache that still rises up sometimes, in the quiet moments when Milo's not at the mic and I catch myself staring at it, wondering about the girl I used to be. The one I might have been.

"Nah, it's fine. Follow your weird, unpaid-advice-columnist bliss." I'm getting at least 50 percent eye contact from him now, so I know he means it. "But judging from that caller, I'm guessing people are going to use 'Call-in Friday' for more advice. So we're going to need some kind of plan, because the only advice I have begins and ends with 'have you tried another cup of coffee.'"

"I'm sure you won't get any more callers," I say, but just then Shay taps the computer screen to get our attention.

Somehow we've amassed a dozen new emails overnight. Not from people sending events or information for the broadcast, but people directly asking for advice. I click on one of them and skim the words, You answered back a friend of mine, so I was wondering if I could ask you . . .

"Shit," says Milo. I can't tell if he's horrified or impressed.

"Okay, um—if someone else calls I can . . . type out an answer really fast for you?" I suggest.

Milo leans down to squint at the computer screen, close enough that his shadow feels like some kind of heat lamp. I'm so aware of the edges of him that I sit as still as I possibly can until he pushes his wheeled stool away. "Or you could just go on and give advice yourself."

My stomach drops. "Oh. No way."

Milo frowns. "Why not?"

"Because *The Knights' Watch* is—" The air has that too-thin quality it used to get when the stage fright reared its ugly head. Before I realized it was insurmountable and gave up on crowds altogether. "It's just supposed to be the Knight. It's always been that way."

Milo shrugs, spinning slightly in the chair. "Doesn't mean it always has to be."

"It does," I say, more forcefully than I intended. Milo stops spinning and Shay glances up from her planner. "I mean . . . they picked you for a reason."

Milo puts his hands up in surrender. "Alright. But if you change your mind . . ."

"I won't," I say quickly, turning my attention back to the computer. "I'll just get through these in the meantime while you guys plan."

I'm left mostly to my own devices after that, but even as I blaze through the rest of the emails, I have one ear perked to their conversation. Less paying attention to what it's about, and more to the tone of it. Milo laughs a bit more than usual. Cracks a few jokes that for once don't sound like they were stolen from a deadpanning Disney villain. When we leave for the night, Milo heading out to get dinner with his siblings and us back to the dorm, I swear there might even be the slightest of springs in his step.

"I think it's about time I introduce the next phase of the decaffeinating plan," I say to Shay.

Shay raises her eyebrows. "You'd be messing with something much bigger than you are, Andie Rose. Bigger than all of us."

Having been raised by Gammy Nell, patron saint of all things delicious, I would never compromise the taste of something so beloved as Eternal Darkness. But now that I'm on my eleventh batch, I've perfected a blend that was every bit as unholy and bitter as the original blend, except without a trace of caffeine.

"It would just be one he could drink in the afternoon. I mean, just look how much better off he is on the half-caf version. He didn't run into one single stationary object today," I remind Shay. She opens her mouth to protest. "*Or* do that thing where he blinks just long enough that you think he's fallen asleep standing up."

Shay sighs, using her student ID to buzz us back into Cardinal dorm. "You're right. But I'm telling you, he's not going to go for it."

"I'll just have him take a taste test tomorrow to see. Even Sean said he couldn't tell the difference, and he's almost as much of a coffee monster as Milo."

My phone buzzes in my pocket and I tense up fast enough that Shay frowns. I've already spent an hour on the phone today with Grandma Maeve and Gammy Nell, and another hour and a half talking to Connor, so there's only one person it can be—except when I look at the screen, it's not my dad. It's Connor's mom.

"I . . . gotta take this," I say, pressing the phone to my chest.

Shay tilts her head at me in a way I've already recognized as "I won't ask now, but I will later." There's this rush of gratitude so intense that I can't help associating it with all the times I've wanted, more than anything in the world, to have a sister. It seems a little wild to think it after such a short time of knowing each other, but this is the closest I've ever come.

"Hi, Mrs. Whit," I say, hovering in the stairwell as Shay walks off. "How are you?"

"Andromeda," Mrs. Whit greets me in her usual even tone. The only reason I don't wince is because Connor's mom has a way of making anything sound dignified, even the original name on my birth certificate that my mom pushed for and then promptly never used. It was a running family joke for years—just one of many spur-of-the-moment decisions my mom had that my dad ran with. But ever since she died, Connor's parents are the only ones who use it. "I trust you are doing well?"

I'm too naive to realize this is less of a question and more of a test, so I answer, "Yeah. Wow. It's great here."

"I'm so glad you're enjoying yourself." Only then do I realize the usual warmth in her voice has taken on a different temperature entirely. "I wouldn't want you to be as miserable as my Connor. I wouldn't wish that on anyone."

My heart stutters in my rib cage. "I . . . I'm sorry?"

The thing is, I've been talking to Connor every day. I've been talking to him a heck of a lot more than we did last semester. If anything, it's been a relief to know we still can. There are a lot of words I'd use to describe those conversations, but "miserable" would probably come in dead last.

"Well, it's to be expected," says Mrs. Whit primly. "Connor's well aware that he's not meeting any of the standards we've held for him by attending a community college. An idea that never would have passed through his head a few months ago."

The tears are already pricking at the back of my eyes before I can get a handle on her words. I love Connor, but I love his parents, too. They've always accepted me as one of their own. Mr. Whit helped me apply to my first part-time jobs. Mrs. Whit took me on trips to the mall to choose my homecoming dress, my prom dress, my graduation dress. I can't even count the holidays and reunions and town events they pulled me into. It's a lifetime kind of debt.

"I . . ." The words come so easily when I'm giving advice to someone that isn't me. But right now, the well of my brain is so dried up I have no idea where to start, let alone end. "I didn't know he was going to transfer, too. Really, I didn't. I was just trying to surprise him."

"Let this be a hard lesson in transparency with your partner, then," she says. "If this is something Connor will even be able to recover from, that is."

I don't remember deciding to sit down against the cool glass of the stairwell's massive windows, but it's all my muscles can take. Mrs. Whit is the closest thing I've had to a mom of my own for so many years now. I never thought I could do anything she'd disapprove of. I never imagined having a conversation like this. We've both always wanted the same things: what was best for me and what was best for Connor.

For the first time I can remember, those two things don't overlap. I close my eyes, and another fresh round of tears spills out.

As generous as the Whits have always been to make room for me in their lives, I've always felt like I have to be careful not to take too much of it—not to presume that I can. A part of me understood that while they love me, some of that love will always be conditional.

And now, despite all my best efforts, I've stumbled into the condition.

"Connor will transfer back," I reassure her. "The transfer won't even show up on his grad-school applications. I checked."

"I sure hope so," says Mrs. Whit, the words clipped.

For a few moments neither of us says anything, and I realize she's waiting for me to speak. "I'm so sorry," I say again, because I can't think of anything else. "I really didn't know."

Mrs. Whit lets out a small *hmmph* noise that would concern

anyone else, but is a comfort to me. I know the ins, outs, and weird noises of her. I know that sound is an admission that I'm at least semi-right, even if she doesn't want me to be.

"Well," she says tersely. "At least we know you'll be behind him, no matter what."

"Of course." I'm grateful she brought it up so I don't have to. "We've always got each other's backs. We're best friends."

"I hope you're right." There's murmuring in the background. I recognize the low tones of Mr. Whit, and wonder if he's every bit as mad as she is. "Just remember that, Andromeda. His success at Blue Ridge benefits him every bit as much as it benefits you."

I try to breathe in without hiccupping, but I can't help it. The words feel like they landed in my ribs and fought their way up to my throat. *And vice versa*, I want to say. But she knows that. She and Mr. Whit have always embodied that themselves. This isn't a matter of Connor getting priority over me because he has more potential; it's a matter of Connor being their kid, when I'm not.

The stupid thing is, I thought she'd be proud of me. I'd imagined a phone call like this so many times, except it started with a "congratulations" and ended with planning a day trip up to campus to check out the historic district of the town.

Mrs. Whit must take my silence as an answer, because she lets out a sigh. "I worry about you on your own out there, too. You're doing alright?"

It's the smallest of bends, but it's enough for me not to break. "Yeah. Yeah," I say brightly. "I'm doing fine."

"I had a feeling you'd find your way to that school. Your mother couldn't have spoken more highly of it."

I rest my head against the window. Mrs. Whit and my mom grew up together in Little Fells. It's one more reason why Connor and I were less of a possibility and more of an inevitability—our shared history goes back further than we do.

It's one more reason why this conversation doesn't just sting, but hurts all the way down. My grandmas were just that—my grandmas. Fiercely loving and quirky and always on my side. But neither of them could ever really be a mom to me. Not in the way it sometimes felt like Mrs. Whit could.

"I'm hoping that this all works out in the end," she says. "And that this semester is over as quickly as possible."

"You and me both," I try to say, but before I can finish, Mrs. Whit cuts me off with, "Our dinner just arrived, so I have to go."

We say our goodbyes and I hold the phone against my ear, the humiliation like a wave that hasn't crashed over me yet. I feel suspended in this moment, like maybe if I just don't get up, maybe if I squeeze my eyes shut, I can send myself back to December. Tell Connor I got in on the transfer. Relive the past few weeks the way we were supposed to, with both of us here, and with Connor's parents still treating me like a daughter instead of some girl who might have just compromised his whole future.

That's when the humiliation hardens and turns into something else. I didn't ask for him to transfer. I would never. And Mrs. Whit must know that—heck, anyone who's ever met me knows that. The idea that she could misunderstand such a fundamental part of me after all this time is the kind of blow that can't fully land.

The thing is, I know why I'm calling my dad back before I even hit the button. He's proud of me. I know he is. And even with everything between us so fractured, I just need to hear his voice right now. Not even necessarily because it's his—but because he's a person who knows what this school means to me. Who would never factor Connor into the equation.

"A-Plus," my dad greets me, his voice booming through the phone. "How's my favorite Blue Ridge student?"

The sound of the nickname makes me press my fingers on the charm of my necklace, and chases the last threat of tears away. He's called me that ever since I can remember. My mom was Amy, the original "A"; I'm A-Plus.

"Good." It's only half a lie. Ten minutes ago, I really was. "How are you? How's the trip?"

"You know, same old, same old," he says. Ever since he took a new job based two hours away from Little Fells he's been taking a lot of trips like this, so he's used to living out of a suitcase. Even without knowing what the Airbnb he's in looks like, I can still picture him now: he's leaning against a counter, his button-down untucked from his jeans for the end of the day, nursing the single Corona he has with dinner every night. "Mostly subsisting off delivery pizza and your gammy's snack cakes. You launched your Blue Ridge advice column yet?"

He's teasing, the pride undeniable in his voice. I wish it didn't grate on me. He still hasn't mentioned the "Bed of Roses" clips I sent to him. I know I should just ask if he's read them, but that's the thing. I don't want to have to ask. I want him to care enough to have read them and brought it up himself.

And then, almost like he heard the thoughts through the phone, my dad asks, "Hey, why haven't you sent me your clips yet?"

I pull my fingers from the necklace in surprise. "Oh. I—I did. A few weeks ago."

"All I got were your transcripts. Great work, by the way," he says. "No wonder you got into Blue Ridge midyear."

I flush. My grandmas always send him paper copies of my grades. My dad keeps a bunch of paperwork in an old-school filing system, and one of the hanging folders has all of my transcripts from kindergarten on. I'm oddly touched that it didn't stop in college.

And embarrassed that I've been annoyed with my dad for weeks now over something that couldn't be helped. I'm so careful to be direct with people and try to consider all the possibilities in different scenarios. But when it comes to my dad, it's all so personal it just goes haywire.

"Um—thanks. Huh. Well, I'll . . ."

"Send them my way, when you get a chance," he says easily. "Figure you're busy taking Blue Ridge's grading curve by storm."

I half laugh, half choke at the idea of it. "Not quite." Before I have to elaborate, I quickly pivot by asking, "Did they put you up somewhere nice?"

"Actually, I'm staying with Kelly."

"Oh?"

I don't mean for it to come out like a question, because it shouldn't be. I know my dad's been dating Kelly for a few months now. From the light stalking I did the one time some friends of mine back home split a bottle of Yellow Tail and went to town on her Facebook, she seems perfectly nice. Big smile, white teeth, shiny hair, a pediatric dentist with a passion for making soap out of offbeat molds like cheese wedges and skulls and corgi butts. My dad asked if I wanted to get lunch with her when she was passing through Little Fells last month, but I blew him off because of finals. And also because the idea of my dad even dating was such a foreign concept to me that watching a dog pop a wheelie on a skateboard would make more sense to my brain.

"Yeah, her family has a house in Lake Anna," says my dad. "So we're just parking it here so we can cut down on company expenses."

He works for a nonprofit, and has always been big on saving money. Even if I can't quite wrap my head around him staying with her, I'm relieved he's not trying to squeeze into another motel.

"A lake house?" I say, wiggling my eyebrows. "Sounds fancy."

"You'd love it here," says my dad without missing a beat. I press my back farther into the wall, not sure how to process this. He's been saying stuff like that lately—these little invitations into his world. The ones I wanted growing up, but never got. I know they coincide with Kelly coming into his life, and I can't decide whether to be bitter or grateful. "Beautiful view. Huge porch. Maybe if you take a long weekend . . . or during the summer, definitely. We'd love to have you."

We. I'm glad he isn't here to see me flinch. I barely heard enough of him as an "I" growing up to suddenly make him a "we."

But I can't say I'm not tempted by the offer. Despite my jam-packed schedule, I've been making an effort to try to explore some of the trails in the arboretum, to try to take a beat and center myself. I was worried it might remind me too much of the hikes I took with my parents as a kid, but instead it stirred up memories I'd forgotten—like this old, beat-up compass my mom always used to keep in her pocket and jokingly pretend she couldn't read, saying we should let the trail decide where it wanted to go. Or when my parents made their special hiking granola with its generous chocolate-chip ratio for us to take along.

Or the few times my mom would be away for work, and my dad and I went out hiking on our own. How he'd patiently stop and explain what different plants were to me, or follow the occasional bird call, or point out the trail signs in case I wanted to go out on my own someday when I was older. How sometimes we'd just walk these long stretches in companionable silence, easy and familiar with each other's rhythms without ever noticing the rhythms at all.

It's strange to think back on now, on the other side of him leaving. I don't think there has been silence with him that I didn't feel compelled to fill since.

"Yeah," I say. "Maybe."

This is usually the part where the awkward silence settles in and one of us finds an excuse to hang up, but my dad surprises me by cutting right through it. "Your grandmas tell me you're in Cardinal," he says, with this hint of a smirk in his voice I recognize more from childhood than anything recent. "It's no Bluebird, but I trust it's treating you well?"

"Yeah," I say again, but this time with feeling. "I love my room-mate. Her name is Shay. She got me a job at the bagel shop near campus."

"Bagelopolis?"

"Yup."

My dad lets out a low whistle. "Listen. Take it from your old man. The strawberry cream cheese with the cheesy garlic bagel?"

"*Dad*," I say, aghast.

"No," he insists, a laugh in the back of his throat, "*trust* me. It's great any day of the week, but it's the best cure for a hango—uh. Well."

"Noted," I say, muffling a laugh of my own. "For all the ragers I'll be attending."

"I do hope you'll get out to some of the parties. Responsibly," he emphasizes. After the smallest of beats, he adds, "Not that I ever worry about that with you."

Usually I'd be annoyed that he feels like he gets to worry about me at all. But tonight feels different. Maybe because we aren't talking just as father and daughter—we're talking as father and *grown-up* daughter. Not quite equal ground, but closer than it's ever been up to this point.

"I'll take your unholy bagel pairing into consideration," I say.

My dad lets out a chuckle. "You're welcome in advance."

"Any other food recs while I've got you?"

"Oh, too many," he says. My sweet tooth probably came from all sides of this family, but my dad takes it to the next level. Cookie Monster would bow down to him. "How much time do you have?"

"Plenty." I pull up the Notes app on my phone. There's a smile on my face so sneaky and wide that the conversation with Connor's mom might have never happened at all. "Hit me with them."

"Okay, first of all, in the historic district of town there's a candy shop with giant peanut butter cups. It's bright pink, you can't miss it. And if you walk a little farther from it, there's a hole-in-the-wall crepe place—your roommate probably knows it, most of the students there— What's that? What happened to your bunny?"

I blink. "Sorry, what?"

But my dad doesn't hear me. The pitch of his voice is slightly higher. I recognize it; the memory goes so far back that I feel like I've been snapped into another time. A time my mom was still alive, and I was little enough that I could still stand on his toes, and he used that same voice with me.

"Don't worry, that's an easy fix. We can sew it right up."

And then I hear the sounds of sniffling. More specifically, little-kid sniffling. I freeze with the phone still pressed to my ear, my heart beating like a drum. It realizes what's happening a few crucial seconds before my brain does.

"Whiskers will be fine. Trust me," says my dad.

There's a muffled reply. I can't make out the words. Or maybe I just don't want to.

"Sorry," he says, using his normal voice again. "A stuffed-animal medical emergency."

"Whose stuffed animal?" I ask, even though I already know. Even though my throat's already thick, and I already feel guilty for it. Even though I already resent this kid I've never met, knowing she's done absolutely nothing to deserve it.

"Kelly's daughter, Ava," says my dad, as if to remind me.

A tear streaks down my cheek. "Right," I say, my voice so perfectly even that the tear might not even exist, if it didn't just stain my coat. "I, uh—didn't realize she had a daughter."

There's a pause. "Your grandmas didn't mention it?"

I bite my tongue so I don't say, *Wouldn't that have been your job?*

And this right here is a bitter taste I know all too well. Every time we have a conversation that seems normal, we hit one of these snags. Like we have all the construction of what could be a normal parent-child relationship, the walls all secure, a roof overhead, but if I let myself step in, it's only a matter of time before I take a step that opens a hole in the floor. We never built a foundation to stand on.

But this feels different. It feels personal. We've spent so long being cordial with each other, this surface-level getting along—part of it is because we barely know each other, but another part of it was so I would never have to worry about something like this. So none of his choices would feel like they had anything to do with me, and they couldn't affect me.

It's hard to let myself keep pretending that when there's some other kid he's playing dad for. Some kid who brought back that voice of his I barely even remember myself.

"Guess not," I say. "But, uh—I just got a text to grab dinner with my roommate, so I actually have to run."

He sounds surprised, but not enough to think I'm lying. "Oh. Where are you headed?"

"Dining hall," I lie, booking it out of the stairwell so I can make it to our room. None of the usual tactics are going to work. I am going to cry, and I am going to cry *hard*, and I can practically feel my body counting down to it like a ticking time bomb. "Talk to you later?"

"Yeah, I'm around whenever," he says. "Keep me in the loop."

It's the closest he's ever come to telling, not asking, me to stay in touch, but my brain can't even register it. I'm too busy trying to keep my face intact. After we hang up I manage to make it to the door when the key gets jammed, and even that second costs me—a tear slips out, and then another, and then *finally* the stupid door opens. The room is pitch-black and Shay-less, so I heave a breath of relief, shut the door behind me, sag into my bed, and just let myself cry.

Chapter Twelve

"I've called him like, fifteen times," says Shay, pacing the tiny space of the recording studio. "He's not picking up."

"Maybe because he's driving?" I wish out loud.

"As much as I admire your unflappable optimism, he clearly overslept. I've been calling for almost a half hour, and his parents' house is a ten-minute drive from campus." She pulls the phone away from her ear, letting out a groan. "And we're *five* minutes from doomed."

Now four, according to my phone, which I've also been using to text him. I try not to wince. This isn't *not* my fault. This, and everything else that's gone haywire on campus these past twenty-four hours.

See, yesterday Professor Hutchison nearly had a fit when not one, not two, but *three* different students fully conked out during statistics. Shay told me her English professor let class out early because he, direct quote, was "going to fall asleep standing up." And Milo was so tired that after dinner at his parents' place, he decided to spend the night there.

He was already asleep when I got a text from Sean and discovered that in my plan to un-zombify Milo, I'd flown too close to the sun—Sean had forgotten to look at the labels I put on the fully decaffeinated Eternal Darkness blend, and in doing so, accidentally decaffeinated half the student body. Including one very sleepy, unsuspecting Milo Flynn.

Which leads us to this moment now.

"Isn't there like, a backup or something?" I ask Shay. "Someone who can go on if Milo can't?"

She presses her finger and thumb to her eyelids, rubbing them hard enough to bruise. "He was supposed to find someone for that, but of *course* he never did."

"Well," I say, "you already know all the information for today's broadcast like the back of your hand. Can't you go on?"

Shay pauses, only so she can frown. "I mean . . ."

I sit up a little straighter in the swivel chair by the computer, clutching my tea. "Actually, this could be another great opportunity to explore a potential major," I realize. "I could totally see you as like, a professional podcaster. You have a great voice, the sense of humor—"

"Why don't you do it?" Shay counters.

Embarrassingly enough, I choke on my own spit. "That'd be silly, I only got here a few weeks ago," I say after I collect myself.

"Weeks you've spent answering a bunch of listener questions over email." Shay gestures at the microphone. "Today is 'Call-in Friday' anyway. Judging from last week's, you'd just be doing the same thing, except out loud."

I shake my head, feeling sweat sting at the line of my temple, itch under my arms. "I, uh . . ." I clear my throat. "I'm bad at doing stuff on the fly. I . . . I need a script. I need to practice."

"So do it like a conversation. Like you're leading Werewolf at the dorm, or you're just talking to me," says Shay, tapping the backside of the chair. "You sure don't need a script when you're telling *me* what you think I should do."

I let out a laugh so breathy that it feels like my throat's being squished. "Shay, I can't."

"Why not?" Shay asks.

"Because . . ."

I don't even notice the ache as much these days, because it's been a constant. But in this moment it's changing shape again. Hardening. Reminding me of the early days after my mom died, when for a while, it felt like the only feeling at all.

The first time I publicly humiliated myself was a few weeks after my mom died, at a school assembly about road safety. I was one of the student crossing guard helpers and was all set to do a skit with Connor about bike helmets. But he clicked the strap on his chin and waited for me to say my line, and I looked out at all the other kids—saw them all watching me in a way they never had before, with some mix of intrigue and pity—and I felt like a stranger to my own self. Like I wasn't the same girl I was in their eyes, or mine, either. I choked.

It's not like I gave up after that. For a while, I'd actively volunteer for the morning announcements or to help host the school talent show. It was like some kind of amateur exposure therapy—I thought I could shake the fear if I just confronted it. Instead the fear just shook back, harder than I could take. I'd never feel nervous in the lead-up, but then I'd feel people's eyes on me and the words that used to come so easily would dry up on the spot.

All these years I'd spent as "the brave one"—the years I spent mapping out these dreams about big platforms, talking on stages, and flying into television studios—and without any warning, all of the nerve that drove it was simply gone.

It was Connor who convinced me to go easy on myself. To find other ways to channel what I wanted to do. "What if you did something behind the scenes instead?" he said. "If you were doing stuff and nobody knew it was you, would it scare you then?"

It was the seed that grew into "Bed of Roses." Into the quiet acceptance that there were some parts of my dreams that were going to change when I changed, too. And an even quieter relief that I wouldn't have to worry about my mom's legacy anymore, because I was taking myself out of it before I could do anything to hurt it.

And that's just it. The kind of fear I feel about this—it's not because of some dumb assembly skit. Not because of a potential talent show blip. It's . . .

"Because of your mom?"

Only then do I realize my eyes drifted toward the wall again. I snap them back onto Shay's fast enough to give my retinas whiplash.

"Andie," Shay says quietly. "I've caught you staring at that picture more times than I can count. Didn't take too much to Google Amy Janson and make the connection. You're here because your mom was the first-ever Knight."

I close my eyes. Not out of any kind of sadness, but appreciation. I'd been so fixated on keeping this part of me tucked away that it didn't occur to me Shay would figure it out on her own. That instead of shying away from it like so many of my friends did growing up, she would quietly keep it to herself until the time was right to talk about it.

"Yeah," I say, trying not to let myself get overwhelmed by the surge of gratitude, of strange relief. "But it's not just that. I really do love answering the listener emails and spending time with you and Milo. It's the best part of my day."

Shay reaches out and puts her hand over mine, squeezing it for a moment before she lets it go. "Well, that's fucked up, because I wouldn't wish this sleep schedule on anyone." I let out a sharp laugh, and she adds, "We like having you here, too. And it seems to me like this whole thing is kind of in your blood."

"That's just it." I'm not looking at her, but the mic. "I feel like . . . like if I did badly, I'd be letting her down."

Shay's mouth twists to the side. "Your mom was what, eighteen when she started this? You really think she was perfect?"

It's not that I expect that she was perfect. It's that I used to be — or at least, my little-kid self thought I was. It used to come so easily, so thoughtlessly, and even if I try again, it will never be like it once was. I will never again be that guileless kid with the mic, the one who made my mom smile.

"Maybe . . . maybe some other time Milo's out for the count." My voice sounds pathetic even in my own ears, but it doesn't change the facts. "When I've had some time to think about it."

"Or overthink about it," says Shay.

But she holds my gaze for a moment and relents with a sigh. I feel that light-headed swoosh of post-adrenaline and expect the relief to soften it, but the feeling is heavier than that, mingled with a strange disappointment.

"Fine," she says. "But you have to sit next to me with the notes, so you can point out anything I'm missing."

I push past it, hopping to attention. Shay positions herself at the mic. I position myself right next to her, scanning the notes so intensely that within thirty seconds I've managed to tattoo them to the insides of my brain. "Construct on Main 2–6, ribbon LA building 5, talent show signups @ portal . . ."

"Okay," I say to myself, soaking it all in. "Okay."

"Okay?" says Shay, holding the music stand with the notes on it closer to me.

I nod. "I got it."

"Good," she says. Then she inexplicably slides off her chair, and pushes the mic toward my mouth. "You're live in five . . . four . . ."

I reach out to grab her arm, but she's already out of reach. "*Shay.*"

She taps the record button to show me she is extremely not messing around, and mouths the words, *Three . . . two . . . one.*

A few seconds of dead air follow. Me with my mouth wide open, Shay with her eyes possibly even wider, the two of us locked in a game of chicken that may or may not end with me tossing my literal cookies (Ellie shared a massive box of Oreos with us last night) into the mic.

I suck in a breath. And then I say, "Hi."

Shay scowls and mouths back, *Hi?*

I shrug, my shoulders jerking up so fast it's a miracle they don't knock off my ears. Shay points at the mic. I take a breath, but it gets stuck halfway up my throat.

"Um, hello. Friday."

I wince, looking over at Shay, certain she'll bail me out. This is the point where someone steps in—a teacher pulls me offstage. Another student steps in to grab my dropped line. And Connor tells me it's okay, that we all have different strengths and I am lucky to have so many others in the first place.

But Shay doesn't do any of those things. Instead she looks me right in my semi-hysterical eyes and makes a "go on" gesture.

"What I mean is—it is Friday. Today. So . . . good for us."

Yikes. I look at the notes that I helped Shay compile mere minutes ago and they look like they're written in hieroglyphics. At some point I must have started to sweat, because I can feel it itching at my armpits and my brow. Right along with the familiar churn in my gut.

I put my hand over the mic and mouth the words, *I can't do this.*

"You're already doing it!" she whispers back, with this unyielding, no-nonsense look that has some real Grandma Maeve energy to it. "Keep going. Anything other than dead air."

Dead air. I remember my mom explaining to me what that meant. When she'd first gotten sick, they hired a temporary host for the radio station while she was in and out of chemo—"There's enough dead air in his broadcasts to put people to sleep," she'd complained. And when I innocently asked if that meant there was alive air, she'd laughed harder than she had that whole week.

I smile thinking about it. Thinking about her eyes gleaming back at me in the studio the days she brought me in for quick segments, the two of us like twin flames in the little booth. Thinking about a time when this wouldn't have seemed like a nightmare, but an opportunity. A beginning.

My shoulders loosen and my lungs fill up with the cool air of the studio.

"Well, in case my voice being a full octave higher didn't give it away, I'm not the Knight," I say, scooting my butt farther into the stool to get my mouth closer to the mic. "I'm . . . I'm the, uh . . . Squire."

Shay pulls up her sleeve so she can dampen a laugh with it. I grin back, and some of the spell is broken. For a moment it really does feel like it's just the two of us having a conversation, just like she said.

"'Call-in Friday,'" she prompts me.

I nod vigorously. Then remember, of course, that none of them can see me. "I'm, um—I'm also the person who's been answering your emails asking for advice, so if you have anything to ask, go ahead and give us a ring when we get to the call-in section of today's broadcast." My voice is still wavering, but it could be worse. "But first—the latest."

I take another breath and it feels like I'm breathing in my own fear, like I'm swallowing it before it can swallow me.

"The construction on Main Street is, much to nobody's surprise, taking longer to finish than a triple major in their fifth year, so you're going to have to avoid that area between two and six today." I'm not great with the pacing, saying some of it too fast. I take another breath, half channeling my mom, and half channeling Milo. "But if you'd like to make use of the time you're taking the long way around, you might want devise a talent act for the annual Blue Ridge Talent Show, because sign-ups for individuals and groups are opening up on the student portal starting today. And if you happen to be near the literary arts building today, congrats! You're about to get front-row seats to the bloodbath of freshmen trying to get ribbons for the next round of the Knights' Tour trivia tonight at five P.M."

Shay gives me a thumbs-up, but it's short-lived. The sound-board is lighting up. We have a caller.

"Looks like we already have someone ringing in for 'Call-in Friday,'" I say, so nervous at the idea that I am trying to reach into the back of my brain for what Milo usually says. It comes up empty. All I hear is my heart pounding in every vein in my head.

"*Knights' Watch*," I say once I hear the call connect. "What's on your mind, friend?"

"Uh . . . well . . . wow. I guess, first I want to say thank you? Cuz if you're the same Squire that helped my roommate with her finances, she's like, way chiller now?"

"Oh." My heart does this happy little *thunk* of a thing, and I smile at Shay again without meaning to. She's already smirking back. "Glad to hear it."

"Same. Which is why I was wondering if you could maybe give me some advice with my job? I signed on to be a part-time general assistant for the company, and . . . my boss is super rad and all. But she's always asking me to do things like pick up her kids from school and get stuff for her sister. And that kind of seems like it's not in my purview?"

"Oh, wow. Been there, navigated awkwardly through that." It's true. I've had enough part-time jobs that blurred the lines between "I just need a receptionist in the afternoons" and "actually, can you pick up my family's groceries on your way home?" to relate. "So first, how's your relationship with your boss?"

In the next ten minutes, we hash through the caller's work history, make a solid plan to approach talking to their boss about it, and even form contingency plans if their boss reacts badly. After that we take two more callers, and then—much to my surprise—Shay taps an invisible watch on her wrist, letting me know to wrap it up.

"Well, you know where to reach me. Happy Friday, everyone," I say, before panicking and ending the show with a graceless "Ta-ta!"

And then it's over. I survived. I gave advice in real time, while actual people listened in. Sure, it was anonymous. Sure, I couldn't actually see anyone. But the rush of it is so intense that for a moment, it doesn't matter. For all the time I've spent trying to make myself fit in here, it feels like I just carved out a piece all my own.

The swell of pride lasts for approximately two seconds before I remember the train wreck of the rest of the broadcast. I wait until Shay turns off the mic, then pull up my sweater and bury my face in it.

Shay pats me on the arm. "Ta-ta?"

"Murder me," I moan.

"I would, but then who would take my bird's-eye-view Instagrams when my hands are busy holding books?"

I pull my face out of the bunched-up cotton to see Shay still grinning at me.

"C'mon. We'll come up with a killer sign-off for you later. But we have a shift to get to," she reminds me, tossing me my coat.

After it lands in my lap I extend my arms out to let my armpits breathe. "I'm sweating through several layers of clothes."

"Precious. Please tell me more." I open my mouth and she holds up a hand to stop me from doing just that. "Andie. You were *fine*."

I will myself not to look at the picture of my mom on the wall, shrugging on my coat. I may be able to ignore the picture, but I can't ignore that all-too-familiar seasick feeling. The kind of sick where I know I'm not going to throw up, but my stomach will still feel like it's in a knot I can't undo for the rest of the day.

"I should've been better," I mutter.

"And you will be. Next time." Shay cocks her head toward the door. "Now let's get out of here before Milo shows up and figures out you poisoned the coffee supply."

Milo does not, in fact, figure this out on his own, but is quickly informed of it an hour later. He rolls up to Bagelopolis in an oversized corduroy jacket and jeans, his eyes bright but wary, his hands in his pockets and his posture apologetic. He locks eyes on me first.

"I can't believe I overslept. Yesterday was nuts," he says, running a hand through his curls. "I'm so—"

"It's my fault," I cut in before he can apologize. "Remember that decaf version of Eternal Darkness I made?"

Milo says without missing a beat, "I can still hear my Italian ancestors weeping, so yes."

I wince. "I left it in the back and Sean accidentally brewed it yesterday."

For a few moments Milo just blinks. "So you're telling me yesterday I drank three cups of lies."

"And then you overslept, and I did that *terrible* show this morning, and you have every right to be—"

"Oh, I listened to the show. You were great," Milo says, so casually that he's not even making eye contact with me when he says it, but focusing on the cream cheese display case.

My jaw nearly drops. I'm sure it goes against some RA policy to shred what's left of my ego, but he doesn't have to rewrite history here.

"Milo. I bombed."

He waves me off. "You picked it back up. Anyway, consider your Friday mornings booked. I need a day off."

That's extremely not happening, but I'm too thrown off to press the point. "You're really not mad?"

"Oh. To be clear, if you ever mess with Eternal Darkness again, I will take that Earl Grey tea you love so much and dump it in the lake like it's the Boston Harbor," he says, leaning into the counter. His eyes are on mine in that wholly focused way of his, but there's something different about it now. Something wry. Something amused. "But no. I am not mad. Annoyed, maybe. But also impressed."

"I really am sorry," I say.

"If you're sorry, then pay me back with an Everything Pretzel Bagel with bacon egg and cheese."

The almost-smile on his face lilts a bit, just enough that I feel like I'm tipping sideways right with it. But then the guilt of screwing him over today kicks back in, and I tear my gaze away.

"Of course," I say, typing his order into the screen.

Milo's brother Sean clears his throat from behind me. "What, you didn't scam enough free meals from home this week?"

"Thought I'd keep on theme, after scamming your old jacket from the house, too," says Milo, stepping back and putting his hands in its pockets.

I feel Sean frown from behind me. "That's not mine, bro. That's Harley's."

Milo's expression goes static, his almost-smile so unmoving that I find myself stopping in place, too.

"Or, uh . . . maybe it was mine first. Can't remember. Too many little brothers," Sean recovers. "It suits you, though."

Milo's entire demeanor changes as he pulls his hands out of the pockets. Before I can read too much into it and double down on my "don't get involved" mantra, he's looking at me again.

"I mean it, new kid."

I step back away from the counter, swallowing down some of the residual nausea. "Milo, I—"

He holds his hand up to interrupt me. "If it makes you feel any better, my first broadcast, I was so nervous I . . . basically burped uncontrollably."

I don't mean to smile. I only do because I remember his first broadcast. I rarely miss a show, and certainly not any show where a new Knight is introduced. He was endearing as always, but he burped enough times to sponsor a soda brand.

He catches the smile and rolls his eyes. "Yeah, yeah. See you in the studio."

Sean returns with a bagel and Milo sinks his teeth into it right there at the register, which gives me just enough of a beat to panic about the fact that I am not good enough to be doing any broadcast, let alone a weekly one.

"Damn," says Milo through a mouthful. "How do these bagels just get better and better?"

I take in a breath, resolved. "I'm not going to —"

"Nope. I'm sleeping in on Fridays now. You owe me," say Milo. "No ifs, Andies, or buts about it."

Before I can protest, he takes the coffee Sean brings him and says, "If this isn't the real thing, you both better hope I don't die first and haunt you for the rest of your lives." But he gives me a slight smile as he raises the cup to me and heads back out into the street.

In the lull between customers I stand uncertainly, waiting for the ache to harden again, or to roil in my stomach. Instead it seems to do something it's never done. It reaches up and up, and it yearns.

Chapter Thirteen

"Okay," says Shay. "I'm ready to get turned into a human slushie."

"You really don't have to do this," I say for maybe the umpteenth time today.

We're not sure what the ribbon event is this afternoon, just that we're supposed to meet up in the quad and "dress warmly," because it has something to do with the fresh coat of snow over campus. It's a miracle we've even gotten that much of a hint from this morning's broadcast—whereas all the blue-ribbon events of January were strictly trivia-based, the red-ribbon events of February seem to be anarchy-based. There's no rhyme or reason to them. So far I've been sent to the student life building for a challenge to make silly meme versions of our college brochure, to the yard outside the physics building to help paint the school logo on a brick wall, and now, I suppose, to the quad to freeze our tails off.

Shay throws on her coat. "I know. And if it's dumb, I *will* bail," she jokes. "But I meant what I said. I'll help you get your ribbons so you and your Lifetime movie cutout of a boyfriend can get your happily-ever-after." She pauses as she reaches for her gloves. "Also, I heard a rumor about free hot chocolate."

I bite down a smile, because we both know full well Shay has access to free hot chocolate at Bagelopolis for no less than eternity. We pass Milo's room on our way out, both of us glancing at the shut door that means he must be in an afternoon class. This morning was the second Friday in a row he tried to get me to take over the show; I've still adamantly refused, and he's still adamantly stuck to his new catchphrase of "next week, then," and I've still pretended it doesn't matter to me when it might just be the one thing that matters most.

"So how exactly did you end up working with Milo on the radio show?" I ask Shay as we make our way to the quad. The flurry of snow from this morning has long since stopped, and now the entire campus is under a blanket of white, the little roads and sidewalks cleared like paper cutouts. "And how did *Milo* end up working on the show?"

"He told me he started out in the cafeteria for work-study his freshman year. He'd have to do announcements on the loudspeaker sometimes, like if they'd run out of a certain dish, or if campus safety wanted to reiterate something for the fiftieth time while everyone was eating. I guess he added some Milo flair to it and . . . boom, recruited."

"Do I even want to know what kind of flair?"

"Eh, you know his thing with the work-studies. Apparently he started mouthing off about the program when he saw all the students elbowing each other for positions in the cafeteria and did some digging into it. Probably good thing he got recruited for *The Knights' Watch*, because he was probably one snarky remark away from getting fired."

"But who recruited him?" I ask.

Shay shrugs. "Some faculty member. Anyway, I ended up finding out at the beginning of first semester because Milo was taking a power nap during his break at Bagelopolis, and he talks in his sleep."

"He confessed to being the Knight while he was asleep?"

"Oh, no, worse. He was full-on doing the morning broadcast in his sleep, Milo radio voice and all. Except his weather forecast was about flying dogs."

I look up at the gray post-snow sky. "I can get behind that."

When we reach the quad, we find at least a few hundred freshmen also gathered in anticipation. After a few moments of hovering on the edge of it, a hand catches my eye, and I see Harriet and Ellie not too far off. I wave back and we start walking over to them just as someone gets on a loudspeaker to address all of us.

"Your task is to build a snowman. Your team has to have a minimum of three people, max of six, and your snowman has to be at least five feet tall. The more creative your snowman, the more ribbons you'll qualify for," says the upperclassman, holding a fistful of red ribbons. "You have one hour. Go!"

Before we even reach the other girls, students start diving into the snow like they're going to run out of it. Ellie freezes, her eyes going wide, and Harriet scans the quad with mild amusement. I shove a hand into the space between all three of us, using the knowledge from the one or two sports movies I've seen in my life to say, "Hands in."

Then I make eye contact with everyone in turn. "Shay and I will get the snow for the base. Harriet, you can get the snow for the middle tier. Ellie, you're on top tier, and also we're going to need your belt. Okay, three, two, one, go!"

We all scatter, and Shay and I both start haphazardly gathering snow and rolling it as I try to come up with a plan. "We can make it upside down," I say, out of breath. "So it'll stand out."

A bunch of kids I grew up with in Little Fells perfected the art of upside-down snowmen when we were nine or ten. It was my dad who taught us how to do it one winter, when we seemed to have endless snowstorms and endless energy. A lot of the neighborhood parents would send their stir-crazy kids out into the quiet street to burn it off, but if my dad wasn't working, he was always the first to join in and lend all his know-how on igloos and snow angels and homemade sno-cones.

My throat tightens—not just at the memory, but the guilt. I

haven't sent the "Bed of Roses" clips to him yet. I haven't said much of anything to him since I found out about Kelly's daughter. I wonder if he's in the snow with her right now, teaching her the same tricks.

"If you think we can pull that off, sure," says Shay, pulling me out of the thought.

I push it further down and smile at her cheekily. "Maybe it'll ignite your passion for architectural soundness, and *that* will be your major."

"As someone who once accidentally sat on her sister's doll-house, I sincerely doubt that," says Shay. "Do we have a theme?"

She took the words right out of my mouth. "There are some bagels in my bag?" I think out loud. "For like . . . Mickey ears or something?"

Shay hums doubtfully, and I rack my brain for some other idea. I usually work well under pressure. What I don't work well under is the shadow of a tall person staring down at me. I blink up and see Tyler squinting at the four of us, a Chipotle burrito in hand.

"Okay, I'm late," he says. "But is it okay to join your team if I have an idea?"

"Permission granted," I say breathlessly, after heaving our snow-ball another few feet. "What do you have in mind?"

Tyler's eyes gleam. "Well . . . if you're committed to the whole upside-down thing . . ."

Tyler runs off to a neighboring dorm and comes back five min-utes later with one large bucket and zero explanation, and twenty minutes later, we've perfected our snowman. He is just over five feet tall—we used my five-foot-one self as a measuring stick, as did several other teams nearby when they overheard us doing just that—and upside down . . . on top of a "keg." Ellie sacrificed her BB-8-themed belt, so it's now protruding from the snowman's mouth into the bucket. The bagels in my bag make up the eyes and nose, which Harriet artfully added a spare nose ring to. And after several doomed attempts to name him, Shay was the one who decided on "Slushed," which is precisely what we tell the judge when she comes around.

"Top-notch work, Knights," she says, clearly delighted by our creation. When we present our white ribbons, she hands me and Harriet and Ellie each three red ones, which I already know from watching the other judgments is the most you can get in this round. "I'm impressed."

We're still admiring our work when the first hit takes Harriet down—a snowball that lands squarely in her side with enough force to knock her into Ellie, who then falls into Tyler, like human dominos. We hear someone yell "SNOWBALL FIGHT!" just as the quad erupts into lawless, snowy chaos around us.

I turn to Shay, expecting her to bail, but she's already scooped up a fistful of snow straight from Slushed's butt and is aiming it at the crowd. "Not on my turf," she mutters.

I file away a note to re-add "Drama" to her prospective majors, because this scene is nothing short of theatrical. It's like Werewolf night in the dorm, only with a bajillion more people, no clear alliances, and—

"Honey Nut *Cheerios*!" I yelp when someone clocks me right in the hip.

Shay attempts to snap her gloved, snowy finger at me. "Keep your head in the game, Rose."

I shove my ribbons into my jacket pocket and do a quick spin around to see if there are any more incoming snowballs headed my way when I spot a tall, mildly alarmed head bob briefly above the fray. Milo must have been distracted by his phone and walked straight into the melee.

"Target acquired," says Shay, "aaaaand locked."

When her snowball makes contact with him square in the chest he doesn't so much as flinch, glancing over at us mirthlessly.

"Uh-oh," I mutter, wondering if we've actually upset him. But then he pulls a snowball out from behind his back and returns fire at Shay so fast that he must have been hiding his ammo the whole time.

"Watch out!" I yell, diving in front of Shay.

It would have been action movie-worthy. Slow-motion splendor, an orchestra welling up in the background, a close-up of my heroic but determined face. That is, if the snowball didn't end up lodging itself precisely between my coat and my jeans.

When I manage to recover from shock as the ice leaks from my hips all the way down to my knees, I see Shay laughing hysterically and Milo with his mouth tweaked in that almost-smile of his. Maybe it's the near frostbite, or the sleep deprivation, or the sugar from all the cookie dough cream cheese I've eaten today. But something compels me to follow that hint of a smile by loading up a snowball of my own, and charging straight for him.

"Aw, c'mon, new kid," says Milo, standing still as a statue in the midst of the chaos. "Cut me some—oof!"

Ellie, bless her heart, has tag-teamed with Harriet to hit him with two snowballs from behind. I launch my own at him while he's distracted, but apparently he's not distracted enough, because he opens a gloved hand and catches it.

"Hmm," he says, examining it, then examining me. "What ever should I do with this."

We're at close range now. If he throws it I'm going to become a human icicle. "You wouldn't."

One of the corners of Milo's lips quirks. I quirk mine right back, but only because I can see the scene unfolding behind him. Tyler has returned with another bucket full of snow, and he shows no mercy. Before I can give myself away by laughing, Tyler has emptied it directly on top of Milo's head.

This time he's the one to give out a graceless yelp, and he launches himself forward so fast that I don't account for how little space was between us until he is, quite literally, on top of me. He seems to realize we're toppling to the ground before I do, grabbing my shoulders and pivoting us around so that we land in the snow with him hitting first, me landing on top of him with a breathless thud.

For a second we're both too stunned to move. The noise of the snowball fight drowns out around us, and we're both wheezing into each other's faces, Milo's rib cage expanding and contracting under mine with enough force that it feels like our hearts are pressed together. I'm about to apologize profusely, but before I can I'm blinking into the green of Milo's eyes, and there's this heat creeping under the surface of my skin that feels downright unnatural given the amount of snow currently lodged in my pants.

It's Milo who breaks the silence. "You okay?"

I have no idea, but I nod slowly anyway. It's like my mouth has forgotten how to make words. Milo reaches a hand up then, pulling something out of my hair—a chunk of snow. I only notice it in the periphery. I can't seem to tear my eyes off his.

I can feel my common sense slowly returning to me—that "get your body off of your RA" voice starting to clear its throat in the back of my head—but my phone pipes up before it can, blasting "Immigrant Song" by Led Zeppelin.

"Connor," I gasp, rolling off Milo so fast I end up in the snow with yet another frosty thud. I yank the phone out of my coat pocket and swipe open the call as fast as I possibly can. "Hello?"

"Hey, Andie."

"Hey," I say back. "How are—"

"Wow, it's—can you hear me? I can't hear you—"

"Yes, I can—sorry, I'm just in the middle of—"

"Andie?"

I scramble to my feet, looking for the quickest exit out of the quad I can find. It's easy enough, only because it's the path that

Milo's taking. He's already far enough away that I can barely see him through the fresh snowfall that just started coming down.

"Yeah, hold on," I say, readjusting my soaked coat and pants. "Just a second, I'll . . ."

I try to follow Milo out of the maze, but when I look back up, he's already gone.

Chapter Fourteen

If I had a superpower, it would be avoiding math.

"So . . ." I lean into the library table, subtly pushing the statistics textbook to the side. "*Kingdom of Lumarin* was meant to be a romance, but the heroine doesn't actually end up with the love interest in the end?"

Valeria sighs, her dark hair skimming the table as she lowers her chin into her hands. Her fingernails are a delightful shade of pink for Valentine's Day, with little heart-shaped gems in the middle that twinkle in the early morning light streaming from the windows.

"The ending is *ambiguous*," she says. "You don't know if she ends up with her or not."

I point a finger at her. "But Shay told me romance has rules. And that your ending between the heroine and the enemy sorceress she teams up with to save the kingdom . . ." I try to remember the indignant words that followed her equally indignant look upon finishing Valeria's manuscript, which she devoured faster than a Bagelopolis special. "'Goes against the genre.'"

Valeria's lips purse in an adorable little frown. "I should never have let her read it. I don't even know what possessed me. We just— sang so much that night we went to karaoke that I must have been drunk on the ABBA of it all, and she asked to read it, and I just . . ."

She makes this loose gesture with her arms as if her 350-page manuscript fell out of the air instead of an email attachment.

"So how *do* the characters end up? In your head, I mean." I haven't read it, but I got the gist from Shay, who has been launching into conversations about it apropos of nothing every other hour.

Valeria winces. "Honestly? I don't know. It just felt like there was too much pressure to tie up the romance with a pretty bow at the end."

"Huh. So are you going to change the genre or the ending?"

"I don't know." She yanks her purse up on the table and plants it there with a thud, rifling through it to find a calculator. "I mean, it doesn't matter. Nobody else will ever read it."

Her phone buzzes on the other end of the table. I'm about to open my mouth to tell her I don't mind if she takes it, but she waves me off. "It's probably just my ex again. He's been texting all day."

"He's *still* bothering you?"

"It's the weirdest thing. He did this whole 'let's be friends' thing and didn't answer my texts for like a *month* after we broke up, but now he'll randomly text me or watch all my Instagram stories. I've had exes get back in touch before, but never ones that seemed to go off and on like this."

"You could always block him."

Valeria pushes a TI-84 toward my end of the table, but her eyes are in some far-off corner of the library, clearly mulling something over.

"I would. But I mean . . . a part of me is relieved. He ended things so abruptly that I wondered if he cared at all. But the other part of me is just so mad. At him, of course, and at myself for caring in the first place." She runs a hand through her hair, fingers bunching around the thick strands. "And for letting it mess with my head about this stupid story."

"Understandably," I acknowledge.

Then I don't say anything at all. Usually the big truths about people's feelings come in the quiet. Sure enough, Valeria pulls in his heavy, shoulder-raising breath, clearly about to go on, when we're interrupted by the sound of cheering in the corner of the library that snaps her out of it.

"Right. Chapter five," she says, squaring her shoulders. "You said you were having an issue with . . . oh, whoops."

When she pulls the case off the calculator, a white ribbon falls out and flutters to the table.

"Is that one of the starter ribbons?" I ask immediately.

"Yeah," says Valeria, looking at the ribbon and then down into the depths of her purse. She carefully zips it shut.

It takes every fiber of my being not to just take it and run. "Aren't you a sophomore?"

"I, uh, found it the other day. Nobody claimed it though." She glances up toward the trash cans in the cafe. "I should probably just toss it."

"Wait."

Valeria's hand hovers just above the ribbon, raising her eyebrows.

"Um—I'll take it," I say, lowering my voice. "If that's okay."

"I thought you had a starter ribbon," says Valeria, puzzled. "Isn't that why you missed the TA office hours to go over your missed test questions last Saturday? Because you were trying to get a red one?"

My face flushes. Not that I'd ever admit it to Valeria, but last week's little incident is not the first time a ribbon collection has conflicted with my studying. There are intentionally a ton of events so you can easily miss some of them and still get all the ribbons you need, but the thing about collecting them for two people is you can't really afford to miss any at all.

It's also why I've been scrambling to keep up with my "Bed of Roses" column, and why I haven't been able to go back to Little Fells to visit my grandmas, or even to visit Connor. I know it's early in the semester to be worrying about that kind of thing, but I miss them. The idea of having to wait to see them until the ribbon hunt is over in March makes me ache.

But at least if I have this starter ribbon for Connor, it won't be for nothing.

"My boyfriend doesn't have a white ribbon," I admit. "The one who transferred out. He's trying to come back."

"Oh. Then knock yourself out," says Valeria, sliding it across the table. "Happy Valentine's Day."

It feels like magic when I touch it. Some of the guilt of Connor's situation is flushed out by this immense, ridiculous relief— I'll still be able to do this for him. I'll be able to make this right. I'll be able to—

"*Oof.*" My chair gets unceremoniously sideswiped by a group of students rushing out the door fast enough to leave a gust of wind in their wake. "Wait, did the fire alarm go off or something?"

"No," says Valeria, glancing at a notification on her phone. "It wasn't my ex. Turns out it's Skip Day."

This tradition is so notorious at Blue Ridge State that campuses all across the country are jealous of us for it—once a semester, the university lawlessly cancels classes for the day without warning. Last semester, Connor used it to come surprise me at the community college with a picnic, waiting for me outside the psych building.

I check my phone at the thought of him, but there's nothing so far. Not even a "Happy Valentine's Day" text. I remind myself that he's busy with his dad, and we did spend the better part of last night co-watching old episodes of *True Blood* together.

"But we should still finish up since we're here," says Valeria, her eyes on the pages but her body undeniably tilted toward the door.

"Absolutely not," I tell her, scooting back in my chair and closing the textbook with a satisfying *thunk*. I gesture toward the students leaking out of the building in a steady stream. "Run. Be free. Math isn't real today."

Valeria hesitates. "You're sure?"

"Six thousand percent." I point at the textbook. "That's a statistic, right? You've done your job here today."

Valeria leans in for a quick hug. "I'm gonna go back to my parents' house for the day and work on that ending where there's peace and quiet. But we'll pick this up later this week, okay?"

I squeeze her back hard. "Sounds good," I say, which is only half a lie. Valeria is quickly becoming a close friend, even if math will forever be my mortal enemy. "You mind if I read your book, too?"

"Manuscript," Valeria corrects me. She bites her bottom lip, considering. "Yes. But only if you give the ribbons a rest this weekend, so you can get in some more study time?" she suggests.

I wince. It's hard to get anything past her when she's assessing my stats skills every week. I'm guessing they have not improved all that much, based on her request.

"Send it my way when you work out the ending!" I call after her, sidestepping.

She laughs on her way out of the library. "You have more faith in me than I do."

By the time I get back to my room, Cardinal is a ghost town. I find a note on my bed from Shay saying she left to go visit her parents. I consider trying to hitch a ride to Little Fells, but Connor's still busy and my grandmas are both out of town visiting D.C. so they can do a macaron and cupcake tour in Georgetown.

But there's no point in getting down about being by myself. I rally quickly by doing what I always do if I sense myself circling the drain of a self-pity spiral: I take a shower, making a mental list of all the things I can tackle today with the unexpected free time.

"Dear god. It's a sentient teddy bear."

I don't even register the words until I'm looking over at Milo, who is facing me in the hallway looking mildly astonished and impressed at my robe. He is far from the only one to comment on it—it's floor-length and ridiculously fluffy, and it comes with a matching hair towel that may or may not have little ears poking out of it.

I stop in my slipper-clad tracks. "You're still here," I say, self-conscious. Not just because I am poofier than a cloud, but this is the first time the two of us have been around each other without any kind of social buffer since our tumble in the snow.

I search his face cautiously, but Milo just seems like Milo—edges rough and eyes soft, no trace of the awkwardness I worried we might be putting off. I feel my shoulders loosen in relief as he lifts his hand and jingles car keys at me, his long fingers fanned out just above my head.

"Not for long," he says.

Only then does a plan B occur to me. "Does Sean need help at Bagelopolis?" If I can get more work-study shifts in now, I won't have to worry about them during finals. "I've got nowhere to be."

Milo cuts me off with a sharp shake of his head. "It's Skip Day. It's illegal to work a shift."

"Ha ha," I deadpan. "But actually."

"But actually, the store's closed. Skip Day means everyone's going to be getting hammered tonight, so Bagelopolis is changing its hours to capitalize on the drunk upperclassmen wandering the streets in need of cream cheese come nightfall."

"White cheddar Cheez-Its," I mutter under my breath, pointing myself toward my door. "Well, I'll see you later, then."

I'm expecting another quip about my ensemble, but instead Milo lets out a sigh, leaning against the wall. "You really want to knock off some of your hours today?"

I pause, turning back.

"I got some extra hours with one of the groundskeepers, is why I ask. And I'm sure she wouldn't mind an extra hand."

"Really?" I ask, way too quickly.

Milo pulls out his phone, leaning farther into the wall and making himself comfortable. "Can you be ready in five?"

I hold up a finger. "Give me six."

Once I'm in my room I yank my wet hair into a quick braid, slap on some tinted moisturizer, then tug back on the outfit I'd met Valeria in—dark-wash jeans, a cozy red cowl-neck sweater, a pair of ankle boots that were clear Old Navy knockoffs of the ones Connor's mom wore all last year. Even then I feel bare walking out in the middle of the day so much less polished than usual, but Milo doesn't even bat an eye when he looks up from his phone.

"I only have one rule for this excursion," he tells me. "You have to be nice to Stella."

By "Stella," Milo means a navy blue 2006 Jetta that has seen better days, likely several Flynn siblings ago. The bumper has several layers of crusted-over stickers like the car itself is having an existential crisis, with a Disney half-marathon-finisher sticker half ripped off next to some kind of faded Star Wars sticker half hidden under a sticker that appears to say MY LABRADOR IS DUMB, BUT CUTER THAN YOUR HONORS STUDENT. The interior is perfectly clean, but smells like coffee and old french fries. Still, there's something about watching Milo seamlessly jam the keys in the ignition, check to make sure my seat belt is buckled, and back out of the lot behind the dorm that makes Stella feel like a getaway car.

On the ten-minute drive through the campus and arboretum we mostly talk about *The Knights' Watch*—I am still patently refusing to take over the Friday show, Milo is still patently refusing to try tea as a coffee alternative, and by the time we get out of Stella we're both laughing so hard at each other that I don't even see the woman approaching until her very tall shadow is over me.

"Who might this giggly person be?"

I uncurl myself from the doubled-over laugh and stare up into celery-green eyes too distinctive to mistake. I straighten up immediately—the plaid-coat-wearing, curly-haired woman in front of me can only be Milo's mother.

"Hi. I'm Andie," I say, extending my hand out to her. "A pleasure to meet you."

She takes my hand in both of hers, shaking it hard enough to rattle me. "Jamie." She turns to Milo. "You said you brought reinforcements, but she's dressed like a doll."

I turn to Milo in mild panic, but he just shrugs at her. "She can still paint just fine, Mom."

"Not in this cute sweater, she can't," she says, clucking at Milo. She hooks the crook of her arm in mine. "C'mere, I'll get you something we can wreck. We're painting the chicken coops today."

I follow her. "Oh—I don't want to inconvenience you, Mrs. Flynn—"

She snorts. "Jamie," she corrects me. "With an 'ie.' How about you, doll?"

"Also an 'ie,'" I tell her.

She pulls our elbows in close enough to knock our bodies together. "That's what I was hoping."

Jamie leads me into a redbrick house on the edge of the arboretum, one with bright blue shutters on the windows and a big yellow door and Christmas lights that still haven't been taken down. In the front hall there's a bench loaded with dozens of mismatched shoes and boots and sneakers and loafers and sandals, all splayed out like people are coming as often as they go. There's this quick cinch of nostalgia in my chest for something I never had—the big family, the chaos of holidays, the perpetual undercurrent of noise—but before I can feel it too deeply, Jamie lets my arm go and says, "I know exactly what you need."

I stand uncertainly in the hallway for all of thirty seconds before she comes back with a gray Henley and a pair of overalls, beaming as she plops them into my arms.

"Milo's, from back when he was short as you," she says, bopping me on the head. "Bathroom's down the hall. Go change and we'll get you a paint roller."

She pivots and disappears again, leaving me to change into Milo's well-worn, floral-scented hand-me-downs. I wander down the hall, the walls clad with photos of Flynn kids cheesing at the camera, all dark curls and big grins and gangly limbs hanging over one another, until I find a bathroom. The end result of my outfit switch is by no means cute, but decidedly more paint appropriate.

"*Mom?*" I hiss at Milo once I join him back out in the cold.

He hands me a paint roller with one hand, the other occupied by a large can of hot pink paint. "Not the first Flynn family member you've worked for, and probably not the last."

"Yes, but I look like a mess," I point out.

Milo scowls. "You look just fine. Now let's get this over with before we turn into Popsicles."

He leads us to a spot in the arboretum a few hundred yards away from the house that I've never seen before, with a chicken coop and a gated area with goats in it and a bunch of little gardens. He explains it's partially here for the agricultural majors—one that Shay crossed off the list *real* fast—but mostly here because as Blue Ridge State's head groundskeeper, his mom decided the school needed chickens, so chickens they would have.

I just barely dodge some of them moseying out, their feathers ruffled by an old Labrador Milo affectionately calls "Bozo" before grabbing him a treat from a little container strapped to the chicken coop door. He turns to me with a slight smile, the winter sun sharp on his face, brightening the red tinge in his pale cheeks.

"Here," he says, dabbing my shoulder with pink paint.

I step back. "Milo!" I splutter. "This is *your shirt.*"

"I'm well aware. And I also know you were about to spend the next hour panicking about staining it, so I went ahead and did it for you before the perfectionist vibes could kick in."

"I don't have perfectionist vibes," I protest, tearing my eyes away from the wall of the chicken coop I was already mentally taping the edges for.

Milo leans down to pry open the can of paint. "Sure you do."

I crouch down next to him, the two of us at eye level for a rare moment. "Based on literally what evidence?"

Milo doesn't hesitate, picking up our conversation from the car as he spills the paint out into a bin. "You love the radio show. I know you do or you wouldn't be rolling into the studio with us at hours too unholy to name." He pauses, the paint can empty. "And you won't do it . . . why? It seems like giving advice on air isn't all that different from what you're already doing with your column and the emails."

He dips his roller in the paint and I follow suit, biting the inside of my cheek at the mention of the column. The truth is, I'm behind on that, too. Not just because of the ribbons—but because I realized after I finished the column this week that nothing I wrote suited the format of a high school newspaper. I'd written it like it was a script. Like it was something I might say on air, too casual and with too much open space in it, like I was anticipating a dialogue with whoever was asking.

I know I have to rewrite it soon, but I've been anticipating it with a weird kind of dread ever since. Like I already know I won't be able to shape it the way I meant to, now that I've seen another version of what it could be. Imagined some other version of myself I could be.

By the time I look back up he's already started one side of the coop and is tilting his head at me, waiting for an answer.

"Because . . ."

Because I'm afraid of letting my mom down. The thought is a reflex, even if I know it's not true. I could never let her down. The thing is, it's that thought that creates a very cushy barrier between me and the real truth, which is that I'm afraid I'll keep letting myself down. That for all these grand designs I have for helping people, even just at Blue Ridge, I still feel so far from them—from the easy way they seem to move through the world, the way everyone else seems to *fit*—that I feel like an intruder. That I get so far in my head about it that I can't connect in real time the way I can when there's no pressure, no watching eyes. When nobody knows who I am.

When I can hide.

"It's not like I want to be perfect," I hedge. "I just—I like situations I can control. Writing things down alone in my room is a situation I can control, but a live show is something else entirely. And I feel like there are already so many things we don't get to control."

He's already watching me, the paint roller paused. He nods, because of course he knows. I think of all the shoes littered by his front door and ache for the pairs of his dad's that must be missing from them.

"But I can still make plans. And stick to them. My major, my career plans, my—"

"Boyfriend?"

I raise my eyebrows. Milo doesn't see, focused on a crisscrossed line of hot pink paint as if he's determined to pretend he didn't say anything.

And I'm happy to pretend with him, even if it does strike a dissonant chord. Connor is steady and safe; not a factor I can control, but can definitely account for. But I don't love him because of that. I love him the way I love looking at big stretches of the sky, or feeling the grass under my toes; he's a feeling I've always known.

My throat tightens. Without meaning to, I pull my phone out of my pocket and glance at it. No messages.

"If anything, he's something I can't plan for," I say, trying not to grit my teeth as I put the phone away. "His parents are like—super strict. They're the ones calling the shots, not me. They have high expectations."

"For you too, then."

The urge to defend them comes faster than a reflex, but it doesn't change the truth. "Yeah."

Milo doesn't say anything for a few strokes of paint, me focusing on the bottom end and him reaching up to the top.

"Well, for what it's worth. Some of the fun in radio *is* what you can't control. Even the embarrassing parts." He tilts his head just enough so I can detect his slight smirk. "I can crack jokes without choking on my own spit now, but you must remember my first few shows."

I smile to myself, remembering. It wasn't perfect by professional radio host standards. But it was its own kind of perfect, with his blunt delivery mixed with a string of candid swear words the few times he lost track of his notes. And, of course, the ill-fated burping.

"I remember the part where you immediately dressed down the entire administration with that first segment about the work-study program," I say.

Milo holds up his paint roller at me like he's pointing a finger. "And thanks to the show, I've managed to get them to actually listen to the businesses that wanted to work with the program off campus and get more positions available."

"Hence Bagelopolis."

Milo nods. "And a few others so far. It's only a temporary fix, though. The problem is just that tuition is getting too damn high, and now they're either shoving people into work-studies where there aren't enough spots or putting them into massive debt."

Anyone who knows the history of *The Knights' Watch* knows about the Knights all choosing a particular topic or running segment, so I know Milo understands what I mean when I ask, "So why'd you decide to make work-study your thing?"

Milo's eyes are intent on the paint roller as he speaks, but his focus seems to go somewhere else entirely as he thinks on his answer. "Well, you know my mom works for the school. My dad did, too. So all my brothers and sisters went here, all of them with work-study positions—and over the years, they've been harder to get." He pauses in his painting for a moment, glancing back in the direction of his family's house. "Now most of my siblings work either for the school or for the community, so Blue Ridge State will always be important to me. I want it to live up to its promise. It's a state school, it's supposed to be accessible. And right now it just isn't, and if we don't do something about it now, it's not going to be the same kind of community I grew up in. The one that people could come to and make a home."

It's more than I expected Milo to say on the matter—more than I think I've heard him say on anything this close to his heart. Even I've paused in my strokes to watch him, struck again by a recognition, by something I didn't understand until this moment that we shared: a connection to Blue Ridge State that goes a whole lot deeper than the ground it sits on.

"You really love this place, huh?" I ask.

Only then does Milo notice my eyes on him, and when he turns his face back to the pink paint, his cheeks flush almost as bright. "Yeah, well." He clears his throat, resuming his painting, but not without shooting me a pointed look. "All this to say, I had no idea what I was doing going into this. Just that I had stuff to say. But people who only like to do stuff they're already great at? They end up limiting themselves. And they end up regretting it."

The words settle in the air between us, taking their time to sink in. It's not that I've never heard some variation before. It's that it means something else, coming from Milo. Coming from someone who is doing something I always wanted to do, and worked hard to improve at it. Someone who believes I'm capable of the same.

"And you said you didn't want to give advice on the show," I tease him quietly.

His expression is rueful when he looks down. "It's not my advice, really. It was my dad's. 'Anything worth doing starts with a mess.'"

We let the words settle in the air, holding their own quiet weight. Then Milo lifts his head to look at me again.

"I like that," I say. "Like—getting a new start doesn't mean you have to wipe the slate clean. Just pick up the pieces. Begin again."

"Yeah," Milo agrees, and then we both fall quiet. As if we're both thinking, in that moment, of the pieces we've been trying to leave behind. The ones that will never really leave us. The ones that will only pull us back the longer we try to pretend they don't exist.

"Sounds like a good guy," I say.

His voice dips low. "The best of them." His eyes sweep back to the ground, and he takes a quick breath and says, "Now pay attention before Tommy here clucks your eye out."

Only then do I notice curious chickens circling us underfoot. By the time we finish, I learn all their names, the chicken coop looks like a free-range, worn-down Barbie Dreamhouse, and Bozo has scammed three more treats from Milo.

We walk back into the house and are greeted with the unmistakable smell of grilled cheese. I wash my hands at the sink and Milo ducks out to change into a pair of pants that isn't streaked pink. When I sit down Jamie takes the seat across from me and leans in conspiratorially.

"You're the girl who staged the coffee coup, huh?"

I rub my hands together, warming up. "My reputation precedes me."

Jamie winks. "Glad someone's looking out for him on the big bad Blue Ridge campus. Pardon the chicken joke, but you and Shay seem like good eggs."

My cheeks warm up faster than the rest of me does. "We're glad he took us under his wing."

She lets out a barking laugh and pats me on the hand. "I like you."

I blink as she turns around to take the grilled cheese off the stove, startled by the impact of those three simple words. It's just so easy, is all—to talk to Jamie. To sit in her kid's worn-out overalls and slouch in her wooden kitchen chair. When I'm with Connor's parents I'm constantly pre-screening every word that comes out of my mouth, taking cues from his mom, trying to keep up with his dad. When I'm with Connor's parents, I never quite know where I stand.

"Smells good in here," says someone who is decidedly not Milo. I look up and see a boy who looks just like him—same dark hair, same green eyes, but with several days' worth of stubble and an entirely different bearing. He seems sharper, his movements quick and his gaze fleeting. Behind him is a strikingly beautiful girl with long red hair who seems to instantly soften his edges when she stands next to him.

"Harley, honey," says Jamie, knitting her brows. "I thought you two were going to that brewery."

I freeze in my seat the way you do when you're bracing for a crash.

"Yeah, we were, but—"

"What are you doing here?"

And cue the crash. I turn to see Milo standing in the hallway with his eyes wide and his cheeks redder than I've ever seen them, his arms so rigid at his sides that I feel my own muscles twinge in sympathy.

"Hey," says Harley, his voice unmistakably nervous. "I didn't realize you'd be home today."

"Like hell you didn't," says Milo, his voice tense, but every bit as shaky as Harley's.

"Milo," says the girl softly.

Milo shakes his head with one singular, sharp motion. "Don't. I'm leaving."

I push my chair back to follow him. I have no idea how much context I'm lacking for all this, but I know Milo. If he's out, so am I.

"Don't be silly, Milo," says Jamie, taking a few steps toward the hall. "This is your home, too. Maybe this is an opportunity for the two of you to work this out."

Milo yanks his arms into the sleeves of his coat and walks out the door, a storm-out only made slightly funny by the way he carefully closes the front door behind him. Jamie lets out a sigh, turning to the grilled cheeses.

"Excuse us," she tells me, wrapping them in paper towels for me and handing me a bag with my clothes in it. "Never a dull moment in the Flynn family."

"Thank you," I say. "It was really nice to meet you."

"You too, doll."

I feel the eyes of Milo's brother and his ex on me as I hustle out the front door to find him leaning against Stella with his nostrils flared, staring down at the concrete of the driveway like it committed a crime against him.

"I'll drive," I offer.

Milo looks up in surprise, like he hadn't expected me to follow "You don't have to."

"Give me the keys. I promise I'll be nice to Stella."

Milo sighs but relents, handing them over. I move the seat up closer to the wheel by about a mile, and that at least is enough for Milo to let out a breath that almost qualifies as a chuckle. I hand him the grilled cheeses.

"Thanks," he says.

I nod, checking the mirrors before I back out. "So that's Harley."

Instead of answering, Milo deliberately shoves at least half a grilled cheese into his mouth. An Andie Rose conflict-avoidance move if there ever was one. I wait until he's finished chewing and ask, "Are you okay?"

"Peachy."

"Milo."

He sighs yet again. "He's a jerk. He knew I was coming home today. I told Sean to tell my mom to tell Harley. And then he just comes marching in there with Nora like a damn ambush, I just . . ."

"So Nora's your ex."

Milo rubs his eyes with his thumb and index finger, propping an elbow on the console. "Yeah. Shit." I can practically feel the way he's trying to scowl but can't quite make his face do it, everything wobbling even in my peripheral vision. "Feels weird to call her that. We were . . . I mean, I thought we were . . ."

"Endgame," I finish for him.

He straightens back up. "So much for that."

"I'm sorry," I say quietly. I'm careful not to say anything else. It's not that I'm out of my depth, but more that I worry we're out of Milo's right now.

"What," he says after a few beats. "No Andie Rose advice?"

I pull out into the main road. "Do you want it?"

Milo stares down at his feet, talking more to them than me. "I feel like I'm going to get it at some point either way."

I clear my throat, pointedly ignoring the edge in his tone. "We can talk about it some other time, then. I don't want to say anything you don't want to hear right now."

"No," says Milo, a bit of apology in the hardness of it. "I want to hear it."

He watches me from the passenger seat, waiting. I let a few beats pass, half certain he'll deflect like he has before. When he doesn't, I say carefully, "I mean—you're still hurting. It's going to take time."

Milo is unmoving as a statue, still watching.

"But at some point . . . you'll have to resolve it, right?" I say. "You can't just avoid him and the rest of your family forever."

"I'm not avoiding the rest of my family."

"You just did," I say gently. "You said Harley knew you'd be home. Maybe it wasn't an ambush. I think maybe he wanted to talk."

I only catch the edge of Milo's deepening scowl before he directs his face away from me.

"And whatever happened—I think when it comes to grief, the more you can process it together, the easier it'll probably be to heal."

It's my dad I'm thinking of then. The way he fell out of orbit more and more with each passing year. How there were pieces of myself that would have been a lot easier to put back together with him there to make sense of them.

"The thing is," I say, pushing past my own hurt, "family is forever. But this thing with Nora . . . I think you'll get over it eventually."

"You think so?"

The directness of the question catches me off guard. "I mean—I hope so."

"Would you if it were Connor?"

I purse my lips. "Milo, we're talking about you."

"Yeah?" says Milo. "Because it seems like you're telling me to get over my ex when you can't get over a guy you've been running around for all semester, who can't even be bothered to text you on Valentine's Day."

He flinches before I do, more surprised to have said it than I am to hear it.

"That was uncalled for," I say anyway.

"I'm sorry," says Milo, all the anger punctured out of him. He runs a hand through his hair, and even in the periphery I can see the slight shake of it. "Shit. I'm just . . ."

"I know."

We drive the rest of the way in silence, me with my eyes on the road, Milo fiddling with the zipper on his coat and sneaking glances at me. I'm coolly composed, a neutral version of the syndicated-talk-show smile. Only then do I realize that the awkwardness I was anticipating this morning—the tension I thought we'd been dancing around since that moment in the snow—it's here now, thick in the air between us. Like it was only waiting for a catalyst, for one of us to brush up against the other too close.

"Really, Andie—I'm sorry," says Milo, as I ease the car into a parking spot.

I hand him the keys to Stella. "I'm here if you ever want to actually talk about it, okay?"

His hand grazes mine when he takes it back, and then lingers for a moment, like he's going to say something else. I look up and see something in his face start to crack open, something honest and miserable and real.

"Andie!"

We both tear our eyes away so fast that the sound of my name might as well be the sound of a car backfiring.

"Connor?"

Chapter Fifteen

There he is, like some kind of golden-haired, broad-smiled apparition, stepping out of his car in his Little Fells varsity soccer jacket with a handful of pink roses, my absolute favorite. He turns to set them on the seat of his car before I even start to run, knowing full well I am coming at him like a small projectile.

"*Oof*," he jokes when I slam into him, easily absorbing the impact and sweeping my feet off the ground. "Hey, you."

"Hi hi hi hi hi," I say into his ear, so giddy I feel like someone just injected a Fourth of July fireworks show straight into my veins. I squeeze him hard and he squeezes back, and for a moment time is at a total standstill. There's just me and the crush of Connor's body against mine and the steady, thrilling *thump thump thump* of our hearts beating in rhythm.

"How are you *here*?"

"My dad gave me the day off. And I just got in the car, and . . ." We pull apart, arms still intertwined, his eyes shining. "Happy Valentine's Day."

I knock my head into his chest, breathing in the grassy, familiar scent of him. "I've missed you so much."

"I missed you more."

I doubt that, but right now it doesn't matter. I can't see anything beyond the familiar shape of him, the overwhelming rush of relief.

He presses his thumb just under my eye. "But what's wrong, Andie?" he asks, the rumble of his voice pressing into my chest. "You looked upset."

"I . . ."

His eyes edge toward Milo, who already has his back turned to us and is walking into Cardinal.

"Who is that?" Connor asks.

"Just my RA," I say. It's easier than explaining that we weren't just in an argument between friends, but one Connor made a cameo in not five minutes ago. "It's been a long day, is all."

"Did something happen with your dad?" says Connor lowly.

I hesitate. Technically yes, even if it's not what has me worked up right now.

Connor doesn't wait for my answer, pressing a kiss into my temple. I melt into it, feeling the weight of too many weeks apart lift off my shoulders and into the cool winter mist.

"C'mon," I say, tugging him by the sleeve. "I'll show you my dorm."

Once we're up there, I show him everything—the books Shay is letting me borrow, my new course curriculum and the wild amount of homework that comes with it. And, of course, the ribbons I've collected so far—half of them for me, half for him.

"I don't even know what to say," says Connor, palming all the ribbons one by one.

I try not to feel possessive of them as he sets them across my comforter, out of the box I carefully stash them away in with my mom's ribbons. But there is still some reflexive part of my brain that wants to pull them back, like he's trying to steal some piece of my mom away.

"How did you manage to get all these?"

"I've been going to every event," I say proudly.

"Aren't they every single weekend?" Connor asks.

I nod. "But I haven't missed one yet."

Connor laughs. "Wow, your classes must be a hell of a lot easier than the ones I was taking here, if you can swing that."

My smile falters, something crackling quick and sharp under my ribs. "Well. Sometimes I miss some studying time." And writing time. And time seeing him and my grandmas. I keep my voice even as I push the thoughts away and add, "But it's just one semester."

"Yeah," says Connor, nodding. "Just one semester, and then . . ."

I push the smile back into place. "And then you'll be back, and we'll both be in one of the secret societies, and it will all be worth it."

Connor reaches out and strokes my cheek. "It's hard enough getting by at Blue Ridge. And you'd still give up all this time to make this happen for me?"

When he puts it that way, the next breath I take feels tight in my chest. It's not like that, I want to tell him. It isn't just for his sake. I've got way more on the line than he does.

"Of course," I say emphatically. I'm not being fair. He has no idea what the ribbons mean to me, and that's my fault, not his. "You'll come back," I add, the words earnest, but my jaw tight. "And everything will be fine."

Connor leans in and presses a gentle kiss to my lips, the kind we both sink into, gripping each other's arms as we lean into the mattress. "Everything will be fine," he repeats with the kind of ease he always does. With that same quiet confidence that comes with being Connor Whit and knowing that, most of the time, what he wants is what he'll get.

He reaches out and tucks a loose strand of my hair behind my ear, securing it there. "But tell me. What happened? With your dad, I mean?"

I close my eyes, resting my forehead on his shoulder. "Nothing."

"Hmm." The hum of his voice is quiet and sure, but his expression doesn't settle. He knows me well enough to know what I mean by "nothing."

"Nothing I should be surprised by, at least," I amend. "He . . . his new girlfriend has a daughter. Seems like he wasn't allergic to fatherhood after all."

"Andie," says Connor lowly.

I'd hate it coming from anyone else—this part of me laid bare, this part of my life that I feel a strange kind of shame for, even knowing it's not my fault. But with Connor it just feels like talking to an extension of my own self.

Even then, my voice sounds small. "I've just felt for so long like I must have done something wrong. Like I wasn't enough. But it feels like some other kid is, and he must have known I'd be upset, because he didn't even bother to tell me about her."

"*Shh*, Andie." Connor presses my face into his shoulder, ready to absorb tears that just don't come. There's something about this moment—the strangeness of Connor colliding with this new world of mine—that has knocked me too far off course to feel much beyond it. "He's . . . he's a lot of things. But he should have told you. Shouldn't have left you in the first place. You deserve to be loved. You deserve people who stay."

There's this distant voice in my head that slithers back in, reminding me that Connor may not be one of those people. That last semester he was close to giving up on us. But maybe that's just it—we persevered through that, the way we always will.

I chase it out of my mind. I'm in his arms, and there are so many ribbons gleaming on my desk, waiting for the two of us to use them to stake our claim here; waiting for me to unravel my mom's mystery, and for the two of us to stand at each other's sides on the other side of it.

"I'll always be here, Andie. You know I will."

"I know you will," I repeat, burrowing my head into his shoulder. It feels good to say. Feels better to let myself believe.

"My parents think my transfer essay could use a bit of work, though." I hear the knowing smile in his voice. "Probably needs a good, thorough reading from a girl who's not afraid to tell it like it is."

I laugh into his shirt sleeve. "Who might that be?"

"I don't know. Maybe the same one who saved this dumbass's GPA time and time again."

I feel an unexpected, but no less familiar, twinge at that. The same one I felt sophomore year of high school, the year Connor's grades started to dip and I focused so much of my energy trying to help him that mine dipped, too. Dipped enough that I never really recovered. That even with all my other grades and extracurriculars and decent test scores I didn't get into Blue Ridge State on the first try.

My eyes skim the ribbons laid out on the bed, Valeria's warning about my study habits pushing back into my brain. I push right back. I'm here now. And soon Connor will be, too. We'll make it where we need to be the same way we always do, taking turns pulling each other up along the way.

"I helped, is all," I deflect. "You're plenty smart."

"And you're plenty kind to put up with me." Connor kisses the top of my head. "I love you."

The words hover in my chest before they reach my throat. "I love you, too."

Chapter Sixteen

The next morning Milo beats me and Shay to the studio. I barely make it through the doorway before he strides right up to me and hands me his familiar beaten-up thermos with the Blue Ridge State logo on it. I take it from him, glancing up into eyes that look every bit as tired as I feel.

"This is tea," Milo tells me. Then, after a beat: "Allegedly."

For a moment neither of us speaks, his eyes careful and searching mine. He may have apologized yesterday, but I feel the full weight of it now. It's in the caution behind his gaze, the faint shame in the curve of those tall shoulders. I'd already forgiven him. But I feel a warmth seeping into my chest just the same.

Shay strolls in behind me, eyeing the thermos curiously. "Why don't I get a random tea?"

Milo turns back around abruptly, heading for his stool. "Because I wasn't an asshole to you yesterday."

My ears burn warmer than the thermos in my hand. Shay raises her eyebrows at me with a clear "we're going to discuss this when we don't have a show to run" in her eyes before attending to the computer.

"Then can you be an asshole to me today?" Shay asks. "I love free beverages."

"I'll try to pencil you in," Milo quips.

I press the thermos to my chest, feeling its steady heat through my jacket. "Thanks, Milo. But you didn't need to do this."

"Don't thank me yet. I've never brewed tea in my life."

I take a sip. It's got enough sugar in it for an entire batch of one of Gammy Nell's famous snickerdoodles and the half-and-half is so thick I can barely detect anything even adjacent to tea. But as terrible as it is on the tongue, it's infinitely warm on the heart.

"Wait." I look down at the thermos, then at his empty hands. "What about your coffee?"

Milo waves me off. "I can survive an hour without my first cup."

I almost feel ridiculous for the way my chest seems to swell at this small but strangely personal gesture. But then Shay blinks, looking at each of us in turn, every bit as stunned as I am.

"Well, I guess even in the Upside Down the show has to go on," she says, peeling the notes off the printer and sticking them in front of Milo. "You're up in five."

After he finishes the show, Milo lingers by the recording mic, his eyes skirting to mine. Shay pats me on the shoulder and ducks out for class. I take the few steps over to Milo, the room suddenly feeling smaller than it did when Shay was still here, and offer him back the thermos.

He opens his mouth and I shake my head, already knowing what's about to come out of it.

"Seriously, Milo. You don't need to apologize," I insist. "I shouldn't have said anything in the first place."

He lets loose a sheepish breath, taking a step back and sinking onto the stool. Even with him perched on it, I have to look up at him to meet his eye. He takes back the thermos, careful to hold it from the bottom, not to let our fingers graze. His next words come out in a mumble.

"I didn't give you much of a choice."

"Still. It probably wasn't my place." I lean in closer, willing him to meet my eyes so he can see the teasing glint in them. "Just my, uh—fix-it thing, as you and Shay call it."

But when Milo looks at me, his expression is surprisingly serious. "I shouldn't have said that, either. I don't think you have a fix-it thing."

I feel a sliver of my composure slip out from under me. "You don't?"

"No. I think you love to help people." His voice is steady, with no trace of the quake from yesterday. Like he's been thinking about having this conversation ever since, or maybe even longer than that. "But I also think you put a lot of pressure on yourself about it."

I feel an unfamiliar kind of itch under my skin. The too-close feeling of someone seeing things that you don't want them to see.

"Well, it *is* what I want to do for a living," I say, my voice high in my own ears. "I want to do my best."

"No, I don't mean like that. I mean . . ." Milo reaches a hand for the back of his neck, his jaw working like he's considering his next words carefully. When he decides on them, he looks down at me and says, "You know you don't *owe* anyone your help, right? Like, you don't have to prove anything to anyone."

My throat tightens. "I'm not—I know that. That's not it at all."

He doesn't back down the way I expect he will, letting me say the words but not letting them sink in. "Maybe it's not, but I think you need to hear it," he says.

My palms are so sweaty that I can't help rubbing them against the edges of my coat. I scramble for something to say, some way to dismiss him, but it's almost as if my lungs won't let me. They can't seem to find the air.

"Sometimes your friends will need help. And sometimes *you'll* need it. But that doesn't mean that we have to solve everything for each other." His mouth twists to the side. "That's the point of having friends, plural. A support system. Everyone helps when they can. They don't spread themselves too thin."

"But I'm not," I say quietly, stubbornly.

"Aren't you, though? I mean—you've been so busy trying to fix things. Shay's major. My sleep schedule. These ribbons for your boyfriend. Every single email to the show *and* your old column. You're telling me nothing in your own life is falling through the cracks?"

I need to shut this down. Need to find some way to gracefully end this conversation before it leads somewhere I don't want to go myself, let alone with someone else.

"I just . . ." I swallow hard. Try to fall back on the same reason I gave him a few weeks ago, walking back from trivia, when he first brought the fix-it urge up. "It makes me happy, being able to help."

But this time Milo just tilts his head at me, as if to say, *Does it?* As if to silently call me out on something that's too complicated to give a name to, too closely woven into my being to define.

"I think you should be happy in your own life first," says Milo.

My eyebrows lift before I can stop them. "Do I seem unhappy?"

Milo shrugs. "Well—yeah, sometimes. But we all are sometimes," he says. "I think the only difference is whether you're willing to acknowledge it. And sometimes I think your whole obsession with fixing things is you *not* acknowledging it."

There's this moment then, when it feels like something in me breaks away; some kind of barrier between me and a truth I've been avoiding so long that despite all my attempts, it's buried itself in me. It's suddenly so loud that I know if I peer at the feeling—if I really let myself sit in it, instead of pushing it down the way I usually do—it's less happiness, and more relief. Not the addition of something good, but the absence of something else.

Because the truth is, knowing I can be helpful means that I'm not a burden. And in the years when my dad was away—the years he left me with two women who may have loved me deeply and endlessly, but certainly never imagined having to raise me in their retired years—I couldn't help feeling like one a lot of the time.

They didn't know what to do with me. Not my dad, who suddenly just stopped being a dad; not my grandmas, who tried their best, but could never fill that space my mom left behind; not even the Whits, who could treat me like a member of the family, but only ever to an extent.

And yeah, when I was a kid, wanting to help came naturally. My mom helped with her quick tongue and ability to shed light on issues. I helped them by listening and shedding light on *people*. We were bonded by the mutual satisfaction of knowing we'd been able to use our abilities to make other people feel heard, feel cared for.

But after she died, after I started feeling so separate from everyone else, it started to feel less like an instinct to help, and more of an itch. A compulsion. The more people I helped, the easier it was to shove that feeling of being a burden away.

You don't need to prove anything. Even as the words are trying to settle in me, I can't help resisting them. When you get used to living a certain way—used to measuring your life, and maybe even your worth in a certain way—it's so much easier to keep going in an old rhythm than to try to pick up one you've never known.

My eyes burn, a strange convergence of realizations all hitting me at once. Not just the mindset that's driven me these past few years. But everything in my life that I've put on hold because of it.

And there it is—the heart of what Milo's dad meant. These are the pieces I haven't picked up. The mess I've been ignoring. I can't scorch the earth and pretend it never happened. Blue Ridge State is my chance to begin again, but I still have to look back if I want to look ahead.

"I want . . ."

The two words are so overwhelming in their potential. I've always known what I wanted. Always had my life mapped out. But those were concrete, measurable achievements. The things that I *want* are things I haven't let myself consider. Things I'm not sure I can even have.

I want to love and be loved without ever having to wonder if it's conditional. I want a life that is sometimes just my own, without feeling like I'm responsible for anyone or anyone is burdened with being responsible for me. I want back what I lost—at least however much of it I can still get.

"What?" Milo asks quietly.

I clench my fists at my side, steeling myself with a confidence that feels borrowed. Like I'm pulling it out of the past, out of my younger self's heart. It takes a few long moments, but then it settles in me, adapts to my new edges, to the new cracks in between.

I look him square in the eye. "I want to do the Friday show," I say, just barely louder than my thundering heart.

Milo smiles this slow, satisfied smile, one so disarming that for a moment it takes everything in me not to stare directly at it. Not to wonder about the origin of it—if it was a smile that he used to smile often, or one that has only ever been reserved for rare moments like this.

My next breath rattles slightly, but the words are firm. "I'm not ready to do things on the fly yet. But if there's a way to give advice as a segment—something I could record in advance—then I think I could do it."

Milo's smile seems to soften then. It suits him—brings out the mossy green of his eyes, the small crinkles in his cheeks and eyes that I don't think I've seen before.

"Welcome to *The Knights' Watch*, Squire."

Chapter Seventeen

The first time I record my segment in advance of the show, I rehearse no fewer than twenty times and sit with my notes so close to my face that when Shay shows me a picture she took of me, it looks like I'm trying to eat them. For the second one I'm still a jumble of nerves, but manage to maintain a respectful distance from my notes. By the third I only have to look at them a few times, anchored enough in my rehearsal that I even throw in some comments off the cuff.

But the real stress comes every Friday morning, when Milo plays my segment in the middle of the show. By the fourth week of it, I'm somewhat used to the strange dread and thrill of hearing my own voice play back at me, but I'm more than a little relieved when the recording ends and Milo takes the first call for "Call-in Friday."

"Hi, I'm, uh . . . I'm calling because, well. I need some advice. Mostly about being in a long-distance relationship."

My eyebrows fly up. We haven't gotten live callers asking for advice since I started the segment. On our request, they've just been writing in.

"You got a name, or should I just call you Long-Distance Listener?" Milo asks.

The voice on the other end is throaty, like they have a cold. "You can call me . . . Bea?"

Milo makes brief eye contact with me. I'm already sweating like I'm competing with a puddle.

"Okay, Bea," says Milo. "Shoot."

"So I have this situation. I have this long-distance . . . almost relationship? I'm not sure exactly. We both say we're open to making it work, but I'm not so sure how committed he is. Things have been really uncertain for a while. And I want to give it a chance, but I'm also kind of crushing on someone else. Someone who's here."

"Crushing, huh?" Milo repeats wryly.

"Well, yeah. I guess I don't know if it's because we're actually right for each other, or just because we're like, actually, physically close. So I was just wondering if maybe . . . you or the Squire had any advice?"

"Well," says Milo, cutting another glance at me, "the Squire's segment is already done for the morning. So, uh. You've got me. And my professional advice is just chuck the whole thing out, love's a scam."

"Milo," Shay hisses.

"Which is, you know. Unhelpful," he recovers. "So my actual advice is, uh . . ."

Only then do I realize Milo isn't looking over at me in acknowledgment. He's looking over at me because he has no idea what to say. He's looking at me because *I* know what to say, and we both know it.

And then, for the first time, I'm not reaching for the braver version of myself I once was. This time she seems to reach out to me. This time she seems to shove.

I nod once at Milo, and he slides off the stool so I can take his place and lowers the mic down to my mouth. I'm expecting my heart to pound. Expecting to feel that same strange distance that makes me feel like I can't connect with people as my actual self nearly as well as my practiced one. But when I open my mouth, I feel more myself than I've ever been.

"You've got the Squire, Bea."

"Oh, good. Hello, there."

I find myself smiling. "Hello to you, too. And listen . . . I know how hard long-distance relationships are. Trust me, I do."

"Yeah?"

"Yeah. So I'm not going to tell you what to do, because I can't. But let me ask you a question. Do you love the person you're long distance with?"

It feels like slipping into an old skin. One I've been easing into now for a while, and am starting to make new again.

The caller blows out a breath. "I care about him."

"Then you know the distance isn't forever," I say effusively. It's my words I hear, but Connor's broad grin I see. "Do you think if you can wait it out, you can make it work?"

Milo's eyes are on me again, this time with a different weight. I try to ignore it to keep focus, but that's the curious thing about Milo. I'm always aware of him. Where he is, the way he moves, the littlest of forces that push and pull and make up his world. Even my own self, when I'm one of them.

"Yeah," says the caller on the other end. "If we both can wait."

I settle onto Milo's stool with the kind of ease I haven't felt in all my weeks of doing this. With an ease I don't think I've felt in years. "In the end, you have to follow your heart," I tell the caller. "But if it's just the distance you're worried about? I've got faith that you can make it work."

The caller lets out a sigh of relief. "Thank you. Thank you, whatever your actual name is. This . . . helps. A lot."

I smile as if the caller's in the room with me, and can feel every inch of it. "I'm glad," I say sincerely, even though something rings false. *Whatever your actual name is.* Like calling myself the Squire is creating a distance between me and this caller that isn't just airwaves, but something I've put up myself.

I shift to give Milo back the stool, but he doesn't move—just points at the mic and makes a wrap-up gesture.

"Me?" I mouth, incredulous.

"We're out of time," he whispers. I forgot he went on a work-study rant a little longer than his usual fare before the segment.

I stare at the mic. The segment is so self-contained that I've never needed to do a sign-off before—at least one that isn't my ill-fated "ta-ta" the day Milo overslept. I scramble, trying to remember Milo's, even trying to remember one of my mom's, but it's like my brain's gone static.

But then I shift my gaze from the mic over to Milo, and the static takes shape. It's a mess. It's pieces that need to be picked up. It's looking forward and looking back. It's everything I've been trying to do, and everything I want to instill in the advice I give from now on—not starting over, but starting with what you've got.

"Well, that's all from us today," I say. "Go make the most out of it, because every day is a chance to begin again."

I feel Milo's smile from across the small room, and smile one of my own into the mic.

After Shay turns off the mic, I sit and wait for the aftermath to hit—to start overthinking everything I said in a twenty-four-hour infinite loop, and pick apart every word of it—but it never comes. We collect our stuff to leave, and on the way out I let myself take a long, hard look at the picture of my mom and for once, smile back at her.

Milo's waiting for me at the main door to the building, holding it open. "Too bad I'll never see you on Fridays again, since you're taking over the show."

I let out a breathy laugh, still in a state of happy disbelief. "That was wild."

"That was great," Milo counters.

I fight the impulse to shrug off the compliment, but can't help adding, "Well, at least it was an easy one to answer, since I'm in the same boat."

Milo shoves his hands into his coat pockets. "I'm glad it's working out," he says, the words quick, but sincere.

"Thanks," I say, momentarily thrown. Milo hasn't even referenced Connor once in these past few weeks. The deliberateness of it feels strange, like it's testing some boundary between us. "Me too."

But before I can feel it out, Milo salutes me in goodbye and splits off to another path to get to work.

I reflexively pull my phone out of my pocket. I should text Connor. Tell him about the broadcast. But the idea of it seems to puncture some of the magic, the feeling I've been riding since I first took Milo's mic.

What if you did something behind the scenes instead? Connor had said to me. Every time I pushed myself, every time I tried to get past this fear, he was there with some variation of those words. *If you were doing stuff and nobody knew it was you, would it scare you then?*

Back then I thought it made me feel safe. But looking back, I think it might have just made me feel small.

When I reach the dorm, I compose an email to my old AP Psych teacher telling her I'm ready to pass the torch on the "Bed of Roses" column. I don't hesitate to send it. Some part of me has known this was coming for a while now. But nothing confirmed it more than this—more than the energy of talking to someone in real time, of rising to meet a challenge as it was presented; more than the fire coursing through me, hot enough to fuel but not so much that it burns; more than the friends who quietly believed I could do it, and waited for me to believe in myself.

Chapter Eighteen

"March is a nothing month," says Shay, scowling at the slush on the sidewalk as we make our way to the library.

"You're literally a Pisces," I remind her.

"And as one of the more emotionally aware signs, I feel more deeply than anyone how boring this time of year is," Shay says, capping it off with a long sigh.

She's not wrong. There's a restless kind of energy all over campus. That post-midterm, pre-knowing-whether-you-passed-the-midterms feeling that has everybody a little bit on edge.

At least it's been getting marginally warmer, because for reasons I cannot begin to fathom, so far every single yellow-ribbon event has been outside. I can't say I've minded it too much, since it's given me plenty of excuses to explore the arboretum. I've even run into Milo's mom a few times taking care of things on the grounds. After I lingered one afternoon watching absolutely transfixed as she moved a beehive, she asked if I would be interested in joining an outdoor volunteer society she led. I loved the idea of it, but told her it would probably have to wait until next semester—or at the very least until the ribbon hunt finishes up.

"If it isn't my fellow reigning trivia champions," says Valeria, already set up at a front table for today's tutoring session when we walk into the library. "Happy Friday."

Shay leans in for a quick hug, easily more familiar with Valeria than I am by now. The All-Knighters have started grabbing the occasional coffee and hanging out outside of trivia, but the two of them both read so fast they meet up to swap books several times a week. They've even done reading sprints at that crepe place my dad talked about, enough times that Shay has more than a few Nutella-stained cardigans to show for it.

"The lit mag meeting should only last an hour or so," says Shay, glancing at the cluster of armchairs where her other friends are starting to assemble. "What time do you guys finish?"

"Right about then, too. Want to grab pre-trivia dinner after we all wrap up?" Before Shay answers, Valeria reaches up and strokes the rosy-orange chunky knit scarf Shay's sister made her. "Ooh, I love this. So soft."

"Thanks," says Shay. "The, uh—the glitter eyeshadow you have on. It's really cute."

Valeria smiles that full cover-girl smile of hers. "I'll bring it to next week's trivia so you can try it."

"Sweet." Shay presses a hand to her scarf in the same place Valeria touched it. "And yeah, dinner sounds great. I'll come find you."

I bite down a smile as we settle in our respective library corners. Every now and then Valeria and Shay seem to go on a mutual compliment train that nearly veers off the tracks, and I can't help wondering if there's more to it than that.

Alas, any secondhand joy I might have felt at the idea of that gets immediately squashed by math.

"You got stumped by that kind of problem last time, too," says Valeria when I've reached an impasse where my brain simply doesn't know what to do next. "Did you ever end up going to the TA's office hours?"

I bite my lip.

"Andie," says Valeria, her tone chastising.

"I know, I know." I don't bother to make excuses about the ribbon hunt or prepping for *The Knights' Watch*. They're all getting old. "But I think the midterm went okay, at least."

We both stare back down, me frowning at a problem I haven't mastered, but Valeria going eerily still. I glance up at her in surprise, wondering if she's really that upset about me bailing on the TA. Then I follow her narrowed eyes across the room, toward the literary magazine meeting. There's a student at the podium holding this month's edition, beaming at the small gathered group.

"If nobody else wants to read from the excerpt of *Kingdom of Lumarin*—a working title, I'm told—I'll go ahead and read it," she says. "But I do hope whoever wrote it comes forward! It is such a phenomenal writing sample, we were so excited to publish it in this month's edition."

I turn my gaze to Shay, whose eyes are wide enough to serve bagels on. But then we both tear our eyes back over to the podium as the student begins to read.

"*The night of Prince Colton's ball was the very same night the witch's prophecy came true,*" she narrates, the lit club group listening with rapt attention. "*I was meant to be finishing up the final touches on my gown. Instead I was scraping spectre guts off my mother's vanity.*"

By the first paragraph of the excerpt, Valeria has already gathered up all her books and shoved them into a bag. I quietly follow suit, trying not to cringe as it becomes abundantly clear that whatever's happening here, it's the last thing Valeria wanted. I try to make eye contact with her, but her lips form a tight line and her eyes are staring holes into the floor, determined not to let me.

Toward the end of the reading, Valeria rises abruptly to her feet. Shay and I both follow, meeting her at the entryway. People are applauding, but all I hear is Valeria addressing us through her teeth.

"Outside," she says. "*Now.*"

Despite the heels on Valeria's knee-high boots, Shay and I can barely keep up with her as she stalks out of the library and down the front steps, leading us to one of the giant trees on the path just outside it. Before we even fully stop, Valeria whips around and finally meets my eye.

"Andie, what were you thinking?"

I blink. "Huh?"

"You submitted my *personal writing* to the school literary magazine?"

I raise my hands up like some kind of surrender. "Heck no."

Valeria's lip wobbles, clearly reluctant to continue accusing me but unsure what else to do. "But you were so fixated on me figuring out the ending. Who else would—"

"I did it," says Shay.

This knocks all the hurt right off Valeria's face. When she turns to Shay, her voice is quiet with disbelief.

"*You* did?"

Shay nods slowly, her eyes searching Valeria's like she's trying to find a foothold. "I didn't think they'd publish it. Usually they run it past the writer first, let them pick a stock photo to go with it. But I submitted it without a name, so I guess they just went for it."

Valeria looks down at the ground, her fingers clenching at her sides. I take a small step back, unsure which would be the worse move: ducking out and leaving the two of them on their own, or standing here and witnessing something I'm not sure they want me here for. But then when Shay opens her mouth to speak again, she looks at me first, the "please stay" clear enough to root me in place.

"The plan was to run it past you if they wanted it, so you could think about it," says Shay. "So you'd see people actually *want* to read it."

"That's not the problem, Shay!" Valeria's eyes are wet, her face puckered with anger. "The problem is *I* don't want them to read it!"

Shay just shakes her head. "Val . . . you're phenomenal. Why not?"

Val lifts a hand up to her forehead like she's steeling herself before the compliment can sink in. "Because—because it's not ready yet," she says. "And it's mine. It's the only thing that's just mine, and I trusted you with it, and now it's out in the world where twenty-four thousand students can hate it or make fun of it or use it as toilet paper."

"Or love it just as much as we do," Shay cuts in stubbornly.

Valeria lets out a strangled, verge-of-tears kind of laugh. "It's like—like, if someone took my diary, and just posted the whole thing on the internet. That's what this is. Don't you get it?"

Shay reaches out to touch Valeria's shoulder, but Valeria jerks herself away as Shay says, "I never meant for it to get published without you knowing."

"You shouldn't have done anything with it in the first place. That was my decision, not yours." Valeria runs her hands through her hair, shutting her eyes. "Just—dammit. There's no way out of this, is there?"

"Nobody has to know it was you," Shay says quietly.

"But that doesn't mean I won't hear what they think about it. And I'm . . . I'm not ready for that."

The late winter wind picks that particular moment to gust in that rib-chilling, unexpected way it sometimes does near the arboretum on campus. All three of us tense up, looking at one another like something will suddenly resolve itself, as if one of us will have the magic words to make it okay.

"I'm sorry," says Shay again.

Valeria's shoulders slump.

"I know you are," she says. "But I just . . . I'm gonna go."

"Val," Shay pleads.

Valeria turns around, swiping at her eyes with her coat sleeve. "I'll talk to you later, okay?"

Neither of us answer her, watching as she turns the corner of the library down the path that leads to her dorm. The sun was already setting when we walked out here, but now a cloud has blotted it out completely and made the darkness fall with unnatural speed.

"Shit," Shay mutters under her breath, turning on her heel in the opposite direction. Yet again, I have to adopt a half jog to keep up.

"It'll be okay. She just needs some time to cool off," I tell her. "One stupid thing isn't going to ruin an entire friendship."

"Friendship," Shay says with a bitter edge.

I pick up the pace to match hers, unsure how to respond. "Or anything else," I hedge.

When Shay answers, the words come out so loud with frustration that several heads swivel in our direction. "I really, really *like* her."

"Oh," I manage.

Because I had imagined this conversation before—I hoped she might say something on a walk home from the broadcast, or one of those nights when we're both practically drunk on sleep deprivation cramming for exams. That at first she'd be shy about it, but eventually that giddy, new crush feeling would win out, and she might tell me then.

What I *didn't* imagine was her blurting it out in the middle of campus, fleeing the library like we just set it on fire.

"Yeah," says Shay. "*Oh.*"

Okay, then. Giddy crush feelings later. Damage control now. The gears in my brain are already turning, thinking ahead to tomorrow, to next week, to the conversations that need to be had and the understanding that needs to be shared. "We can fix this."

Shay stops so fast that I almost skid on the slushy pavement to follow.

"No, *we* can't," she says. "I fucked up, Andie."

I open my mouth to say she didn't mess up so much as make a well-intentioned mistake, but she shoots me a warning glance.

"Okay, yes, this wasn't ideal," I say, shifting course. "But it's not like—the be-all, end-all of you guys having a relationship."

Shay holds up a hand to stop me. "I can't even think about that right now." She takes a breath, then glances around the quad like she's worried someone will overhear. But for once, it's just us. There's no mistaking the finality in Shay's tone when she looks at me and says, "I don't want your help with this. Just don't get involved, okay?"

It stings more than the bitter wind, but it's not about me. I know that. So I nod. "Okay. I won't."

Shay lets out a long breath. "Sorry. I'm just—so mad at myself."

"I know," I say, keeping my voice low, too.

She gestures out toward the main road off campus. "I'm going to just . . . walk for a bit. I'll see you back at the dorm."

After she leaves I stand on the edge of the quad for a few moments, trying to decide what to do with myself. But before I can, my phone buzzes in my hand. I wince, certain it's going to be my dad—I have been passive-aggressively playing voicemail tag with him for weeks—but it's an email letting me know the score from my latest statistics test is in.

Sixty-seven percent.

The blood in my body pretty much stops moving as I scroll farther down, certain I read it wrong or the Scantron got bungled in the machine.

"Chocolate-covered pretzels," I mutter. "*Oof.*"

My nose is deep enough in my phone that I walk right into a very tall human being's arm. I smell coffee and faint citrus and know exactly who it is before his hand reaches out for my elbow to steady me.

"Sorry," Milo and I both blurt at the same time.

He gestures at his phone. "I was . . ."

"Same," I say, holding up my phone with an embarrassed laugh.

But Milo doesn't laugh back. In fact, he looks like he's had a run-in with the ghost everyone claims haunts the arboretum's lake.

Just like that, the exam score is completely out of my mind. "Are you okay?"

Milo blinks. "Yes. I mean."

Instead of telling me, Milo hands me his phone, which is also open to an email.

"*Congratulations, Milo Flynn,*" I read out loud, "*on your acceptance to . . .* wait." I keep waiting for the words to change, but they don't. "Isn't this school in California?"

"Yeah."

So basically as far from Blue Ridge State as he can possibly get. I hand him back the phone, trying to smile, but my face feels all wobbly. He doesn't notice, still staring at the screen like it's going to start talking to him.

"They've, uh—they've got a good broadcast program there," he says.

I bite down on the inside of my cheek. *So do we.* But he knows that. He's been so diligent about keeping his identity as the Knight under wraps that Shay and I just assumed he was applying to Blue Ridge State's program. The broadcast program still resents the show for existing outside their jurisdiction, so it could only hurt his chances if they knew.

Maybe that's why this feels like such a surprise. I knew he was trying to transfer. I've known since the literal day we met. But somehow over the past months of early mornings in the recording studio and afternoons at Bagelopolis and late nights at trivia, I let myself forget.

This is the part where a good friend would ask him how he feels about it, or what he thinks he's going to do. But as soon as I think up the questions I know I don't want to hear the answers. All I see is our little friend group falling apart before it even really had the chance to solidify.

"Well, good for you." My voice is too tight, too chipper. I take a breath and ground myself. "I mean—I know how hard you worked for it."

He nods. I nod back. A group of students spills out of the science building, and we both use the commotion as an excuse to wave and keep walking in opposite directions, the weight of those emails feeling heavier with every step.

Chapter Nineteen

That weekend a cold front comes in that has everyone burrowed indoors—everyone except Shay, who's home for the weekend. After spending most of Saturday and Sunday sitting on my bed overthinking every thought I can possibly think and not getting a single thing done, I regret not going home, too.

The thing is, there is plenty to overthink. Namely the fear that's rippled like an undercurrent ever since I got my acceptance letter—the fear that I don't belong here. That I'm not cut out to match pace with these ultrasmart, supercompetitive kids in this top-tier school the way my parents were. That I'll never have the same easy sense of belonging it seems like everyone around me has, that even Connor seems to have even though he doesn't go here anymore.

Then there's Shay and Valeria, a problem I've still managed to unpack from a hundred directions even though the most obvious one is *stay out of it*. And I have. But it doesn't take it from the forefront of my mind, knowing Shay is out there angry with herself and Val is out there embarrassed to have people reading her words and I'm just sitting here unable to do anything to help.

In the periphery I keep trying to ignore is . . . everything else. The overdue call to my dad. Milo's news. The ribbons I'm worried I'll never have enough of. Those are the sharper thoughts, the ones

I have to push down before the edges catch me by surprise. So I ignore them. I make lists that go nowhere. I draft an email to my professor about the exam I never send. I stare at my phone long enough to burn a hole in it.

And then the phone rings. There's this instant, almost desperate kind of relief. I'll tell Connor everything. Maybe he'll know what to do, what to say.

"Hey." My voice is so hoarse I realize I haven't spoken to anyone all day. "How's life?"

"It's, uh . . ." I hear a door click shut and imagine him in his bedroom at his parents' house. "Well. I guess it could be better."

"What's wrong?"

"You'll be so disappointed in me."

I sit up straight in bed. "I could never be disappointed in you."

Connor sighs, like that's the last thing he wants to hear right now. "I'm, uh . . . , I'm not doing so hot in my classes. It turns out."

There's an immediate sympathy chased by an overwhelming relief. "Oh. Well—me neither, really."

"Yeah?"

"Yeah," I say, my spirits already lifting just hearing him on the other end of the line. "I just bombed an exam, actually. How about you?"

There's a beat. "I'm, uh. I'm failing two classes."

I'm glad he called and didn't FaceTime, because I can't stop my eyes from widening. "Well. There's still time to turn things around."

"Yeah, but . . . my application to transfer back. They'll see those." Connor takes a breath so heavy I can feel the weight of it even all these miles away. "Andie, I don't think I'm going to get back in."

The words sink under my skin like an ice bath. I want to unhear them, but there they are anyway, already sinking in. It's as if they numbed my brain cells, because all I can say is, "But your ribbons."

He's quiet for a moment. "I'm so sorry, Andie. All I wanted was for us to be together."

I close my eyes just to give myself a moment to think, but a tear comes spilling out. I may not have asked him to, but he transferred there to be with me. And now he can't get back.

"I could . . ."

I know what I'm supposed to say, but I can't say it. Instead I'm replaying this version of our lives I've been writing in my head since I got here. How next semester Connor would be here sharing an apartment with his friends across the street from an apartment where I'd live with Shay. How he'd join our trivia team and I'd cheer him on at his games. How we'd weave each other into the fabrics of the lives we made here, introducing each other to our friends, to our favorite spots on campus.

But now when I try to conjure the images, I come up empty of them. Like all it took was reaching out to realize they were made of smoke.

"You could transfer back?" Connor finishes for me.

I know it's what we were both thinking. But that does nothing to ease the sharp hurt of hearing him say it. Of knowing he *expects* it.

I press my lips together, swallowing hard. The hurt doesn't go with it. "It's not over yet," I say. "Maybe you'll get in."

"Maybe," says Connor doubtfully.

I close my eyes again, trying to ground myself in the reality of what's happening, to decide what comes next. It should come easily. By now I'm used to things falling through. I just thought if I could hold on hard enough, Connor wouldn't be one of them.

But it feels like even in asking that of me, a part of him is already gone. As uncertain as the future is, one thing I know for certain is this: I would never, ever ask him to do the same for me.

The rest of the call I feel like I'm half in my body and half not. We talk about classes and our friends at home and the future. We tell each other "I love you" and hang up. My eyelids are so heavy that I fall asleep before Shay even gets back from the weekend, and

I stay asleep so thoroughly that she has to shake me awake for the Monday morning broadcast.

Milo doesn't say anything about the acceptance letter when we get to the studio, and neither do I. Not that morning, or for the rest of the week, which whips by in an aimless, uneasy blur. On Friday comes the only bright spot—not only do I give my whole segment without looking at my notes, but I even take two more callers on the fly.

Milo offers me a smile as tired as mine when he takes over the mic and wraps up. "Anyway, that's the latest, unless you're one of the freshmen only tuning in to get your hands on more of those ribbons. I've been told you're supposed to meet at the gazebo in the arboretum at three P.M. I have no idea what's going to happen to you there, but seeing as I'm not harebrained enough to go outside in this cold, that's not my problem."

That's it. A place I can funnel all this loose, chaotic energy. I'll get another ribbon, I'll put it out into the universe that I'm not giving up—not on the ribbon hunt, not on Connor, not on my mom's legacy.

After class I head back to the dorm and gear up, adding extra layers when I hear the howl of wind outside the window. It's still freezing when I head out for the little path that leads to the gazebo, but for the first time in days there's a singular sense of purpose driving me onward, and with it comes a numb kind of calm.

That is, until I realize whoever reported the Blue Ridge State weather forecast this morning was standing in front of a green screen of lies.

"Sourdough *cheese* toast," I cuss, the wind strong enough to blow me sideways. "What on *earth*?"

I stare up ahead, dumbfounded. It's snowing. No, not just snowing—all at once it's snowing hard enough I can barely see ten feet in front of me.

At first it's so breathtaking I stop in my tracks to stare at it. It's a sheet of white, powerful and beautiful, erasing everything in its path. I feel it falling all around me and there's this sense of awe so overwhelming that for a moment I almost forget why I'm here.

Then there's a flash so close it looks like flames shooting down from the sky, and a rumble so loud and deep I can feel it in my bones.

My hands fly to my mouth. *"Thundersnow."*

It's not my first time experiencing it, but it is certainly my first time being reckless enough to get caught in the middle of it. I reach for my pocket to pull out my phone as if the weather app is going to somehow save me from my own stupidity, but just then a gust of wind blows enough snow into my eyes to knock me back a few feet.

"Andie!"

I glance up, but there's nobody there. Just the wind howling and the snow flurrying. I narrowly avoid falling on the path, but once I find my footing, it's almost impossible to tell which direction I'm facing. It's like being in a snow globe getting violently shaken by a kid in a gift shop.

I try to stay calm and pick a direction, reaching for any advice my dad might have given me back when we were outdoors in all kinds of elements. I think of my mom's old compass, how she'd never use it herself but she'd sometimes hand it over to me, let me see if I could lead us. I wonder where it is now. If it could lead me out of this mess the same way the memory of my mom led me into it.

There's another flash of lightning, close enough that this time I can't help letting out a yelp. The boom of thunder is so immediate that at first all I can hear is the rumble of it, followed by a series of cracks and a deep, unsettling rustling—the sound of a tree coming down.

I've done some stupid things in my life. Forgotten book reports.

Worn jeans to Mrs. Whit's birthday tea. Gotten myself in the middle of friend fights I had no part in. But this is a different level of stupid, I realize all too soon and way too late. This is the kind of stupid where you end up dead.

The tree falls just a few feet away, and all I can do is stare at it, the branches splintering so intensely that they spray me. A twig flies right at my face. I throw my arms up, but not fast enough—something slices my forehead, and I back up so fast my feet slip on a sheet of ice that's somehow collected under the snow.

"*Andie*." Someone grabs my elbow, steadying me before I can fall.

My arms are still braced, my entire body tense. Somehow the voice I'm hearing is even more implausible than all of Mother Nature ganging up on me at the same time.

"Milo," I splutter. "What are you . . ."

He grabs me by the shoulders and spins me around to face him. "Shit. Are you okay?"

My forehead is stinging and my body's shaking and I'm cold enough to chip like ice. "Yes," I say anyway, because right now not being squished by that tree is okay enough.

Milo frowns just above my field of vision, but his eyes are on mine before I can figure out why.

"My mom has a supply shed close by. Hold on to my arm, okay?"

I'm on autopilot, clutching him like he's the last solid thing in the world, my mind replaying the fallen tree over and over again. We slowly make our way through the impossible onslaught of snow with Milo leading the way, our bodies pressed against each other and braced against the snow. Something keeps messing with my vision. I blink and I blink, but it only gets worse.

The door slams behind us before I even realize we've made it to the storage shed, a dimly lit building that's half the size of a dorm room and crammed to the gills with shovels and fertilizer and orange cones. Then everything's quiet and still except for Milo, who whips around and looks at me again, letting out a low hiss.

"What?"

He doesn't answer as his fingers graze my face, pushing my hair back behind my ear. "Your forehead. You're bleeding."

My own hand flies up to my face, bumping straight into his. "*Ow*," I exclaim, the pain of it registering the moment I can feel the warmth of blood against my fingertips. "Oh, no. Oh, *shoot*. Is it bad?"

Milo takes a step closer, lifting his hand again to push back my hat and peer at it. "It's just bleeding a lot, I think. It'll be fine."

My lips form a knot, unwilling to ask the actual question on my mind, which is whether it's going to need stitches and just how much of my face it's going to affect. I see Milo watching me and brace myself for a well-deserved teasing, but instead his eyes soften.

"Seriously, Andie. Once it's fixed up I don't think anybody will even notice it."

I still keep my palm pressed on my forehead like the pressure will undo it happening in the first place. "How did you . . . how did you know I was out here?"

Milo finds a giant box full of supplies and sets his foot down on it, testing its weight. When he seems satisfied, he gestures for me to sit on it.

"I knocked on your door, and when you didn't answer . . ." Milo pulls the hood off his head, rooting through the shelves of the dimly lit shed. "I remembered you talking about how your school app never synced, because of the transfer. There was an alert everyone else on campus got. Telling us about the storm and canceling everything, including the ribbon event for today."

"So you realized where I was," I say, very close to blubbering.

Milo sits down next to me and presses a clean piece of cloth to my head. "Hold that there," he tells me.

My hand grazes his as he pulls away to find something else in the first aid kit he pulled out. "You walked through this circus because of *me*."

"Well," says Milo, with a hint of a smile, "I am the broadcaster who led you out here *and* the RA who's responsible for keeping you alive. So if you were killed by thundersnow, your grandmas probably would have killed me next."

I'm not expecting to laugh, but the image of six-foot Milo cowering at my tiny but vengeful grandmas immediately demands it. The hint of a smile on his face deepens, like he's pleased with himself, but he turns his attention back to the alcohol wipes in the kit before I can fully see it.

"Do you have a hair tie or anything?" Without waiting for me to answer, Milo turns back to the shelves. "I'm sure my sisters left some in here somewhere . . . this was always more their hideout than ours."

I can tell by "ours" he means his brothers. Even with my head bleeding and the sky throwing a full-on tantrum outside I am careful of where I verbally step. "Where was your hideout?"

"Nice try, but you're not getting all the Flynn family secrets out of me today."

He produces a scrunchie that looks older than we are and hands it to me. I pull the cloth from my forehead and Milo leans in to peer at it, the pale green of his eyes so close and so focused that I don't even bother to stop myself from staring at them.

"This is gonna sting."

I wince when Milo dabs at my forehead with the alcohol wipe, but the adrenaline is still too loud in me to really feel all that much. Another gust of wind hits the shed and rattles the walls and the doorknob like a giant is trying to smash the place down. Milo doesn't even seem to notice, pressing a bandage to my forehead with such careful precision that even I stop breathing for a moment.

"Thank you," I say.

Milo just shrugs, taking a seat next to me on the box and frowning at the tiny little window next to the door.

"I can't believe how hard it's coming down out there. That was like something out of a movie."

"And yet you were willing to get squashed by a tree for a ribbon anyway," says Milo, his tone a mix of exasperation and the kind of familiarity that feels deeper than it should, with the two of us so close together.

I close my eyes, the embarrassment swooping in faster than the wind outside. "You probably think I'm an idiot, huh?"

Milo just stares at the floor thoughtfully. "You want to be in one of these societies that bad?"

I grab at the damp fabric on the knees of my jeans. "Yeah. I . . ."

It's not a secret, but it's still mine—mine and Grandma Maeve's and even my dad's. A piece of my mom that doesn't belong to anyone outside of us, at least not anyone I've ever known. But it doesn't feel strange to tell Milo, once the words start spilling out. It feels like a relief.

"My mom was in one of them. I don't know which. You don't get to find out which society alumni were in unless you qualify for them, and I'm just . . . so worried I won't have enough."

Milo watches my hands, still clutching at the denim like I'm holding on to the ribbons themselves. "You're on track to get plenty."

"Yeah, for me. But I need more for Connor." I bite my lower lip to stop myself from saying it, but it doesn't work: "Not that it matters now."

"What's that mean?"

I'm almost grateful for the sting of my forehead. It's just the distraction I need to keep myself from tearing up again. "He's failing some classes. I don't think he'll be able to transfer back."

Milo seems to have taken that argument we had in his car to heart, too. "So you'll just be long distance," he says.

I don't answer because I know if I do, it'll be some way of dancing around the truth. And the truth is that Connor and I are no good at long distance. I probably knew it last semester. I still didn't want to believe it when I was giving advice about it on the broadcast. I know it for certain now. If we're going to have a future together, we have to *be* together.

And if Connor can't be here—if that future is really gone—then every other part of it shifts, too. The same way it did when my mom died. The same way it did when I lost the nerve I used to have for talking to crowds. I don't know what losing Connor would look like, but I've lost enough now to know it will leave a mark.

I swallow hard. I don't want to think about transferring back. I don't want to think about giving it up: not Shay and Milo and Valeria, not our friends at Cardinal, not Bagelopolis or the radio show or even this moment right now, stranded in the middle of a thundersnow storm with a boy who has an uncanny knack for cutting through the things I don't say to the things we both know.

"Wait," I say, sitting up straight. "Why were you knocking on my door earlier?"

"I . . ." Milo blows out a breath. "It's not important."

I bump my shoulder into his. "C'mon. It's not like we're going anywhere anytime soon."

Milo sighs. "I have to put a deposit down soon if I'm going to California."

I can't help myself. "And you wanted my advice?"

"Yeah, yeah. Don't get too cocky about it, new kid." The words are undercut by the decidedly fond look on his face. "But you've been known to have a level head about things."

I look down at my boots so he doesn't see my smile falter. I usually do have a level head—when it comes to strangers, that is. When it comes to giving advice to people whose decisions won't affect me. And at some point in the last couple months, the decisions Milo makes became exactly that.

"Well." I clear my throat, stalling for time. Most of the time the advice just snaps into place. If I have enough information I can bird's-eye-view the whole situation, look at it wholly and objectively and compassionately before I say anything at all. But all I see is Milo chugging Eternal Darkness and Milo coming to life in front of the studio mic and Milo fist-bumping us after a trivia-night win. "Have you thought about what your life would be like there?"

It's Milo's turn to look down at his boots. "More like thought about what it'd be like to get away."

Another clap of thunder rattles the entire shed, knocking us into each other. I don't even bother pulling away. There's nothing to overthink, nothing to consider—there's just fear and this mutual trust that seems to blot everything else out.

"Shit," says Milo, just as I mutter, "*Frosted* Flakes."

He lets out a short laugh.

"What's so funny?"

Milo opens his mouth. "You with your—" Another flash of lightning.

"Salted caramel Oreos!" I mutter, just as Milo lets out a low "*Jesus.*"

We brace ourselves for the rumble of thunder that follows the jolt of lightning, laughing at the same time.

"Oreos?" Milo wheezes through his laughter. "Where did these swear words of yours even come from?"

"My favorite foods, of course."

"Is that it? Bad things happen, and you just think of foods you like to eat?"

Another burst of lightning. I yelp in surprise, but Milo yells, "Pretzel bagel and unicorn *cream* cheese!"

And just like that, I'm laughing so hard that the rumble of thunder barely even registers. "*You* like the unicorn cream cheese?"

"Indiscriminate fruit is my favorite flavor," says Milo without a hint of shame. "Lucky Charms, Gogurt, whatever the heck we're putting into unicorn cream cheese included."

"I never knew. You drink Eternal Darkness black, I never thought you'd like something so sweet."

"I contain multitudes." He leans back against the box, propping himself against the wall. When he speaks again his voice is so low it's hard to hear over the wind. "So. What do you think?"

I take a beat, but I already know my answer. I just don't think he's going to like it.

"I think . . . well. Both schools have amazing broadcast programs."

Milo's lip quirks again, realizing I must have done some side research on my own. My cheeks flush.

"And I know you initially switched out of biology because you were mad at Harley," I add quickly, before he meets my eye. "But that also makes sense, since you were clearly meant to do this."

"High praise," he says, with his usual wry deflection.

"Honest assessment," I correct him. "And an important one, because the thing is—you got lucky, with that part working out. Doing something because you were mad at your brother, I mean. But I don't know if you'll luck out again. What I mean is—I want you to make sure that if you're making this decision to go, it's just for you."

Milo's jaw tenses. "The other program is more well-known." He picks a corner of the shed and stares at it, then concedes, "Blue Ridge State's is smaller. More competitive, but more chances for hands-on experience."

I don't mention the radio show he's technically supposed to lead until graduation, when he helps train another Knight. It wouldn't be the first time one of them had to leave early. It'd just be the first time it was someone who mattered to me.

"Both good programs," he says, echoing me.

I nod. "But the thing is . . . you're never going to know if you're going for yourself or because of Harley unless the two of you settle things first."

Milo blows out a breath. "I've got a few weeks for the deposit, not twenty years."

I nudge my shoulder into his. "He's your brother. And it sounds like you were close."

Milo doesn't nudge back, but he doesn't move, either. Our shoulders stay just faintly touching, this quiet, grounding thing in the tumult of the storm.

"Yeah. Especially after . . . well, after our dad died. We were the youngest. We got the least amount of time with him. So we just kind of—I mean, we were always close." For once, Milo's words aren't as ready and blunt as they always seem to be. He has to pause. Has to consider. "But I think after that it was like—yeah, we were all hurting, but there was this specific kind of hurt that our older siblings didn't quite get."

I think of the way Grandma Maeve and I have our own little unit of grief, this lens we see the world through that it feels like nobody else quite does. One I know my dad must too, if we ever really talked about it.

"I can see how that would happen," I say softly.

"Honestly, I think Harley wanted to go out of state himself, but stuck around to stay near me." Then Milo clears his throat, blinking hard. Something in his posture changes. Hardens. "But I guess it wasn't just for me. I guess it was for Nora, too."

I choose my next words carefully. He asked for advice about college, not this. Trouble is they're one and the same.

"It sounds like he didn't mean to hurt you."

"But he did." Milo's fingers curl and uncurl into his palms, some of the knuckles popping as he fidgets. "Nora was my . . . I mean, shit. She was my best friend. He's my brother. And here I was, just the biggest *jackass*, thinking how lucky I was to have them in my life even after everything went to shit, and the two of them were just . . . waiting, probably. Who even knows for how long."

Best friend. The words stick to my ribs. The way he said them first and only. It's the way I think about Connor, too—my best friend first.

"And the way I found out was just—so humiliating," says Milo, shifting his body slightly like the memory is itching just under his skin. "What did they think was going to happen?"

He says it with the tone of someone who's asked it a hundred times since, and tried to wrap his head around the answer even more than that. I wince, imagining him in the theater that day, his eyes falling on the pair of them. The hurt. The embarrassment. But probably more than any of it, the surprise.

"It's not like I would've been okay with it if they *had* just told me," Milo admits. "But the way they went around my back, it's like—shit. I knew things weren't perfect, but I thought she and I were happy. And I thought Harley and I were pulling each other along. I thought the deal was that I needed them, and they needed me, but I guess they just really needed each other." He takes a breath, some of the tension in his body giving way, making space for words pulled up from somewhere deep. "So was I just not . . ."

He shakes his head roughly. *Enough*, he was going to say. My throat is thick with the familiarity of the feeling. It's followed me through my family falling apart, through the years I spent trying to make myself fit in someone else's. Sometimes I'm scared it might follow me my whole life.

I reach out for one of his hands, gently uncurling the fingers. Once his hand is in mine I squeeze like I can will that feeling out of him. I know that words alone aren't strong enough to fight it; at least not right now, when he's staring down to the deepest part of it. I can't make it go away, but we can share some of it for a little while.

He stares at our intertwined fingers, shifting the warmth of his further into mine, easing his own pressure into it. And this—*this* is why I love what I do. Why I want to spend my whole life doing it. For these heart-stuttering, breathtaking moments when you realize that if you carve us all down to our barest parts, we're all the same.

"I think all of those things can be true," I say. "That you need each other. That you love each other. Sometimes life just changes the nature of it. But it doesn't make it matter any less. And it doesn't make it anybody's fault."

Milo lets out a terse laugh, but doesn't interject.

"You're good, Milo. To the people you love and the people you don't." Milo might not be willing to look at me when I say the words, but I can feel him letting them settle all the same. I press on. "And they know that. Anyone who knows you does. And I bet you anything that's why they lied. Because you would never do anything to deserve it."

Our hands are still tangled, his gripping mine like it's anchoring him to the spot. Before I can think the better of it, I add, "You must miss them."

All of the hard lines in Milo's face soften at once. Like the opposite of bracing yourself; something that lands before you even saw it coming.

"It sucks," he says, the words dull on his tongue, without their usual edge. "Knowing they probably don't miss me half as much."

I let out a hum of doubt. We both know it's not true, even if it makes him feel better to say.

Something in the room seems to shift then. A change in the light outside, the sun briefly gleaming behind a storm cloud, jolting us back to our senses. Whatever spell Milo was under seems to flash through right with it. He gives my hand a quick squeeze before letting it go.

"Unlike you lot, who probably won't miss me at all," he jokes, his throat still thick with emotion. "Probably go changing Eternal Darkness's recipe again the minute I leave."

I stare out the tiny window like the light might come back. I'm so fixated on it that the words slip out of me before I know whether I really mean them. "I don't know if I'll be here, either."

"Wait, really?"

I swallow hard, casting my eyes away from the window but still avoiding his gaze. "I mean . . . even if it weren't for Connor. I'm not doing so hot in my classes either. Maybe it'd be for the best if I just went back."

I brace myself for a scoff or some remark I no doubt deserve, but instead Milo asks the kind of question that cuts right past all the tangles of the situation and to the core of it.

"What are you scared of?"

I open my mouth, but I'm too stunned to think of a response. At least one that doesn't feel like more of a reflex than the truth.

"Because leaving Blue Ridge State . . . maybe for me, it'd be running away," says Milo. "But for you it'd be chickening out. And you're no chicken."

"Says who?" I mutter. "You've seen me on the radio show."

Milo swings his foot out under the chair to gently knock mine in the back of the heel. "I've seen you get braver and braver every week. So what's different about this?"

The difference is what's at stake. The difference is that despite everything—despite the plans and the dreams and carefully curated lists I've made all on my own—I sometimes feel like I have no sense of who I really am. But knowing I always have a place to belong with Connor and his family makes me feel solid in a way nothing else has.

It's the first time I've ever admitted the full extent of it to myself, even privately. There's almost a relief in the understanding. But with it is the magnitude of everything I might lose.

"It's like you said," I manage. "About Nora being your best friend? He's mine. And his family . . . they're my family, too."

"So you'll get past this. If that's really how it is."

I don't want to test that boundary again, the way I did when I transferred here. But Milo's right. I know he is. It's like the bird's-eye view I can have for strangers—suddenly, seeing it through his eyes, I am starting to see it for myself.

If Connor's parents really love me—if *Connor* really loves me—it'll be okay. We can be okay.

"And in the meantime—the ribbons. If they're that important to you, just get them for yourself." Milo nudges my foot again, this time with some playful force behind it. "And maybe, you know. Study."

"Called out," I say with a wince. "I was just trying to be fair about it. Ribbons for him and ribbons for me."

"Well. Maybe just try ribbons for you, huh?" says Milo. "I mean—it's about your mom. He must understand that."

Except he doesn't. I've never told him. And that never seemed all that strange until now, when I realize I told Milo without a second thought.

"And you're too smart to be bombing a class."

I feel my head droop, my eyes fall into my lap. That's the most embarrassing part of this, probably. I have all these standards and expectations for myself, these carefully laid plans, and somehow I'm so far off track from them that it seems impossible to find my way back. It feels like a confirmation that I shouldn't be here at all. That I'm not good enough to make it in this place where my own parents thrived.

"So go fix it," Milo presses, before I have to think of something to say. "What else is all this work-study bullshit for if not the study part?"

I smile grimly. "Free bagels?"

"Absolutely that. But also for all those ridiculously ambitious color-coded dreams of yours to come true."

This time when the resolve hardens in me, it's not demanding. It's gentle and easy, like something I already know the feeling of coming back. It occurs to me, meeting Milo's gaze, that the ache I'm so used to feeling is quieter now than it's ever been.

"I guess I could go to the TA sessions, too," I say. "Catch up before the end of the semester."

"That's the spirit, new kid." His leans back a bit to check the bandage on my head, then adds, "Hey, maybe if you stay, you'll even take over the radio show for me."

I shake my head vehemently enough that Milo's eyes widen in mild alarm.

"Well if you're *that* put off by being my successor . . ."

I find myself starting to grin even as the thunder keeps rumbling above us, distant but fierce. "It's got nothing to do with you."

"Sure it doesn't," says Milo, clutching his chest and pretending to be wounded.

I lightly kick his foot with mine. "Drama king."

"Drama *dictator*," he corrects me. "Go big or go home."

Then the grins are genuine, both for him and for me. It feels like a break in the storm even as it rages on, enough of one that we lean back to wait it out, content to be in this moment now, and not the uncertain ones ahead. At some point the shed starts to dim, the early evening setting in and sharpening the angles of light from the one dim bulb in the shed, and the two of us realize the storm has long since passed.

Milo gets up first, leaning down to look at my forehead. "First stop, the student health center."

"I'd rather just burrow under the covers for the rest of the night and curse every air molecule that caused this."

"Too bad I'm the RA. What I say goes, or you'll get in trouble with the residence hall director."

"Scare me."

"*And* lose privileges to the rec room," says Milo, his eyes gleaming. He knows he's got me. Our weekly games of Werewolf have gotten so out of hand that seven different dorms pile into Cardinal to pretend to murder each other and eat snack cakes. We've even started a betting pool over whether Tyler or Ellie will ask the other out first. Like most competitions with Blue Ridge State students, it's all gotten pretty intense.

"Fine," I say, getting up from the storage box and dusting my-self off. "You got me."

I don't miss Milo's slight hover, the way his hands are just far enough from his sides to catch me if I stumble. But I am touched to see it just the same.

That is, until we reach the door of the shed, and Milo pauses with his hand on the door. He turns to me, his gaze so deliberate I feel almost weak under it, but in a way that I don't necessarily mind. In a way that makes me feel *too* seen, but just enough at the same time.

"Andie . . ."

And then the fear hits. It's irrational and comes out of nowhere, but I have this stupid thought that he's going to say something that'll upend us. Something I've felt in a few jolting moments we've been alone, that's been humming between us for the last hour we've been locked in here together.

But I'm wrong. For better or for worse, I'm wrong.

"While we're just butting into each other's business like this—talk to your dad."

I look up at him in surprise. I hadn't even mentioned the calls I was dodging. Not for the past few weeks, and not even in this time we've been more open with each other than ever before.

Milo stares at his own hand, still touching the doorknob. "If I had the chance to talk to my dad again—well. It's different. But you know."

I nod. It *is* different. Milo's dad didn't choose to leave. But we both know what it's like to lose a parent and all the moments that would have come after.

Ever since he tried to get in touch, I've been willing to forfeit those moments with my dad. I may have had no choice in his leaving, but I do have a choice in him coming back. And I can't help resenting him for having to make it. I can't help resenting him knowing that, if the roles had been reversed, my mom would have stayed, and I'd never have to make a choice like this at all.

It isn't just Milo's words that sink in then. It's my dad's, too. The voicemails he's left. The giggle of a little girl I've never met. The sound of my own voice wondering when things would go back to the way they were, when I'd get my dad back again.

My fingers curl into my palms. He is back. He's trying to be. But I don't even know what that looks like anymore, so I have no idea how to let him back in.

Just then Milo opens the door to the fresh, post-storm air, to the too-white snow and the too-bright sky. We blink into it for a moment, both of us processing the arboretum like we've stepped into some alternate reality. No storms. No dead parents. No doubts about the future holding us back.

"For the record, Milo," I say quietly into the new air, "I would miss you."

It doesn't change anything, but it feels important for him to know. Or maybe just important to say it out loud. Like maybe I can make the hurt of missing him a little less if I own up to it now instead of later.

Milo turns away from me, carefully shutting the door behind us. When he looks at me again, there's something resolute in his eyes that I can't get to the bottom of no matter how hard I try.

"For the record, Andie—same to you."

Chapter Twenty

I have every intention of calling my dad that night, except the entire dorm descends on us when we get back. Apparently getting four small stitches at the crown of your head is all it takes to become a Blue Ridge celebrity. Shay makes us tea and knocks on Harriet's door to commandeer enough cash to pull all the dusty Cheetos and Reese's out of the vending machine, and Shay and Milo and I sit on the floor in a pile of pillows Shay fashioned by her bookshelf.

Milo sniffs at his own mug—the one covered in chickens that I now recognize as the chickens in his mom's coop—and takes a tiny sip. "I will admit this isn't the worst thing that's ever happened to me."

I snort. "It only took a tree almost killing you."

Shay raises her eyebrows at us, not for the first time since we got back. "I'm never going outside again, huh."

"We angered the weather gods," says Milo grimly. "Should we call Valeria? She might get—" Milo squints at the label on the tea box—"herbal coconut macadamia FOMO."

Shay sighs. "Well."

And that is how she ends up telling Milo about the whole mess with the literary magazine and the crush and the very unfortunate tension between her and Val, in that frank, resigned manner of someone who has gotten over the initial shock of something and doesn't know what to do next. Milo lets out several sympathetic hisses between his teeth and a "See, this is why love is a scam. Run, Shay. Run."

Shay rolls her eyes, and then meets mine. "I need a plan B. I'm assuming you already have them through Z, though."

"I could, in fact, offer the alphabet," I say. "If you do want my help."

Shay puts a hand on mine like she's one of Connor's soccer coaches and says, "I'm tapping you in."

I take a sip of my tea and spend the rest of the night scheming.

Well, most of it, at least. I can't help checking if the next yellow-ribbon event is still on for the next day, but even before I see that it is, I make a choice. A choice to commit to something that seems truly disrespectful to the institution of Saturday: math.

Only when I show up to the TA's office hours, there is no TA waiting for me. Instead there is Professor Hutchison, sitting on the swivel chair in front of her desk, her steel eyes catching mine like a trap before I even walk through the door.

"Oh," I say, unconsciously taking a step back. "I must have gotten the time wrong."

"Christine's home for the weekend. I'm running office hours." She hardly moves a muscle, but speaks with enough authority to run a small country when she says, "Sit."

I swallow so hard that I'm half expecting a *gulp* sound effect to echo through the hall. She's already pulled up my midterm score on her giant monitor before I manage to get to the chair. Turns out the only thing worse than seeing a "D" is seeing it four times larger on someone else's screen.

Without another word, Professor Hutchison leans down and pulls out a stack of papers, thumbing through them until she finds the exam pages where I made all my notes. She passes them to me from across the desk and then, to my horror, stands up and positions herself directly behind me.

"Try that first problem again. Talk me through what you're doing."

Somehow I manage to bleat out an explanation under her intimidating shadow. She doesn't once interrupt me, not even when I've concluded by getting the same wrong answer as before. In fact, she asks me to do it with the second problem I got wrong, and then the third.

Abruptly, her shadow lifts from behind me, and she's moving back to her seat.

"You're too focused on the math," she informs me.

I splutter, trying not to laugh. She raises her eyebrows at me.

"Sorry, it's just—those were words I never thought anybody would actually say to me."

"Why's that?" she asks sharply.

"Because I'm terrible at math."

She shakes her head with the impatience of a person who has heard that excuse too many times to accept it. "More likely you were taught to come at it from an angle that doesn't work for you." She thrusts my own notes from the test back at me. "Here. Read the scenario. Actually *read* it in its practical sense, and what it's trying to achieve."

I glance down at the problem I absolutely skewered—a longitudinal study examining couples' self-reported happiness over time. We were asked to isolate different groups within the study to pull more specific findings out of it. All I'd found, it seemed, was a failing grade.

But now that I'm actually looking at not just the data, but the context of it—the weight of all the years that went by during the study, and the implications of that raw data—my thinking starts to shift.

"Does the number you came up with seem to fit the scenario?"

"No," I realize. It doesn't necessarily help me figure out *how* to solve it, but once I look at it within the context of what I've been given, it's enough to recognize there's a problem in my reasoning.

"You've been trying to separate the math from the psychology. It's common for students who aren't confident in statistics to try to stick to the black and white of the original formulas and separate their feelings from it. But that's how you let yourself miss other variables. The math and the psychology behind them—they go together."

I bite down a smile. "Math has feelings, too?"

Professor Hutchison comes just short of rolling her eyes. "If it did, it would be disappointed in your trajectory this semester," she says mildly.

I turn my attention back to the page. "I've been going to a tutor," I tell her.

She taps her fingernail on the desk between us, snapping my attention back up to her. Her steel eyes lock me in place again, drilling each word into me: "An hour with a tutor every week doesn't replace practice. And it certainly doesn't come close to the best kind of practice—learning from your mistakes."

My ears burn. It feels like I've been doing a lot of that lately.

"I know you haven't been to these office hours," she continues. "It's a shame. Most of the students who were struggling were able to get a better foundation once they grasped the problems they got wrong."

"I've been . . . busy," I hedge.

But Professor Hutchison bulldozes. "At those weekend ribbon events, I presume."

My sheepish expression is answer enough for us both.

Professor Hutchison leans forward. "Tell me. What do you want out of this experience?"

I straighten up. "I want to get good grades. I want to be able to apply to a competitive graduate school."

"No, I mean this *experience*. Not what you get out of it." She gestures out the window, toward the view of melting snow on the quad gleaming in the early morning sunlight. "What do you want to remember about this place after you leave?"

The words puncture deeper than I anticipated. But when my smile falters and the pencil poised in my hand finally eases onto the page, it's clear that the words struck just where she intended.

The answers are poised on the tip of my tongue, but thick in my chest. I want to remember laughing with my friends. Passing nachos around on trivia night. Setting my ribbons down next to my mom's. Quiet walks in the arboretum. Taking the mic from Milo on Friday mornings and feeling a hum of potential in the airwaves.

"You kids are all so focused on doing too much. So much of everything all the time. What you need is balance. Priorities." She makes sure I'm looking at her when she says, "You need to decide what's important to you, or then nothing is important. You understand?"

I duck my head, feeling the truth of it. The way I've been throwing myself into so many things that I can't quite give my whole self anywhere. Not to the things that matter most. Not just the things that matter while I'm here, but during whatever comes next.

"But what you also need is to show up to these study sessions," she says sternly. "That is, if you want to pass my class."

"You don't think it's too late?" I ask.

"I think that's for you to decide," says Hutchison. "Now walk me through your logic on that first problem again so we can talk about where you went wrong."

The next hour is equal parts illuminating and excruciating. Professor Hutchison might have insights that Valeria had, but she has none of her gentleness. When I'm wrong I can practically feel it radiating off her before she opens her mouth. But I leave with my exam newly marked up in my own handwriting with correct answers this time, plus an old version of the exam from last year so I can try my hand at similar problems. I leave with a sense that I'm not just skimming the surface of learning this, but digging in deep.

It's only as I'm walking past the quad, thinking over her words — *what do you want out of this experience?* — that when I put myself on the spot, I didn't think of Connor at all.

Chapter Twenty-One

Every now and then I still get emails to my defunct "Bed of Roses" email account, and forward them over to the new columnist who took over at Little Fells. But a few days later on my way out of class I open it to an email from an address I recognize on sight. Trying to get my very accomplished, extremely busy daughter at Blue Ridge State to call her old man back, it reads. Any pro tips?

My entire face flushes, embarrassed and oddly touched at the same time. I haven't intentionally drawn this out to be some kind of test, but it's still reassuring to know that for once he's not taking the excuse to stay away.

I wait until after my first class to call him back. He picks up on the first ring.

"A-Plus!"

He sounds so happy to hear from me that for a moment I feel absurd. All this apprehension, all this overthinking, and he's just glad that I called in the first place.

"Hey, Dad," I say, rounding the corner to a quieter part of the quad. "How are things?"

"Busy and good. Just like you with all those ribbons, huh?"

I blink, surprised to hear him mention them so readily. We never discussed them before—not when he decided to put my mom's in storage and certainly not since I got in here. I can only assume my grandmas filled him in.

"Yeah," I say, slowing my pace as I process.

"You having fun on the hunt?"

I blink, the image of that falling tree and Professor Hutchison's stern gaze a little too fresh in my mind.

"Yeah," I say. "Mostly."

"Those were some of my best memories there. Aside from . . ." He trails off, his voice taking on that soft quality it always has when he seems to sink into a memory too far to take me with him.

"Mom," I supply, the word sharp.

It's a challenge, in its own way. A rebuff. But my dad doesn't go quiet the way he usually does.

"Yeah," he says instead. "I'm glad you're getting to enjoy it, too."

"Definitely," I say tightly. I take a second to compose myself, and it occurs to me that I never knew my dad did the ribbon hunt, too. I'm about to ask him about it, but he beats me to the punch.

"Listen, I—well. The last time we talked, you seemed a little thrown off. So I just wanted to check in with you."

A few other students vacate a nearby bench, so I decide to walk over to it and plop myself down despite the late March chill. "Thrown off," I repeat. "Dad, I had no idea Kelly even had a kid."

I can practically hear him wince through the phone. "That's my fault. Her name's Ava. She's eight. I should have told you. I just figured it had come up that time you and Kelly met, or that your grandmas had already mentioned it."

I feel an unfamiliar twinge of paranoia. "Did they meet her or something?"

"No, no. I just asked them for some advice on things."

"What things?" I ask too quickly.

"Well—mostly asked your Grandma Maeve about dating some-one with a kid," he says sheepishly. "Since she's had a few boyfriends with kids of their own. It's new territory for me."

There's a pinch of relief. I thought maybe he was asking for advice on kids in general. The rub would have been a little too close—the idea that he can do better this time because he's willing to learn in a way that he wasn't for me.

But that's the thing. When I was eight, he was everything he must be for Ava now: someone funny and dependable and kind. Someone who cut shapes out of peanut butter and jelly sandwiches and ate my crusts. Someone who drove circles around the park during Christmas because I couldn't get enough of the lights display. Someone who was *there*.

So it's not like he doesn't know how to be someone's dad. He just forgot for too many years, and now that he's remembering, I don't know whether to trust it or not.

"That makes sense," I say. "So. Ava. Is she . . ."

I'm not sure what I'm asking, really. If he likes her? If she's at all like I was when I was her age? I'm still so unused to the idea of her that none of it feels natural in my head, let alone coming out of my mouth.

"I'd love for you two to meet at some point," he says. "I've told her a lot about you. She thinks you're pretty cool. And I think you'd get a real kick out of her, too."

That's the first time the word "stepsister" floats through my mind. It isn't accompanied by any kind of jolt, though. Because the weird truth in all this is that I'd be happy if my dad married Kelly. I may not know her well, but I'm a good enough judge of character to know she's a good person. And even if I weren't, the evidence is right here: in this new version of my dad, or more fittingly, this version of my dad she's helping bring back. Someone I recognize.

But I've been let down too many times to pin my hopes on

anything. Too many missed holidays and broken traditions and memories shut up in a storage facility outside of town.

"Yeah," I say anyway, steeling myself for a future that may or may not come to pass. "I'd like to meet her, too."

Just then there's a very loud *beep* on my phone, and I let out an "oh" of surprise.

"What's up?" my dad asks.

"Oh. Um—an alert from the campus app." I pull the phone away from my ear to read the notification. After the thundersnow debacle, Shay personally marched me into the student office to get someone on the tech team to sync my phone to the campus alerts. "A ribbon scavenger hunt event in the library. I should . . ."

I shake my head. Not one week ago Milo was reminding me that the ribbons should be an *Andie* thing, not a compulsively-get-as-many-as-I-can-for-Connor thing. And not five minutes ago my dad inadvertently reminded me why we are all hunting for ribbons in the first place. Not as something to cross off a to-do list, but something that's meant to be fun.

"Always there for the hunt, just like your mom," says my dad with a laugh.

The frankness of the words knocks me off-kilter. The warmth of them. The confusion of hearing them at all.

"I won't keep you. But take a look at your calendar, okay?"

I'm too stunned to push back. I should keep him on the phone. See if he'll say anything else about my mom, now that we've gotten this close—almost closer than we ever have.

But I'm too overwhelmed by it to think of anything to ask. *Just like your mom,* he said. The words are already pressed somewhere too deep to reach.

"Yeah. I will," I tell him.

"Love you, A-Plus."

I press the phone closer to my ear. "I love you, too."

Chapter Twenty-Two

"Well, what do you like to do together?"

Today's call is an older woman asking for advice on emotional distance in her long-term relationship, and I can already tell she might be a tough sell. Her voice has that exasperated tone of someone who can't quite believe she's doing this. I'm expecting it to rattle me, but the adrenaline doesn't have that sour, too-quick feeling it once did. It feels warm and energizing. Like a challenge.

"Maybe that's the problem. We've got our own separate interests."

Her voice is tightly controlled, like she's holding the rest back. I wait for a moment, even through the dreaded dead air. The more I've transitioned from hiding behind my old column to actually connecting with people in real time, the more I've started to understand that there are a lot of circumstances where people aren't necessarily looking for advice. They just want somebody to hear them. They just want to know that they're not alone. I suspect that's what this woman might be doing, even if she doesn't know it.

And that makes this whole thing less intimidating—the idea that you can help sometimes just by being there. No fix-it urge. Just understanding.

Sure enough, the caller lets out a sigh and says, "At first it was nice, having that kind of independence from each other, but now . . . I don't know. Over the years it's kind of distanced us."

"How do you mean?" I ask.

And then, almost reluctantly at first, she tells me. Not necessarily the specifics, but the feeling of it. And yet again I'm brought back to that moment in the supply shed with Milo, that feeling more universal than most: that constant, human worry of wondering whether you're enough.

I suspect most of the benefit from this came from letting her say it out loud, but this *is* an advice segment. So I still offer what I can.

"Is there any place you know they'll really shine? Something they're good at, something you can learn more about yourself?" I ask. "And same to you—some place you can take them and let them a little more into your world?"

"Well, now that you mention it . . ." The caller clears her throat. "I suppose. He's been talking about a conference that I could attend with him."

"You could make a weekend of it," I say encouragingly.

There's a gratifying hint of bemusement in the caller's voice. "You're right. I could," she says.

"Good luck to you both," I say sincerely.

"Thank you," she says wryly.

"Anytime," I say, as the call disconnects. "That's all from us today," I say, because we've just started making my segment the end of the show. By now the sign-off is so easy that it rolls right off my tongue: "Go make the most out of it, because every day is a chance to begin again."

I find myself beaming as I hop off the stool, an energy flowing through me so far from the old ache that it sometimes feels like the insides of me have shifted. I feel solid. Like what I'm made of finally matches what I want. Milo has to bounce to get to Bagelopolis for his shift, but not before leaning in and saying close to my ear, "Seems like you've got a handle on things. Maybe my friend the Squire will let me sleep in next Friday?"

I'm still in the afterglow when I meet Valeria for tutoring at the library a few hours later.

"Someone sure is chipper on this rainy day," she observes.

I set my bag down, fishing my stats textbook out of it. "Trivia tonight," I remind her. "We're going to crush Team Knight Owls."

Valeria's lips press into an uncertain line. "I wasn't sure if I should come or not."

Usually I have more subtlety than a falling brick, but I'm too eager for an opening to stop myself. "Shay's really sorry."

Valeria eases back in her chair like the idea of it has been weighing on her. "I know she is," she says quietly. "And I'm sorry, too. For making a big deal out of it."

I shake my head. "It's important to you. It's not 'making a big deal' out of anything."

She smiles appreciatively. "Thanks for saying that."

I tilt my head to the side. "Of course."

She leans forward again, her eyes so steady on my textbook that I'm certain she's going to brush past it. "It's weird," she says instead. "I know you guys are close, so I just . . . was worried maybe you'd just stay close. Without me."

So that's it. For all the time I've been worried about fitting in here, it didn't occur to me that someone who's been here as long as Val might feel a degree of that, too. I wish I'd realized that sooner, before she had to wonder about us.

"Val. Of course not," I say, reaching out to put my hand over hers. "The All-Knighters are a team. One for all and all for whatever fried-potato situation Shay can scam from the back kitchens."

I feel a twinge then for the sake of said team—as far as I know, I'm the only one who knows Milo might be on his way out. But I push the thought aside, focusing on Valeria.

This time her close-lipped smile is deeper and more genuine, puckering the dimple on one of her cheeks. "You're right. I'll, uh—I'll be there, then."

I give her a beat, but not enough of one to let her shift from feelings to math. "I feel like I have to ask," I venture carefully. "You want to be a published writer someday, right?"

Valeria sucks in a shaky breath. "I mean, yeah."

I tilt my head at her. "So what's the plan then?"

I'm expecting her to hesitate, because she isn't sure of either the plan or whether she wants to tell me, but instead she seems to relax in her seat. When she speaks, it's with so much resolve that I can see the vision taking shape in my own head.

"A pen name, is what I'm thinking. My middle name's Beatrice. It's my grandma's, and she—well, she was the one who introduced me to romance novels in the first place," says Valeria, a smile playing at her lips. "I like the idea of it. Using her name so she'd know how much it meant to me, but also so I could still hold a day job in something else without the Google search for my name skewing in one direction or the other."

I frown, not sure how to interpret this. "Plenty of people hold day jobs and write romance. It's not anything to be ashamed of."

"Oh, I'm not," says Val, with more confidence now. "I just . . . it's not shame at all. It's just that the things I write? They're mine. They're *just* mine. And I like the idea of sharing them to the degree that people can read them one day. But not the idea of losing the part of them that's for me, you know?"

I nod slowly, the understanding starting to settle in, even if it's not coming with anything all that helpful to respond with yet.

"I think if it were so public—if it were my actual full name on a book one day, and I had to go out into the world and speak on its behalf as myself—I don't know. It would feel less like it belonged to me." Valeria runs a hand through her hair. "I'm not making sense. I know."

"No, you are. I mean—I'm anonymous, too. I get it."

Just as I'm saying it, though, I realize that I don't get it at all. I'm anonymous right now, but it's not out of wanting to keep the advice on the old "Bed of Roses" column or even *The Knights' Watch* to myself, the way Valeria holds her work close to her heart. For me, that distance I put in place is something else. For me, it's fear.

I shift in my seat, tucking that worry away for later, then lean in close to meet Valeria's eye.

"Either way, I think it's clear you have a bright future in writing ahead of you. Shay says people loved it so much that they got a record number of readers emailing asking where they can get the rest."

Valeria flushes so red I'm almost worried about her cheeks. "I'm glad people are enjoying it."

I nudge her foot under the table. "Well. Get used to it, *Beatrice*."

And it's only then, when I'm saying the name myself, that it taps into some recess of my brain. Beatrice. *Bea*. As in the caller a few weeks ago who was torn between an ex trying to make things work and a new crush they vibed with. Valeria *definitely* has feelings for Shay, too.

Up until now I'd been holding back on any concrete meddling—Shay may have asked for my help, but I haven't felt out Valeria yet, so I wasn't sure whether to make a move. But just like that, Operation Help Val And Shay Find True Love is a go, along with an idea inspired by the conversation I had with this morning's caller.

"Hey," I ask on our way out after we finish tutoring, "you got any plans for tomorrow?"

Maybe it's testing my luck. I've only just managed to convince Val to come to trivia with me. But I know full well that she and Shay will blurt apologies to each other and we'll all go back to eating potato skins and yelling out answers to stuff like "Who was the second Sailor Scout found in *Sailor Moon*?" like nothing happened. I've got an opening here to see if Shay and Val might actually want something more than friendship, and I'm not about to let it go.

"Not really," says Valeria, tossing her hair to the side so she can prop her bag over her shoulder. "Why?"

I face the library doors, a conspiratorial smile stretching across my face. "Consider it booked."

Chapter Twenty-Three

"The thundersnow didn't kill us, so you thought you'd freeze us to death to finish the job, huh."

I halfheartedly swat at Milo's arm, my gloved hand barely thudding against his giant coat. He's not wrong, though. It's brutally cold for late March. I'm surprised the lake isn't frozen over.

"You volunteered to help," I remind him.

Milo peers out at the lake, at the thick woods at the edge of it and the towering mountains beyond. It's a sight every bit as breathtaking as the cold. Glittering frost and still water, woven trees and jagged peaks, a crystal blue sky.

"Did I?" says Milo, shoving his hands deeper into his pockets. "Seems irresponsible of me."

Just then Milo's older sister Piper pops her head out of the kayak rental stand. She's every bit as tall and lanky as her siblings, her dark curls spilling haphazardly out of a frayed beanie. "You said four people, right? Four kayaks?"

"Yes, but—if you could do two single kayaks, and one double," I tell her.

Piper frowns. "We've got plenty of single kayaks. I can pull two more out."

"Nope, no, one double and two singles would be great," I say quickly, flashing her a very large and perhaps too aggressive smile.

Piper casts her bemused eyes from me over to Milo. "Gotcha, boss."

Milo lets out a sigh deep enough to cloud the air in front of us. "At least Piper will tell Mom I loved her after the hypothermia ends us."

"Thanks again for pulling these strings," I say, sidestepping his morbid declaration. He can pretend all he wants, but the only reason we're here this late in the afternoon is because he made us wait until after he got off his Saturday shift. "I didn't think I'd get this close to re-creating the boat scene in Valeria's manuscript, but you know what? It works. Like, if you squint."

Squint hard enough to pretend you're on a summer sunset ride to steal a bejeweled, enchanted crest from a secret ocean cave when you're living in a place so cold that your eyebrows are threatening to accumulate ice, that is.

Milo shrugs. "What is having all these siblings lingering around campus for if not to get discounts on our own icy demise?"

Just then my phone rings with Connor's familiar ringtone. "Quick sec," I say, walking toward the snowy end of the parking lot.

"Try not to lose a toe," Milo calls after me.

Connor's voice is warm but rushed. "Hey, I've only got a minute but I saw you called last night. What's up?"

Maybe it's the cold or the week I've spent working my ass off or the god complex I am somewhat flexing now trying to get Valeria and Shay together, but I feel oddly buoyed. I don't hesitate.

"I've been going to office hours. Pulling my grade up. I told my professor how serious I was about trying to get back on track. She's trying to help, and I—I feel a lot better. Even if you don't transfer back, it's probably not too late for you to turn some of your grades around, too."

Connor lets out a breathy laugh. "Blue Ridge has grown on you, huh? You really don't want to come back to Little Fells."

The hurt is so quiet, so unexpected, that I have to hold the phone from my ear for a moment.

Grown on me. As if this weren't my parents' school. As if this weren't my mother's school. As if I hadn't planned to be here for so long that it was practically one of the first conscious thoughts I could remember having—that one day I'd come to Blue Ridge and be a Knight, too.

Does he really think I only transferred because of him? That he's the only driving force that brought me here, that could compel me to stay?

I've been walking up the edge of the parking lot, but this is the thought that stills me: It doesn't matter what brought me here or what didn't. Blue Ridge isn't just a school for me anymore. It's starting to feel like a home. Not because it grew on me, but because I've grown in it.

"No, I'm not coming back," I say, quiet but firm. "I want to be with you. I'm not coming back, though."

It doesn't feel that scary to say because it doesn't quite feel like a risk. At least not yet. Not before we know what is going to happen next year or where we'll even be. It's like Milo said—*So you'll just be long distance.* We've loved each other for years. It shouldn't be that hard.

Connor's quiet for a few moments.

"Okay," he says.

"Okay?"

"I hear you. I get it." He eases out a breath. "And who knows? Maybe I'll get back in, and none of this will even matter."

I don't miss the implication behind that. "And if you don't?"

"Let's just—say I will, for now. We can cross that bridge if we ever get to it. And hope we don't."

"Right." My voice sounds chipper, too bright against the bright piles of leftover snow. I realize my face is stretched into a smile. The syndicated-talk-show one.

"I mean, I've gotten out of tougher spots before."

The words feel like the whine of a car brake. I've watched Connor face enough "tough spots" to know he doesn't always get out of them by trying. When push comes to shove, he's either relied on charm or his parents for help.

It's something I've been able to dismiss in the past, calling it luck, or part of his nature. Maybe even something I've been able to dismiss because there were undoubtedly times I benefitted from it, too.

But maybe I'm being unfair. It's not like either of those factors means anything up against the Blue Ridge State admissions team.

I swallow down my unease and say, "Let me know how it goes."

"Yeah. And I'll send you some more of my essays," says Connor. "You always know just how to tweak them."

As soon as the call disconnects and his words sink further in I feel a flash of anger that jolts me with how immediate it is, like it's been waiting for me to notice it for much longer than I've felt it. But there's no time right now. I wad it up in myself and push it back down, hustling back over to the rental shed where Milo's waiting, crunching some frosted grass with his boot.

"All good?" he asks.

Shay and Valeria mercifully interrupt, laughing so hard about something that we hear them before we see them coming from the parking lot. "Sorry we're late. There was the *dumbest* deer in the road. Truly just like. Magnificently dumb."

"We must have honked fifteen times," Valeria giggles.

Shay shakes her head, grinning. "That little dude thought we were singing him a lullaby."

I'm so relieved to hear them back in their usual rhythm that for a moment I forget that in this little stage I've concocted, I've got the next line.

"Do you guys mind sharing a kayak?" I ask. Before Piper or Milo can interrupt me, I say, "Milo's already a pro and I'm kind of new at this, so it's probably better if we're in our own kayaks. And since you're both at the same level, it'd make sense for you two to share the double, right?"

Valeria's not the only one who can mess with the only-one-bed trope in this squad.

Luckily, she doesn't seem to notice anything amiss. "Sure," she says. "Good with you, Shay?"

"Fine by me. Gonna need a hell of a lot of Eternal Darkness to warm us up after this though, huh?" she says with a mirthful look at Valeria.

Valeria shivers, leaning in closer to Shay. "Amen to that."

I clench my fist triumphantly as they walk ahead of us, waiting until they're out of earshot to say, "Phase one is a go."

"*Be* more emotionally invested, I dare you," says Milo.

I stick out my tongue. Milo rolls his eyes and cocks his head toward the water. "C'mon. I'll help you get started before you capsize trying to eavesdrop on them."

I almost wave him off—it's a silly little boat, it's not *that* complicated—but approximately five minutes later I am drifting off and making absolutely zero progress in so much as holding the oars correctly, let alone using them to move.

Milo paddles behind me, following my aimless zigzag through the water with embarrassing ease.

"This is how sailors get lost at sea, isn't it?" I mumble, despairing as Valeria and Shay get so far ahead of us there's no way to overhear them. "Someone's going to have to write a sad sea chantey about me."

"It just takes some getting used to," says Milo, narrowly avoiding the splash of me cutting my oar in the water with accidental violence. "You'll get the hang of it."

Not before I end up clear on the other side of the lake. The woods look more than a little haunted, but at least Milo seems committed to making sure we all get back in one piece.

I sigh. "Well. Maybe it's for the best. I've set all the conditions, so now it's up to them."

"Well, hey." Milo's breath makes its own little cloud of fog that hovers for a moment, just as hesitant as he is. "Since we're out here and all. I was wondering . . . if I did leave."

"If," I say, more to myself than to him. I'm glad it's still an "if" and not a "when."

"Well. I know you'll probably say no. But I thought I'd ask just in case."

Despite the absurd chill, my cheeks are suddenly blazing. "Ask me what?"

The words come out too fast, my teeth chattering and my heart skipping a beat. I can't even explain why. But there's some kind of potential energy in waiting for his question, something thrilling and scary, something I want to hear and don't want to hear at the same time.

That is, until he asks something I'm not expecting at all.

"I just wanted to be clear that it was an actual offer, not just a joke—if you'd be interested in taking over the radio show."

The confusion hits before the panic slides on in, knocks it aside, and fully takes over.

"Oh. Yeah. Um, still no."

Milo's oars go still, our two kayaks drifting closer to each other even in the still of the water. "Can I ask why?"

"Because . . ."

It's not that I'm afraid anymore. I mean, at least not petrified, the way I was. And it's not even the pressure of trying to live up to my mom. Being on the radio was her dream; it's just one means of many ends for me.

"I like being the Squire. It's what I want to do. The broadcast element of it—it's not really my thing."

For a moment I expect some kind of shift beneath us, like the lake is going to spontaneously whirlpool and swallow me whole.

Some kind of punishment for disrespecting my mom's legacy, when it's been closer to me than it's ever been.

But I'm startled to realize it's the truth. What I do as the Squire is meaningful because it's mine, because it's connecting me to people in a way I've shied away from for years. But now that I've been in the thick of *The Knights' Watch* for so long, now that I can see past my fear and the whole enigma of her legacy, I can appreciate it for what it is: something my mom accomplished. Something I don't need to prove myself worthy of, now that I'm finding my way back to goals of my own.

"Well, you know each of the Knights has their own 'thing.'" Milo tilts his head at me, like he's inviting me to consider something. "Advice giving could be yours. You can make the rules as you go. I mean, we've technically been pirate radio since the nineties. I say 'fuck' enough times in the first ten minutes of each show to make the people who assign movie ratings cry. Who's gonna stop you?"

I laugh, even as I set aside the idea to mull over later. The trouble is that it's hard to picture it right now. Hard to picture anything right now, with so many factors up in the air. "I guess that's true," I say.

Milo nods, accepting that as the only answer I can give for now. "Well, if I do leave, at least go easy on my replacement," he says, the mirth in those clover eyes distinct even in the fog. "Unless they're wildly more attractive than I am, in which case, feel free to bully them."

I mime splashing him from the lake.

"So you're still trying to decide?" I ask.

"More like putting it off," says Milo. I'm too cold to give him a hard time, but he ends up beating me to the punch anyway. "I know, I know. But procrastinating on major life decisions is a Flynn family varsity sport."

"That and actually knowing how to maneuver one of these neon death traps," I say, referencing the kayaks under us.

Milo lets out a low chuckle. "Yeah, let's figure that out before we turn into Popsicles. Here. I'm gonna pull up ahead. Try to mirror my oar strokes."

He cuts through the water with the kind of grace that has me watching the cut of his shoulders, the smooth, steady way they propel him forward. I shake my head, turning to my own clunky oar.

"Your extremely tall-person, long-armed oar strokes?" I say before he gets too far ahead.

He lets his kayak glide for a moment so I can catch up. "I'll keep it at Polly Pocket arm speed."

"I resent that!" I call after him.

"Good. Use it as your motivation not to freeze to death."

Shay and Valeria have long since left us behind, going on a thorough and controlled loop around the perimeter of the lake. Milo and I are aimless in comparison, mostly just trying to keep our kayaks from bonking each other's as he helps me figure out my strokes. At some point we make it to the dead center of the lake, where everything's so hushed and still it feels like we've slipped into some other world.

We both stop unconsciously, breathing it in.

I turn to meet Milo's eyes, but his are already on mine, waiting with this small, conspiratorial smile. For once, I don't feel the need to say anything, to fill a silence or worry about setting another person at ease. We just sit in the quiet of it. Soak everything in.

Eventually a bird flies low in the fog, surprising us both. I laugh and Milo startles and we both look over at the dock, where Shay and Valeria are drawing near.

"Cool Ranch Doritos," I mutter, trying to jerk the kayak around. "I lost track of them."

"Slow down there, sailor," says Milo. "It's not like they're going to leave without us."

"But I had *one job* and it was to try to fix this thing."

"Why's it your job?" Milo asks, rerouting his kayak to follow me as I tear into the water.

His voice is careful, the way it was when we first talked about my "fix-it thing" all those weeks ago. *You know you don't owe anyone your help, right?* he'd said. *You don't have to prove anything to anyone.*

And the words hit home. Enough that it feels like half a lifetime has passed since he said them, because I've considered them in everything I've taken on since. But this time feels different.

"Because—because I'm the one who might have blown it," I confess. "I think Valeria was the one who called in the other day. About being hung up on an ex?"

"That caller who sounded like they swallowed a bug?"

Sheesh, can't these stupid oars go any faster?

"I think she was trying to disguise her voice. And anyway, if it's true, then I totally put her off Shay by pushing long distance with some other guy, and like—maybe that wasn't the right call! Maybe I was just saying that because of my own stuff, you know?"

"Maybe you should slow down."

"And if I'd known that it was Valeria, no way in heck would I have pushed for the other guy, because he's a dishrag who left her in the middle of nowhere and made her cry a whole bunch of times, so—"

"Andie, your *kayak*—"

"—if she and Shay have a shot, which I think they do, don't you? I kind of owe it to them to set the right conditions to—"

There's this lurch in the kayak followed by a lurch in my stomach, the kind that recognizes impending doom. I'm especially grateful for Piper's long lecture on life jackets and safety protocol as the kayak unceremoniously flips both itself and me over into the icy lake.

After that, pretty much my only thought is that nature had a *lot* of nerve letting water get this cold.

Fortunately Milo's wits are still about him, because mine are almost too numb to move. Before I can even fully process the depth of my stupidity, he yanks me by the hand and pulls me over to his kayak.

"Shit. Are you okay?"

I splutter lake water, my teeth already chattering so violently they don't feel like they belong to me anymore. "I think I saw the kraken."

Milo sets my hand on the surface of his kayak to keep me there, then busies himself with flipping mine back over. "Well, he's a friend of the family, so he probably won't fuck with you."

"L-Let him," I moan, my legs kicking frantically underneath me despite the life vest and the anchor of Milo's kayak. "Then I don't have to die of embarrassment later."

Milo pats my kayak. "I'll hold it steady. I'd get back in fast if I were you, before the adrenaline wears off."

I hook my arms back over the kayak. "Don't look at me," I moan, trying to flop myself back in and feeling like a baby seal.

"I feel morally obligated to never look *away* from you, considering the sheer amount of nonsense you've gotten yourself into this week." I wince at the legitimate edge of concern in his voice. The last thing I wanted to do was make anyone worry about me. As if he senses this, Milo adds, "Remind me to never team up with you on *The Amazing Race*."

As I'm clambering back into the kayak, every single one of my nerves starting to scream from the cold, I catch sight of Valeria and Shay on the dock. They're locked in a tight hug, Shay's arms wrapped around Valeria's puffy coat, Valeria's chin resting on Shay's cheek.

"Oh no," I mutter.

I can't pinpoint the precise genre of this hug, but judging from the faint disappointment on Shay's face, it's not the one she was hoping for.

Milo nudges my kayak with his oar. "We're not that far. Are you good to get back?"

"Yeah," I say, although I'm none too eager to get there.

I really thought I was on the mark with Shay and Valeria. I'm not used to being wrong, but it's not just that. I'm not used to being wrong about people I know this well.

But maybe I'm just leaping to conclusions. First priority: talk to Shay and figure out what actually happened. A priority that gets unfortunately pushed aside when Shay claps eyes on us approaching the dock and lets out an audible gasp.

"Holy shit. What happened?"

I wave a hand at them, only to realize said hand is so numb from the cold that I can't actually feel myself doing it. "I, uh. Fell in."

Valeria's eyes are just as wide as Shay's. "Your lips are fully blue."

"There's like—*frost* in your hair," Shay exclaims.

"Elsa isn't the only one who can pull this look off," I joke, hoping we can get off the subject of my complete and utter idiocy so I can gauge what happened here. That hope is further abandoned when Piper offers her hands to pull me onto the dock and I realize it's not just my hand, but my entire body that's gone numb.

Luckily Piper's got some muscle on her, because she heaves me back up with the ease of someone who is used to fishing terrible kayakers out of the water.

"Aw, crap. You better get her to the house," says Piper.

Milo has somehow already gotten himself on the dock and lightly puts his hands on my shoulders, steering me toward the parking lot. "C'mon. Let's get to Stella before people try to rent you out as an ice sculpture."

I follow his lead, but not without looking back at Shay and Valeria. "B-but—what about you guys?"

"We're gonna go grab some coffee," says Shay, deliberately nodding toward Milo's car with an unmistakable *Go*.

So maybe my hopes aren't completely dashed after all. It doesn't exactly bring back any of the feeling in my limbs, but it's restorative nonetheless. I follow Milo to Stella, confused that my legs are still moving me forward even when I can only half register that they're still attached to me. I'm busy staring down at them when the weight of Milo's coat is unexpectedly over my shoulders. It doesn't do much to warm me, but that familiar smell does—that mingling of citrusy soap and coffee and warmth.

"Th-thanks."

"I'd say anytime, but I'm optimistic that's the last time you'll catapult yourself into a below-freezing lake," says Milo.

He jerks the heat all the way up in Stella despite the house being right down the road, casting a glance to take quick stock of me before he pulls out of the lot. Piper must have sent their mom a text to expect us, because Jamie is walking out the front door and clucking sympathetically at me before the car even fully parks in the driveway (no easy feat, considering the chickens nipping around).

"C'mere, doll," she says, grabbing Milo's coat and helping me shimmy out of my other one. "We'll get you in the shower. I'll leave you out a change of clothes. Nobody's lost a finger to hypothermia in this house yet, and I'd like to keep our record clean."

I stammer some frankly unintelligible thank-yous before bringing my human body slowly back to life in the guest shower. There's a pair of boy's jeans, a T-shirt, thick socks, and an oversize flannel waiting for me just outside the door, with my underwear that Jamie stuck in the dryer for a quick cycle. I pull them on gratefully, most of the chill finally shaken off, and pad out to the living room.

Milo stands up from the couch when he sees me, making Bozo the dog whine petulantly at the loss of his body heat. There's a split second his eyebrows lift when he takes me in, the floppy socks and the faded jeans, the flannel that goes all the way down to my knees. It occurs to me then that these used to be his.

"Oh, good," he says, his expression neutral by the time he settles on my face. "You're alive."

"Yeah. Thank you again." Bozo hops off the couch and comes over to nuzzle me on the leg. I lean down to scratch his ears and he lets out a low, appreciative woof. "I should, uh—get back to campus. Figure out what's going on with Valeria and Shay."

Milo sucks in a breath. "Sorry. No can do."

I knit my brows in confusion, pausing mid–ear scratch. "Is Stella broken?"

"No. But your priorities might be a little on the fritz."

"E*xcuse* me?"

Milo does that deep "I'm the RA" sigh he usually only reserves for drunk co-eds yelling in the halls.

"Andie. Shay and Val are adults. They'll work their own stuff out." He takes a step closer, and only then do I see that he has my backpack full of textbooks on the couch. He pulls it up by the strap incriminatingly. "You need to study."

"Well. Yes. After I figure out how to help."

The itch is back, the compulsion. It wasn't when I first planned this whole thing for Valeria and Shay. But it came back the instant Connor and I hung up the phone. That knee-jerk reaction to prove myself. To make myself useful. To know that even if the rest of my life might be a mess, there's one thing I can do right.

Milo crouches down on the other side of Bozo, leveling with me. "I'm no Squire, but is it possible that you're hyper-focusing on someone else's problems to avoid your own?"

I narrow my eyes at him. "Touché."

He tilts his head toward a door on the other side of the room. "We call that Flynn Family Jail. No distractions. No internet connection. Just couches and textbooks and like, one window, because we're not total monsters."

"You're . . . putting me in study jail?"

"Scarlett's already in there. Grad school thesis. So at least you'll be in good company."

Before I can think of any further protests, he unceremoniously walks over to the door, opens it, and deposits my backpack on the other side. Bozo follows me hopefully until Milo sticks a leg in front of the door to cut us off from each other.

"See you in two hours."

With that, he shuts the door behind me, leaving me in a small, white-walled room occupied by a very stressed-out-looking person I immediately identify as Piper's identical twin. The only differences are Scarlett's hair is slightly longer, her eyes are entirely more sleep-deprived, and her outfit is decidedly more cottagecore to Piper's wilderness-guide chic.

"Hello, fellow inmate," she says, as if it is perfectly normal for strangers to get locked in a room full of inspirational prints that say things like WHAT DOESN'T KILL YOU WILL MAYBE AT LEAST MAKE YOU SMARTER and DON'T FUCK THIS UP! BUT IF YOU DO AT LEAST THERE'S CAKE.

". . . Hi," I say, settling into the chair across from hers and pulling a blanket over myself, half certain I'm hallucinating.

Scarlett shoves an open box of Oreos at me. "Godspeed."

Four Oreos and a boatload of statistics problems later, Scarlett lets out a loud yawn. I look up from my pages to see that it's entirely dark outside.

She taps my book. "We need sustenance."

"Yeah." I am still trying to wrap my brain around the fact that the Flynn family just short of academically kidnapped me, but I've gotten a lot of work done. More than I thought I'd get done today, with Shay and Valeria top of mind and Connor just behind them. Scarlett stands up and stretches and I follow suit, closing up my books and wandering out with her.

The lights are dim in the living room and even Bozo is nowhere to be seen. Scarlett ventures out toward the kitchen, then stops abruptly. I figure out why a beat later: The kitchen table is empty save for two people. On one side is Milo, his shoulders tight and his eyes trained on his hands, which have worked themselves into a knot. On the other is Harley, slumped in his own chair, tired eyes set solely on Milo.

I open my mouth in a silent *oh* of realization, backing up before Scarlett does.

"Okay if I drive you home?" Jamie asks quietly, appearing behind us with the kind of quiet that probably only a mom of seven could master.

I nod, pulling my backpack up over my shoulder and following her out to the family minivan.

"Thank you," she says, once I'm firmly in the passenger seat.

"Thank—for what? Thank *you*," I say. "You're the one who just took in a random icicle for the evening."

Jamie's lips press into a very Milo-esque, knowing smile.

"Those boys . . . they've needed to work their shit out for a while. I've got a pretty strong feeling you've got something to do with Milo finally being willing to listen."

I'm glad for the darkness of the car, because my cheeks immediately flush. "I don't know about that."

Jamie reaches out and nudges my shoulder none too gently. "Take credit for your shit."

I let out an unexpected laugh. "I mean—if I did help—I'm glad. I know Milo isn't sure what he's going to do about school yet, but I think this will help him decide."

She nods at me in the rearview mirror. "He's lucky to have a friend like you."

I'm beaming like a star, directing all the energy into my lap, only because it's kind of embarrassing how much her praise means to me. The only thing I can compare it to is Mrs. Whit's approval, and that feels so much harder to earn.

But this—this feels just as earned. Just as meaningful. The difference is I didn't have to jump through a bunch of hoops to make it happen; Jamie seems to just appreciate me for being me in the first place.

Jamie catches my eye in the rearview mirror, her smile teasing. "I'm hoping your little swim didn't scare you off looking into the outdoor volunteer group next year."

Next year. The words feel more solid, more like a promise than they ever have. The call with Connor may have left a lot of things up in the air, but it solidified the thing that mattered to me most: I'm staying, no matter what.

It feels like I've lived a lot of my time here only letting my roots sink in halfway. Trying to hold on to the old parts of me—the "Bed of Roses" column, the fix-it urge, the ribbons for Connor. But now that I know I'm here for good, it's like the last of the old strings holding me back are falling away. Like I can really find that balance Professor Hutchison talked about, because nothing about my time here feels conditional the way it once did.

And part of what I want—what I've wanted since I got here—is to spend more time exploring these grounds. To reconnect with the kid I was back when my parents took me out for adventures, and I soaked up every word they taught me on them so one day I could take them on my own. To find satisfaction in something that feels like it's just mine.

It would mean kissing the idea of more yellow ribbons goodbye, but for the first time, it doesn't send a streak of panic through me.

I'll either have enough of them for the group my mom was in or I won't. That's something I can't control, but this—this is something I can.

"Actually, my weekends are freeing up," I say. "I'd really love to join now."

Jamie's eyes are warm as she says to me, "Well, take your time. You're welcome whenever. But I'll get your email from Milo and send you some details."

We spend the rest of the ride exchanging funny stories about Milo—me tattling on him for the time he set a "no crying to Disney power ballads in shared spaces after eleven P.M." rule in the dorm, her sharing that Milo is the one who individually named each of their chickens and gets extremely offended when other members of their family mix them up. On my way out of the car, she hands me two aluminum-foiled sandwiches and two containers of tomato soup. The warm weight of them suddenly makes me want to cry.

"For you and Shay," she explains. Then she winks. "One of these days you'll eat grilled cheese with us at a table, huh?"

I grin back. "Sounds good to me."

As I bound out of the car and head back to the dorm, I let myself imagine it: a crowded table. People talking over each other. Massive amounts of food and laughter and eyes to catch anywhere you look. Something I've wanted my whole life; something I thought I'd just have to wait for.

But maybe it isn't. Maybe that kind of table is a lot closer than I think, if I just give it a chance.

I pull out my phone and check the calendar app, then text my dad the next Saturday I have free. He responds within the minute: *Works for me, A-Plus! See you then.*

Chapter Twenty-Four

Between the two of us, there are probably ten shades of nail polish bottles on the floor. I am opting for rainbow, with a different color on each finger overlaid with sparkles. Shay is going for a moody purple with crescent moon stickers, claiming she needs the witchy energy after all the happenings today.

"You're right," Shay says to me. "Like, looking back—I really think that *was* Val on the radio show."

I wince, smudging my bright purple pinky nail. Fortunately or unfortunately, I have a full hand of smudged nails to match—I'm too preoccupied to focus. "I wish I could go back in time. Answer her differently."

Shay shakes her head. "She's still hung up on him. I mean, that's what she said to me on the dock."

We've been over this a few times now—once when we were eating our grilled cheese, another time when we were eating the emergency stash of Twix bars under my bed (to be clear, most days are "emergencies"), and now in the aftermath, cultivating our nails so that we might move on from the embarrassment of this day: Shay for being politely rejected by Val, and me for becoming a swamp monster.

But the more I try to dissect this entire situation, the less sense it makes.

"I mean, on the list of things that concern me about the whole thing, the fact that Val might still like this guy who put her through the wringer is pretty close to the top," I say, my brow furrowed.

Shay shakes her head. "I don't think she does at all. I just think she's still really hurt by the whole thing." Her eyes sweep the floor. "And considering everything he put her through, I don't blame her."

I set the purple polish down, staring at the same spot on the carpet like it's going to clarify anything. "Yeah. She was pretty upset when we met. Whoever this loser is . . ." I let the words hang in the air, only because we've said some variation of them a dozen times already tonight. "And she didn't say anything else while you guys got coffee after?" I ask.

"No. It was pretty normal. I mean . . ." Shay sighs. "It's gonna hurt for a long time, I think. But I'm glad we can be friends in the meantime. It would have really fucking sucked otherwise."

Despite myself, the smallest of smiles tugs at my lips. I've had this sense that though our little friend group may be new, it has a strong foundation. Today might not have shaken out the way we wanted, but it still proves it. That no matter what rocks us — crushes or feelings or falling face-first into a frozen lake — we've still got one another's backs.

"Thank you, though." When I look up, Shay's brown eyes are warm on mine. "For your help with this."

There's a warmth in my chest that feels entirely different from the relief I used to get from a successful fix-it. One that burrows deeper and takes a stronger hold. This is the kind of friendship that doesn't come with conditions; the kind so solid that you never have to wonder if you're enough. We'll ride out our problems together, one at a time, and be grateful we're there to see each other through them whether we can fix them or not.

Shay stretches her leg out to knock her foot into mine. "At the very least, the whole drama with the literary magazine is over. Val's writing again. Even going back to her sister's place tomorrow to try to work on her ending." She starts collecting the nail polishes off the floor. "And I've learned my lesson. No more shouting about other people's work without their permission."

And only then does something in my brain finally click. I slam my hand on the carpet between our beds.

"Shay."

"Hmm?"

It feels like there's glitter in my veins, and it's shooting straight up to my brain. "Switch your major to marketing."

"Ah, yes. Because I don't deal with enough entitled frat boys on this campus as it is."

I leap up on my freshly painted feet, yanking my idea board for Shay's major out from under my bed in a dramatic swoop. It's a heck of a lot messier now, given all the things we've tried and rejected. It's also a little useless, given the fact that the answer isn't on the board, but basically screaming all over the room.

"We dismissed publishing way too fast."

"I told you. I only read the books *I* want to read."

"Exactly. And then you shout about them. Like with Valeria. And all over your Instagram." I gesture at her bookshelves so wildly that Shay takes a cautious step back.

"If bookstagramming were a full-time job, trust me, I would not be here," she says, continuing to calmly put the nail polish away even as I am having what could arguably be my most important revelation of the semester. "You'd have some bushy-tailed Southern belle for a roommate and I'd be reading on a beach."

"I don't know about the beach, but Shay. If you only read books you want to read, and then you're championing them as aggressively as you have for years—I mean, couldn't you try being an agent? Or someone on a book marketing team? Someone who gets *paid* to shout about books?"

Shay blinks at me, half of her considering my words and half of her clearly trying to reject them. "I do this because I love it. The whole idea seems . . . sellout-y. I don't like the idea of having to champion books I don't connect with, and that's the whole point of the Bookstagram—to be able to talk about queer stories and Black stories and stories that deserve a whole lot more attention than they're getting. To have some control over the narrative."

I seize on this so fast that even Shay, who is more than used to my theatrics by now, raises her eyebrows in mild alarm.

"Agents get to pick and choose who they represent. So you'd get to champion stories like that right from the start, right?" I ask. "And as for marketing, if you don't like the idea of not getting to pick what you read—go to a smaller imprint. One where you'll know you actually like the books they publish, and you'll have a hand in helping put them on the map before they're even released." At the beginning of the semester I didn't know enough to even give her this advice, but after overhearing Shay and Val's conversations about the book world, there are weeks of publishing knowledge rattling in my brain. "You'd have to find the *just right* opportunities, and it might be hard, but it'd also be *you*."

I know I've reached the "aha!" part of Shay's brain because she hasn't even attempted to take a breath to talk me out of it. Instead she's chewing on her bottom lip, her eyes skimming the bookshelf in all its color-coded, overly stuffed, cozy glory.

"Maybe" is all she says in the end.

And maybe we've made some progress, opened a potential door. Maybe we're right back to square one. But where there might have been a fix-it urge before, there's just a respect that life isn't that simple—that the things that matter most take time. And as we go to bed with our nails a lot more colorful and our hearts a little fuller, I'm grateful that Shay and I have plenty of it between us.

Chapter Twenty-Five

I'm on the quad squinting against the glare of the sun when I see a boy who looks just like Connor walking toward me.

No, scratch that—*Connor* is walking toward me.

I stop in my tracks, the day welling up around me like a storybook page. It's all too perfect. The way the sun is beaming down. The smell of fresh-cut grass and the slight warmth in the breeze. The sounds of students laughing and arguing out on picnic blankets on the quad. And my boyfriend, my handsome, steady, magnetizing boyfriend in the middle of it all, like the beautiful day just conjured him here.

He's come to surprise me. There's this simultaneous thrill and *ache* that I can't make fit in me at the same time, that freezes me in place. I want to be happy. But mostly I'm just relieved. And maybe even a little bit of something else—something that settles low in my stomach, quiet and confused.

As if he senses me watching, Connor turns his head. His sandy hair catches the light, the tousles gleaming gold, his brown eyes already wide with anticipation. I steel myself—this is the beginning of something, but the end of something else, too. The end of the future I made myself imagine without him in it, the one I've been easing into since it became clear that he wasn't coming back here, and we might not last, either.

But if he's really here, it must be to tell me he still wants to make it work. I should be happy. I should be *happy*. I should be—

"What the *hell* are you doing here?"

It's Valeria, her dark mane of hair sweeping between me and Connor so fast that it whips behind her like a cape. I watch them the same way I'd watch something unfold in a dream—like I've suddenly forgotten I'm a part of the scene, so fixated on what's happening in front of me that I'm only half in my body.

"I told you to leave me alone," says Valeria. "You can't just show up here in the middle of the day and try and—what is it you even want, Whit? To get me back? To have me around as some kind of backup girl?"

It's weird enough that Valeria's talking to Connor. It is somehow even weirder to see him talk to her right back.

"I-I'm not here for you, I swear. I thought you were at your sister's place."

She points an accusatory finger at him. "I was on my way, but good to know you're still creeping on my stories even after I blocked you."

"Look, I'm—just seeing some friends," says Connor, holding up his hands as if in self-defense. "It has nothing to do with you. Just go to your sister's. Pretend you didn't see me."

Valeria lets out a hollow laugh. "Of course you don't want to talk. Figures, since I only hear from you when you're lonely or drunk."

"I'm sorry, Valeria. Okay? I'm sorry. But I've got to get going before—"

"Before what, Connor?"

My voice is so steely even I don't recognize it. Connor jerks his head toward me with almost comical speed, but I'm as still as the statue at the end of the quad. My body knows something my brain hasn't processed yet, and every bone in it is telling me to stand my ground.

"Andie. Hi." His voice is strained, and there's this smile I've never seen on his face before, something that crumbles before it fully reaches his lips. He perseveres, his eyes still wide on mine. "I was—I wanted to surprise you."

Usually there are so many words in me that they're threatening to spill out like a Scrabble board. Now there is just this clean, concise hum, like some other Andie has taken over.

"This is certainly a surprise," I say, crossing my arms over my chest.

Valeria's eyebrows fly up. "You two know each other?"

"Yeah. He's my . . ." The word has never had a sour taste to it before. "Connor's my boyfriend."

"Whit's your boyfriend?"

Whit. It didn't occur to me that he'd use the nickname outside of the team in college, or maybe Valeria would have recognized him as the Connor I've talked about long before now.

This is the part where I'm supposed to say something like, *Not anymore, he's not.* I've seen the rom-coms. I've given plenty of advice to people who have been cheated on. It's just that never once in thinking about this kind of scenario did I ever put myself in it.

That's when it really starts to sink in. *Cheated.* While I was working my butt off not just to get into Blue Ridge State but to keep our relationship intact last semester, Connor had already moved on from us. And instead of telling either of us the truth, he'd strung us both along—me last semester, and Valeria now.

It's all so immediately, brutally crystal clear that it feels like walking straight into a glass wall. Something I should have seen coming. Something that's so embarrassingly easy to process and accept that it's probably been right there in my periphery all along.

Connor lowers his voice, using the tone he only ever uses when we're alone. Gentle. Intimate. Like there's a secret we've known our whole lives that most people never figure out.

It used to make me feel so special. Right now it makes me feel anything but.

"Andie, let's just—let me take you to lunch," he pleads. "I can explain."

"Oh, I'd love to see you try," says Valeria, putting a foot between the two of us like a bodyguard. It is clear to me in that moment that her anger for me is bigger than her anger for herself, and I've never been more grateful for her friendship than I am right now.

Even so, I want him to explain. I *need* him to explain, because I need a way to forgive him for it. I'm scrambling for some way to make this okay, for some solution that'll fix this the way I've fixed so many things between us before.

But at the crux of it is a question that can't do anything but break. I don't want to ask it, but I don't have any other choice.

"Why did you transfer back to Little Fells for me, if you'd already found someone else?"

Connor reaches for my hands. I snatch mine back before he can reach them, and the hurt in his eyes is so immediate that it feels like it ricochets right back at me. I'm so used to feeling what he feels that even in this moment I can't stop myself.

His eyes briefly dart to Valeria's like he wishes she'd disappear. Valeria straightens her spine, cutting an intimidating figure in her ruby-red coat and unyielding gaze.

"I didn't find someone else," says Connor, shaking his head. "It was just a confusing time, and I'm so grateful to you for—"

"You miserable jerk. Tell her the truth." Valeria's so riled that there's a vein popping in her forehead I've never seen before. "You ditched half your classes and got academic probation. And I—I felt so *sorry* for you. I let you cry on my shoulder about it for weeks. And this whole time you were lying to Andie about it and making her feel *worse*?"

My ears are ringing. It's not hurt. It's not sadness. It's something I'm not used to feeling, something that curls in my fists and burns from my chest all the way to my cheeks.

"You ditched your classes," I repeat.

Connor's brows knit in desperation, like he's trying to meet my eyes even though we're already looking at each other. "I was overwhelmed. You know the kind of pressure I'm under—"

"And you lied to me, and—and to your *parents*. To *everybody*." I finally take a step forward, and he doesn't dare move to meet me. "Do you have any idea how guilty I've felt? I thought I'd messed with your entire future. You watched your mom come down on me. Your mom, who's the closest thing to a mom I've had for years."

And then the rage simmers out so fast I can feel myself reaching for it again, trying to use it to tether me. It's too late. The tears are already streaming down my cheeks, putting the fire out.

Connor stops trying to talk. Even Valeria's anger seems to be stunned right off her face.

It's not just that I've lost Connor. It's that he's been gone for longer than I knew. At some point, without knowing it, it all slipped away: being in love with my best friend. The future we had planned together. A set of parents who loved me like I was their own—who took care of me when my mom couldn't, and my dad wasn't around nearly enough to try.

I can't move, but I don't have to. The ground already slipped out from under me before I had the chance to fall.

Connor says my name like a lifeline. "Andie."

I ignore it. It's Valeria I turn to, grabbing her hand and squeezing it. "I'll talk to you later, okay?"

There's a quiet nod of understanding, one that speaks to something we both already know: Whatever we find out today, we trust each other. This isn't going to rock our friendship. It's enough of a comfort for me to take a breath and temporarily stanch the tears as I turn to go.

"I'll come with you," Connor offers.

The words form tethers in the air, try to wrap around and soften me. His voice is as familiar to me as my own; the first sound I want to hear when I have news, good or bad or anything in between. Right now it can't even skim the surface of me.

"Don't."

I point myself toward the psychology building, on autopilot until I'm finally standing in the dimly lit studio, face-to-face with the picture of my mother. Staring at her earnest, cheeky smile, at the gleam in her eye, at the determination in her posture. A ghost of a ghost—a version of her I never met, who in the last few months might have become more familiar to me than the one I knew.

The tears start streaming again. "I messed up," I tell her, touching the frame. "I messed up."

I don't even know what part I'm referring to—this thing with Connor might be a grenade thrown into my life, but it was already plenty messed up before then, wasn't it? My own grades. My own fear. My own fixations on other people's problems, instead of facing my own. My own way of holding myself back, time and time again, and telling myself I'm not worth the chances people have taken on me. Blue Ridge State for letting me in; my professor for giving me a second chance; Milo for letting me on the show.

"Andie. Shit. Are you okay?"

I'm too stunned by the sound of Milo himself to stop myself from turning around, ginormous, embarrassing tears and all.

"Oh, hi," I say, and whatever else I was about to attempt is swallowed by an embarrassing hiccup. I open my mouth, trying to collect myself, but it doesn't end up mattering. Milo has already crossed the small room and wrapped his arms around me so fast that I instinctively crush my eyes shut right into his chest, so grateful for the presence and the pressure of him that I can't do anything else.

I spend the next minute scrambling for something to say, some way to recover. Some way to laugh this off and walk away—he may have seen me at my worst, but he doesn't have to *continue* seeing me at it. But at some point it becomes very clear that he's just going to hold me like this for as long as I need it, that he's just going to let me muck up his jacket with my tears, that's he's just going to ride out this storm with me the same way he did back in that little shed in the woods.

And so I let myself cry. I don't know how long, but long enough that it feels like I'm empty of something, something that needed to leave. Something that's been weighing me down so much that it feels like it had its own gravity, and now without it I might float away.

"Valeria told us what happened," Milo says quietly, once most of the tears have stopped. "We were looking for you. I don't know why, but I just . . . had a feeling."

When we pull away the room feels a little colder. Milo's eyes search mine with this careful concern that makes me feel more raw than I've ever been; like he's not just seeing me on the surface with my puffy eyes and red nose and hurt, but all the way down to whatever just left me. His eyes only stray for one moment to the photo behind me, so quick I almost miss it. He must have seen me staring at it when he walked in.

It feels important to tell him then. Like we've seen so much of each other that it's only right he knows. Maybe even long overdue.

"The original Knight," I say, turning to face her again. "Amy Janson. She's, um. My mom."

"Oh." Milo may be caught off guard, but it doesn't take him long to recover. "Is that why you've been here all this time?"

I shake my head. "Well, maybe—maybe a little, at first. But then I was just . . . I fit here. With you and Shay."

Milo gently knocks his shoulder into mine, a quiet way of saying he feels that way, too.

"Your mom was Amy Rose, huh?" He looks between the photo and me, registering the slight surprise on my face. "I should have made the connection. I listened to her show every morning for years."

"You did?" I feel the sting of tears again, but this time I don't shy away from them. They're not the happy kind, but they're still the good kind. It hurts to hear, but it also means more than I can possibly ever say.

"Yeah." Milo looks away, giving me some space to react. "She was amazing."

I nod.

"I didn't get enough years with her, but I . . ." I swipe at my eyes with the heel of my hand. "I know people romanticize the past. That things are always sweeter when you look back. But my mom, she was kind of just magic, you know? Always wanted to go on adventures, whether it was driving all the way up a mountain to see the stars at midnight or check out an ice cream store three towns away."

The tears feel like a relief now, like a way of letting my love for her out into the world; like maybe the energy of it is bigger than I am, even though I've spent so many years trying to hold it in for myself. "She could set anyone at ease. Make anyone laugh. Turn any dull thing into a game."

"I remember," says Milo quietly, his eyes trained just as carefully on the frame as mine are.

I tear my eyes from it, looking up at him meaningfully. "So you get it. I can do my best with all this, but I'm never going to be like she was—she just made everything shine."

Milo lifts his hand toward my face like he's going to hold my cheek in it, like he might brush away the tears. He stops and shakes his head, something more urgent pressing in him, something that roots me to the spot as he says it loud.

"You're right. You're not like her, Andie," he says, with a certainty that cuts right past his usual bluntness. "Your mom was an entertainer. She knew what people needed to hear, whether she was cracking jokes or giving their problems a voice. She helped people get through their shit, and so will you—in your own way. By helping them face it head-on."

For a moment I'm too stunned to answer, not sure which is more overwhelming: how well Milo understood my mom, a person I never even imagined in the same world as his, or how well he understands me.

"I think I'm always going to worry I'm riding her coattails," I admit. "I don't think I even got in here on my own merit. I was the only transfer in my class. I'm worried they just realized who my mom was and let me in because of that."

Milo dismisses this so easily I almost envy him. "Well, I know that's not true. I mean, look at this place."

"Exactly," I say miserably. "I'm a pity admission."

This time Milo does reach out, putting a hand on my shoulder. "There is no such thing."

There is a quiet part of me that has trusted Milo since long before either of us earned it from each other, a trust I feel in the warm pressure of his hand. A trust that makes me want to believe those words are true, and understands, objectively, that they must be.

But as the words settle in me, a sad, but strangely comforting understanding comes right along with them. It isn't just about the school; this feeling is tangled in so much else. In everything that I do, every moment I won't be able to turn over my shoulder and ask my mom what she thinks, or feel her pride.

Whether or not I belonged here has felt like a thing I could measure. I'd be worthy of her legacy, or not. But the truth is that moments I've lost with her are immeasurable, and no amount of wondering about admissions or how well I do on the show or any other measuring stick I can hold to her legacy is going to bring them back.

This feels like one of those moments right now. The kind where I'd be able to call her or come home to her. Maybe even a moment that would never have happened if she'd been around, because Connor wouldn't have had to fill a space she left behind.

The whole mess comes crushing back then, heavy in my chest.

"And on top of that . . . this thing with Connor," I say.

I grit my teeth. It's the hurt. The humiliation. It's too much to process right now, or maybe even forever; there are pieces of myself starting to unravel right now that I've known my entire life. I think of that stupid memoir I've been planning to write for half my life, all these chapters I tried to fit neatly into place.

Now the pages are all at my feet, scattered before I could even put them together. I can't believe I was naive enough to think I could write them in the first place. I can't believe I let Connor be one of the strings that tied them together. Only now do I understand it's because I just plain didn't have enough faith in myself to begin with, and that's maybe the most brutal realization I've made in this whole mess.

"I feel so stupid," I admit. "I really thought . . . I really thought I could make this work. I love him."

Love. Not loved. I can't make it go away, can't shake an entire lifetime of love from under my skin; even trying to see as far into the future as I can let myself in this moment, I'm not sure if I ever will.

But I don't have to explain it to Milo. He's spent months with the same hurt in his heart. With the strange way you have to rearrange yourself when you can't make the love you have for someone go away, but have to wait for it to take a new shape. Connor will always be my childhood best friend and my first love, the same way Nora was his.

"Well, it's like my dad always said," says Milo, squeezing my shoulder gently. "Anything worth doing starts with a mess. Maybe . . . this one is yours."

It's not the first time I've thought of those words since Milo said them to me all those weeks ago, but it's the first time I can fully appreciate them. I've spent my whole life with a plan. Neat, tidy, organized. Fitting myself like a key into other people's locks just so I could call their homes my own.

But just because Connor's family won't be mine anymore doesn't mean I'm on my own. Maybe I'm a mess now, but I'm in the middle of everyone else's mess, too. Milo's and Shay's and Val's. We might not know where we fit yet, but we've got a strong grip on one another, and maybe that's all you get to ask for at this point in your life. Maybe it's the only thing you really need.

"You're right. He's right," I amend. I take in a shaky breath, trying to explain—not to excuse the time it's going to take for me to get past this, but so he'll get it. "I think for a while, I was just . . . I mean, my parents met here. They were best friends first, and then they fell in love. And they were happy." I tilt my head as if the world is tilting with me, as if I'm trying to understand the new view. "I just thought—that I could try to have that, too. I could re-create the same magic my mom made. Have her same shine. It felt like the universe wanted me to—I mean, Connor and I have known each other for practically our entire lives. Our moms were best friends. And his mom was like . . ."

Milo nods in understanding. Doesn't try to tell me I'm wrong to think of her that way. Doesn't try to talk me down from the importance of it all, or the magnitude of what just happened.

"I gotta pull an Andie Rose right now. So forgive me for asking." Milo's teeth graze his lower lip in a moment of hesitation, and I know what the question is before he even asks it. "Have you talked to your dad about these feelings?"

I lean forward, gently knocking my forehead into his chest. "No," I tell him. "But I did get in touch."

Milo lifts his hand from my shoulder and presses it to the back of my head, holding me steady. "Good."

"Seems like you made some headway with Harley last night, too."

He takes his hand off and we separate again, Milo looking sheepish like he'd forgotten all about it until now. "Yeah, well."

"Where did you leave it?"

Milo rolls his eyes affectionately. "Can we please have five whole minutes where you're not worried about anyone else's shit?"

But that's just it. Somewhere along the way, his issues started feeling like mine, too. Not the way they were at the beginning of the semester, when I wanted to fix things for the sake of fixing them. But because I want to be with him through it, the same way he has been for me. The same way I sense we will be far beyond this.

"Milo," I say quietly, imploringly.

His gaze is utterly still on mine for a moment, a hush in the air between us. Then he blinks a few times like he's pulling himself out of something. "Well. You were—I mean, I'm glad you told me what you thought about the whole thing. Because you were right. About where Harley was coming from. And about . . . how the stuff with our dad played into it."

"Yeah?"

"Yeah." Milo clears his throat. "It turns out they fell for each other before our dad's accident. She was always going to break up with me, then she and Harley were going to wait for a while to actually do anything. But after what happened to our dad, there just wasn't a moment that felt right for any of it. And everything just kind of—escalated, after that."

I nod. We both know by now that grief doesn't play by anybody's rules.

Milo lowers his head, his shoulders easing with it. "I'll always be hurt about how it happened. But I can understand more of it now. Mostly because I could tell they meant it. The last thing they wanted to do was hurt me. But they were both hurting too much to be apart from each other, and I—I guess I get it. Now that I'm actually trying to."

"That must be a relief," I say softly.

Milo lets loose a heavy breath, reaching a hand for the back of his neck. "I mean. We've got a long way to go. But I've—missed him. And Nora." His voice is tight when he adds, "And talking to them—they said they've missed me, too."

There's something uncertain, almost boyish in his expression. Some side of him that I've always known was there just under the surface, but he's letting me see for the first time. Something cautious. Something searching. Like he's only letting this part of himself go in this moment because he knows I'm a safe place to land.

"I hope it works out," I tell him.

Even with his overly tall height our faces are inches apart, so close it feels like we're not just separate from the people beyond the door, but everything else.

"Me too," he says. "And I do feel a lot more clearheaded about this transfer thing. I might not know what I'm doing yet, but . . . at least I'll feel good about it when I do."

My throat is tight, but I still manage to say, "Good." I may have to look down for a beat when I say it, but we both know I mean it.

"Hey, Andie."

I glance back up at him, into the depths of those mossy eyes.

"I know you want to be like your mom. Trust me, I do." Milo's voice takes on this rasp to it, like he's on the edge of something he usually tries not to touch. "Even forgiving Harley . . . part of me was open to it because I know it's what my dad would do. I want to be like him, too."

His head ducks down, curls almost covering his eyes. I want to reach up and brush them out of his face, want to silently let him know he doesn't have to hide from me. But he knows that. By now, we both do.

"I wish I could have met him," I say quietly. "But I don't have to have known him to know he's proud of you."

Now it's Milo's eyes that mist up, so fast that I catch him trying to laugh at himself to cover it up. In the end, though, he just stares back at me and lets the words sink in before hitting me with a few choice words of his own.

"Well. Same to you," he says. "And you know, you don't need to re-create your mom's shine. You've got that all on your own."

It feels kind of wobbly, and another tear threatens to fall in the process, but I can't help the smile blooming on my face.

I want to tell him he's wrong. Want to brush it off before it can sink in some place where it doesn't feel deserved. But then there's this moment—this hypnotizing, heart-stalling moment where his warm palm is cupping my cheek and my own hand is bracing against his forearm and our eyes are locked, and it all falls away. The self-doubt. The hurt. The impossibility of everything that just happened today, and all the ways it will impact every corner of my life.

My calves burn and my legs quiver with anticipation as I lift myself up to my toes, Milo already leaning in to meet me. Our foreheads touch. I feel his breath on mine, coffee and mint and Milo.

"I . . . want to kiss you," he says quietly.

The words reach something deep in the core of me before they reach my ears, making my limbs feel weak in a way they never have before. My eyes slide closed. It isn't a feeling I recognize—it's not desperate, it's not pining, it's not scrambling to keep up. But it still burns. It burns in a way I never thought something could.

"But . . ."

And then something shifts. Some piece of reality edges its way back in, slices us both down the middle. He presses his forehead into mine even further, but with the pressure of an apology, not a release.

"Shit. I'm—I'm your RA."

I let out a strangled laugh. "*Milo.*" I don't bother pointing out that so long as we let the housing committee know, it doesn't really matter. I can't point out anything just about now, because I'm reeling from the shock of it all. The immensity of these feelings that are swimming their way up into the surface of me like they've been there for longer than I was ever able to admit.

I look up at Milo with a hesitancy that feels intimate, like I am less scared of what I'll see in his face and more scared of what I'll feel when I see it. But Milo's eyes are trained on the floor.

"And I . . . I don't even know what I'm doing next year," he mutters.

There it is. The truth that I wasn't ignoring, but in the heat of the moment, I forgot. It isn't one I can resent him for in the slightest—the truth is, I'm proud of him. Proud that he put himself out there. That he might take a chance across the country. And more important, that he's working to resolve everything with Harley first.

So this tumult of emotion I'm feeling. This pull, this burn—it's reactionary. My life has just spiraled out of control, and now I'm spiraling even more. Spiraling straight into Milo, who is too important to drag down with me.

"And I guess—well," I say, my voice flimsy even in my own ears. "I'd say I just broke up with Connor, but we didn't even get to that part."

It's weird to think he might still be here somewhere. That this world we built together could just implode and we could be closer to each other than we've ever been. I feel this wave of nausea and dread, the reality of it sinking back under my skin.

Milo looks uncertain about what to say next, so instead I try to lighten the mood, teasing him. "And you don't believe in love anymore anyway," I say lightly. "What is it you said at the beginning of the semester? 'Love is a scam'?"

I'm expecting him to laugh, but Milo's eyes darken, sweeping to the floor. "Well. I think . . ." He swallows hard. "You're right. This is just—it's been a weird day."

I'm not sure whether to press the point. Of all the day's surprises, this might be the strangest of all—the way my heart isn't just slamming in my chest, but seizing, pieces of Milo suddenly so woven into it that it must have changed its shape.

As I'm trying to decide, my phone vibrates in my pocket. I pull it out, unsurprised to see Connor's name lighting up the screen.

Before I answer, I feel the weight of Milo's eyes on mine. It's not a look that says, *Are you going to answer?* Or *What are you going to do?* It's a clear *Do you need me?* And it lands somewhere soft.

"Thank you for . . . for everything," I tell him. Then I nod, more to myself than to him. "I'm gonna finish this."

Milo nods back, reaching out to squeeze my shoulder one last time. "You got this, new kid."

The warmth of it lingers long after Milo is gone.

Chapter Twenty-Six

But I don't finish it. I open my phone to find Connor has texted me a stream of apologies, pleas to hear him out. Then a direct: Please don't say you're breaking up with me. I text back a short I need you to leave me alone right now. Then I pocket my phone. I walk to the arboretum and sit on my favorite bench and wait—wait for enough time to pass that the sun has gone, and Connor will have to have gone home with it.

I know what I have to do, but it's too much, too soon to let it all go. How do you quit an entire person? How do you give up on someone who has defined almost every version of love you know?

It seems doubly unfair that I have to be the one who does the hardest thing here by ending it. The same way I've been upset with my dad for leaving me to decide whether he gets to be part of my life, I'm at another impasse where a choice has been forced on me. One I can't will away. One I can only put off until I'm ready to deal with it. And with the shock of this still so fresh, I know I can't.

When I finally get up from my perch, my plan is to dive face-first into my pillow and sleep until Shay's alarm wakes us both up for the Monday broadcast. What happens instead is I turn the doorknob to my room, and find Valeria and Shay sitting on Shay's bed and Milo sitting on my desk chair, the little collapsible table

Shay sometimes uses for bookstagramming overloaded with a half-empty bottle of room-temperature rosé, Tastykakes, and Goldfish.

The sight of Milo splits something in me, opens me up to a feeling I know too well because I've felt it before. That afternoon we fell into each other at the snowball fight. The first time I saw him slip into his Knight persona in the studio. The rub of his shoulder on mine in that shed in the woods. Earlier today, with his springtime eyes and the warmth of his forehead on mine.

So many countless moments I've bulldozed past and dismissed. Moments I press back down so fast that they pinch in my chest, sharp and painful, too much to be contained.

"You're *here*," Valeria exclaims.

Luckily, the room full of complete and utter lightweights doesn't notice my momentary pause; despite only being half a glass deep each, Shay is positively glowing, Valeria appears to be missing both a sock and one of her dangly earrings, and Milo is—

Well. Milo is Milo. Clear-eyed and staring at me with a wry expression the same as he always does, that somehow makes me weak in the knees in a way I've never let it before.

"I was never here," he says, raising his hands up. "Legally, I was in my room the entire time, unaware of underage drinking taking place on my floor."

"*You're* underage, you dope," says Shay, kicking her foot in the air for emphasis.

Valeria has already leapt off the bed, enveloping me in a hug so tight and so effusive that bones in my back crack during the impact of it. I squeeze her right back. Only then do I understand that I wasn't waiting for closure with Connor. What I needed was this. My friends, all here and waiting for me with my favorite snacks and their unwavering love and, judging by the unmistakable sound of Kelly Clarkson's "Since U Been Gone" blasting from Shay's laptop, a breakup playlist that is already in full swing.

"Fuck Connor," says Valeria. I can tell she was crying at some point today from the slight congestion in her voice, but she's all indignation and rosé now. "I'm so fucking sorry, Andie."

And frankly, I'm too overwhelmed with how grateful I am for the All-Knighters to even think of Connor right now. "You guys . . ."

Before I can get too weepy, Shay chucks a wrapped twin set of Tastykakes at my head, a knowing smile on her face. I let out a guffaw—maybe the first time I've fully laughed all day—just barely catching them before they hit the floor.

"I've taken the liberty of changing the group chat's name to 'Fuck Connor Whit,'" says Shay, holding up her phone proudly.

"Ah, yes," says Milo dryly, taking a swig of what appears to be Semi-Eternal Darkness. "The group chat I've begged to be removed from all semester."

Valeria releases me, only so she can bop Milo on the head on the way to rejoining Shay on the mattress. Milo looks so gloriously affronted by this gesture that I end up laughing again despite myself.

"You love us," says Valeria.

"Don't put words in my mouth," says Milo. "I affectionately tolerate you."

Then he uses his foot to hook the chair from Shay's desk and pull it closer to him, beckoning for me to sit next to him. I settle into it with a mingling thrill and guilt, the two of them a perilous cocktail of emotions I can't process right now. Fortunately, a solution for dealing with them comes in the form of a mug half-full of rosé, which Shay hands me with absurd ceremony.

I recognize Milo's chicken mug on the spot. "Oh my gosh. It's Rosaline," I say, pointing at one of them.

I turn to look over at him, and his grin is broad enough to make my heart stutter. He waits until I take a sip, then he leans in to point at the other chickens and says, "And here's Patricia. And James. And Abigail, and Camille . . ."

We take a brief and much-needed pause to tease Milo to high

heaven for not only naming all his mother's chickens, but recognizing them on sight. I sag a little deeper into the desk chair, some final tension leaving me. The emptiness doesn't feel so empty now, but more like it's making room for something else. Something a whole lot like this.

"Seriously, though, Andie," says Shay. "I'm so sorry. And when you want to talk about it for real . . . we're all here for you."

"Always," Valeria iterates.

I should tell them it isn't really over yet. Not the way they think it is, at least. But Shay has her head on Valeria's shoulder, and Valeria's hand is resting on her thigh, and Milo is smiling this sleepy, exasperated smile that ignites something so tender in me I can't bear to put it out.

We all lift up our mugs for a "good riddance" toast. There's the clink of ceramic and the love in the air between us and the solidarity of our long, drawn-out sips. There's another hour of eating and drinking, of swapping stories about our exes, of intermittently breaking out into fits of giggles over things that happened or things that could have been.

And then there's Shay trying to leave with Valeria quietly, saying she wants to meet her roommate's cat. There's Milo still hovering at the open door, his mug of coffee empty, his dark curls tousled, his cheeks flushed.

"Hey," he says quietly, so the rest of the hall can't overhear. "I know you, so. I know shit's going to be okay."

I raise up his chicken mug, biting down the surge of guilt. "Same to you."

He salutes me, sliding out of the entryway, but not before I see something telltale in his eyes. Something that aches the same way I ache; something taking shape before I understand the depth of it. The understanding that no matter what happens—if we both stay here, or we're flung thousands of miles apart—we are important to each other, and we will be for the rest of our lives.

The moment everyone is gone, I flick out the lights. No more thinking. No more feeling. I fall asleep so quickly and so thoroughly that my body can forget it all, even if the *beat, beat, beat* of my heart pulses it the whole night through.

Chapter Twenty-Seven

The next morning is so familiar in its rhythms that I could almost forget that my life capsized faster than that ill-fated kayak on the lake. Almost, if it weren't for the way I suddenly don't know how to safely look at Milo, the same way you're not sure how to look at an eclipse. I want to look. I *have* to look. I just know that it'll be bad news if I do.

Apparently yesterday I opened the floodgates to something, and now it can't be stopped. I gave an inch and my body took a mile. Suddenly I can't hear Milo's laugh on the air without thinking about how when he held me yesterday, I could feel his voice in his chest. I can't look into his eyes without my brain conjuring words like "seagrass" and "springtime" and "mint." I can't hold a conversation with him without staring at his lips and thinking about how close mine came to them. The *almost* of it all.

The feelings are so intense that they should be a full-body shock. I should be WebMD-ing "sweaty palms" and "complete inability to rationally function in front of a person you mutually friend-zoned months ago." But that's the telling part—it isn't a shock. It's almost a relief. Like I've just been waiting to let myself feel it, and now that I do, it's clear I'll never be able to unfeel it again.

Just in time for Milo to transfer, and me to be stuck in the kind of limbo with Connor that my brain is unhelpfully refusing to process right now. Cherry chocolate *jam,* am I done for.

It doesn't help that Milo's in top form during the broadcast, even while Shay and I are blinking our post-rosé selves awake. Whatever it is that happened with Harley, it looks like some kind of weight has been lifted off his shoulders. I don't know if anyone else would notice, but it seems like he laughs a little more readily. Like his wry remarks are 10 percent less grim. Like he's more excited for the day and less bracing himself for it.

Because the universe has decided to show me one mercy in this very confusing time, Milo immediately has to duck out for a shift at Bagelopolis, leaving me and Shay to deal with packaging the radio show into podcast form before we start our shift an hour later.

"So," I say, sidling up to Shay at the computer. "How was Valeria's cat?"

I don't miss the dimple puckering on Shay's cheek as she tries to bite down a smile. "Darcy's a brat. I'm gonna cat-nap him."

I twist a strand of my hair innocently. "Before or after you change out of yesterday's clothes?"

Shay swats at my shoulder. "Andie Rose," she scolds me with a grin. "It wasn't like that. It just got late, is all."

"Yeah, well. With her ex *extremely* out of the picture . . ." I shudder, an image of her and Connor arguing in the quad still just as jarring in my mind as it was in real life. "Eh. Sorry. Too soon for jokes."

Shay focuses back on typing and I assume the subject is dropped. That is, until she stares at the screen for a few moments and says, "I think . . . I mean, last night was really fun. It's like I said. I'm glad we can just be friends." Her lips pucker thoughtfully. "Actually, I think after yesterday, I kind of . . ."

The drop in her tone is uncharacteristically self-conscious, even cautious. Like she wants to say it, but doesn't want to put whatever it is on me.

"Kind of what?" I press, making it clear I don't mind.

Shay shakes her head. "I mean, no offense, since he's your ex and all. But Connor's a tool. *That's* the guy she was so hung up on that she didn't know whether or not to date me?"

I bite down the reflex to defend him, embarrassed at how readily it comes. "I don't know if I'd look at it that way," I say, both for Valeria's sake and for mine. I hate to admit it, but Connor has always had a magnetism to him. The confidence, the small-town charm, the way he makes me—well, makes people feel special when he takes the time for them. When you know everyone in the room wants to be at his side, but he only has eyes for you.

I will the two pangs in my heart to just go away, but they don't. One of them is aching from losing Connor; the other may be tiny, but it's still wild and desperate, reminding me that technically it isn't over, that I don't have to let this go.

"Sorry. I shouldn't even be—I mean, I can't even imagine how you're feeling about the whole thing right now," says Shay. "Breaking up with him after all this time."

I let out a weird hiccupping laugh. "Well."

"Anyway. I know what'll take our minds off all the bullshit," says Shay, tapping the notes Milo was using as a script for today's broadcast. "The dance party in the quad."

I tilt my head at the screen. It's a dance party, sure, but also billed as a surefire way to get ribbons—the upperclassmen organizers legitimately throw every color of them into the crowd. The whole thing is perfectly timed out, too. I know the exact playlist for the event, because one of the organizers set it up to play from our station and taped it up on the booth for everyone's reference. It's one of the rare times anyone who isn't one of the three of us ever comes in here, but the dance party being broadcast from here instead of someone's playlist on a loudspeaker is a nod to the ribbon hunt's roots.

I wait for the clench of my stomach, the same one I've felt worrying before every ribbon event. Instead there's just a flood of relief. An anticipation that isn't dread, but excitement—the idea of going out with my friends and dancing for the fun of it, without any other goals or plans in mind.

"It starts at three," Shay reminds me.

That's just in time to get back from our shift, if we go straight there from Bagelopolis. Plus it ends at five, which gives me plenty of time to get to the statistics exam I spent all the time at Milo's studying for.

"Do you think it's okay if I just leave my stuff here for the day?" I ask, knowing full well that a shoulder bag will only hinder my ability to jump up and down while shouting lyrics at the top of my lungs.

Shay glances over at the mound of stuff the sound engineer and DJs left in the corner. "Knock yourself out."

"Given my dance skills, that's a real possibility today."

Shay pats me on the arm. "We'll protect you from yourself."

I'm expecting the rest of the day to grind as painfully as the day before did, for the shadow of what Connor did to cast everything in ugly colors. I ready my syndicated-talk-show smile and throw myself into work, hoping if I keep moving fast enough, I won't have to think.

But at some point I stop willfully forgetting what happened; I just forget. It's a busy day at Bagelopolis, the kind that marks a difference between who I was in January and who I'm becoming now. The Andie who isn't just tethered by the idea of this place, but the people in it. By Shay, who spends the entirety of our shift making me giggle by inventing horrific bagel combinations for famous book characters (Peeta Mellark's won with "a bagel inside of a bagel with bagel-flavored cream cheese, because bread"). By Valeria, who shows up during our lunch break to bring Shay a book and drill me on a few extra stats questions before the test. By Milo, who is in the back for most of his shift, but still manages to make me laugh out loud with a new name tag that reads ANDIE ROSÉ in deference to our mild hangovers.

By the time we're all released for the dance party, I'm already in absurdly high spirits, buoyed by friendship and cookie dough cream cheese and the thumping bass of a Beyoncé song in the distance. Milo waves us off to go meet up with one of his sisters on campus, and Shay and Valeria and I head straight into the maelstrom of Blue Ridge students getting dangerously amped by the key changes to "Love On Top."

"Andie," says Shay, jostling my shoulder in an up-and-down motion. "You have to *dance*."

"I am dancing," I protest.

Valeria shakes her head at me. "You're doing the a cappella bop."

Shay snickers, not unkindly, and I ask, "The what?"

"That thing where you . . ." Instead of explaining, Valeria demonstrates, doing an all-too-accurate impression of me shifting my weight between my feet and vaguely moving my arms with them. "That bop."

I stop my bopping. "Well, I can't dance."

"Bullshit," says Shay, yanking me by the elbow with one hand and yanking Valeria by the elbow with the other. "Dancing isn't a skill, it's a goddamn right. And you're a single woman now. Nothing to hold you back."

I feel the press of bodies against us, the sound of the music nearly drowned out by people whooping and shouting and singing along to the words. My heart starts beating like it never has before, so high in my chest it feels like it might burst. I glom onto Shay and Valeria, equal parts thrill and terror, feeling less like I am walking into a crowd of strangers and more like I'm walking into a new version of my life. Something I couldn't fully see on my own, but is all too clear with two of my best friends on either side of me, pulling me through.

"Now dance like you *mean* it," Shay yells over the noise.

I grin back at her, pinching my nose with one hand and making a sea-diving gesture with the other as I lower myself to the ground.

"Still counts!" says Valeria, letting out a hoot of approval.

Shay's laughing hard enough that she's doubled over, almost as low to the ground as I am. "What else have you got, Andie?"

I jokingly pretend to drive a bus with one hand and use the other to open an invisible bus door and welcome a passenger in. Valeria enters my "bus" without missing a beat, getting into the back seat and grooving right alongside me in a manner decidedly more graceful, but dorky nonetheless. Shay groans and knocks on the invisible bus door until we let her in and starts grooving beside us.

"Where is this godforsaken bus going?" she asks.

"The Kingdom of Lumarin!" I exclaim.

I can practically feel the heat of Valeria blushing next to me, but it's as if now that we're in the middle of this crowd, all our usual self-consciousness has worn away.

"Then you'd better fasten your seat belts," she says, "because there's a *whooole* lot of witchcraft and confusing romantic shit ahead!"

Shay unsheathes a fake sword. "Bring it on!"

And then for a long while, the rest of the world just falls away. We're goofing off and jumping and dancing and yelling, three people in a crowd of hundreds, ribbons flying everywhere but none of us even bothering to reach for them. We're just sweaty limbs and ridiculous cackling and breathless energy, like there isn't a past to worry over or a future to account for. The kind of moment that forms a tattoo in your heart before you even fully understand how much it means to you, living in it and outside it at the same time, making it a part of your story before you know how the story ends.

There's a brief scheduled pause in the music so the upperclassmen can do a recap of this year's ribbon hunt, which I know from asking around that they do just before they unleash a bunch of ribbons on the crowd. I reach out and hug Valeria and Shay, the three of us sticky and grinning and smushed against one another.

"I'll be back in a few minutes," I tell them.

Valeria points to the other end of the quad. "I'm gonna grab us some water bottles."

Shay glances to the left. "And I gotta pee. Meet back here in a few?"

"Sounds good," I say, pulling out my phone before I even reach the end of the crowd. I'm all buzz and adrenaline and bass, but it's grounding. Clarifying. I don't know if my thoughts have ever been so clear, if I've ever felt so certain about anything.

It will be brutal. It will hurt for longer than I can say. But I can't put it off anymore—I have to break up with Connor.

Once I can hear my own thoughts instead of the chattering of the crowd, I press the phone to my face, letting it ring. It rings and rings and rings, my heart still beating so hard I can feel it in my ear, my jaw, every part of the screen against my head.

I'm about to get Connor's voicemail when instead I get Connor's voice.

"Andie?"

I pull the phone away, trying to figure out why he sounds like he's right in front of me. Then I realize that he is, in fact, right in front of me.

His hair is mussed, his eyes practically bruised from lack of sleep, his clothes all wrinkled. I'm so stunned to see him that it barely registers, my brain trying desperately to catch up to what's right in front of me.

"I, uh. I didn't leave last night," he explains. "I stayed with some soccer buddies."

I hold up my phone. "I was just . . ."

Calling to break up with you, is what I should say.

But Connor gives me a rueful smile. "Even now we're on the same wavelength, huh?"

I'm not the one saying the words, but somehow they still leave a bitter taste in my mouth. I step farther away from the quad, like I don't want Connor's presence to taint the magic I'm still coming down from. Connor follows one step behind, his eyes trained on me.

We reach the outside of an academic building where the crowd has thinned out and I stop. "Connor, I'm sorry, but . . ." It feels so weird to say. The finality of it. The way a few small words can finish something bigger than I can measure. "I'm done."

His expression crumples so quickly that I can't help the way my heart sinks—like watching him fall during that soccer game where he screwed up his knee, or when we were little kids and someone made fun of his slight stutter. There's this urge to comfort him, to wipe the hurt from his face, that feels too loud to ignore.

"Andie. Andie, please," he says, tears already clogging his throat. "Just . . . is there somewhere we can talk? I have so much I need to say. Things I should have said a long time ago."

I glance down at my phone, willing myself not to waver. "I have an exam. You can follow me to the studio to get my stuff. But after that, I have to go."

"Of course," says Connor, his head bobbing. "We can talk there?"

I blow a breath out through my teeth, surprised at my own impatience. "Yeah. Sure."

We walk over to the studio without another word, Connor

slouching with his hands in his pockets and watching me closely, me shooting a quick text to Valeria and Shay not to wait up for me before picking up the pace. I need this to be finished.

I've spent too much time worrying about my future with Connor. I don't think I even understood how much until I spent most of this day not worrying about him at all. I've always had space for him the way I have space in myself for everyone I love—but after today, after feeling so light and oddly free, I realize his space had its own weight. I've been pulling it for ages, and it's only gotten heavier this past year.

I can't hold on to it anymore.

If Connor senses the finality of the conversation we're about to have, he sure doesn't show it. The instant the door to the studio closes he takes stock of the place like this is a social visit, like he's expecting me to give the whole tour. Music from the dance party set list is playing lightly from the booth, and Connor even tries to jokingly dance to it, like he can lighten the mood. Then he spots my backpack in the corner, sees the ribbons poking out of the front pocket.

"I can't believe how hard you must have worked to get all of those," he says, the waver in his voice undermining all his bravado.

My own voice is unyielding. "Yeah. Maybe someone else will want them."

Connor takes a step toward me and I take a step back, so quickly that he startles.

"You mean it, huh?" he asks, deflating again. "After all this time, you'd really just give up on us."

There's this sweeping tone in his voice, romantic and tragic, the kind that might have made my heart skip a beat in some other circumstance.

"You cheated on me, Connor," I say, shattering the spell of it. "And lied to me and to everyone we know about your transfer in a way that made me look like the biggest jerk in Little Fells."

"And I'll never not be sorry about it," says Connor. "You know how much pressure I was under. I was so embarrassed. I didn't want you to know the truth."

"But I suppose it was okay for your *other* girlfriend to know it," I say.

"Everything with Valeria happened because I was so ashamed. She was tutoring me. She already knew, and I just— It's not an excuse," he says quickly, when he sees my scowl deepening. "I just needed to explain."

He runs a hand through his hair, taking a seat in the chair by the sound console. Shay's chair. He glances at the chair next to it, clearly expecting me to sit down next to him. But if I let myself get settled, he'll have more time to try to talk me out of this, and that's the last thing I need.

"I mean, I know I can't expect you to forgive me right away . . ."

He leaves the sentence hanging like I'm going to set terms, or give some timeline for that forgiveness. "Connor, you've been the one saying over and over how difficult the distance was," I say instead. If I can't appeal to the fact that he's hurt me, I might as well remind him what it'll do to him, too. "That's not going to change. You'll be in Little Fells and I'll be here."

"About that."

I tilt my head sharply, narrowing my eyes at him.

"Uh—so my dad has a friend. It'd be a big favor, but . . ." Connor takes a breath, a shaky smile forming on his face. "He might be able to get me back into Blue Ridge next year."

My jaw goes tight enough to chip a tooth.

"Good for you," I say tersely.

Connor is earnest. Insistent. Like this blow to his pride is something he's doing for my benefit, and nobody else. "We'd be together."

"No. We wouldn't," I say calmly. "I'm breaking up with you."

"After everything we've been through? Just like that?"

Connor leans back on the console, trying to seem confident, like he knows exactly what to say next. He looks more like his father than he ever has.

"I know you, Andie. Past, present, future. I've been there for everything. Do you think we'll ever find other people who know us half as well as we know each other?" He sits on the edge of the seat, pressing a hand to his chest. "I know how to make you happy. I *want* to make you happy."

I say it as gently as I can, even though I'm saying it through my teeth. "I don't think either of us has been happy in a long time."

Connor just continues on like he hasn't heard me, not even giving the words a chance to land. "This is all just—it's growing pains. Or maybe it's being away from Little Fells so long. I mean, maybe this place is the problem. We weren't supposed to be in a place like this." He gestures out at the campus beyond these walls. "Do you really feel like you belong here?"

"Excuse me?"

Connor recognizes the edge in my voice and tries to recover. "What I mean is—we have so many friends in Little Fells. We were so happy. We never had problems before then."

"You created the problem, Connor. Not me," I say clearly. "And now on top of everything, you're going to sit here and imply I'm not good enough to be here?"

"Well. Andie. You didn't even get in the first time around."

It takes a lot to make me angry. And up until now, I didn't even think I had it in me to kick it up a notch to actual rage. But it comes swarming through me anyway, this roaring, fiery blaze that starts in my core and rushes through me so fast I'm almost dizzy with it.

"I didn't get in because of *you*, Connor."

I'm not yelling, but the way Connor's jaw drops in surprise, I might as well be. I've never seen myself this riled, so of course, neither has he.

But it's been years of holding this in my heart. The anxiety over my grades and the heartbreak from the rejection and the exhaustion of doing everything, *anything* I could to find my way back here to my mom. To the dream I had for myself long before I knew she wouldn't be there to see it.

"I spent our entire sophomore year focusing on *your* classes and *your* pressure from your parents and I ended up with a bunch of Cs," I say. "You asked for my help. You asked and asked and asked, and I gave it. And I never held that against you because that was my choice, but—" I have to pause, only because I've never felt this kind of fury before. I don't know how to hold on to it, but I need it. I need to say this here and now, to let it out of myself so I never have to carry it again. "How dare you bring that up. When you should know full well why I didn't get in the first time. Why I had to work twice as hard to get in on a transfer."

"But—it's not like I wanted you to fail at my expense," Connor says defensively. "I mean, come on, Andie."

I shake my head. He knew I was skipping out on my own work to study for his back then, the same way he's known about it this whole semester. For a moment I'm back to Valentine's Day, sitting on my bed, Connor's voice low in my ears: *You'd still give up all this time to make this happen for me?*

"And now I'm doing it again, aren't I?" I say, letting out a strangled laugh. I felt so lost here in the beginning that I relied on something that I knew I could do: help Connor. All this work scrambling around to get his ribbons when I should have been studying, or exploring campus, or spending more time with my friends—I was so worried about keeping my place with him, with his family, that I barely let myself find a place *here*.

But I don't need that crutch anymore. I'm not lost. And I can tell Connor knows it when he suddenly stands up, not quite matching my anger but coming close. "You're acting like I'm the only bad guy here."

"Oh yeah?" This time I'm the one who takes a step toward him. He has half a foot on me, but I've never felt taller in my life. "And what did I do?"

"You clearly fell for another guy."

My skin feels hot enough to ignite. "Be careful what you say next, Connor, because there's only one cheater in this room."

"Don't pretend you don't have some dumb crush on your RA."

The guilt is so immediate that for the first time, I know it's true. I *do* have a crush on Milo. It's been simmering for months, and only now has it started to boil and burn.

But that's just it—the difference between me and Connor. I never would have acted on it. I know myself, and I know Milo. I would never cheat on anyone, and he never would have let himself be a part of it.

Connor takes my stunned silence and rolls with it. "I mean, for Christ's sake, you just dragged me into a windowless room with his *picture* mounted on the wall; who knows what you've been up to in—"

"This is a recording studio. He's the Knight," I spit back.

"And you're in here all the time because . . . ?"

It's not like I mean to say it. But seeing the way his eyebrows raise in this suggestive, accusatory way makes my stomach roil, both on my behalf and Milo's.

"Because I'm the Squire," I tell him.

Connor lets out a laugh that borders on mean. "You're the *what* now?"

"Forget it," I mumble. Given the state of this conversation, it'd be a waste of breath to explain. "It doesn't matter."

"It does. I know you. And yesterday you weren't going to break up with me. You were going to give me another chance." He gestures at Milo's picture on the wall, unintentionally also gesturing right at my mom. He doesn't even notice her there. Somehow that stings worse than everything else he's said so far. "Tell me if that Milo Flynn guy didn't exist, we wouldn't still be together."

I open my mouth to tell him how wrong he is, but the door crashes open. A very wide-eyed sound engineer stares at the two of us with undisguised panic before diving toward the console behind Connor and flicking off a switch. A light turns from green to red. I stare at it like it's something unholy, the realization dawning on me before the engineer even opens her mouth.

"Um," she says, "so—you were broadcasting live."

Connor must have knocked it on when he was leaning on the console. And we're both too close to the mic for it not to pick us up.

"The dance party in the quad," I say, my voice flat with horror.

The engineer winces. "I got here as fast as I could. But the whole thing played over the music."

"Oh, no. Oh, *no*."

Those are apparently the only two words left in my vocabulary, because when I reach into my brain, that's all I can seem to think, too.

"Great," says Connor, blowing out a breath and clearly not recognizing the magnitude of what we just did.

I'm not sure if I can even recognize it myself. I'm rooted to the spot, my brain replaying our conversation like some kind of horror-movie film reel as the engineer backs out of the studio like she just walked in on a crime and doesn't want to be implicated in it.

"We just revealed the Knight to the whole school."

I don't say it to Connor so much as to the room. It feels like he's not even here anymore. It's just me and my complete and utter self-hatred, me and the knowledge that I've let both Milo and my mother's legacy down.

"Why do you even care so much?" Connor asks.

I turn to look at him. This boy I've known and loved. This boy I folded up paper fortune-tellers with and kissed in school parking lots and shared a blanket with at homecoming games and picked out wedding songs for. This boy who knew me with my mom and without her; this boy who has shared his parents with me for years, even when I could never fully feel like I belonged; this boy who shaped so much of me that he'll always be there, even when he's not.

And still, I never told him the truth about my mom being the Knight. I used to wonder why it was so important to me that the secret be just mine. But now in this moment, I think I understand— it's not that I don't belong at Blue Ridge. It's that I never really belonged with Connor. I might have been able to convince myself in every other way that I did, but the memory of my mom was the one thing too precious to put on the line.

"I have to go," I tell him.

Connor has the nerve to look bewildered. "So that's just . . . it, then?"

All the anger is blown out of him now. There's just Connor, eight and eighteen at the same time, looking so lost that it feels like I'm going against every instinct not to guide him.

Maybe someday we can be friends again. Once we're both un-tangled from the pressure and the hurt that brought us here, and can find some new kind of baseline to meet each other. But for now all I can say is, "That's it."

He hangs his head. There are a few beats of quiet. Of accep-tance. "I really fucked up," he finally says.

I don't deny that. I walk over to the chair where he's still seated and put a hand on his shoulder. "Tell your parents what happened last semester, Connor. They love you. They want to help."

He's shaking under my palm. He nods without looking back up at me. I walk out, closing the door on him and so much else in my wake.

Chapter Twenty-Eight

On the way to my statistics exam, I call Milo. It goes straight to voicemail. I call a second time, and a third time, and a fourth.

"Unicorn *cream* cheese," I mutter, shoving the phone back into my pocket.

I consider trying to make a break for it, running over to Cardinal to apologize to him face-to-face and risk being late for the exam and blowing it. But I know Milo. He'd be more upset with me for missing the exam than if I didn't immediately try to make this right.

Still, I check the time just to do some mental math and see if I can swing it. If I sprint, I can—

"What the hell, Andie?"

I look up from my phone into the eyes of one extremely indignant Shay, who is waiting for me outside the psychology building in her sweaty, post-dance-party glory with both of her hands on her hips.

The moment I make eye contact with her, the anger softens. My face must look a heck of a lot worse than I thought it did.

"I can't reach Milo," I blurt.

Shay lets her arms go loose at her side, kicking at a stray twig on the sidewalk. "Yeah, no shit."

I step closer to her. "Is he okay?"

Her eyes search my face, like she's still trying to decide how to process what just happened. What she and Valeria must have heard out on the quad with half the student body.

"I don't know," she says after a few moments. "I can't reach him either. But *come on*, Andie. After a whole year of keeping his identity under wraps . . ."

I basically put Milo's big secret up in neon lights.

"I'm so sorry," I say, the magnitude of it hitting me in waves.

"It's not just that. It's . . ." Shay glances past me toward the journalism building, as if she's expecting to see Connor trailing behind me. Given my luck today, she just might. "You let us all think you broke up with him."

It'd be easy to make excuses, but it wouldn't change the truth. Shay doesn't ask for an explanation, which somehow makes the whole thing worse. She doesn't need one. She already knows why I did it, because apparently not only am I a sucker, but I'm a predictable one at that.

"I'm sorry," is all I can say, is all I'll be saying until the end of time.

"I know you are." Shay presses her fingers to the bridge of her nose. "But now we've got a whole other host of problems to deal with, starting with the show."

I hate to say it, because most of me is still hoping it's not true. "He might be leaving anyway."

"Oh, he's definitely leaving." Shay says it with this finality that somehow manages to jar me despite everything that's happened today. "The sister he was meeting up with earlier? She works in admissions. I'm sure he was just . . . settling everything here before he left." Her scowl deepens. "But even if there were a chance he was going to stay for our school's program, I guess that's out the window now."

Then the full extent of Shay's worry hits home. Now the Blue Ridge State broadcast program will know who was behind the mic of the infamous pirate radio show, and they might take none too kindly to it. Even if they still let him in, the other students will undoubtedly resent him for snapping up the best broadcast experience someone can get out of the school without actually majoring in it. I might as well have just bought Milo a one-way ticket to California.

My eyes flood too quickly to hide. Shay's own eyes flit to the cement, unwilling to meet mine.

"I just don't want things to change." Shay sounds close to crying herself. "Before this semester it was like — my old roommate didn't want to be here. People in our hall barely talked to each other. It felt really lonely, but we're like a weird little family now. And I really like what we have."

My throat is thick with a new kind of regret. When I crash-landed here in the middle of the year I was so worried about fitting in that at first I couldn't see past it. I didn't understand that I may have felt out of place with my weird upbringing and the loss that shaped it, with my shaky grades and my old fears, but I wasn't the only one who felt like the odd one out. I wasn't the only one looking for a place to belong.

Only now do I understand that we never found one. We worked together to build one. And now, thanks to me, it might just come crashing down.

"Me too," I say softly.

Shay reaches out then to hug me. A quiet forgiveness. One that I don't feel like I deserve.

"I hope it's not too late to fix it," she says.

It can't be. It won't be. I may not have the ability to do anything right now, but just as soon as I'm out of this exam, I will figure it out.

Shay lets me go, hustling me into the psychology building. I make it there with a minute to spare, the other students already seated and ready to go. There's only one seat left—the very same seat

I had on my first day. The one with the iconic "A" scratched into it. After a grim moment of acceptance, I start walking over, hoping nobody will comment on my near lateness.

That is, until I end up face-to-face with Professor Hutchison walking up the aisle, blinking at me as if she's looking at a ghost.

"You're here," she says.

A hundred pairs of eyes turn to look at me. It's that nightmarish first day all over again.

"Yes," I say warily, sliding my bag off my shoulder.

She shakes her head, rattling herself out of some thought. "After what just happened on the radio show, I thought . . ."

My stomach drops. The hundred pairs of eyes all lean in a little closer, hanging on her every word, watching me for my reaction. And then somehow it gets worse—a low mumbling ripples through the room.

I can't hear much, but I hear plenty. "Squire." "Radio show." "Fucked up."

I've been so terrified about outing Milo that it never occurred to me that I might have outed my own self. Connor said my name out loud. If a professor immediately made the connection that I was the Andie he was with, who's to say other people didn't, too?

I'm on autopilot, stepping closer to her. "Is this the exam?" I ask too loudly, trying to drown the class out.

"Yes. Yes, here," she says, handing me one of the stapled sets of papers and a Scantron.

"Thanks," I say as cheerfully as I can manage. I try to whip out the syndicated-talk-show smile, but it turns into something else— steelier, and more defiant. It's aimed at all the students trying to get a better look at what's going on in the back of the room, but to my surprise, Professor Hutchison's eyes widen at it in something that looks almost like recognition.

I dismiss it as I sit down, trying to focus my attention on the exam. But the moment I sit, it's like some kind of cue to my body. The adrenaline stops rushing. My heart stops beating in my throat. There's just the hush of the lecture hall, and too many of my thoughts to fill up the silence, thoughts that spiral faster than any statistical anomaly on this test possibly could.

Professor Hutchison knows. Which means anyone could know. Which means not only did I blow Milo's cover, but everyone knows precisely who did it. I'll go down in infamy as the girl who ruined *The Knights' Watch*; the girl who took her own mother's creation and set it on fire fast enough to blaze everything else in its path.

I stare down at the questions on the paper. I will myself to focus. But my eyes just drift to the swirling, swooping "A" carved into the desk until it's all I see.

"Okay, you lot. Time's up."

My head jerks up to see that I'm one of the last twenty or so people in the lecture hall. My exam is just barely filled in, and I can't even remember most of the questions.

I don't even have it in me to feel anything about it. All the studying I did with Valeria, the pages I pored over in the dorms and at Milo's, the office hours where I ran Professor Hutchison's unsuspecting TAs ragged with questions. All of it was for nothing.

As I lay the exam down on the pile with everyone else's, it occurs to me that if I fail this exam, I'll fail the entire class. I won't be able to take all the other psychology courses that this is the pre-req for; all the other courses I'm supposed to take next year and beyond. It'll set me back an entire semester, likely make me graduate late, and accumulate even more debt than I've already accounted for.

I can handle that, though. I've never gotten emotional over money issues. They're just a fact of life.

It's something deeper than that. It's the rejection letter I bawled over in my senior year of high school, when no amount of Grandma Maeve's anecdotes or Gammy Nell's peanut butter marshmallow pie could soothe me. It's Connor asking me if I feel like I really belong here. It's the Blue Ridge State mug my mom drank out of every morning, her fingers tracing the little map, taking me places in our minds that she'd never get to take me herself.

Professor Hutchison's gaze is heavy on mine as I set the exam down. It's all I can do to nod at her, pivot on my heels, and book it out of the lecture hall as fast as I feasibly can.

The next thing I know I'm knocking at Milo's door, the pit in my stomach wide enough to become a crater. When he opens it, he looks just about as tired as I feel, his eyes just as red-rimmed and weary as they were the day I first met him, his dark curls in disarray.

"Milo."

He opens the door a little farther. Jerks his head toward his room, letting me in. I'm weak with relief until he uses the door-jamb by his desk to leave the door wide open, checking up and down the hall before he lets me in, clearly worried we'll get spotted alone together.

I close my eyes. Of course. I forgot the other layer of this—the part where he's my RA, and even the idea of one of his charges having a crush on him is bad news, let alone a crush literally broadcast to the entire student body.

He leans against his desk, those green eyes sweeping over me with gentle caution.

"Are you okay?" he asks.

Something in my heart splinters. "Are *you*?"

Milo blows out a breath, leaning against his desk. "It is what it is."

"I'm so sorry, Milo. Exposing you—you know how seriously I take *The Knights' Watch*. I hate that I did this to you. I'm so, so sorry."

Milo's brows lift in surprise. "Andie . . . I'm not worried about the radio show."

"You're not?"

He shakes his head, gripping the edges of his desk like he's anchoring himself there. "I mean, I know what it means to *you*. I get why you think that's why I'm upset, but . . ."

His eyes meet mine fully for the first time since I walked into the room, and it almost feels like a collision. Like I'm not just feeling the full force of what I feel for him, but what he feels for me.

"I'm upset that you'd stay with him," he says quietly. "Not—not because of anything to do with me. But because you deserve better than that. And you know you do. Your *friends* know you do. You wouldn't have let us all believe it was over last night if you didn't know that."

I'm still so unused to this layer of him—this deeper, solemn layer under the sarcasm and the rebuffing and the occasional sleep deprivation. This part of him that cuts to the core faster than I ever imagined it could.

"I was never going to stay with him," I say. "I was just wrapping my head around what happened, and I needed time. Everything's just—been up in the air, for a lot of my life. But not Connor or his family. They've always been this one constant thing." I make myself hold his gaze as I confess it. "I worked really, really hard to make myself fit into their world. And now it's just gone."

None of this is a revelation, but saying it out loud is the thing that makes it real. Not just the years I spent fixated on it, but the future I have to face on the other side.

"You shouldn't have to make yourself fit, Andie," says Milo. "That's not a constant. That's you changing all the time for other people's sakes."

I bow my head, staring down at my feet. For all my changing, I've never felt more grounded, more separate, than I do right now. It's freeing, but it's terrifying. A burden has been lifted, but a strange responsibility has taken its place—my choices, and the consequences, are wholly my own.

"If there's one thing I've learned from you aggressively inserting yourself into my business and making me socialize against my will, it's that there are going to be all kinds of constants in your life," says Milo. "And I know you. You have plenty of them. Your grandmas. Valeria. Shay."

There's a beat where Milo's breath seems to stall. I close my eyes, steeling myself, then open them.

"But not you," I say, so he doesn't have to.

Only then does Milo look up, his eyes so immediately on mine that it's arresting. Like someone flicking on a light when you've slept in total darkness; like looking up from a long, lonely walk in the woods to see someone directly in your path. "Why's that?"

I try to smile. For once, I can't manage it. "Shay said you're leaving."

When his gaze falls away from mine, the room is noticeably colder. "Yeah," he says, his hand gripping the edge of the desk so tightly his knuckles go white. "I guess you're right."

I didn't mean to confirm it like this. If anything, I was hoping to float the idea of him leaving so he could tell me I was wrong. It's like Shay said. We're a *family*. As prepared as I've been for him to leave, it does nothing to stop the ache in my chest from widening, knowing I was wrong. Embarrassingly, ridiculously wrong.

"I'm sorry," I say again, my voice small. "I know you said you're not worried about the show, but—but I am. So I need you to know, I really am sorry. For that and for everything else."

"I'm sorry, too," he says. "I mean, you and I . . ."

I hang on the end of that sentence even when I understand he's not going to finish it. He's giving me an opening here. But no matter what Milo wants me to say, I can't take it. Not when I know he's about to cross the country. Not when his future is on the line.

I spent half a lifetime feeling held back from a relationship. And if there's one thing Milo and I have in common, it's that we both want the other to soar.

"I'll miss you," I say.

Milo just nods, more to himself than to me. An acceptance. "I won't disappear, Andie," he says. "We'll always be friends."

I don't want his friendship. I want to shut the door. I want to cross the distance between us and put my hands on the back of his neck and pull him down toward me, want to feel the heat of his body against mine again, want to know what yesterday's almost-kiss will feel like when it isn't a "what if," but a "what now."

"Of course." My voice doesn't waver. My hands don't shake. "Always."

I turn to leave, but not before his expression sears into my memory—it's not acceptance, I realize. It's resignation. I unlock the door to my room, fishing for the light when my phone lights up for me, a notification from the student app popping up on the screen. I swipe, my heart already sinking even before I see the exam grade. It's a big, unrepentant D.

Do you really feel like you belong here?

This time the doubt feels different—brutal and sour. This time when I sweep my eyes out the window to the campus below and let the doubt seep in, I don't have anybody but myself to blame.

Chapter Twenty-Nine

When Shay's alarm goes off I burrow under the covers and let her leave without me. I wake up again when the sun is up, long after the radio show has been recorded. I can't bear to listen. I have no idea how Milo handled the aftermath of everyone knowing his real name, and selfishly, I don't want to—it'll just make what I did more real.

I put a blast out to the rest of the students in the work-study to find a replacement for my Bagelopolis shifts for the rest of the week, and once they're snatched up I start packing, tossing odds and ends into a suitcase without any clear intention of what I'm doing or why. I just know I need to get off this campus. Away from the studio, away from the glaring D on my exam, away from my friends, and away from this stupid, fragile feeling in my heart, like it's one conversation with Milo away from cracking in two.

I pull out my phone. I'm going home for a bit, I text Shay. Let me know if there's anything I can do to help with the show.

I'm about to call the home phone to ask my grandmas to come get me, but before I can, my dad's number pops up on the screen. It's an unusual time for him to call, so I pick up without thinking.

"Hello?"

"Hey, A-Plus," says my dad, his voice normal enough that I rule out any weird freak accidents right off the bat. "I know you said you wanted to meet up next weekend, but I'm nearby today, if you wanted to grab a bagel or anything."

It's an embarrassing relief to hear his voice. I feel like a little kid, pressing the receiver to my ear.

"Oh." The reflex to brush him off almost kicks in, but then some other reflex beats it to the punch. "Well, um—I was actually— thinking of going home today?"

My dad doesn't miss a beat. "Well then, let me take you."

I stare down at the mess of pink and denim in my suitcase. "Don't you have work?"

"Eh. It's a slow day. Half hour from now sound good?"

I'm too stunned to question it. "Um—yeah. Meet you at Bagel-opolis?"

"Sounds like a plan," he says cheerfully. "See you in a bit."

The whole thing is so seamless and so . . . casual. Like the way Shay talks to her dad on the phone, or the way people talk to their dads on television shows. I know we've had a complicated history, but it didn't occur to me that it could just be that easy. *Come get me.* And a dad there to do just that.

I grab a few more random things to pack, unsure of how long I'm planning to be home, then call Bagelopolis and order the cheesy garlic bagel with strawberry cream cheese and the pretzel bagel with cookie dough cream cheese. Mercifully, Milo and Shay aren't on today, so I grab it from the pickup shelf without anyone noticing me or asking about the suitcase. My dad pulls up seconds after I grab our order, rolling down the driver's side window.

"Top of the morning!" he calls, in this dorky dad way I'd be embarrassed by if I weren't so grateful for it. He's grinning that same unselfconscious grin I've seen more often on Gammy Nell than I've seen on him, and he's wearing the flannel Grandma Maeve and I picked out for him for Christmas at Little Fells's one strip mall a few miles from our house. I clamber into his car, im-

mediately comforted by the smell of his beloved vanilla-flavored
Dunkin' Donuts order and gasoline.

"I got your favorite," I tell him, setting the distinctive white
Bagelopolis bag between us.

My dad immediately reaches for the bag, deeply inhales, and
then—like some kind of bagel savant—lists the flavors of not just
his bagel, but mine, too.

"Whoa. I'm impressed," I say, fastening my seat belt.

"And I'm grateful. Do you want to eat them now, or get out of
Dodge?"

I'm glad he asked, even if I'm a little suspicious of the offer. Last
I checked, all he wanted to do was show me around campus. But
he must know something's wrong if I'm heading back to Little Fells
smack-dab in the middle of a school week.

"Let's, uh—let's just head out for now."

"On it," says my dad, revving up the engine and leaning back
behind me to check for traffic. It's a familiar gesture, one I was
used to seeing from the back seat when I was little. My dad checking the mirrors, then resting his hand on the back of my mom's
seat and leaning back to check behind him again.

I blink it out of my brain, and we drive. My dad asks me about
Shay's major. About what the current seasonal bagel is at Bagelopolis. About the outdoor volunteer group I'm joining. All these little
things that make it clear he's been keeping up with me, even when
I've been tacitly avoiding him.

And for my part, I hold it together. I answer all his questions as
thoroughly as I can, even though I am staring out the window, just
waiting for us to get home to my grandmas so I can safely fall apart.

But when my dad stops the car, we aren't at the house. We're
in the parking lot of the Big League Burger a few miles away from
it, the one next to the outdoor playground he and Mom used to
take me to every weekend when I was little. I'd split a big milkshake with Connor and a plate of fries with my mom and chicken

nuggets with my dad and chase all my friends through the tunnels and slides that seemed so big and infinite to me then, a maze of technicolor and plastic, like a separate little world.

"You always loved this place," says my dad.

I nod. He takes it as a cue to cut the ignition, to open the door to the car. I follow suit, feeling numb as we walk toward the picnic tables where my parents and Connor's used to sit.

"I could go in and grab us a milkshake to go with the bagels," my dad offers, jerking a thumb toward the actual building. "You still like chocolate caramel?"

The universe only knows why, but for some reason this offer is the straw on the camel's back. My chest goes tight and my hands go wobbly, opening up the bagel bag so shakily that I end up ripping it.

"I messed everything up."

My dad is somehow unsurprised by this emotional display after two hours of normalcy, taking a seat and pulling the bag from me to shell out the bagels himself. "I'm sure that's not true."

I shake my head. He sets my bagel in front of me and all I can do is stare at it like it's some kind of evidence of my failure.

"You don't even know," I say miserably.

For a moment my dad doesn't say anything. He's never been great with emotions. Or more that he's never been great at being around for them. I'm expecting him to sidestep the whole thing when instead he says, "Well. If you're referring to that whole thing with *The Knights' Watch* . . ."

I stiffen. "You heard about it?"

It's mortifying enough that it's campus-wide knowledge. Has it somehow spread to the entire *state*?

My dad calmly uses a plastic knife to cut my bagel into fourths for me, the way he used to do when I was a kid. "I listen to the show every morning. I heard the Knight reference something that happened yesterday, and did some prying to figure out just what."

I mindlessly pick up one of the quarters, trying to make his words make sense. I've listened to the show for years, but I've had good reason—I wanted to keep up with Mom's legacy. Last I checked, my dad was avoiding that like the plague.

"You listen to the show?" I ask cautiously. And then, with decidedly less caution: "Because of Mom?"

My dad shakes his head. A little boy squeals on the slide as a little girl plumes down right behind him, the two of them crashing together at the base of it in a fit of giggles.

"I checked in on it from time to time because of your mom," says my dad. "But I recognized your voice a few weeks ago. I've been tuning in ever since."

The revelation doesn't know where to land. For so long the studio has been a hideaway, this quiet place where nobody can see me except for Milo and Shay. It feels like discovering there's been a secret window the entire time.

"You have?"

Only then do I realize that my dad's call was no coincidence. He already knows exactly what happened. His call this morning wasn't an offer—it was a full-on rescue.

"Course. You're made for the air." My dad busies himself with a piece of his bagel, watching me process all this out of the corner of his eye. "Plus, I had to do something to get my 'Bed of Roses' fix, since you never sent me your clips."

I blink down at my own bagel. "I, uh . . . I've been busy." My throat is thick. "I didn't realize you were listening."

"I always want to know what's going on in your world."

I look over at him so quickly that I can see him bracing himself, his hands paused on the table, his shoulders set against the breeze. This is the part where I'm supposed to say something like, *You've got a funny way of showing it.* Something combative, something to cause even a fraction of the hurt I've felt for years.

My dad clearly is ready to take it, but suddenly, I don't have it in me. I don't want to hurt anymore. I just want to understand.

So I level with him. "I appreciate you trying. I really do. I'm just . . ." I can't look at him when I say it, so instead I stare off at the shadows of the kids barreling through the tunnels, palms and knees knocking against the plastic in the distance. "There were times when I thought you were going to be more involved, and you weren't. I don't want to get my hopes up so you can just . . ."

Start over with someone else, I want to say. But I already feel raw enough taking it this far. I can't say anything else without knowing what he'll say, how he'll react.

"The time I was gone — it was longer than I thought it would be," my dad says.

I can tell it's the beginning of an apology, but it can't start like that. If we're blowing this open right now, we're blowing it wide open. "Longer than I thought it would be" isn't going to cut it.

"You were gone for years."

I'm surprisingly calm. Part of it, I think, is that I've been imagining some version of this conversation for a long time. Versions where I cried, versions where I yelled. Versions that eventually boiled down to the core of the issue: what I needed to say, what I needed him to hear. After that it was just a matter of working up the nerve to do it.

The other part of it is Milo's voice in my head. *If I had the chance to talk to my dad again . . .*

I want to have that chance. Not just for this conversation, but all the ones that can come after. The kind that will only really mean anything if we try to fix this first.

"It felt like you were running away." I sit up straighter, the bagel forgotten, the sounds of the kids fading away. "From Mom. From Little Fells. From me."

My dad's eyes close for a moment. "I never wanted to be away from you, Andie."

As I watch him start to gather his thoughts, I realize I imagined this all wrong. It's not what I need my dad to hear. It's about what

I need him to say. So I don't protest, don't point to moments in the past we both already know. I just keep watching him and wait.

"You're right. I was trying to avoid Little Fells." He glances past the playground to the row of trees beyond it, to the road that leads to the main part of town and branches off into side streets full of everyone we know. "It was sort of like . . . Groundhog's Day. I kept trying to move on—for both our sakes. But every person here, they knew your mom. They loved her. And every conversation I had . . . it started with this grief. This pity. Everyone was hurting, every single time her name came up." He shakes his head, like the words aren't quite matching what he's trying to say. "And your mom wouldn't have wanted that. She would have wanted people to smile when they thought of her. But they didn't understand that, and sometimes I'd just be so angry that—that they felt like they could understand, that they knew what we'd lost, when—when it felt like they didn't know her at all."

I hate that I know exactly what he means. It's the same private kind of grief Grandma Maeve and I have always shared. There is a part of Amy Rose that belonged to Little Fells, and a whole of her that only belonged to us.

"And everywhere I went it was like—being at the funeral. All over again." He adjusts the baseball cap on his head, lowering it over his eyes and then setting it back again. "The grief already felt like a mountain. It just got heavier and heavier the longer I stayed here. Like we were carrying it for everybody else, too."

It's more than I've ever heard him say about losing Mom. It didn't occur to me that he'd be this frank. That maybe he'd been thinking of this very conversation as long as I have.

When he meets my eye again, it's clear that he has. "I wanted you to come with me."

I remember him offering. It was a courtesy offer, really. One he only made two weeks before he was planning to move.

"I could never leave Little Fells. Not then, at least." I shift in my seat. "But I know what you mean. I felt that way, too. Like it wasn't just our lives that changed, but everyone around us. Like we were never going to be the people we were to them before it happened. I couldn't figure out if everyone else changed or I did."

He dips his head. "I wish I'd talked to you more about it back then."

I mirror him, glancing down at my lap. I think about that first school assembly where I choked, and everything changed. How it felt staring out at the other kids and feeling like I was on an island, and no matter how hard I paddled back, I could never step foot on the old shore. How the feeling only got worse over time with every year my dad stayed away, every year I struggled between trying to be my old self again and trying to find a new version who could be better. Who could fit somewhere else, since the old world didn't fit anymore.

"Me too," I say, glancing back up. "The whole thing just— made me feel so alone."

His eyes are misty when he meets mine. I swallow thickly and press on.

"Especially because I couldn't figure out why you did it. I thought for the longest time—maybe I was just too much like her, or something. Maybe that's why you felt like you had to stay away."

My dad lets out a soft laugh, surprising both of us. "Oh. Andie. You and your mom are nothing alike."

The sudden jolt is almost welcome, after the heaviness of everything else. "Excuse me?"

The smile on his face softens like the edges of a memory. "I mean, you are in some important ways. But you—you're a planner. You're methodical about things. You put a lot of care into them. So did your mom, of course, but she was a whirlwind." He's talking to me, but staring outward at something else. "Never liked a plan. Always just went where the winds took her."

Just then the wind happens to pick up, and for the first time in a long time, I feel my mom's presence so strongly that it's as if we've conjured her here—like she's watching, part cheerleader, part referee. The idea of it buoys me, makes me dig deeper. All the way to the bottom of this, so we know how far it is back to the top.

"If it wasn't that, then what was it?" I ask. "Because it wasn't just the distance. It was everything else. You barely even called. When you were here, it felt like you had one foot out the door."

I feel my fists curl with the familiar frustration. Sometimes I'd feel like a little windup toy when my dad was around, trying to think of anything I could say or do to hold his attention, to keep him in town. I'd make lists of movies we could watch together. Show him school projects. Text him pictures of things Gammy Nell and I were making in the kitchen. But I could only go on spinning for so long.

My dad is quiet for long enough that I'm worried he's going to deny it. "I didn't mean to," he finally says. He lifts his head back up to look at me, and it's with the kind of regard I'm still getting used to—like he's not just seeing me as a kid, but someone fully formed. Someone he can be honest with.

"But that whole thing with planning—that's something you got from me. Your mom would spin big ideas. I'd make the plans, help set them into motion when I could. We balanced each other out. I think that's the most you can hope for when you're in love; that you balance each other out. Make each other stronger."

I try to think back to my memories of my parents together, but all I remember is the haze of knowing your parents are in love, and never questioning it. Never having a reason to, because what they had was built to last.

"But that's the thing about being the one who makes the plans," says my dad. "When they all fall through . . ."

I hear a car engine start behind us. At some point the kids in the play place were gathered up by their parents, and now it's so still out here that it feels like we're the only people in Little Fells. Nobody else's grief to handle but our own.

"Everything was just gone. I was overwhelmed. This entire life I'd planned for the three of us—I just—she was my anchor," he says. "I needed her. I didn't know how to be without her."

And then come the words I've been avoiding this entire time. The ones that have dug under my skin for years, the ones so private and so raw that they were too much to even let myself think.

"I needed *you*," I tell him.

He lowers his head then, nodding just once before staring down at the picnic tabletop. Another breeze sweeps past us, and it feels like a separate wind has been knocked out of me. One I've held inside for so long that it felt like a storm in my heart.

But now there's just quiet. The kind I still need him to fill now, even after all this time.

When my dad speaks again, his voice is hoarse with feeling. "I never meant to avoid you. It's just . . . you were so happy with your grandmas. You came back to life in this way that you never were with me, and I knew that was my fault. That I was pulling you down." He clears his throat. "That's all I've ever wanted, Andie. For you to be happy."

The words fall out of me too quickly for them to be anything but the truth: "I'd rather be miserable with you than happy without you."

For a few moments, he doesn't speak.

"I should have known that then." He flattens his palms out on the top of the table like he's grounding us in this moment. Pressing it somewhere into himself so we can't cast it away. "I wish I could change it. And I'm not asking to start over. But I'm . . . I'd really love a chance to start something, Andie."

When his gaze meets mine, some of the lingering bitterness falls away. I see it plainly now—the grief. The regret. And deeper still, the shame. It clouds his eyes, but makes something else all the more clear. The part that he'll never really be able to say, because

I don't know if he fully understands it himself; he never wanted me to see this weakness. It just took all these years, maybe, for his need to fix this to be louder than that part of him that wanted me to think he was strong.

But this—it's the strongest I've ever seen him. I wish there were a way to tell him that. But at least now it seems like I'll have plenty of time to find one someday.

"I know I haven't made it easy," I admit.

My dad presses his lips together, collecting himself. "I'm not expecting you to. And for what it's worth, I'll keep trying. As long as you're okay with it."

My eyes well up unexpectedly. That's the crux of the whole thing. I've been pushing him away before he can leave. Even now I'm scared—even as this supposedly adult, eighteen-year-old version of myself who shouldn't need him, who shouldn't be in a position to be disappointed by him anymore. But part of me is peering over the same edge I did at eleven and fourteen and seventeen, waiting to be let down.

"I don't know if it'll ever feel fully normal," I admit. "But I never gave up on you. So . . . don't give up on me, either."

"Never."

He pulls me in gruffly, wrapping an arm around my shoulders and pressing me into his. Then he relaxes his grip, the two of us just leaning on each other, watching another group of little kids pile out of a station wagon and sprint for the slides.

"I really do want to meet Ava," I tell him.

"Yeah?"

"Yeah."

He taps the table with his finger. "I don't want you to think you have to be a part of that just for us to be a family. I'm going to be here no matter what. Okay?"

I nod, too overwhelmed for a moment to answer. For so long the word "family" has loomed over me like a threat, like something

I stood to lose. But the way my dad says it, the word doesn't feel like something I have to earn. It feels like something that just is.

Maybe it's not so scary now that I'm starting to recognize that families take shapes of their own, and I'm lucky to have more than one. It's like Milo said. I have my grandmas. My friends at Blue Ridge. This town that's still here for me, even when I'm far from it. Things I never took for granted, of course, but maybe didn't appreciate for what they were—the peace of being known. Of always having soft places to land.

If I'm lucky, Kelly and Ava might just be another one of them. But I'll never find out if I don't let myself move on from the past and give them a chance.

"Thank you for saying that," I say sincerely. I needed to hear it. "But really. If you're still free next weekend . . . I'd love to see them, too."

My dad just nods, wisely not making any plans, giving me space to change my mind. It's the kind of thing I'd be thinking about, too—trying to see into the future for someone else, into all 360 degrees of the decisions they're making or trying to make. It's weird to see this similarity in the two of us. For so many years I've been so fixated on following my mom's footsteps that it never occurred to me that mine might be closer in shape to his.

I feel a sudden surge of questions I want to ask him, but there's a relief in letting them come and then letting them go. In knowing I don't need to ask them right now, because the door isn't going to close. He's back, and I'm finding my way back, too. We finally have time.

Chapter Thirty

As I'm setting our giant Big League Burger milkshake in the drink holder I accidentally knock my backpack over, the ribbons spilling out from the front pocket again. "Oops," I mutter, pulling them out from the console. But not before my dad lets out a hearty laugh.

"What?" I ask with a self-conscious smile.

"Oh, nothing. Just—of course you have more ribbons than you could possibly know what to do with," says my dad, helping collect a few that scattered over to his seat. "Truly your mother's daughter."

I take the ribbons from him, securing them back in my front pocket. "Yeah?"

"Oh, yeah. She was insufferable about them," he says, wiping a tear of laughter from his eye. "Got more than anyone else in her year."

I balk at him, so stunned that my body decides to forget how seat belts work. "You remember that far back?" I demand, finally getting it to click on the third try.

"Course I do." He pulls out of the lot, the laughter dissolved into a sly smile. "I was one of the students who started the ribbon tradition in the first place."

It's clear from the way he takes his sweet time pulling out that he's enjoying every second of my shock. "You *what*?"

"Oh, yeah. That's how we met."

"E*xcuse* me?"

My dad laughs again, easy and low, a laugh I remember from a long time ago. It's less like I am discovering things about him today, and more like I'm finding them again. I wonder if he feels the same way about me.

"Your mom was incensed that she didn't get a ribbon at the pie-eating contest. Claimed she should have won because the girl who upchucked halfway through should have been disqualified—I think her exact words were, 'That was at least half a pie she tossed, so I beat her.'" My dad shakes his head with laughter. "She came knocking down my door at ten o'clock at night—"

"You never *told* me this," I accuse, the words bubbling with a laughter of my own.

"Oh, your mother would have killed me." He glances at me conspiratorially. "But I figure she'd have let you know by now."

Oddly, I have no trouble imagining my mom finding true love in a pie brawl. It's the other part of the story that I can't quite process. "You started the ribbons?"

"Yeah." He clears his throat, suddenly sheepish about the whole thing. "Well, with a dozen or so other kids."

"What?" For someone who wants to answer people's questions for a living, I suddenly can't form a single coherent one to save my life. "How? *Why?*"

My dad shrugs. "It's like I said. I liked making plans. We needed a way to get around the new organization ban on campus, so . . . I ran with it. Turned it into a series of events that would turn *into* organizations. They couldn't ban something that technically hadn't formed yet. Which is why," he says, pointing at my white ribbon, "anyone playing had to have one of those. To prove they were there for the game, and not to rat us out."

My brain feels like it's about to explode, trying to process all this at once. For so long I thought of the ribbons as something belonging to my mom that I never once factored my dad into it. Never once did I consider that he might have other reasons for tucking her ribbons away for all these years. That the memories behind them weren't just hers, but theirs.

I glance at him cautiously, but he's shaking his head with a fondness that makes him look younger than he is. "As for your mom—the instant I heard her ranting about the pie, I knew. Her voice was unmistakable. She was the Knight who clued us all in to the mishandling of administration funds that led to the ban. The one we'd been working with to drop all the clues."

In a strange role reversal, it's me who has to look away from him; me who needs a quiet moment to collect myself as I absorb this piece of their story, as I make it a part of my own. I'd known all this time I was walking on the ground where they'd trod, but I didn't understand how directly, how luckily, it led to everything else. To them falling in love. To them sharing a life together. To me.

I find my voice and manage, "That's incredible."

My dad's smile quirks. "We were fairly badass back in our day."

We stop at a light. I've waited for this secret for so long. Too long. And now that all these other secrets are unraveled, I need to know.

"So . . . you know what they're for? Each of the colors?"

My dad plucks the milkshake from my grasp, taking a comically long sip, his eyes teasing. "You have friends who aren't freshmen. None of them have told you?"

I make a mental note to harass Val and Milo as he passes the milkshake over to me. "Nope."

My dad raises his eyebrows. "I am deeply impressed by everyone's commitment to the secret. Damn. It's been—what? Twenty years?"

"The secret?" I repeat.

The light changes. His eyes are on the road, but still full of mirth. "You're sure you want to know?"

I can't help myself. "I just want to know which one Mom was in," I blurt.

My dad's head tilts back in surprise, but then settles in a quiet appreciation. Like this means more to him than any other question I might have asked. "Oh. Well. That's easy—she was in the red one."

I can't even explain why my eyes flood with tears. Red doesn't even mean anything to me. I have no way of differentiating it from the others. It's just that for every fragment of my mom that I can still hold, I know there are a thousand others I'll never know about—things she might have told me, things I might have found out on my own. It doesn't matter how I get them. They're all precious just the same.

"Yeah?"

"Yeah," says my dad fondly. "And I was in blue."

I'm fully aware I'm pushing my luck when I ask, "So . . . what do they mean?"

My dad makes a show of pretending he's not going to tell me for a moment with this near-clownish expression. It is, perhaps, the most aggressively like a dad he's ever been.

"Well—you've got more than enough to qualify for any of them, so I guess there's no harm in telling you. They're all volunteer societies." He glances down at my backpack. "You might have noticed there are some themes to the qualifying events. Social and campus activities are red, academic ones are blue, nature ones are yellow. If you get enough ribbons for any of them, you get to choose which society to join and help do volunteer work with."

Volunteer societies. My heart suddenly feels full enough to burst. I've been trying to trust in the idea of these "secret societies" because I trust my mom not to tangle herself in anything bad, but it's still such a relief to know that I was right to trust her. That I was right to trust them both.

"These days they're not really a secret. The volunteer societies are open to anyone, freshmen included—the ribbons just give you an opportunity to cast votes on their activities sophomore year instead of waiting for junior year," my dad explains. "You can only cast votes for one of the groups, but you can still be in any of the other groups you want. Heck, you might have been recruited into one already."

I almost laugh when I realize he's right. All this time I've been so fixated on following my mom's path, and in joining the outdoor volunteer group, I'd already picked one myself.

I wait for the worry to brew, or the disappointment to sink in. Depending on the choice I make, all this effort to be in the group that she was in might have gone to waste. But louder than the worry is the comforting thought that maybe I didn't need her as much as I thought I did. That I may have taken the long way, but maybe I ended up where I needed to be on my own.

"And you helped come up with that?" I ask.

My dad presses his lips together. He's never been great at taking credit for things. Gammy Nell's been on his case about him advocating for himself at work ever since I can remember.

"Yeah. But your mom really turned things around after she joined the red squad."

Only now can I appreciate some of the differences between Dad then and Dad now. Appreciate why he felt like he needed to get away from here. He used to talk about my mom with this impossible kind of weight, but now the amusement in his voice is undeniable. Like he can finally look back and see the joy of things the way they were, instead of the pain of what might have been.

"She was the one who had an imagination for what else we could do with the program—some of our best events were all her doing. The snowman contest, cleaning up the litter in the arboretum, that big dance party . . ."

My eyes widen. All the events that have punctuated and defined my short time at Blue Ridge, for better or for worse. The ones that helped me build friendships, helped me push past the limits I set for myself, helped me realize what was actually important to me, and what wasn't. It's as if all this time she was holding my hand.

My dad mistakes my reaction, thinking I'm still worrying about the radio-show-dance-party incident.

"Hey," he says. "I know you're upset about what happened. But Milo played it off really well. You should listen to the recording, you'll see."

I try not to wince, glancing out the window on the passenger side, watching the little strip of Little Fells's main street go by. A sidewalk I've walked thousands of times, full of people who have always known my name.

"I blew Mom's big secret."

"Oh, A-Plus." I can hear the smile in his voice without seeing his face. "I can promise you that wherever your mom is, she is laughing her ass off about that right now."

"You think so?"

"There's nothing your mom loved more than a plan gone awry." My dad pulls down the street to my grandmas' house and slows the car more than he needs to, taking his time. "And I know this goes without saying, but—she'd be so damn proud of you."

I rest my head against the cool glass of the window. "Even after everything I messed up?"

"Especially after everything you've fought for," says my dad assuredly. "These years? They're not meant to be easy. But I've got no doubt you'll tackle them head-on, the same way you always do."

It's not that I am unused to people having this kind of unshakable faith in me. My grandmas always have. Shay and Valeria and Milo do. To some degree, I've even had that faith in myself. But it means something entirely different coming from him—not like it counts for anything more or anything less, but it counts in a way more meaningful to me than I thought it would.

I lift my head back up as he pulls into the driveway, and say something I haven't in years: "Thanks, Dad."

He doesn't nod. Just looks at me like the words weren't meant to be something I accepted, but something that should be a given. "For the record," he adds, "I'm damn proud of you, too."

My bottom lip quivers. "You're gonna give me an ego."

He laughs out loud again, finally shutting off the car. "If you ever get one, it's from those badass grandmas of yours, not me."

I smile this new, wobbly smile, one that's genuine and confused and grateful all at the same time. "I got plenty of things from you, too."

My dad's eyes soften, looking between me and the house where I grew up, full of the women who built me. "Well. If that's true, I'm one lucky dad."

Chapter Thirty-One

The rest of the day feels like something out of some storybook version of my childhood. The four of us spend the entire day together. We make the dough for Gammy Nell's famous caramel-stuffed peanut butter chocolate chip cookies. We all muck ourselves up outside to help with Grandma Maeve's side of the garden (read: most of the garden, since she's decided Gammy Nell can't be trusted with hers) as she chain-smokes and tells us stories about her college years in San Francisco. We start up a forest-themed puzzle someone got my dad for his birthday years ago that he never opened, and continue to work on it as my grandmas put on their coveted DVD of *Definitely, Maybe*, which only gets whipped out on special occasions. We order takeout from our favorite pizza spot in Little Fells, and have a small army of neighborhood kids on the porch by the time we pull Gammy Nell's cookies out of the oven.

I'm eating them on the rocking chair by the front door when Grandma Maeve walks into the hall to join me and says, apropos of nothing, "I hope whatever got fucked up feels less fucked now, chicken."

I finish chewing on the cookie, not quite finished chewing on the massive pile of regrets I've been ignoring all day. "I'm glad I'm home."

She pats my cheek. "And we're glad to have you. But also, it's a damn Tuesday." Her penciled-in eyebrows fly up on her wrinkled forehead, filled with more laugh lines than anyone I've ever met. "Smells like some conflict avoidance, if you ask me."

She cushions it with an offer of her last pizza crust and the tub of butter, knowing full well how I love to dip my crusts in it. I accept them both with narrowed eyes.

"I'm guessing my dad already told you the gist of what happened," I say. I can't even pretend to be annoyed about it. It's actually kind of nice, the normalcy of it. A parent being overly involved in something for once.

"Sure did," says Grandma Maeve with a broad grin. "And can I just say, from the bottom of this feeble old heart . . ." I brace myself for some candid, sassy end to that sentence. But my grandma's eyes lose their edge and keep all their sparkle. "You were always miles above that Connor Whit."

Gammy Nell walks over, holding up a mug of tea. "Hear, hear."

My eyes widen enough to rival planetary moons. "Wait. How did you know about . . . I mean, I haven't even mentioned him."

Gammy Nell winks. "We have our sources."

"Sources that asked for our address approximately two hours ago," says Grandma Maeve, glancing at the door expectantly.

As if on cue, there's a knock.

"Hmm. Better go get that," says Grandma Maeve with a wink.

I take my emotional-support pizza crust with me, trying to think of who it might be but drawing a complete blank. I don't get much time to guess, because Valeria's already talking before I fully open the front door.

"We fucked up," she informs me, looking windswept and agitated, her usually sleek hair in tangles and her chic red coat buttoned up unevenly.

Grandma Maeve lets out her signature cackle. "I knew I liked you. Come on in."

Valeria's eyes widen in mild alarm—she's met my grandmas twice now from their campus visits, but she's always been at her utmost polite self for the occasion—but before she can sputter an apology, Gammy Nell has already started wrestling her coat off her, and Grandma Maeve has shut the door.

"What else did I mess up?" I ask. "Also, how are you *here*?"

She looks me up and down like she was half expecting to find me in pieces. "Um, where's your phone, Andie?"

Tucked so far deep into my backpack that it might as well be in the earth's molten core. "Kettle corn," I mutter at myself, crouching down to wrestle it out. "What did I miss?"

The phone screen answers that for me before she can. Four texts and a call from Milo. Are you around? the first one reads. Sean says you took off the whole week?? says another. Seriously, though, where are you? Did you leave campus?

And then the fourth text, just before the call: Let me know when you get these, you're freaking me out, new kid.

My face burns hotter than the aforementioned molten core.

"I texted Shay—"

"Yeah, uh." Valeria winces. "Shay's with her sister."

I set my backpack down. "Is she okay?"

Valeria blows out a breath, shifting her weight between her feet. "So, um. I may have confessed my feelings for her out in the quad this morning. And she just kind of like—bolted?"

My grandmas have already vacated the premises, taking their tea and wine out to the back porch where my dad is still frowning methodically over his puzzle. I usher Valeria into the living room, which is every bit at odds with itself as my grandmas: half dainty florals, half flashy hot pinks and jet blacks, like the cozy love child of several eras of Taylor Swift mashed together.

We take a seat on the old pink velvet sofa, Valeria too distressed to notice me subtly moving the LIVE, LAUGH, FUCK OFF throw pillow to the side. Now that we're sitting and the shock of her being in my house has worn off, I see her eyes are puffy and bare, like she must have cried her mascara off a while ago.

"What exactly did she say?" I ask.

Valeria sinks into the sofa looking more miserable than I've ever seen her. "She, um . . . said she couldn't handle the whiplash of the whole thing. I don't know if she believes me. And after I shut her down last week, I guess I don't blame her."

The gears in my brain are already starting to grind when Valeria says something that slows them to a temporary halt.

"Also, Sean told Milo he saw you at Bagelopolis with a suitcase? I called him in case he knew where Shay went, but he was already freaking out because he thought you were like, full leaving Blue Ridge State."

Ah. That explains why Valeria used "we" when she showed up at the front door. I've officially run out of choice foods to cuss with today, so all I can do is put my face in my hands and try not to groan.

"Which—you're not, right?" Valeria asks cautiously.

I snap my head back up. "No. I . . ."

I know I can't run away. But the crush of it all comes rushing back just the same—the grades, the radio show, my deeply inconvenient crush on a boy who is leaving me behind. The things I've been avoiding all day that will still be my problem tomorrow.

"Let me just send a quick text to Milo."

I try to bite back my guilt with little success, texting a profuse apology and letting him know I meant for Shay to tell him I was with my grandmas and I'll be back soon. I want to go into more detail or just call back, but if I am triaging the little disasters in my orbit right now, a near-tears Valeria who just up and drove two hours for my help is priority number one.

I set the phone down, shifting on the couch to level with her. "You really have feelings for Shay? Like . . . you know for sure now?"

I ask both for Valeria's sake and for Shay's. I don't want either of them risking each other's hearts if they're not both 100 percent on the same page—and if I know Shay, I suspect she still is. She's just worried about getting hurt all over again.

"I've always *known*," says Valeria, withdrawing into some quiet place in herself. "Now I just have to make her believe it."

She glances over at me then like she needs confirmation I believe her, too. Which means that it's probably time for me to fess up.

"I've known, too," I say. "You were the Bea who called into the radio show, huh?"

Valeria presses her lips together sheepishly. She must have made the connection that I was the Squire she'd confessed to after I accidentally put myself on blast yesterday. "Yeah."

One of her hands is resting on the couch. I lean forward and put mine on top of hers, giving it a small squeeze. "I gave you bad advice."

Valeria stares down at our hands, the words coming out in a mumble. "I didn't give you the full story."

I tilt my head at her. "What is the full story, then?"

"I don't think I even understood it until this weekend," she says. "This thing with Connor—it was about him, but I think it was also about me. I've just been scared."

"Of what?"

Valeria draws into herself a bit more. "I've been writing romance for so long, but with Connor everything was so different from other people I'd dated. It was the first time I understood how a single person could affect me that much. So much that it bled into everything else." Valeria looks at me with caution in her eyes, worried she's said too much. When I hold her gaze, she adds, "I was just afraid of that, I think. Of letting love in, knowing that it could have that power over me."

"I think it's supposed to, to some degree," I say carefully, ignoring the pang in my chest when I realize I understand exactly what Valeria's talking about with Connor. How if I'd really taken a good, hard look at my life, I would have known it for years. "The difference is how you use that power. Whether you use it to undermine or support."

Valeria sinks deeper into the couch. "And that's the kind of person Shay is," she says. "Someone who's got your back no matter what."

"Yeah," I agree, and not for the first time, send a silent thank-you to MTV for scooping up her last roommate so she could be mine. "She is."

"I just needed time to heal that feeling, before I could really let myself trust it again," says Valeria. "Because what I feel for Shay—it feels even bigger. And at first that made it scarier. Easier to try to ignore. But with Shay . . . I really hope I haven't messed things up too much. Because whatever we're going to be to each other, I hope it's for a long time."

I nod, knowing exactly what she means. Milo, Shay, Valeria—at some point we crossed that line with one another, and I can feel the full force of my gratitude for it in this moment now.

"I'm sorry, Andie," says Valeria. "I know that's how you thought of Connor, too."

This day has been long enough to feel like a year, and there's a strange relief in that—even thoughts of Connor feel faraway.

"I think we've wasted more than enough headspace on him."

This time Valeria's the one to squeeze my hand. "I know. But I still want to say—I'm sorry. I know it wasn't either of our faults, but I'm sorry that it happened to you."

I don't know if I'll ever get any real closure from Connor. If we'll ever be able to talk again, or if it will always be this open-ended, confusing thing that defined my life until it didn't. But there is closure in this. Certainty in it. Something more unshakable than what I had with Connor.

"I'm sorry it happened to you, too."

We hold our hands there for a moment, a beat punctuating the understanding we already had. Then Valeria shifts her hand away with a quiet smile.

"Well," she says, "the good news is, this whole realization kind of freed up my brain. I . . . actually have an ending to the book now."

"Oh yeah?" I ask. "What is it?"

Valeria looks at her shoulder bag shyly. "Do you want to read it?"

It's strange how I already know the ending before she hands it over—how I can see it in the gleam in her eye, in the hopefulness of her brows. How my chest is already warm with the same certainty of it the way I am with this moment now.

"Immediately." As she dutifully starts fishing it out, I can already feel the spark of a plan coming to life. "And you know what—I think I've got some ideas for fixing things with Shay and Milo."

"You like him too, don't you?"

Even if I had it in me to lie, Valeria's eyes are all too knowing on mine.

"He's leaving." When I swallow the words down, my entire throat feels like a bruise. "I just need to fix our friendship, is all. I can get over a little crush."

Valeria searches my face for a moment, but doesn't pry. Just rolls up the sleeves of her cardigan and asks, "What can I do?"

I nod, grounding myself as I pull up a recipe on my phone. "Hope you're not scared of food dye."

Valeria takes the phone from me as she hands over the manuscript, a smile blooming on her face. "Never a dull moment with the All-Knighters, huh?"

I grin right back. "Not a one."

Chapter Thirty-Two

Valeria and I are up half the night, me reading through her manuscript and sending it to Shay, Valeria in the kitchen creating an unholy rainbow concoction as I walk her through tomorrow's plan and start gathering supplies. The next morning Gammy Nell kisses both our cheeks, Grandma Maeve sneaks us a bottle of cheap white wine in the trunk, and my dad hugs me and tells me he'll see me on Saturday. We may be piling into Valeria's car with the terror of two people with a whole lot on the line, but at least we're on that line together.

Valeria drops me off at Cardinal first, where I feel more than a little silly carting my full, mostly untouched suitcase back up the stairs. I'm only halfway down the hall when Milo emerges from his room with the same bleary-eyed countenance he has after doing the show on very little sleep.

I open my mouth to say hello, but he spots me first. I grip the handle of my suitcase, expecting Milo to tell me off for disappearing yesterday.

"You're here," he says instead.

There's no sarcastic remark. No pretense of annoyance. He just crosses the hall like this moment is something inevitable, like there is no other thing to do except pull me into his arms. His embrace is so firm that I can't help melting into it, can't help wrapping my arms around him too, and we pull each other in.

"I thought . . . shit," he says, his voice so close to my ear that I can feel the low rumble of it all over my body. "I don't know. I'm glad you're back."

He rests his chin on the top of my head, and I bury my face in his chest, inhaling the warmth of him, the Milo-ness of him. All the thoughts that have been scrambling in my head for the past few days are gone now, replaced by this steady, low hum.

I reach for something to say before we pull apart. An apology. A joke to ease the tension. Anything other than the words "I love you," which are the only words left in my bones.

I close my eyes then, the magnitude of them rushing through with full force. These feelings I've had for Milo—the burn, the ache, the *need*—it's like Valeria said. They're so much louder, so much scarier than anything I've ever felt. At first it made them easy to dismiss. I've never let myself be led by my feelings before; I've only ever been the architect of them. I told myself how to feel, and I felt it. There was order. There were rules.

And now there is this boy with his hands pressing into the backs of my shoulders and the whole of him beating in every pulse of my heart, smashing every one of those rules to pieces.

It's not a crush. But whatever it is, it's about to crush me.

When we pull apart I nearly stumble, suddenly unmoored. He looks every bit as unsteady as I do, those green eyes searching mine like he's finally spotted a lighthouse in a storm.

"I'm sorry," I say, pulling my suitcase closer to myself. "I thought—"

"C'mere," he says, dismissing the apology before I even get a chance for it to land. "I wanted to show you something yesterday."

I follow him to his room like I'm in some kind of trance, the words *I love you, I love you, I love you* like a mantra in rhythm with my every step. He leaves the door wide open again, not even checking to see if I've followed before grabbing a small stack of papers on his desk.

"I was supposed to meet with my sister Cleo the other day. The one who works in admissions. After the radio thing sidetracked us I ended up meeting with her yesterday, and . . . well."

He hands me the pile of papers. I'm expecting them to be Milo's transcripts, or some kind of official documentation for his transfer. Instead I see the familiar "Bed of Roses" logo that heads all the articles I did for our high school paper.

"Where did you . . ."

"You said you were worried about a 'pity admission.' That it had something to do with your mom." He taps his finger on the papers in my hands, insistent. "They had no idea who your mom was, Andie. *This* is why they let you in. It's all in your file. Cleo showed me the whole thing."

I leaf through the pages, realization dawning on me. There were two envelopes the day I sent these. One had a paper copy of my transcripts to supplement the electronic files for my Blue Ridge State application. Another was the "Bed of Roses" clips my dad had asked to see.

"That's why you went to see Cleo?" I gather up the papers and hold them to my chest. "All this time . . ."

All this time I spent worrying about what kind of person I'd have to be to fit here, and it turns out it was just myself from the start. What really brought me here was something that went deeper than anything else they could measure about me. Something that evolved here in small ways each day, with every answered listener email, every segment, every push to be braver about it than I had in years.

I break out into a grin so wide that it feels like it might split my face. I've been slowly blossoming here all semester, but now thanks to this, I know I'm the one who planted the first seed.

"I had no idea I sent these in," I explain to Milo. "These clips were supposed to go to my dad."

"Well, maybe now you can send them again," Milo says, both with hope and with caution. "Get a chance to talk."

"Actually, we did. That's where I was yesterday."

Milo leans in closer. "How did it go?"

"Better than I expected." I stare down at the clips in my hand. I want to tell Milo about the conversation with my dad, and I will. But right now I'm still too floored by what he did to revisit it. "I'm . . . I just can't thank you enough for doing this."

"You belong here, Andie." The conviction in Milo's voice sounds different now. More quiet and more sure. "You always have."

I set the papers back down so haphazardly on his desk that they're already sliding off when I lurch forward, hugging him again, this time hard enough to bruise. Milo lets out an *oof* more for effect than actual surprise, not hesitating to hug me back.

"Thank you," I tell him.

He just tightens his grip and shrugs mid-hug. I don't have to see his face to know his cheeks are tinged red in that affable way they do whenever he's pleased someone.

"Well. I mostly just did it to prove I was right," he says. "That, and Cleo owed me lunch."

"Uh-huh," I laugh as we pull away from each other. "Hope it was worth your while."

Milo's smirk is slow, his eyes entirely on me in this way that makes the rest of his room tilt. "More than."

Then I perk up fast enough to make him blink in mild alarm. "I have something for you, too."

I unzip my backpack, producing a plastic container. Milo opens it carefully.

"It's Unicorn Bark," I say, on my tiptoes so I can peer into the container with him. "Inspired by unicorn cream cheese. Rainbow-swirled white chocolate, rainbow sprinkles, a ton of Froot Loops, and a dash of Trix. Like you said—'indiscriminate fruit.'"

"You," he says, with more fondness in his voice than my heart can take, "are one ridiculous human being."

If the Unicorn Bark was meant as an apology, the look on his face is all I need to know that he's accepted it. For a moment we both just stand there mere inches from each other, my neck craned up at a ridiculous angle to look at him, his own bent down so I can feel the shadow of him all over my body. I open my mouth to say something. I'm not even sure what. I suddenly can't trust myself to know what I'm going to say, what I'm going to do. All the usual functions are taken over by too many overwhelming things at once—this gratitude I have for this boy who understands me in ways nobody else has. Who knows me well enough not to try to fix me, but to give me the space to fix myself. Who is standing there with this flushed, perfect face it is taking everything in me not to lean upward and kiss right now.

The door is still wide open, so when Tyler yells, "No, it's *your* turn to decide this Friday's date spot!" and Ellie giggles back, "You're gonna regret reminding me of that when you're stuck in the drive-in theater's back-to-back Marvel feature!" we both snap back to attention.

Milo scratches the back of his neck. His dark curls have gotten longer this semester, a little more unruly. I will myself not to look at them. Not to imagine running my hands through them.

Because that's just it—it doesn't matter how I feel about him. There won't be date nights and drive-ins. There won't be afternoons watching the chickens cluck around the coop and inside jokes with his brothers and sisters and trivia wins and terrifying bagel-related experiments. There will be Milo in California and me here. Excelling at things that we love, but entirely apart.

"There was something else I wanted to tell you," says Milo.

Just then, my phone chirps in my pocket. I ignore it.

"What?" I ask, holding his gaze.

But Milo is glancing at my pocket. "Uh—you should take that."

"No, no, tell me," I say.

I need him to rip the Band-Aid off. I need him to tell me he's leaving so I can nip all this in the bud, or at least as much of it as I can. It's already overgrown in me, tangled into too many places, rooted in my heart.

But Milo shakes his head. "That's the notification you get when a professor reaches out to you directly. So you'd better take it."

My jaw drops. "Oh. *Oh*."

I pull my phone out of my back pocket, half my attention on the screen, the other half watching Milo pluck a piece of Unicorn Bark out of the container and make an endearing little happy noise when he takes a bite.

The message is from Professor Hutchison. I'm holding office hours at 11 am. Can you make it?

Eleven A.M. That's five minutes from now.

"I've—I've gotta go," I blurt. If there's a chance I can do anything to turn my grade around, I've got to take it.

Milo nods, already wheeling my suitcase out of his room and across the hall for me. "Everything good?"

"Gosh, I hope so," I say sincerely, just short of catapulting the backpack into my room once we open the door. Before I go I reach up and hug him again, brief and tight, the gesture more heartbreaking than it has any right to be. Already I am counting down to the moment he leaves. Already I am bracing myself for the hurt of it all. "But what were you going to say?"

Milo just jerks his head toward the elevator. "I'll tell you later today. I've got my last shift at Bagelopolis."

Last shift. The words are a gut punch, but I'm too wired for them to register. "I'll come find you," I promise.

He doesn't bother to hold me to it, ushering me out with a "Go, go, go."

And then I'm off like a bullet, running through campus fast enough to outpace the entire Blue Ridge State track team mid-morning workout. I reach the psychology building at 10:59, taking a minute to wheeze and attempt to collect my sleep-deprived, deeply unathletic self before knocking on Professor Hutchison's office door.

"Come in."

It's the first time I've actually seen her in this office since our one-on-one meeting. Since then it's always been TAs leading the sessions, and plenty of other kids here to do the walk of statistical analysis shame with me. I hover in the doorway, glancing back as if someone else might turn up at any moment.

"It's just us this morning," says Professor Hutchison without tearing her eyes away from her laptop screen.

My voice decides to go up about three octaves when I squeak out, "Oh." Professor Hutchison doesn't look away from her screen when she gestures for me to sit. I do just that, my skin suddenly itching like the failure is poison ivy, the kind that spreads fast.

For a few moments, Professor Hutchison doesn't say anything. When I can't stand it anymore, I break the silence myself.

"I did study. I really did. I'm so sorry for bombing it, but—but I don't want you to think I don't take the class seriously. I really have."

"Oh, I know," she says mildly. She minimizes the window on her screen and moves her swivel chair over to her desk, tapping on a folder. "The TAs keep track of everyone who comes in here. You've been in here more often than anyone this past month."

I sink farther into my chair. It's true. This office is practically as familiar as my dorm.

"So you should have done better," she says.

I close my eyes. "I know," I say miserably. "I just . . ."

"Was recovering from that very embarrassing incident with the radio show."

By now I know Professor Hutchison is not one to pull her punches, but I find myself letting out a sharp laugh of surprise just the same.

"Yeah," I say. "There was . . . that."

"I believe you, you know. That you would have done well on the exam if it weren't for that." She taps on the folder again. "It's a big class, but I keep track of everyone's progress. Since that midterm, you've been steadily improving."

It's a relief at least that she doesn't think I slacked off. And while I'm concerned about the state of my grade, I still can't help myself from asking, "How did you know it was me on the show?"

For the first time since I've known her, Professor Hutchison seems to hesitate. Like she's used to having the power in a conversation, used to using it to keep students at arm's length, and she knows whatever she says next is going to make that shift.

"I didn't for a while. Not when you were first starting out, and everything sounded scripted. I even called in for advice once myself," she says, bemused. "But the longer the segments went on, your voice—at some point it sounded too much like Amy's to mistake."

It's jarring, hearing someone call her "Amy"—for as long as I can remember, people have referred to her in relation to me. "Your mom" and not much else. Before I even ask I have this strange sensation of peeling back another layer of her, one I didn't think I'd get to see.

"You knew her?"

Professor Hutchison goes very still. "Well," she says after a moment, "someone has to recruit the Knights."

I think back to Shay mentioning how Milo was tapped from the announcements he gave in the cafeteria, but couldn't explain how. "And you chose my mom?"

Professor Hutchison doesn't hesitate this time, and I get the sense from the sliver of a smirk on her face that she wants to tell the story every bit as much as I want to hear it.

"Oh, no. Your mom chose herself. The year she started she went to as many professors as she could asking questions about the organization ban. I was newer at the time. Tenured professors were careless about gossiping around me. So I knew it was a mismanagement of funds, and I told her so." She leans in closer to her end of the desk, smirk deepening. "Not ten hours later she broadcast what I told her word for word and got herself kicked off the school's main radio show."

She may be smirking, but by now I'm full-on grinning. As hard as it is sometimes to imagine my mom at my age, it's not at all hard to imagine that.

"She came back to me. Asked if I had any more information. I didn't, really," says Professor Hutchison. Her eyes cut to the door, toward the hall beyond it. "But she wanted a way to get back on the air, and I had my original office."

"The studio," I realize. A cramped little space that twenty years ago could easily have been an office for one of Blue Ridge State's newest hires.

Professor Hutchison nods. "I wasn't involved in the ribbon hunt or anything. It all just took on a life of its own, the same way it always has with each Knight. But she asked me when she graduated if I could help keep it up by tapping other people for it, and I've been doing that ever since."

She waves a hand like she never meant to get emotionally invested in the whole thing, but the way she blinks hard before she turns to her laptop screen gives her away. So does the way her voice lowers when she says, "Amy was a force to be reckoned with."

I smile. "Yeah. She was."

There are a few beats where Professor Hutchison takes a

breath like she is going to add something else. It's usually the part where people tell me they're so sorry about what happened to her; how they can only imagine where she'd be today if she were still alive. I see her decide not to. It's not that she doesn't think it. It's that we both knew her talent well enough that it goes without saying.

She clears her throat. "Anyway, I called you in here to talk about your grades. You and I both know you'll have to repeat the class with a grade like that."

I stare down at my lap. There's still candle wax in my nails from last night's shenanigans with Valeria. "Yeah."

Professor Hutchison leans forward at her desk, making rare and deliberate eye contact. "Which is why I'm telling you something I don't tell most. I drop the lowest exam grade at the end of the semester."

My insides feel like they might liquefy with relief. "Really?"

"So with your other failed score dropped and this D, you'd be on track to pull through. So long as you keep going to tutoring sessions and coming to office hours." She pushes a piece of paper toward me. "There are a set number of hours I'm usually here without the TAs. You're welcome to come by then, too."

"Thank you," I say sincerely. I worry on my bottom lip. I don't want to ask it, but I know that the relief won't last for long if I don't get a clear answer right now. "But you're not—this isn't just because you liked my mom, right?"

"It may have taken me a few months to realize you were the Squire, but I knew you were your mom's kid the minute I saw you with that silly ribbon in your bag," she says, leveling me with her usual no-nonsense expression. "If I were going to give any special treatment it would have started then."

I sit up a little straighter, embarrassed and pleased at the same time.

She taps on the paper again. "The grade drop is still a secret, though, so don't let anyone know I told you." She pointedly doesn't look at me when she adds, "I figured I owed you a solid."

At some point in this conversation I connected the dots. We don't get a lot of non-student callers, and hers stuck with me. "It worked, then? You going to the conference."

She still doesn't quite meet my eye, even if I can see a trace of amusement in hers. "We've started getting more involved in each other's interests, yes. And it's been helpful." She presses her lips together and raises her brows just enough for me to know that's all she's willing to say on the subject.

"I'm glad."

She smirks. "Also, I wash my hands of whatever you and Milo decide about the radio show. But you have my blessing either way."

All things considered, it may be the closest I'll ever come to my mom's approval about my involvement with *The Knights' Watch*. But oddly—comfortingly—it doesn't change much. I don't need it anymore, the way I thought I did at the beginning of the semester, when I felt all this pressure to live up to the legacy she built.

Now it finally feels the way I'm sure my mom would have wanted it to—like I've been working toward my own legacy all along.

Professor Hutchison shoots me another pointed look. "So long as you kick yourself into high gear on these grades."

"Absolutely," I say without missing a beat. "I won't let you down."

The moment I step out of her office, I know I've avoided yesterday's radio show long enough. If I ever want to come back—whether as the Squire or Milo's replacement or even just as the person who answers emails—I need to listen and own up to the aftermath of it.

But first I duck out of the campus, off the little windy path that leads into the gazebo in the arboretum. It takes me through sun-dappled trees and new spring blossoms, a world so colorful and so far removed from the thundersnow incident that it feels like I'm stepping into another reality. Stepping carefully, of course, because the last thing I want to do is interrupt Valeria's plan.

Once I finally catch sight of them, though, it's clear that a meteor could fall out of the sky without either of them noticing.

The scene is all set, just the way Valeria and I planned it, but somehow even sweeter. A re-creation of the ending scene when the heroine runs away from her own coronation, revealing that she only attended to obtain a hidden key, the final enchanted object to break the curse on both her and the sorceress's kingdoms—the same curse causing the generations-long feud between them, and the same one that the sorceress has spent her entire life trying to break on her own.

Except once the heroine meets the sorceress in the woods, they discover that the key wasn't the final piece they need. The two of them, with the sacrifice of all their magic combined, are the final piece. So they lay out the candles and the herbs and the crystals they need with the ancient prophecy, and just before they have to cast the potentially deadly spell, confess their love to each other in a sweeping, glittering, romantic moment in the spring sun.

We made do with fairy lights on the shed and tea lights around the picnic blankets, crystals on loan from Harriet's dorm room, and actual food instead of herbs. But it's clear from the way Shay and Valeria have migrated next to each other on the blanket, the food untouched and their fingers intertwined, that the romance did not need to be borrowed or bought for the occasion. It's right there in Valeria's quiet smile, in the glint in Shay's eyes.

My heart feels so full it might tip over. I've never believed in fairy tales; I've only ever believed in our power over our own fates. But whatever happens next, we'll always have this—the kind of moment that proves magic isn't just for pages in a story, but something you can find all on your own.

Chapter Thirty-Three

I feel a pinch of guilt when I put off meeting Milo at Bagelopolis. A few hours ago I wanted him to just tell me he was leaving, so I could make myself face the facts. Now that I am walking away in the haze of Shay and Valeria's happiness, I want to stay wrapped in it like a cocoon. I want to exist for just a little while longer in a world where we're all still here not just until the end of the semester, but for years to come.

I try to tell myself it'll be easier. Milo's not interested in a relationship. With him gone, it'll be that much easier to get over him. No constant reminders of the way he always smells like freshly brewed coffee or the way I can sometimes turn that smirk of his into a genuine smile or how my calves are always tingling after we hang out from standing on my tiptoes.

It's like Shay said with Valeria; they'd still be friends, and it would be more than enough. But enough is a little easier to swallow when it isn't staring you in the face every day.

With that, I force myself to put on my headphones and sit on a bench on the outskirts of campus that borders the main road. Milo's voice floods my ears the same way it has a hundred times, and I lean back like the sound is some kind of balm, letting the familiarity of it wash over me.

"Good morning, Knights. Spent the weekend offline, what did I miss?"

If I'm not mistaken, I can hear Shay's faint snort in the background.

"Really, though. The nice thing about having my identity revealed to you lot is that none of you have any idea who I am anyway. So no point in making it weird. I'm still the Knight, and you're still—well, if the state of the quad after that dance party is any indication, probably hungover. So if it's all well and good, I'll keep giving you campus news and warning you off the dining hall's most recent monstrosities, and you'll keep ignoring me by eating the chili dogs anyway. Balance has been restored."

It's quick, wry, and perfectly executed. Milo really is a pro. He transitions into the daily news without another word about what happened, and I let myself get lulled into the familiar rhythm of events and club announcements. That is, until Milo stops halfway through signing off.

"Oh. We have a caller." A beat. "We have *several* callers. Uh . . . I mean, it's six thirty on a Wednesday morning, why not punish ourselves? Caller one, you're live."

I instantly recognize the caller's voice as none other than Harriet from our floor. "I just wanted to say—I fucking love the Squire. She's the only reason my roommate got her head out of her ass and asked out her now boyfriend. We're all very proud."

Milo lets out a laugh, something he very rarely does on air. "Yeah. She's got that effect on people."

"She does. Whoever that asshole was on the recording with her—well, I for one am Team Squire. And I know I'm not the only one."

Milo lets out a hum of acknowledgment. "Gotta be honest, she's not here today. But knowing her, she'll listen to this later. So noted." And after a second: "And well—we're also Team Squire. So thanks."

I tighten my grip on my phone as the words pool in my chest, warm and known.

"Eh. I'd say 'thank you' back, but I wouldn't want to say it too loud and break quiet hours," says Harriet, a clear if not loving dig at Milo's tenure as the RA.

Milo lets out yet another short laugh before saying, "Well, looks like we've got more calls to get through. Hit me, caller number two."

It's more of the same—people calling in to say they love the Squire. People calling in with rare gems I never usually get: updates on where they are now, after they've asked for my advice. The caller who had the boundary issues with their boss. An emailer who was struggling to get independence from her parents even though they were a junior. Another caller who had issues with their roommate. All people who are better off now than they were before, and willing to go to bat for me because of it.

Their defense of me means a lot, but their updates mean much more. Only with people in my immediate circle have I been able to see the effect of my words. Understanding the full reach of them fills me to the brim, like the happiness of it could tip over my heart.

One of the callers is more candid than the others. "I've always been too scared to call in or even email," she says. "But I-I've seen her help friends of mine. And I listen to her on every Friday broadcast. I'm usually a total cynic, so—she's basically the whole reason I believe in love again."

There's a pause so long that I hear my mom's warning about dead air in my ears. But the air isn't dead. It's impossibly full. I understand that when Milo finally finds his voice again.

"Yeah," he says. "For what it's worth—me too."

The words knock the wind out of me. No, not just the words, but the sincerity of them. I know Milo's voice too well to doubt it.

"So is she coming back or what?" the caller asks.

"God, I hope so," says Milo. "Can you imagine if I were the one giving advice on this show? Campus would be up in flames by the end of the week."

There's a brief pause where the caller laughs and Milo waits them out, clearly assuming she has more to say. When she doesn't, he speaks up again, his voice low but clear.

"I mean it, though. We're all better off with her around. I'm glad everyone else seems to agree." Milo takes in a heavy breath. "Alright, that's enough calls for a lifetime, go bother someone else. And have a good day, I guess. Or as good of a day as we can have with the looming threat of chili dogs over our heads."

The podcast recording of the show ends and I still haven't moved a single muscle, Milo's words pressed into me like ink on a page.

For what it's worth—me too.

I stand up from the bench, the phone nearly falling out of my shaking hands. Milo wouldn't say something like that without meaning it; he never does. He wanted me to hear it. He wanted me to know.

My feet are carrying me to the intersection dividing campus from the main road before I even know where I'm going or what I'm going to do. I've spent too much of my life overthinking things, but this—this is somehow both the easiest and scariest thing I will ever do.

The outside of Bagelopolis is quiet, the inside just the same. Cozy and fragrant and inviting. I expect Milo to be in the back, but there he is, standing at the register for once, his brow furrowed over an inventory slip. His blue apron is pulled taut across his body and his flannel sleeves are rolled up, exposing the lean muscle of his forearms. His hair is a mess of dark curls, overgrown and moving in tandem with every minute shake of his head, and his cheeks are flushed from the post-lunch rush.

I've always known that he's beautiful. But it's when he looks up and sees me standing there that my heart presses against my chest, because he is so much more than that. He is the steady pulse of something known, something understood — not a person to build your world around, but a person to build one with.

"Hey, you," says Milo, his eyes lighting up. He jerks a thumb toward the back. "I'm about to go on break. Want some tea, or — oh."

I make it to the register, sucking in a breath to buoy myself. Then I grab the coffee cup he keeps at the register, the one I know from experience will be full of piping-hot Eternal Darkness. I close my eyes, abandon my last shred of self-preservation, and *chug*.

I nearly sputter it right back out when I reach the dregs.

Milo's expression oscillates between quizzical and concerned. "Why do I feel like I just watched a crime against nature?"

"*How*," I wheeze.

Milo pries the coffee cup from my hands. "More like why?"

I clear my throat, regretting coffee beans for ever being born. "I needed liquid courage," I manage to choke out. "I have something to tell you."

"Uh . . ."

Sean comes up from behind and pats Milo on the shoulder. "Go take your break before she starts swinging from the light fixtures."

Milo leads the way to the back exit, checking over his shoulder like he's worried the caffeine exposure might combust me. And maybe it will. I can feel my heart beating like there are ten of them all over my body, a heat coursing through my veins that might just turn into an inferno. He holds the door open for me and we blink our way into the bright sunshine of the back parking lot.

I take a deep breath. I did not plan to do this in front of a loaded dumpster. I didn't plan to do this at all. But if I've learned anything this semester, it's that sometimes you have to chuck the plans out the window.

"Here is the thing," I say.

Milo watches me so intently that if there's a world beyond his gaze, I can't see it. I should be afraid, maybe. But it's hard to be afraid of anything, looking into those eyes and knowing that I have nothing to lose; that the feelings we have for each other are strong enough that they can take any form. Whether we walk away from this friends or step into something else entirely, we still have each other for life.

So I let the words pour out of me—words I've said plenty of times before, but words that have an entirely new meaning now that I'm saying them to him.

"I love you."

The words feel like hurtling myself off a cliff without knowing where I'll land. I want to crush my eyes shut, want to brace myself for whatever comes next, but I can't. Not when Milo's are still steady on mine, so instantly soft, so instantly deep.

"Andie, I—"

"And maybe you don't feel the same way, and that's okay, too. I—I just wanted you to know," I say quickly, the anxiety catching up to me faster than I anticipated. "I needed you to know. Because either way, I want us to be part of each other's lives. And California might be far, but there are always school breaks, and we could FaceTime, and—"

"Andie," Milo tries again, a hint of a smile on his face.

But I'm not finished. "It wouldn't be perfect, but it's like your dad said, right? Anything worth doing starts with a—"

And then Milo's firm hands are cupping my jaw, bringing my face up toward him as he leans down to meet me, catching my mouth and the last of my words with his. I lean into his touch, into the gentle warmth of the kiss, dizzy with the everything of him.

The burn I felt before, the ache—it was just the beginning of a rising tide, one that is swelling in me now, moving me on its own command. I've never kissed like this before; never *been* kissed like this before. With this sudden, frantic urgency, with the beautiful desperation of two people so overwhelmed that it borders on senseless, standing on the edge of the possibility of it all. This kiss, and all the ones that will come after. This moment, and the infinity beyond it.

I fall into him, his back pressed against the brick wall of the store, his hands still bracing me like I am something too precious to let go. The rhythm of the kiss softens, slow and exploratory. We both taste like coffee and sweetness and something that is just us, something that makes me feel bolder than I've ever been.

When we pull apart, his eyes are a brighter green than I've ever seen them; like spring leaves, like evergreen peaks, like new beginnings.

"Hey, new kid," he says, pressing his forehead against mine.

I'm not even sure who answers, because I don't have a single wit left. "Yeah?"

Milo's hands press into the small of my back, and something in me pools warm and low, feeling the words in every inch of me before he says them out loud. "I love you, too."

For once, I'm all out of words. I just tilt my face toward his and kiss him again. It's sweet and chaste, the kind of kiss that leaves me feeling more exposed than the first one, the kind that defines what we are to each other more than words ever could.

"Also," he says lowly, "I'm not leaving."

The words feel too much like I'm dreaming to let them sink in. "You're not?"

Milo laughs, and there's something different about it. Something unselfconscious, the kind of happiness that belongs in a childhood that we're stealing back right now.

He cups one of my cheeks with his hand, watching my face. "That's what I was trying to tell you earlier."

He's expecting me to smile, but I shake my head into his palm. "Not—not because of . . ." I lean into his touch, trying to make him understand. "Milo, the last thing I'd ever want is to hold you back."

"Same to you," says Milo easily, using his hand to my brush my hair out of my face. We pull apart just enough that his arms are still around my neck and my hands are still on his hips. "But this is Cleo's fault, not yours. She pulled out my application file, too. Showed me my essay. How I wrote about the town that raised me. How going to college at Blue Ridge wasn't just an opportunity to learn, but to take what I learned to give it back to this place."

I smile warmly, thinking of the Flynn legacy and how deeply ingrained it is not just in this town, but in one another. The kind of closeness that isn't just bound by blood, but by love.

"The truth is, every time I thought about California, it didn't feel real to me," Milo admits. "But this is my home. I don't want to go somewhere new—I want to make this place something new. I want to do what your mom did, and be a voice for this community." He lowers his voice, adding, "And I want . . . to spend more time with my family. With my friends."

The words seem to have their own warmth, spreading from the tips of his fingers into every part of my body.

"So you're staying." I lean back so I can smack lightly at the zipper to his jacket. "You scared me. You said it was your last shift."

Milo's eyes widen, only just realizing what I must have thought he meant by that.

"Shit. That's the other thing I wanted to tell you. After you said my name on the broadcast—well, it turns out the local radio station had been trying to scout me for an internship. Paid." He lifts up a hand to tweak my chin and I feel this thrill run up my spine, thinking of all the quiet little gestures like this I'll get to have with him now. "I start next week."

I didn't think I could get even giddier than I already was, but the smile on my face is threatening to burst. "Milo. Congratulations," I say, leaning into him again. "You're going to knock their socks off."

"We'll see about that," says Milo. "But between the internship and starting the broadcast program here, it does mean my schedule's going to take a hit."

"Oh." The broadcast program. I'd almost forgotten. "They're really okay with you being the Knight?"

"Oh, not at all," says Milo, the pride clear in his tone. "But they're letting it slide. I think the fancy local internship probably helped."

The relief rushes like a wave, one that finally settles the fear that's burned in me ever since I found out I'd put his secret on blast. I'm about to ask him for details, but he's already grinning at me, poised to give them.

"But the fact of the matter is, I can't do both. Which means . . . we need a new Knight." His eyes gleam. "Someone who knows the ins and outs of the show. Someone who can do it justice. Someone a little bit nosy, someone short, someone who makes lengthy PowerPoint presentations about their friends' major life decisions for fun—"

"Okay, okay," I say, laughing. "I get the message loud and clear."

Milo's smile softens. "So you'll do it?"

This time I don't hesitate. I don't feel the weight of it anymore—not my mom's legacy. Not the expectations of Connor and his parents. Not the years I spent trying to fit, the years I worried I wasn't enough, the years I felt like I had to prove myself to other people. Now it's only a matter of what I have to prove to myself.

"Yeah," I say firmly. "I'll do it."

Milo leans down to kiss me again. I marvel at how easily my body can respond to something it barely understands the edges of yet. How easily it can trust something that feels both certain and wild, something that was never part of the plan.

How suddenly the world can feel wider than it's ever been, and I've never felt more ready to meet it.

Eight Months Later

"Not to be dramatic, but we need to leave immediately." Shay's hand is poised on the door to our little off-campus apartment in her autumnal knit sweater and denim skirt. "This is my favorite holiday."

I reach up and brush off a lingering glitter fleck on her forehead. "But Halloween was yesterday," I say. And holy moly, do we have a camera roll full of pictures of us all dressed to the nines as *Kingdom of Lumarin* characters to prove it (save Milo, who wore his normal clothes and claimed he was dressed up as a "reader").

Shay responds in kind by pulling an errant fake cobweb strand off my purse. "Forget Halloween. We're about to get free tickets to the most glorious shit show of the *year*."

I knit my eyebrows at Shay in confusion and she just says, "You'll see."

On our way out Shay knocks on the apartment a few doors down from ours, prompting Valeria to call "Just a sec!" from inside. She joins us a few moments later, her curls and makeup immaculate, no evidence of glitter, cobwebs, or the aftermath of us all eating cold pizza on the floor a few hours ago to be found.

"Hello," she says cheerfully, leaning down to Shay for a quick kiss.

As they pull away Shay pretends to grouse, "Morning people should be illegal."

"You and Milo can make it a class-action lawsuit," says Valeria, glancing down the hall of the apartment to his room. Once Milo decided not to be an RA this year and move off campus, he and Valeria figured it would be easiest for them to move in together. We've basically been living in an insufferably adorable state of double dating in this complex ever since.

"But without morning people, who would make our beloved bagels?" I remind them.

Shay sighs. "Touché."

We cut through one of the outer paths of the arboretum to get to campus, the leaves on the trees tinted gold and rusty orange and flame red, the air sweet and earthy, the dirt paths soft beneath our feet. Fall is the final season I haven't seen Blue Ridge State in, and I already know it's going to be my favorite.

"Fancy new trail markers," Shay notes with a nod.

I beam, taking in the reflective circles in different colors that I helped post on the trees to mark the different trail paths yesterday. Just one of the many little maintenance jobs and improvements we've made to the arboretum in the past few months to make it more student-friendly and accessible, a place people can go to get out of their own heads and relax.

Speaking of—"Can I borrow your phone's fancy camera?" I ask Valeria. "I should snap a few shots for the wilderness volunteer Instagram page."

"A social media hero," says Valeria, handing her phone to me. "What would the yellow team do without you?"

I return her slight smirk as I pause briefly to focus on a particularly vibrant branch, the rest of the scenery blurring satisfyingly in the background. I've never *quite* let her off the hook for knowing what the ribbons meant all along. In Milo's defense, he truly didn't care enough his freshman year to find out what the fuss was all about. But Valeria was secretly on the blue team coordinating a bunch of the academic-related events half the time—hence why she had that extra white ribbon in her bag in the library that day, and how she got into volunteer student tutoring in the first place.

"Still can't believe you chose yellow, considering your track record with the elements," says Shay, gesturing out toward the campus lake just beyond the trees.

"Hey," I say indignantly. "I've only fallen in the lake twice."

Shay lets out a snort in lieu of listing my many mishaps since joining the yellow team, which include and are not limited to falling butt-first out of a tree during apple-picking season, toppling off the dock as Piper was teaching me how to lead wilderness tours over the summer, and somehow, against all odds, locking myself inside the chicken coop for several hours before Jamie found me in a sea of feathers and eggs.

Mishaps aside, sometimes I'm still surprised I chose yellow, too. My dad was right in that I had more than enough ribbons to join the voting boards for any of them, and even if I didn't, I was still welcome to join any of them as a member. At first the answer seemed simple: join the yellow team for myself, and join the red team I'd worked so hard to be in, just like my mom.

I had a few weeks to decide for sure, and those few weeks were pivotal—they were weeks when the ribbon hunt was over, and my world opened up in a new way. Aside from studying, my weekends were completely my own. Instead of chasing after ribbons, I found myself wandering around the paths in the arboretum, signing up for different volunteer activities to get to know the area better, even taking a few excursions off campus with a group of students who met up every few weeks.

It was all the magic of the hikes my parents took me on, but with a new kind of magic all its own—the independence of it. Of knowing I could explore anything I wanted, whenever I wanted, and it didn't have to amount to or count for anything. A sense of purpose that wasn't driven by any kind of reward, or a fear of consequences. Something that was just mine.

When the choice came, it stunned me how there suddenly wasn't one to make. I'd join the yellow team, and only the yellow team. It was the current under my skin, the one that felt like the perfect mix of inherited and earned—a love not just for a place because of what it means for your history, but for your future. A love for a place so deep that you feel compelled to make it the best it can possibly be. And so I decided to focus solely on what brought me the most joy: I'd help preserve the natural beauty of this place I'd fallen in love with, water to trees to mountains to sky. I'd make my own path at Blue Ridge State, one winding trail through the woods at a time.

Well. Not without my fair share of tripping on tree roots and poison ivy and near frostbite. But at least Mother Nature always keeps me humble.

"Behold," says Shay as we round the bend into the main street of campus. She comes to a dead stop and puts her hands on her hips, breathing in deeply. "Soak it all in. Twenty-thousand-plus students pretending they haven't just mutually destroyed all their livers as their parents descend on campus."

Only then does it occur to me that November 1 being the school's annual Family Day is either the most careless or the most cruelly calculated move on the planet. Because even in the five seconds we've been on campus, I've spotted a student with Resting "I'm Going To Upchuck" Face lodged between beaming parents, another student with enough mascara under her eyes to put raccoons to shame begging her mom to get her a Gatorade, and what appears to be a still-drunk bee wandering around campus singing the "I'm bringing home a baby bumblebee" song to himself.

I stifle a laugh as what appears to be a world-weary roommate steps in to collect the bumblebee. "Okay. This is quality entertainment."

"Be *nice*," says Valeria, playfully swatting at Shay. "This would have been us if Andie hadn't been in charge of food and hydration last night."

"I'll be nice again on November second. Today?" says Shay, scanning the expanse of our deeply hungover campus. "Today is for me."

We maneuver our way through the figurative and occasionally literal zombies to let ourselves into the back of Bagelopolis. None of us actually work here anymore—Milo spent his last month as the Knight pushing his work-study program agenda more aggressively than ever before, and between his efforts and his newly public identity letting him take a more hands-on approach, it's actually started to work. Since the new program expansion kicked in, Shay's been able to do her hours at the local bookstore, and Piper's taken me on as an assistant for her wilderness tours. But Sean still treats us to our old employee discount, which was never formally explained beyond "take as many bagels as you want as long as Sean gets his beloved chocolate pretzel bagel first."

We set to work, Valeria making standard sesame bagels with honey-nut cream cheese for her parents, Shay going the savory route for hers, and me grabbing my dad's signature strawberry cream cheese with the cheesy garlic bagel along with some plain bagels with cookie dough cream cheese for me, Kelly, and Ava. I'm about to wrap up an extra with unicorn cream cheese when I'm interrupted by a hand swooping from above to grab it, and the familiar press of a kiss against my temple.

"I'm assuming this is mine," says Milo, his mouth already poised to take a bite.

I turn around to find Milo close enough that I can lean my forehead into his shoulder. I breathe in his familiar sweet, earthy scent as I tilt my face up to meet his gaze. "We're picnicking in literally ten minutes."

"Yes, but I've been up since zero o'clock," says Milo. His internship has him up absurdly early every weekday morning, but he only goes on the air a few times a week. I can tell from the gleam in his eyes that today was one of those days. "I need sustenance to stay awake."

I return his grin, eyeing the cup of Eternal Darkness already in his hand. "That hasn't kicked in yet?"

"Oh, this?" says Milo, lifting the cup. "This is just so Ava doesn't kick my ass if we play tag again. That kid's a live wire. Gotta stay on my toes."

I lean in closer, staying on my own toes to reach him for a quick kiss, feeling the slight fall chill under my skin warm at his touch. He helps me finish wrapping up the bagels, chatting with Valeria about her application process to add a creative writing minor and teasing Shay about the semi-drunk reenactment she attempted of a *Kingdom of Lumarin* scene that led to a half-hour-long search for one of her shoes.

Then we split off—Valeria to meet her parents, Shay to meet up with her sister, and Milo to head out with me to the quad, where I already know my dad and Kelly arrived a few minutes ago from the text updates we've been sending. Ava spots us before we spot her, beelining from the massive blanket where Kelly's already laid out fruit and brownies to go with our bagels. Ava collides with Milo first, who lets out a staged *oof* as he leans down to hug her briefly before she pivots like a puppy and nearly bowls me over with a hug, too.

"I got to take the day off school to visit," she crows to us, not waiting to see if we're keeping up when she turns right back around and runs back toward the blanket.

My dad gives me a bear hug and Kelly follows it up with a

happy, tight squeeze of her own, her homemade bracelets jingling under her warm flannel. I visited them in Lake Anna just last weekend, so there isn't too much to catch up on, but Kelly and Ava update me on her science project while my dad and Milo discuss the upcoming annual Thanksgiving game between Blue Ridge State and our rival school. The conversation has an easy ebb and flow I couldn't have quite imagined before we all met, but seems perfectly natural now.

Eventually Milo splits off to show Kelly and Ava where the public restrooms are, leaving me and my dad to perch with all our stuff. He waits until they're out of earshot to move closer to me on the blanket.

"How are you feeling?" my dad asks.

It's a testament to how much we talk now that we can ask each other questions like this—like we've dog-eared book pages on each other's lives, and can jump right back into the middle of them without any context. And as far as book pages go, the next chapter of mine might be a big one.

"Good. But nervous," I admit.

The feeling is so unfamiliar to me these days that it's almost a welcome one. I've gotten so at ease at the mic for *The Knights' Watch* each day that it's just a happy part of my routine. Now being nervous doesn't feel like a sign of disaster—it feels like the energy of a new opportunity ahead.

Because today's show isn't just going to be *The Knights' Watch*— it's also serving as an audition. A few weeks ago I was approached by a Blue Ridge State graduate who ended up working for a media entertainment start-up looking for new and upcoming talent to develop and spearhead their own content. After I went mildly viral on the alumni page for last year's slipup, she started tuning in on the days I segmented, and kept at it once I took over. Now she wants to know if I'd be interested in adapting a podcast for a broader audience loosely based on the show—one that she'd produce weekly, and one that comes with the opportunity of possibly expanding into the network's smaller pool of on-screen talent as well.

It's been a few weeks since then, and I've spent most of them developing a new structure for the potential podcast so I could call the shots on it—a large task, but one I relished taking on, given the experience I already had with building my own version of *The Knights' Watch* this year.

The biggest change made to *The Knights' Watch* right off the bat was the time it aired. Now instead of six thirty A.M., the show goes live at five P.M., giving callers an opportunity to phone in without having to pry their eyes open to do it. That way we can do a prepared segment either on something timely or an issue multiple students have emailed about, then transition into taking live calls. The same way other Knights had their own focuses, I have mine—and both by design and because my identity isn't a secret, it's much more of a dialogue between the show and the listeners than other Knights had in the past.

That said, there are nods to other Knights in my version, too. Because it's so community-oriented, we have a lot of people calling in for more practical advice and concerns, spanning everything from the work-study program reforms Milo spearheaded to more local on- and off-campus causes like my mom once did. And we still update students on campus goings-on at the beginning of each broadcast; I used to think I wouldn't enjoy that part as much, but I've come to understand that being ingrained in what's happening here is *part* of being able to effectively help. So the heart of the show is still there, even if it looks a little different on the outside now.

But the higher-ups from the start-up listening to my broadcast today aren't listening so much for the format as they are to get a sense for me and my on-air personality. It's a test to see what I might be able to do for them—not just for the podcast they're considering me for, but the potential beyond it.

I'm feeling confident, but I think part of that is because I am not so worried about the stakes now as I was when the idea of doing this really scared me. Now that I've started to deal with that fear and rely on the experience under my belt, I understand those goals I made weren't meant to be a road map. They weren't meant to fit neatly in that perfectly packaged memoir I always pictured writing one day, everything decided for me, everything pressed into place. The reality is that nothing about this is going to be linear. It's all going to evolve in its own time.

The same way the show will someday, when another Knight takes it over and makes the show their own. The same way my life will when I eventually move on from it, and figure out which step to take next. I'm just going to have to trust myself along the way.

"I've been digging through some of our old things," my dad tells me. By "our" I know he means his and my mom's things. My dad and I may talk about her a lot more openly now, but I know going through the things he put in storage with Grandma Maeve these past few weeks hasn't been an easy process for him. "I have a lot of stuff saved for you to go through at your grandmas', but I figured you should have this now."

He hands me a worn metal compass, the same one my mom used to take on our hikes and famously ignore. It's still beaten up at its edges, the glass slightly cracked, looking more used than it ever actually was. I smile to myself, the mischief in my mom's declarations clear in my head even if the words aren't exact: *Forget the compass. Let's go on an adventure.*

The memory doesn't well up without an ache, but it's a sweeter one now. As if the more my dad and I have talked about her, the more we've had the chance to heal; like some part of the grief was always going to be suspended in motion until we started coming to terms with it together.

My dad's smile is pressed into a proud line. "Unlike your mother, you and the yellow squad might actually put it to good use."

I thumb the compass, watching the arrow adjust as I tilt it slightly in my hand. I will always need her, I realize. I will need the memories of the way she loved me, especially in moments like this when I can still feel that love in full force. But I don't need her footsteps. I don't need her path to lead the way. I slide the compass into my pocket, knowing wherever it takes me, the paths will be all my own.

"Thanks, Dad," I say quietly.

His own voice is firm and earnest. "Knock 'em dead, A-Plus."

We spend the rest of the late morning wearing out Ava on the quad and walking around campus to show him all my new favorite haunts. My dad regales us with stories from his own time here, waiting until Ava's out of earshot to tell us about his own first Family Day, when Gammy Nell caught him so hungover she threatened to stop sending him care packages stuffed with homemade cookies every week. (Apparently this idea was dropped when she realized it would be every bit as much punishment to her as my dad.)

When it's time for them to make the drive back I hug them all in turn, my dad giving me an extra squeeze and saying they can't wait to tune in today. For a little while Milo and I stay on the quad, Milo finishing up his reading for a class, me going over today's segment on little-known campus health resources. We alternate between using each other as headrests and footrests in the variety of Andie-and-Milo-studying-together positions our bodies have grown accustomed to these past few months until Milo stretches.

"I better head out to meet Harley," he says.

I smile at the words, and the way I hear them a whole lot more often these days. Milo and Harley have slowly but surely been weaving their way back into each other's lives. Enough that we even went on a joint hike once with him and Nora, and are all invited to a Friendsgiving at their apartment before we all leave for break.

"But we'll be tuning in this evening," Milo says. "The whole Flynn family."

I glance up at him from my perch, his cheeks perfectly sun-kissed and his curls messy from the heat, his eyes warm on mine.

"Chickens included?" I ask, leaning in close.

"If they don't fight over which one of them is calling in again," says Milo, closing the distance to press a kiss to my lips.

I grin as he pulls away, then reach up and sneak another kiss. "For good luck," I say cheekily.

Milo's own smile widens as he shakes his head. "Trust me, new kid. You don't need it."

I head over to the studio on my own, breathing in the cool fall air to settle my thoughts. Shay's already at the computer when I get there, doing what she does best whenever I'm nervous, and pretending it's just any other broadcast. Still, I notice she's got an extra printout of my notes on hand just in case.

I pull my own out of my purse, but it's more out of habit than anything else—these days I get into such an easy rhythm that I rarely need to look at them. Then I sit on my stool, feeling the reassuring weight of the compass shifting in my pocket as I settle in.

"Ready?" Shay asks from the control panel.

I nod, grounding myself by glancing around this familiar room. At the four walls that have been home to some of my best and worst moments, and the pictures on them that have watched it all. My mother's beam. Milo's wry smirk. And now my picture just above his, grinning like I've swallowed the sun.

Maybe I should be more nervous than this. Somewhere under the peace that settles over me, I probably am. But there is a deep comfort in that moment in seeing my own happiness reflected back at me. In this feeling of being deeply rooted and known and loved, and the understanding that this happiness I have found here—in the friends I have made my family, in the dreams I've reclaimed and rebuilt, in the heart I've learned to follow—is just the start of so much more to come.

"Going live in five, four . . ."

Shay stops counting out loud and uses her fingers for the "three, two, one." I watch the quiet beats go by, a smile blooming on my face as I take in a breath, lean forward, and let the adventure begin again.

Acknowledgments

As always, a ferocious thank-you to everyone at Wednesday—four books in and I'm still pinching myself every day that I get to work with such wonderful humans. To Alex, for your endlessly brilliant edits and ideas, and for understanding on a soul-deep level my need to hinge every plot on dessert. To Meghan, Alexis, and Cassidy, for helping bring this book into the world and for the wild amount of work and organizing that goes on to make it happen. To Kerri and Vi-An for this cover I am so in love with (and for rolling with my incredibly dweeby punches at the suggestion for the inspiration behind Milo; I won't say who it was here in case anyone reading this wants to take a guess!!).

Thank you infinitely to Janna, who has seen every corner of my chaotic glitter dessert brain by now and continues to support its wild agendas every step of the way.

Thank you to my friends both in and out of Writer Land—WOW, am I glad we all have each other. To Gaby and Erin and Kadeen and Suzie and Cristina for everything and forever (holy guacamole, look at us all now!!). To JQ and David and—you know what? I'm not thanking Harry Styles this time, he's been inactive in the group chat for too long and it feels rude. To Jackie and Ashley and Heather and Noah, the newest member of the squad, who grew into being at the same time as this book, which I think legally makes him this book's cousin.

Thank you to Evan, Maddie, and Lily, who are not only superb siblings, but I'm hoping have forgiven me for years of kicking them off the family desktop to write fanfiction despite our collective Neopets agendas. And the biggest thank-you of all to our parents, who have always believed in and supported us so thoroughly that it was never hard to pick ourselves up from a challenge and—please forgive me as I whip out the title of this book for dramatic effect—begin again.